INTRODUCING

KATIE MAGUIRE

KATIE MAGUIRE was one of seven sisters born to a police Inspector in Cork, but the only sister who decided to follow her father into An Garda Síochána.

With her bright green eyes and short red hair, she looks like an Irish pixie, but she is no soft touch. To the dismay of some of her male subordinates, she rose quickly through the ranks, gaining a reputation for catching Cork's killers, often at great personal cost.

Katie spent seven years in a turbulent marriage in which she bore, and lost, a son – an event that continues to haunt her. Despite facing turmoil at home and prejudice at work she is one of the most fearless detectives in Ireland.

THE KATIE MAGUIRE SERIES

White Bones

Broken Angels

Red Light

Taken For Dead

Blood Sisters

Buried

Living Death

GRAHAM

MASTERTON

LIVING DEATH

First published in the UK in 2016 by Head of Zeus Ltd

9 7 5 3 1 2 4 6 8

A CIP catalogue record for this book is available from the British Library

ISBN (HB) 9781784081416
ISBN (TPB) 9781784081423
ISBN (E) 9781784081409

Typeset by Ben Cracknell Studios, Norwich

Printed and bound by CPI Group (UK) Ltd, Croydon, CR0 4YY

Head of Zeus Ltd
Clerkenwell House
45–47 Clerkenwell Green
London EC1R 0HT

WWW.HEADOFZEUS.COM

'Gach madadh air á mhadadh choimheach'

Irish saying: Every dog attacks the stranger dog

For Katharine Walmsley
with love

One

As soon as she came teetering out of the doorway of the Eclipse Club in her short black dress and her spiky black ankle boots, her eyes circled with scarlet make-up and her hair dyed luminous green, they knew that she was exactly what they were looking for.

It was 2:25 in the morning. She was very drunk; and it appeared as if she might be on her own. She fumbled in her orange hessian bag, which had the wickedly grinning face of a pumpkin stitched on to it, and eventually managed to find her mobile phone.

The two of them were leaning against their shiny black Opel on the opposite side of Oliver Plunkett Street, smoking. They didn't cross the road immediately. They watched her frowning at her phone, jabbing at it with her glittery green fingernails, and then silently swearing because she was finding it hard to focus on the app she wanted. All the time she was doing this, she was staggering to keep her balance and repeatedly slinging her bag back over her shoulder because it kept slipping off.

Milo looked at Garret and raised one eyebrow. Both men were dressed in tight black overcoats, with white shirts and ties. Milo was short and blocky, with grey hair shaved to a carpet-like fuzz and acne-scarred cheeks. Garret was taller, with a waving black fringe like a raven's broken wing, and sunken cheeks, and the kind of thin black moustache on his upper lip that Corkonians call a 'thirsty eyebrow'.

'What you thinking, Gar?' asked Milo.

Garret flicked his cigarette butt across the street. 'Stall it for a minute, do you know what I mean? Just in case she's a scrap with her boyfriend and he'll be coming out begging her forgiveness.'

Six or seven more young people came tumbling out of the Eclipse, all laughing and swearing and pushing each other. One of the boys had painted his face dead-white like a vampire, with lipstick drops of blood dripping from the sides of his mouth. Another had a Ghostface mask from the *Scream* horror films perched on top of his head. Two ginger-haired sisters were dressed as witches in gauzy green dresses and a thin dark-haired girl was wearing a tattered white cloak like a *bean-si*.

One of the young men called out, 'Where we heading on to now, sham? It's too fecking early to call it a night and I'm gasping for another gatt.'

'Don't know, boy,' replied one of his friends. 'Wish I hadn't ate that fecking curry, I tell you. I'm just about ready to barfus maximus.'

'Well, don't you be boking over me. These are brand-new, these jeggings.'

Milo and Garret waited, but nobody came out of the club looking for the girl in the black dress. She continued to prod at her phone and after a minute or two it appeared that she had managed to send a text. She dropped her phone back into her bag and stood in the doorway of J. Casey's furniture store next door, holding on to the black metal gates to keep herself steady, and she was obviously waiting for somebody.

Milo glanced to the left to make sure there were no cars coming and then crossed the street with his hands in his pockets. He went up to the girl and said, 'All right there, love?'

'I'm grand altogether,' she replied, without looking at him.

'Okay. I got a lamp off you there and I was wondering if you needed a lift home, like.'

'No, you're all right. I just called Hailo.'

Milo raised one eyebrow. 'Okay, love. Grand. Just making sure you're okay. Looks like you've had yourself a wicked awesome party the night.'

'Not really.' The girl continued to cling tightly to the railings and although she still didn't look at Milo he could see that her scarlet eye-shadow was streaked, as if she had been crying.

'Do you live far, like?' he asked her.

'Knocka. But it's all right. My taxi's going to be here in a couple of minutes.'

'Ah, okay. Fair play. But I'm just about to go home to Gurra myself, so I could easy give you a lift. It'd be free of charge, like, and we can go right now, so you wouldn't have to wait.'

The girl looked at him at last, and her eyes were sparkling with tears. Although her make-up was a mess, he could see that she was really quite pretty, with wide-apart brown eyes and a tip-tilted nose and full, pouty lips. He kept his hands deep in his coat pockets and he gave her a shrug and a reassuring smile, as if it didn't really matter to him one way or another if she accepted his offer, and that he was only being friendly.

She lurched slightly, and gripped the railings with both hands to steady herself. She said, 'No, I don't know,' and Milo had the feeling that she was going to turn him down. At that moment, however, two more young people came out of the Eclipse – a tall, broad-shouldered boy in a red-and-green striped sweater and a brown trilby hat like Freddie from *Nightmare on Elm Street*, arm-in-arm with a curly-haired blonde. The blonde was dressed in a scarlet Spandex suit with huge red feathery wings attached to her back, and she had two red horns sticking out of her hair – an angel from Hell.

The boy in the Freddie costume caught sight of the girl in the black dress in J. Casey's doorway and immediately turned his back, pulling the red-dressed angel even closer to him and ostentatiously kissing her.

When she saw that, the girl let out a mewling sound in the back of her throat, like an abandoned kitten. The boy kissed the angel again, surreptitiously looking sideways at the girl to make sure that she was watching. It was then that the girl turned to Milo and said, 'All right, yes. If you can give me a lift home, that would be grand. Killiney Heights, do you know it?'

'Of course, yes. Come on, then. Give me your hand. Don't want you falling over in the road, do we, and making a holy show of yourself?'

He helped her over to the Opel, and opened the rear door for her. When she had managed to topple into her seat, he walked around the car and climbed in the other side, so that he was sitting close to her. Garret was already in the driver's seat, his dark eyes floating surrealistically in the rear-view mirror.

'My name's Milo and this is my friend Gar,' said Milo. 'What's your name, love?'

The girl was still silently sobbing. She had raised her left hand to the side of her face like a horse-blinker, so that she wouldn't be able to see Freddie and the evil angel kissing each other.

'Siobhán,' she said, miserably.

'So what's upsetting you, Siobhán? Is it that feller in the stripy jumper – your one meeting that beour with the wings?'

'He's my boyfriend,' said Siobhán. 'Well, he *was* my boyfriend. And that's supposed to be my best friend Clodagh.'

Garret turned around in his seat and said, in his hoarse voice, 'How about I go over and give him a good hard dawk for you?'

Siobhán shook her head. 'No. That'll only make things worse. Just take me home, please. Killiney Heights – the blue house, right at the end, by the playing fields.'

'No bother at all,' said Garret. He started the engine and steered the Opel away from the kerb. As he reached the end of Oliver Plunkett Street and was about to turn left into Grand Parade, he glanced in his mirror and saw the taxi that Siobhán had ordered on her Hailo app arriving outside the Eclipse. He smiled to himself but said nothing.

'That feen's some pedro,' said Milo. 'Look at you, girl – you're twice as good-looking as that so-called friend of yours. But if you can't trust him, like, he's not worth the full of your arse of boiled snow, believe me.'

Siobhán didn't answer but rummaged in her bag for a crumpled tissue, so that she could wipe her eyes and blow her nose.

They crossed Patrick's Bridge, over the River Lee. A crowd of young kids were gathered under one of the streetlamps, smoking and larking about and passing a large bottle of cider around.

After they had reached the other side of the river, however, instead of turning left along the embankment towards Knocknaheeny, Garret drove straight ahead up the steep slope of Bridge Street, and then turned right into MacCurtain Street, so that they were heading east, instead of west.

Siobhán said, 'Where are we going? Knocka's back that way.'

'Short cut,' said Garret.

Siobhán seemed to be satisfied with that explanation for a moment, but when Garret turned up Summerhill towards St Luke's Cross, she sat forward in her seat and said, in a drunken slur, 'This is *totally* the wrong direction, like.'

'I told you – short cut,' Garret repeated.

'Don't worry about it, girl, Gar knows what he's doing,' said Milo. 'This'll save him going all the way round St Mary's Hospital.'

Siobhán sat back for a moment, but when Garret indicated that he was turning right into the Middle Glanmire Road, she sat up again and said, '*No!* This isn't the way at all! You have to go back! Where are you taking me?'

Milo laid his hand on her arm and said, 'It's all right, Siobhán, don't get yourself all steamed up. Everything's going to be fine. Gar has to pick up a couple of things from Mayfield before he drives you home, isn't that right, Gar?'

'That's right,' said Garret. 'I forgot them, that's all. I'd forget me own arse if it wasn't screwed on.'

'Take me back,' said Siobhán, twisting her arm away. 'I don't care what you forgot, I'm not going with you. Take me back.'

'Can't do that, I'm afraid,' Milo told her. 'This is one of them journeys that you have to go to the end of, once you've started. Bit like life, do you know what I mean, like?'

'What are you talking about?'

'Well, think about it. Once you've been given birth to, you might take a sconce at the world and decide you don't particularly like the look of it, but you can't go squodging your way back into your mamma's gee, can you?'

'Stop the car!' shrilled Siobhán. 'Stop right now and let me out of here!'

She tugged desperately at the door-handle, but Garret had switched on the central locking. She turned around and started to pummel Milo with her fists, panting with frustration, her bracelets jingling and her earrings swinging. Milo laughed – a short, abrupt bark – and seized both of her wrists, gripping them so tight that she couldn't move her arms at all.

They stared at each other for a few seconds – Siobhán's eyes were wide with fear and bewilderment, while Milo's eyes were completely dispassionate – grey-green, almost colourless, but there was so little expression behind them that they could have been made of glass.

'Please let me go, Milo,' Siobhán begged him, trying to pronounce her words as clearly as possible, and not to sound too drunk. 'I can call a taxi to take me home, or I can *walk* even, if you don't want anybody to know where I've been.'

'*Walk*, girl? You can hardly fecking stand up. Besides, we're almost there now.'

Siobhán frowned out of the window. All she could see were the grey stone walls that lined Middle Glanmire Road, and hedges. They passed the cream-painted Montenotte Hotel, with its flags and its floodlights, but then they were driving between narrow walls again.

After a further five hundred metres, Garret slowed, and turned up a steeply sloping driveway. Ahead of them, Sibohán could see a large grey house, its walls blotched green and black from decades of damp. A single light was shining in the porch, and one of the upstairs windows was lit, without curtains, but apart from that the house was in darkness. Its gardens were in darkness, too. Apart from the driveway, they were surrounded on all four sides by yew hedges, over six metres high, so that Siobhán could see only the rooftops and chimneys of the houses on either side.

Outside the front of the house stood a painted signboard, *St Giles' Clinic*. Garret drove around to the side of the house and then stopped.

'Are you going to let me out now?' said Siobhán.

'I thought you wanted a lift home,' Milo told her.

'I did, but now I don't. I just want you to let me out.'

'Well, all right, then, if you insist. Gar had to stop here to pick up one or two things, but if you really don't want us to take you back to Knocka—'

'I don't. Let me out.'

Both Garret and Milo climbed out of the car. Milo walked around to open the door for Siobhán, and stood patiently waiting for her while she picked up her bag and shuffled herself off the seat.

She had started to sober up now, and when she got to her feet she said, 'Jesus, I swear to God, I don't know what kind of a stupid game you two think you're playing at!'

Milo shrugged and smiled apologetically, but he didn't tell her that Garret was standing close behind her with a two-pound ball-pein hammer lifted high above her head. He was still smiling when Garret hit her on the left-hand side of her skull, with a hard, hollow crack. She pitched forward, so that Milo had to step neatly back to avoid her, like a dance manoeuvre, and she collapsed face-first on to the tarmac driveway.

'Good man yourself, Gar,' said Milo. The two of them crouched down and rolled Siobhán over on to her back. She was unconscious, but her eyes were still half-open, and the lids were fluttering. All the contents of her handbag were scattered across the ground.

'That was some fierce old wallop you gave here there, boy. Wouldn't surprise me if she was brain-damaged, and the Doc won't have to bother with all the rest of his malarkey.'

'This is a good heavy hammer, this one,' said Garret. 'I bought it at Hickey's day before yesterday. The other one was too fecking light by far, wasn't it? I always had to clonk them about a half-a-dozen times before I knocked them out cold.'

Milo took hold of Siobhán underneath her armpits and started to drag her around in a circle. He positioned her very carefully so that she was lying across the driveway with her knees directly behind the Opel's rear offside wheel.

When he looked up from doing that, he saw that a man was standing in the upstairs window, silhouetted against the light. He didn't wave or acknowledge that he had seen him because he knew that the man wouldn't respond. As far as Milo was concerned, he wasn't there, and he would never say that he had seen what Milo and Garret were going to do next.

Garret lit a cigarette and then climbed back behind the wheel of the car. Milo stepped clear, but not too far away, in case Siobhán suddenly regained consciousness and rolled herself out of position.

Garret started the Opel's engine, although he kept his door open so that he could look over his shoulder and see where he was reversing.

'All right, boy, you're fine,' said Milo, beckoning him backwards.

Garret slowly edged the rear wheel over Siobhán's legs. Her bones snapped like muffled pistol-shots, and this was followed by a soft crunching sound as two thousand kilos of car crushed her knees.

Two

Cleona suddenly sat up in bed and said, 'Eoin! Just listen to the dogs, will you? Something's bothering them! Eoin!'

'What?' said Eoin, blurrily. 'What is it?'

'The dogs, Eoin! Listen!'

Eoin lifted his head from the pillow. The dogs' barking was indistinct, because it was raining hard outside and their bedroom window was closed, with the curtains drawn. All the same, he could hear that they were frantic. This wasn't the monotonous barking of dogs who were impatient to be taken out for a walk, or who were hungry, or thirsty. This was the sound of dogs who were panicking – almost screaming, some of them, like terrified children.

Eoin switched on his bedside lamp, threw back the patchwork quilt, and swung himself out of bed. He went over to the window, opened the curtains, and peered out into the darkness. The window was speckled with raindrops, and all he could see was the wall lights on the end of the two rows of kennels, and their reflection in the wet tarmac yard. His first thought had been that there was a fire, but he couldn't see any smoke, or smell any, either.

He opened the window so that he could hear the dogs more clearly and there was no doubt that they were hysterical. He recognised at least two of them: Bullet, the young Welsh terrier, whose high-pitched yapping was always distinctive, and the throaty barking of Trippet, the Labrador.

'What time are we?' he asked Cleona, crossing over to the chair where his jeans and his brown cable-knit sweater were hanging.

'Twenty past four,' said Cleona. 'What do you think's wrong with them?'

'That's what I'm going down to find out.'

'Well, for the love of God be careful. You can never be sure who's prowling around these days. Hold on a moment and I'll come down with you.'

'No, pet, you stay here. I'll call out for you if I need you.'

Eoin struggled into his jeans, grabbing the side of the wardrobe to keep his balance, and then pulled on his sweater, so that his black curly hair stuck up. His eyes were puffy from lack of sleep and his head was thumping. It had been his thirty-eighth birthday yesterday, and since his birthday was on 31 October, he had celebrated as usual with a monster Hallowe'en party at Hurley's.

He switched on the landing light so that he could see his way down the steep, narrow stairs, but he didn't switch on the light downstairs in the hallway. He doubted if the dogs had been disturbed by anybody more threatening than a petty pilferer – some Knacker looking to see if there were any tools or bicycles lying around. At this time of the morning it was even more likely to be a red fox, rummaging through their dustbins. If it was a prowler, though, he wanted to catch him by surprise, and he didn't want to open the front door and appear as a backlit target. Sceolan Boarding Kennels was very isolated, with the next house nearly a kilometre away, and the village of Ballinspittle more than four, and Eoin was always cautious about security.

Before he opened the front door, he looked out through the semi-circular window in it, but he could still see nothing but darkness, and rain, and the two lights at the end of the kennels. He pushed his bare feet into his wellington boots, picked up the ashwood hurley stick that he kept in the umbrella stand, and stepped outside. The wind was cold and blustery, and even though the gutters were gurgling, the rain seemed to be easing off a little. The dogs were still barking, though, and as he crossed the yard, he thought that they sounded even more frantic. Marcus, a pedigree

Labrador, was giving out a long convoluted howl like the Hound of the Baskervilles.

When he reached the two parallel lines of kennels, he began to see why the dogs were so distressed. At least six or seven of the doors at the far end of the left-hand line were wide open. He broke into a run, gripping his hurley even tighter. The kennel doors were all fitted with alarms, which he religiously switched on at night, but clearly somebody had found a way to short-circuit them.

As he reached the first of the open doors, he saw who the intruders were. Just out of sight of the house, a silver Range Rover and a large black Transit van were parked in the driveway that led down to the road. Two men were pulling a reluctant German Shepherd called Caesar into the side door of the van, while three more were walking back towards the kennels.

Eoin stopped running, and stood where he was, holding up the hurley in both hands. 'Hey!' he shouted. 'What in the *name* of Jesus do you think you're doing?'

The three men said nothing at first, but kept on walking towards him until they were only five metres away. Two of them were wearing black windcheaters, and had scarves wrapped around the lower half of their faces, like jihadis, so that Eoin could see only their eyes. The third man was wearing a long grey raincoat, tightly buckled at the waist. He had swept-back grey hair and the ruined good looks of an ageing actor. A cigarette was glowing between his lips, and it waggled up and down when he spoke, as if to accentuate what he was saying. He spoke very softly, with a slurred Sligo accent, so Eoin found it difficult to hear him over the cacophony of barking.

'Sorry if we've disturbed you, sir! As you can see, we're only after taking a few of your liabilities off of your hands, that's all.'

'Oh, you mean you've come here to pikey my dogs?'

The man's forehead furrowed into a distinctive V. 'Ah stop! That's not a very friendly thing to say, now is it? If I *was* a pikey, like, I'd be pure offended by that. As it is, I'll let it pass. How about we say nothing, all right, in case something's said. But I suggest that you go back indoors and let us get on with our business.'

The other two men had slammed shut the Transit's door by now, and come over to join them. Apart from the man in the grey raincoat, none of them spoke, but they didn't have to. With their hands thrust into the pockets of their windcheaters and their legs braced apart and their heads tilted slightly back, they were making it quite clear to Eoin that if he tried to stop them they would beat him senseless and dance on his face.

It sounded as if the dogs could sense the increasing tension in the air. Their barking not only continued relentlessly, but it grew sharper and harder, echoing from one side of the kennels to the other. Eoin felt as helpless as they obviously did. What could one man do against five, even if he was armed with a seven-hundred-gram hurley? For all he knew, they could be carrying knives, or even guns.

In a cabinet in the dining-room he kept an under-and-over shotgun. Why hadn't he had the sense to bring it out with him? Hadn't his father told him time and again: 'Always be ready for the worst that life can throw at you, boy, because it fecking will'? His father had died of lung cancer at the age of fifty-one.

'All right,' said Eoin. He was trying to sound calm but he felt as if his insides had turned into cold water. 'It doesn't look as if I have much choice, does it? But all I ask is, treat these dogs with respect, and take good care of them.'

The man in the grey raincoat gave him a sideways-sloping smile. 'You don't seriously think I'm going to let you go back inside on your own, do you? As if you won't be ringing the shades as soon as you walk through the door. No – a couple of my pals here will go along with you while the others finish up here, taking what we came for. Oh – and you can drop that *camán*. Don't want you taking a swing at them, do we?'

Eoin hesitated for a moment and then tossed the hurley so that it clattered on to the ground. One of the men stepped forward and picked it up, sloping it over his shoulder as if it were a rifle.

'What are you going to do with them – the dogs?' Eoin asked the man in the grey raincoat. 'You're not going to have them fighting, are you?'

'Oh, will you come round to yourself,' the man replied. 'These are fine dogs these are, best quality. They'll all of them be going to pampered homes, believe me. They'll probably be eating better munch and sleeping in more comfortable scratchers than you or me ever will.'

Eoin was tempted to say something like, 'You won't get away with this,' but he knew how futile that would sound, and the reality was that they probably *would* get away with it. The Garda were tied up with enough serious crime without chasing after dognappers.

He walked back to the house, with two of the men uncomfortably close beside him, including the man who was carrying his hurley. They followed him inside, and with his voice muffled behind his scarf, one of them said, 'Just park your arse in the parlour, okay, sham, and don't be trying anything stupid.'

Eoin went into the living-room and switched on the lights. He could still hear the dogs barking and he prayed that Cleona hadn't heard him come back into the house; that she wouldn't decide to come looking for him.

He sat on the end of the white leatherette sofa while one of the men sat in the armchair by the fireplace. The man with the hurley remained standing, directly behind him, as if he were just waiting for him to make a wrong move so that he could give him a cheeser across the back of the head.

'So what are you going to do with our dogs?' asked Eoin.

Neither of the men spoke, although the man sitting in the armchair gave a loud catarrhal sniff, and then another. Even so, he didn't lower the scarf that covered all of his face except his eyes.

'If you're not going to be fighting them, what? Breeding them? Racing with them? Selling them on, pretending they're yours? They've all been chipped and registered, but then I'd guess you know that.'

Still the men said nothing. They both smelled strongly of stale cigarette smoke and the man who was standing behind Eoin was wearing some strong cheap body spray like Lynx.

'You're not taking them out lamping, are you?' said Eoin. 'You could just get some old mongrel for that. These are all pedigree. They'd catch their death of cold in the woods.'

'Shut your face, will you?' said the man behind him.

'I'm only thinking of the dogs,' said Eoin.

'Well, for feck's sake think about something else, will you? You're wrecking my head.'

At that moment, Eoin heard a creak from the main bedroom, which was directly overhead. The men heard it, too, because they looked up at the ceiling and the man in the armchair sniffed and said, 'Who's that? Is that your wife up there?'

'You leave her out of this,' said Eoin.

'So long as she doesn't start causing bother,' the man told him.

But then they heard Cleona call out, 'Eoin? Eoin, what are you doing downstairs? The dogs are still going mad out there! What's going on?'

'Tell her everything's grand and to go back to bed,' said the man behind him.

Eoin hesitated, so the man prodded his shoulder with the toe of the hurley and said, 'Tell her, will you?'

Eoin cleared his throat and shouted, 'It's all right, Cleona! It was only a fox sniffing around, that's all! They'll settle themselves down in a while!'

There was a long pause, and then Cleona called, 'So what are you doing downstairs? Aren't you coming up?'

'In a minute! There's a couple of things I have to do first!'

Another pause, not so long this time. Then, 'What things? At this rate it'll be time for you to get up before you've come back to bed.'

'Like I said, Clee! I'll be up in a minute!'

They heard another creak as Cleona walked back across the bedroom. A lengthy silence followed, interrupted only by the man in the armchair sniffing.

After five minutes had gone by, though, they heard the creak again. This time Cleona didn't call out, but started to come down the stairs.

'Clee, don't come down!' Eoin called out, and his voice was croaky with stress. 'I won't be much longer, I promise you! Go back to bed, sweetheart! Please!'

But now Cleona appeared in the living-room doorway, her blonde hair tousled, wearing nothing but her short rose-patterned nightdress. She blinked at the two men on either side of Eoin and said, 'What's going on? Who are these two fellers? Eoin? What's going on?'

'You just come in here and sit yourself down, pet,' said the man with the hurley. 'We won't be staying long. All you have to do is sit still, like, and keep your bake shut.'

'Who are you?' Cleona demanded. 'How *dare* you talk to me like that? Eoin – what are they doing here?'

'Are you deaf, missus, or what?' the man retorted.

'I'm ringing the guards,' said Cleona.

She turned around and headed for the stairs, but the man in the chair by the fireplace bounded out of his seat and went after her. Before she was even halfway up, he had mounted the stairs after her, reached out and grabbed her right ankle. She lost her footing and tumbled back down into the hallway, hitting her elbow against the newel post and banging her head hard against the wall beside the front door.

The man bent down, caught her under her arms, and lifted her up. She tried to struggle herself free, but he gripped the neck of her nightdress and twisted it in his fist, and then he slapped her across the face.

She cried out, '*Aaahhhh!*' more in rage than in pain, and attempted to hit him back, but he slapped her again, harder this time, and started to drag her back into the living-room.

'Leave go of me!' she screamed. 'Leave go of me, you bastard!'

Eoin stood up and shouted, 'Take your hands off her!'

He lunged towards the man who was jostling Cleona across the room, but the other man stalked stiff-legged around the end of the sofa with his hurley uplifted and cracked him hard across the back of his head. He fell heavily into a small side-table, knocking off a lamp and a small clock and half-a-dozen framed photographs of himself and Cleona with their prize dogs.

Cleona screamed, hysterical now, but the man who was holding her clamped one hand over her mouth and gripped her hair by the roots with the other. Underneath his scarf, he blurted, 'Shut the feck up, will you, or I'll tear your fecking head off!'

Eoin was still lying on the floor, concussed. The man with the hurley was standing over him, ready to hit him again, but he didn't move.

'Did you see that?' the man said, triumphantly. 'I should of played for the Barrs, me!'

The other man slung Cleona on to the sofa. She had stopped screaming now but she was sobbing in deep, honking sobs, and she was almost blinded with tears. Her nightie had been pulled up on one side, exposing her hip. The man reached down and tugged up the other side. She tried to cross her legs and tug the hem down to cover herself, but he slapped her again, twice this time, and very hard. Both of her cheeks were swollen now, and fiery red, and his signet ring had left a pattern of tiny purple bruises on the left side of her face.

'Don't you fecking try to fight with me, doll, because you'll only end up the worse for it, I can tell you!'

With that, he wrenched her nightie up higher, and then he took hold of the hem in both hands and ripped it open, all the way to the neck, although he wasn't able to tear apart the stitching around the collar. Cleona attempted twice to get up from the sofa, but he shoved her back down, holding her by the throat and raising his left hand to show her that he was quite prepared to slap her again.

Still holding her by the throat, he unzipped his windcheater one-handed, and then he unfastened his belt-buckle and twisted open the buttons of his jeans.

The man holding the hurley leaned against the fireplace, watching him. Cleona was whining for breath now, but she was no longer struggling or making any attempt to cover herself. She was staring up at the ceiling as if she were trying to imagine that she was somewhere else altogether, and that none of this was happening.

'Well now, will you look at these!' the man exclaimed, and sniffed. 'It's a fierce fine pair of diddies you have here, darling!' He let go of her throat and squeezed her large white breasts with both hands, kneading his fingers deep into them and then pinching her nipples between finger and thumb, stretching them out as far as he could. 'If I was your old man, I swear to God, I wouldn't get a wink of sleep all night for playing breast-ket-ball!' Then he looked down and said, 'Not sure about the flange, though! Doesn't fecking match! The lights are on upstairs all right, but it's pitch dark in the cellar!'

'Come on, Keeno, beggars can't be choosers,' said his companion. 'Are you going to give her the McWhinney's or what? Michael and the lads will be finished loading up all them dogs in a minute.'

The man delved inside his jeans and prised his stiffened penis out of his shorts. It was short, but his dark purple glans had baroque curves to it, like a helmet drawn by Leonardo da Vinci. He forced Cleona's thighs wide open and then with his blackened fingernails he pulled the lips of her vulva wide apart.

'State of this la!' he snorted, underneath his scarf. 'Did you ever before see a woman so soggy? She must be *ga-a-asping* for it!'

He climbed awkwardly on top of her and forced himself into her, all the way in, right up to his jeans. As he penetrated her, she let out an extraordinary whinny, more like a young horse than a woman, and her arms and legs convulsed, and then flopped. After that, though, she lay on the sofa silent and motionless while the man pushed at her and pushed at her, grunting and sniffing and cursing under his breath.

The dogs had stopped barking now, and so the only other sound was the squeaking of the sofa and the persistent squelching of attempted intercourse. The man's companion had tucked the hurley under his arm and was frowning intently at his mobile phone. Cleona had her eyes closed. Her breasts wobbled with every thrust and occasionally she let out the softest of gasps, but apart from that she might just as well have been dead.

After a few minutes the man holding the hurley said, 'Ah come on, Keeno. That's enough shagging. Michael and the lads are all set to go.'

The other man stopped humping up and down on top of Cleona but stayed inside her, staring down at her.

'You're not going to open your eyes and look at me, are you, darling? Well, that's a terrible pity, because I think you and me could have let off some fireworks together, if you'd only been a little more obligating, do you know what I mean, like?'

'Will you beat on, Keeno, for feck's sake,' said his companion.

But the man was still lying on top of Cleona when Eoin suddenly stirred, and sat up. Eoin looked around him, holding his head with one hand and blinking, as if he couldn't understand where he was. Then, though, he turned towards the sofa and saw the man climbing off Cleona and bending his half-erect penis back into his jeans.

'Holy *Jesus*! What are you doing?' Eoin cried out, and he was almost screeching. He reached out for the armchair to pull himself up on to his feet, but he was still giddy from being hit so hard on the head, and he dropped to his knees on the shaggy green hearth-rug.

'*What have you done to my wife*?' he screamed. '*What have you done*?'

The man holding the hurley prodded him with it and said, 'Shut up and forget about it, all right? I don't mind beating you again, boy, and next time I'll make sure you don't fecking wake up for a week.'

Eoin turned to Cleona. She was still lying on the sofa, although she had closed her legs and pulled her torn nightie across to cover her breasts. Her eyes were open now and she was staring at Eoin but she looked totally shocked. She opened and closed her mouth but didn't seem able to speak.

Eoin tried again to stand up, but the man jabbed him hard with the hurley in the side of the neck.

'Don't even fecking think about it, okay?' he warned him. 'We bait gap now, you'll be happy to hear. You won't be seeing us again and you won't be talking about us to anyone at all and you won't be squealing about any of this to the shades for sure, on pain of something much worse befalling you, if you follow my meaning. We know where you live, like.'

'Get out,' said Eoin, without looking at him. Instead, he was still looking at Cleona, and he held his hand out towards her. She was still staring at him, too, but he wasn't at all sure that she was able to focus – or even if she could, that she recognised him.

'Fantastic to meet you,' said the man who had forced himself on Cleona. 'Pity we won't be doing this again any time soon. Nice and tight your wife is, sham. Better than some of the old brassers I've had. Some of them, Jesus, it's like throwing a banana up Patrick's Street.'

Eoin was beginning to shake. His head was banging so hard that he felt as if the blood vessels in his brain were just about to burst, and he was so enraged by what these men had done to Cleona, and so humiliated that he hadn't been able to protect her, that he didn't even know if he was going to be able to move again, or if he was going to have to spend the rest of his life kneeling on this green shaggy hearth-rug with his head bowed like a mediaeval penitent.

He watched dully as the two men left the living-room and he heard them open the front door. They must have left the door open behind them, because he could hear a single dog barking, and the sound of the Range Rover's engine starting up.

Cleona whispered, '*Eoin? Is that you?*'

He turned back and looked at her reddened, bruise-decorated face, and at the way she was clutching so pathetically at her ripped-apart nightie, and he took three or four deep breaths. Then – as if he had been jolted by lightning like Frankenstein's monster, he seized the side of the armchair and jerked himself on to his feet.

'Eoin?'

'I'll be back in a second, sweetheart,' he said, although he hardly recognised his own voice. It sounded as if somebody else had spoken, somebody who was standing right next to him.

'Eoin?'

'It's all right, Clee. Everything's going to be grand. I'll be back in a second.'

He walked unsteadily out of the living-room and across the hallway to the dining-room. The gun cabinet hung in the corner, next to a painting by Martin Driscoll of a farmer resting with his black-and-white dogs. He took the key out of the oak sideboard and unlocked it. There were racks inside for three shotguns but he only had one, a twelve-bore Miroku. He lifted it out, and rummaged in the drawer for the box of cartridges.

Still feeling unbalanced and strangely unreal, he broke open the shotgun and loaded it as he made his way towards the front door. It was raining again when he stepped outside, a thin fine drizzle that was illuminated by the wall lamps at the end of the kennels, so that the morning looked ghostly and blurred.

By now the two men were more than halfway along the kennels. Eoin couldn't yet see the van and the Range Rover, but he could hear their engines running and see the smoke from their exhausts drifting across the driveway.

He started to walk faster, and then he broke into a jog. Before the men could reach the end of the kennels, he shouted out, '*Wait!* I *Stall it there, will you?*'

The two men stopped and turned around. The man who had taken his hurley was still carrying it slanted across his shoulder.

'Just hold it right there!' said Eoin.

'Come on to feck, will you, sham!' called the man with the hurley, impatiently. 'We're in a hurry to get away now!'

Eoin was less than fifty metres away from them when the light must have glanced off the barrels of Eoin's shotgun. The man who had assaulted Cleona croaked out, 'Jesus Christ, Jimmy, he's got a fecking gun! Sketch up!' He started to make a run for it, with an odd, hobbling gait, as if he were practising a three-legged race without a partner.

The other man, though, took hold of the hurley in both hands and stood his ground.

'Come on, then, boy! What are you going to do? Shoot me? You haven't got the stones!'

Eoin stopped. The man kept jiggling the hurley and shifting his weight from one foot to the other, as if he could hardly wait to run up to Eoin and give him another hard crack on the head.

The other man had disappeared around the corner of the kennels, but Eoin thought: *all of his fellow dognappers are there, waiting, and the odds are that at least one of them will be carrying a gun. Whatever I decide to do, it's now or never.*

'Come on, then, don't waste the rest of your life!' the man with the hurley challenged him.

Eoin raised his shotgun and aimed it. He waited a few seconds, but only to slow down his breathing and steady himself, so that he wouldn't miss.

The man took two steps towards him, and he fired, jolting his shoulder. Between the two rows of kennels the shot was deafening, so that it sounded like three shots, instead of one. He hit the man directly in the face, just where his scarf covered his nose, and blasted the top of his head off. His entire brain was blown out of his head and landed on the tarmac ten metres behind him.

The man dropped the hurley and half-turned around, as if he had heard somebody calling his name. Then his knees sagged and he collapsed on to the ground, face downward, and lay there with his feet still frantically jerking. Eoin could have imagined that his legs were trying to obey the brain's final instructions to run away.

He reloaded the barrel that he had fired, but then he stayed where he was, in the softly falling drizzle. He was ready for the rest of them, if they came for him.

He heard a dog yapping. It was Gaybo, a small prize-winning Munsterlander. He heard a van door slam, and he cocked his shotgun. But then he heard the distinctive whine of its transmission as the Range Rover drove away, followed by the van, which had a rattling exhaust. Within a few seconds, they had driven down to the main road and gone. He saw their red tail-lights disappear behind the trees, north towards Barrell's Crossroads.

Eoin walked slowly back to the house, past the empty kennels with their doors wide open.

Holy Mother of God, I've killed a man, he thought, as he reached the front door. *I've actually killed a man. He's dead. But in a way, that's my life over, too. How can anything ever be the same?*

It was nearly five o'clock now, but it was still dark, and he wondered if it would ever get light again.

Three

Katie looked up at the clock on her kitchen wall and said, 'Maybe I should ring them again. Maybe they can't find us.'

Barney her Irish setter cocked his head on one side as if to show her that he understood her anxiety completely, but couldn't think of anything useful to suggest.

She put down her mug of coffee and picked up her iPhone, but before she had even had the chance to switch it on, the doorbell chimed. Barney immediately wuffled and trotted out into the hallway.

When she opened the door, there he was, at the bottom of the porch steps, sitting in a wheelchair. Because it was raining so hard, the paramedics had covered him with a yellow waterproof cape with a pointed hood, so that he looked like some kind of giant gnome. Katie couldn't even see his face.

'Good morning to you, ma'am,' said the female paramedic. 'Here he is – we've fetched your friend for you.'

The male paramedic lifted up a dark grey overnight case and said, 'His things are all in here, such as they are, and all his medication. There's written instructions from Doctor Kashani on the dosage.'

John pushed back his hood. Katie had seen him regularly in hospital, of course, since both of his lower legs had been amputated, but under the naked porch light she was shocked at how much weight he had lost, and how much he seemed to have aged. He was smiling at her, and his eyes were bright with pleasure and relief, but his hair was grey and scraggly and cropped short, when it used to be long and black and curly, and his cheeks were sunken in, so that she could see the contours of his skull. When they had first become lovers, he had looked so handsome and muscular and saintly. Now he looked as if the paramedics had wheeled him here on a visit from Glyntown Care Centre.

'Barns, how are you, boy!' he called out, in a wheezy voice, but Barney stayed in the hallway, behind Katie, as if he wasn't at all sure about this strange wizened man in a wheelchair.

'Do you want a hand lifting him in?' asked Katie. 'I'll have to have a ramp installed, won't I?'

'No, you're all right,' said the male paramedic. He turned the wheelchair around and bumped it up the steps backwards. Barney retreated even further into the hallway, making a low suspicious sound in the back of his throat.

'I don't have to sign anything, do I?' asked Katie.

'No, no, you're grand,' grinned the male paramedic. 'He's not a parcel. All the same, like, we don't accept returns. If you change your mind about him within twenty-eight days, you still have to keep him.'

They all laughed, and Barney barked. The paramedic pushed John into the living-room and then said, 'G'luck, so, John. I expect we'll be seeing you again before too long.'

Once she had shown the paramedics out, Katie went back into the living-room. She lifted off John's rain-cape and then sat on the end of the couch next to him. He reached out his hand and she took hold of it, and squeezed it tight, although she couldn't help thinking how cold and bony it felt.

'Would you like a coffee?' she asked him. 'I just had one but I could make some fresh.'

'No, no thanks,' he said. 'I'm okay for the moment.' He looked around the living-room and then back at Katie. 'It feels so weird to be here. But *good*, too. You don't know how good. I haven't been able to stop thinking about our days together, and how great they were.'

'Well, yes, we did have some good times all right,' said Katie. She squeezed his hand again and then let it go. This was no time to bring up all of their blazing arguments, and how much John had resented her strength and her ability to organise his life for him, especially when he had been out of work. Neither was she going to mention the morning he had walked out on her because he had discovered that her impetuous once-only fling with her previous neighbour had left her pregnant.

'Katie, darling, believe me, we can have those good times all over again,' said John. He grimaced as he shifted himself up straighter in his wheelchair. 'Once my stumps are healed they'll be able to take all the measurements for my sockets, and it won't take more than a couple of weeks before my prosthetic legs will be ready. Then I can start proper gait training, that's what my therapist told me. That's what they call teaching you to walk. They should call it "gatch training", shouldn't they, in Cork?'

He paused, and reached out for her hand again. 'Even so, being able to walk, that's not an essential when you're in bed, is it? Look at Oscar Pistorius.'

'Yes, my God,' said Katie. 'And look how *he* turned out!'

'Well, I know, sure, but all I meant was, he was able to make love to his girlfriends even though he didn't have any legs, like me. It won't change me, this, Katie. It won't change who I am, and it won't change the fact that I love you. I know I haven't always treated you too well, but it was only because I was so possessive about you. What's that song? "I'm Just a Jealous Guy".'

He paused again, and then he said, much more softly, 'You've shown me that you love me, too, Katie, so much. You saved my life and ever since then you've stuck by me. I know how deeply you're devoted to your job. I understand that now. But now I've found out that your devotion to me runs just as deep. I guess you couldn't always find the words to tell me, that's all.'

There was a very long silence between them. Katie gave him small occasional smiles but she couldn't think how to answer him. *'Yes, I do love you, but looking at you now, I'm not sure that I find you so physically attractive any more'*? *'No, I don't love you, and perhaps I never did love you – not really, not as deeply as you seem to believe'*? *'I care about you, John. I feel responsible and guilty for you losing your legs, but responsibility and guilt – they're not the same as love'*?

'Bridie will be here soon,' she told him. 'She's a grand girl, very experienced, and very good-humoured. I got her through Seamus O'Shea at Caremark. She'll be looking after you while I'm at work. Jenny Tierney will be coming in from next door to take Barney for his walk, so you don't have to worry about that.'

'I think Barney's taken against me for some reason. Look at him staring at me. If looks could kill.'

'He doesn't reck you, that's all, and he's very protective. He'll get used to you again, the longer you stay here.'

John said, 'Bless you, Katie. Without you, my life wouldn't be worth the living, I can tell you that.'

Katie was about to ask him if he was hungry when her iPhone played the first two bars of 'Tá Mo Chleamhnas a Dhéanamh, The Matchmaking Song'.

Oh I walked east and I walked west
I walked Cork and Dublin's streets
An equal to my love I didn't meet
She's the wee lass that's left my heart broken.

It was Detective Sergeant Begley. By the sound of it, he was standing outside somewhere, in the wind and the rain. Katie could hear somebody shouting in the background, and the sudden whooping of an ambulance siren, which abruptly stopped.

'Sorry to be disturbing you today, ma'am. I know you have the day booked off. But there's been a fatal shooting early this morning out at Ballinroe East, and under the circumstances I thought you need to be informed as soon as possible. You'll have the media wanting to talk to you, if they haven't been chasing you already.'

Katie held up one finger to John to show him this was a serious conversation and that she needed to give it all her attention.

'What's the story, Sean?' she asked Detective Sergeant Begley.

'The victim's a male in his late thirties, no identification on him of any kind at all. He was shot at a boarding kennels just off the R604, a little short of a kilometre south of Barrell's Crossroads. The owner of the kennels is a fellow called Eoin Cassidy. He and his wife were disturbed around four o'clock this morning by a gang of fellers stealing their dogs. Almost all of them are pedigree, spaniels and suchlike, so they're worth thousands, some of them.'

'Go on,' said Katie.

'Well, this Eoin Cassidy took his shotgun and went outside to challenge them, like. They started to come for him, so he fired a warning shot in the air. But that didn't stop them, and he says he was afeard of his life, so he fired another shot at them directly, and blew the head off of one of them. After that the rest of them scattered quick.'

'I assume that Superintendent Horgan knows all about this.'

'He does of course. There's five officers from Bandon up here now, including Inspector O'Brien. They're just waiting around for the Technical Bureau to go over the scene before they have the body moved. But the thing of it is, this gang who was robbing the kennels, they sound like the same bunch of dognappers that we've been having such trouble with around the city. They was driving a Range Rover and a white van and there was about six of them altogether.'

'You're right,' said Katie. 'It does sound like them. What does Dooley call them? The Labrador Lifters.'

'Those are the fellows. And if it's the same gang, like, Superintendent Horgan didn't want to be talking to the media until he'd had the chance to discuss it with you. Didn't want to be treading on your toes, like, do you know what I mean?'

'Well, yes, fair play to him and I appreciate that. But this dognapper getting shot, that puts a whole different complexion on this. They've been nothing much more than a nuisance so far, this gang, but if dog owners are going to start using lethal force to protect their animals—'

'Lethal force? He only blew his whole entire brain ten metres out of his head.'

'Where is this Cassidy fellow now?' asked Katie.

'They've taken him in to Bandon for questioning. As far as I know, he has his solicitor on the way. I'll be heading across there myself in a minute.'

'All right. I have to wait for my home carer to show up, but then I'll go directly to the station. I'll call Superintendent Horgan from there.'

When she had finished talking to Detective Sergeant Begley, John said, 'I suppose that means that duty calls.'

'Yes, I'm afraid so. I had hoped to have the whole day off, but of course I'll wait until Bridie gets here.'

'You're all right. If you want to go now, I can look after myself. I'm pretty nifty in this wheelchair now.'

'John, I'm not leaving you here on your own. Bridie won't be long.'

She stood up and touched his hand and smiled at him. The rain pattered against the living-room window like a soft, regretful reminder of days gone past. They were both acutely aware that they hadn't kissed.

'Are you hungry at all?' she asked him. 'I could make you a sandwich, if you like; or I have some beef hand pies that my father's cleaner Blaithin gave me. She cooks for the Roaring Donkey in Cobh and she always brings me the leftovers.'

'Maybe later,' said John.

She leaned over and kissed him on the forehead. His skin felt dry and unfamiliar. He raised his head and kissed her on the lips, but again she felt as if she were kissing a stranger.

John was just about to say something to her when the doorbell chimed. Barney immediately sprang to his feet and ran into the hallway, wuffling, and Katie said, 'That'll be Bridie now.'

She opened the door and Bridie was standing outside in her raincoat, a wide-hipped round-faced girl with crimson cheeks and crimson lips, which gave her the appearance of a life-sized matryoshka doll. She was carrying a heavy blue satchel over her shoulder and three bulging carrier bags.

'Good morning, ma'am. You'll have to forgive me if I'm a little late. The traffic's desperate through the tunnel.'

'Never mind,' said Katie. 'Come inside and meet John.'

Bridie stepped in and put down her bags and hung up her raincoat. Underneath she was wearing a navy cardigan and a pale blue nurse's overall, which emphasised to Katie that John was now an invalid, and how much care he was going to need. She hated herself for feeling so negative about him, and so depressed. If he hadn't been kidnapped by a criminal gang in order to put pressure on her, and if they hadn't bolted his feet to a bed to keep him from escaping, so that they became septic, he would never have lost his legs. But was it really her fault, and did she really owe him a lifetime of nursing?

'Hallo, John!' said Bridie, brightly. 'I'm Bridie Mulligan and I'm going to be supporting you from now on. Now, I don't want you to be afraid to ask me for any help that you require, and by that I mean any help at all – washing, dressing, going to the toilet. That's what I'm here for.'

John whispered, 'Thank you, Bridie,' and then cleared his throat and repeated it, louder. 'Thank you, Bridie. I'll try not to be too demanding.'

'No, John, you can be as demanding as you like. If you feel like a cup of tea in your hand, all you have to do is say so. If you need to water the horses, don't be embarrassed and leave it till it's too late. I've seen it all before, like, do you know what I mean, and it doesn't bother me at all. I've changed more old gentlemen's nappies than you've had hot dinners.'

Katie showed Bridie around the house. She took her into the kitchen so that she knew where the tea and the coffee were, and how to work the heating.

Bridie said, 'That's all grand. If I have any trouble at all, I have your number, and I'll text you.'

She paused, and then she said, very quietly, 'You're pure distressed by this, ma'am, I can see that.'

Katie nodded. 'It hasn't been easy. Well, to tell you the truth, it's turned out to be much harder than I imagined. And – please – you can call me Katie.'

'There's homes you know, where people like John can be taken care of. It's not his fault, I imagine, losing his legs, but he's going to be a fierce burden to you, and you can't escape that.'

'How old are you, if you don't mind my asking?' said Katie.

'Twenty-seven, ma'am.'

'Well, you're very wise for twenty-seven, Bridie. I wish I'd had half your perspicacity at your age.'

Bridie gave her an uneasy smile, because it was obvious that she didn't know what 'perspicacity' was.

'Insight,' said Katie, and now Bridie nodded.

'I've had a rake of experience, ma'am – I mean, Katie – and some of the patients I've taken care of, they've been a sight worse than your John, like. Blind, some of them, as well as disabled. That makes it so much worse.'

Katie went back into the living-room.

'I'm off now, John. I'll be back as soon as I can.'

'Okay,' said John.

Katie gave him a quick kiss on the forehead again, but as she went to the door, John said, without looking at her, 'I love you, Katie Maguire.'

Four

Siobhán opened her eyes and at first she thought she was lying out in the open air somewhere, because her spine and her pelvis felt numb with cold, and she could see nothing but a pearl-grey fog. Her head was throbbing so painfully that she had to close her eyes again.

Oh, dear God, she thought. *Surely I didn't get as mouldy as all that last night.* She remembered dancing in the Eclipse, and she remembered screaming at Tadgh, and going back to the bar and tossing back at least three Jägerbombs. She couldn't remember anything more after that. Surely she hadn't staggered into the Peace Park and fallen asleep on the ground.

She tried opening her eyes a second time. The fog was gradually dissolving now, and she was beginning to make out shapes and outlines, and she realised that she wasn't lying outside at all, but in a brightly lit room with grey-painted walls. She could see a window, with a dark grey pelmet and curtains, and a cream-coloured blind drawn right down to the windowsill. She could see a door, and a white-painted chest-of-drawers, and a framed black-and-white engraving of a saint kneeling in front of a descending archangel.

Above her head, and off to her left, a large cream surgical lamp was suspended, the kind of lamp that she had seen at the dentist's. There was a strong smell of antiseptic in the room, too, just like the dentist's. What was she doing at the dentist's? And why did her head hurt so much? She closed her eyes yet again. She must be dreaming this. She must be at home, in bed, but she was so hungover that she was having a nightmare.

She remembered coming out of the club and trying to call Hailo for a taxi. A taxi must have arrived and taken her home. All she had to do now was wake up. *Count to ten*, she thought, *and then open your eyes, and you'll be awake.*

She had only counted to five, though, before she heard the door open. She opened her eyes and she was still in the same brightly lit room, so it wasn't a nightmare. She was really here, wherever this was. And her head really hurt, and she still felt paralysed with cold.

A middle-aged woman with a pale freckly face and wild coppery hair leaned over her. She was wearing a green cowl-neck sweater and she reminded Siobhán of her bunscoil teacher, Mrs O'Leary. She stared down at Siobhán, frowning, and then she called out, 'She's conscious, doctor!'

From outside the room, a man's deep voice said, 'Thank you, Grainne. I'll be with you in just a minute.' He sounded calm and educated, with a Dublin accent.

'Where am I?' asked Siobhán. Her mouth was so dry that she could only croak.

'You're safe enough,' said the woman. 'You've had yourself a bit of an accident, that's all. Don't worry. Everything's going to be grand.'

Siobhán tried to sit up but her back felt frozen stiff, and she had no leverage. She dropped her head back down on to the pillow and said, 'What do you mean, accident? What accident?'

'You don't remember? You were hit by a car, dear. Both of your legs are broken.'

'What? Where? Is this a hospital?'

'It's a kind of a hospital, yes. It's a nursing home for people like yourself, with debilitating injuries.'

'Where's my phone? I need to call my mother.'

'I haven't seen any phone, dear. Sorry.'

Siobhán tried again to sit up, but she simply couldn't feel her lower back. She reached down and felt a honeycomb blanket over her legs, of the kind they always used in hospitals, and underneath it she could feel her left thigh with her hand, but there was no sensation at all in the thigh itself. It might just as well have been made of wood.

She saw that her arm was bare, and she realised then that she was wearing a short-sleeved nightgown, white with small blue dots on it, so she must be in hospital.

'I have to call my mother. She'll be sick with worry. What time is it?'

'Half-past two.'

'You're joking, aren't you? She'll have probably called the guards by now. If I'm late at all, I always have to ring her and tell her where I am. Are you sure it's not in my bag?'

'What bag was that, dear?'

'My orange Hallowe'en bag. It has like a pumpkin stitched on to it. Don't tell me I've lost it.'

The gingery-haired woman raised one eyebrow, as if she couldn't even be bothered to think about Siobhán's bag, let alone go and look for it.

Siobhán said, 'Do you have a phone that I could lend a borrow of? I have to call her and tell her where I am.'

'I'll have to talk to the doctor. He wouldn't want you upsetting yourself unduly. And I'm not at all sure that you're allowed any visitors yet.'

'What do you mean? Why not? What's wrong with me?'

'Like I said, dear, it's your legs. You stepped out into the road without looking. I'm making no judgements at all, but from your blood analysis this morning, I'd say you were probably langers. You stepped out into the road and a car ran over you. The trouble is, it looks like you may have some spinal injury, too, and so we can't risk anybody coming to see you and bringing in some infection. You know what it's like this time of year, everybody coughing and sneezing, like. You don't want to end up paralysed for the rest of your life, now do you?'

'But I only want to ring her and tell her what's happened, and where I am.'

Siobhán's eyes were crowded with tears now, and she was beginning to feel that she was in some kind of a madhouse. She sounded logical, this woman, but she wasn't really making any sense.

'Please,' she said. 'Just lend me a borrow of your phone. I'll only be making the one call.'

'Let me speak to the doctor.'

'Can't *I* speak to the doctor? I want to know how bad I've been hurt.'

'Of course you can speak to the doctor,' said the man's deep voice. 'I'm right here, miss. How are you feeling?'

Siobhán craned her head up as much as she could, and saw a very tall man standing on the opposite side of the room, wearing a pale green surgical cap and a full-length surgical gown. The lower half of his face was covered by a surgical mask, so that she could see only his eyes. They were glittery and almost black, his eyes, and his eyebrows were thick and black with a few stray wisps of white.

'I need to ring my mother,' said Siobhán. 'I need to tell her what's happened.'

'You can of course,' said the doctor, approaching the bed and standing close beside her. 'But before you do that, I have to perform at least one more urgent procedure.'

'What? What do you mean?'

'The reason you can't remember what happened to you is that when you were struck by the car you suffered a vasovagal syncope. This simply means that either your ulnar nerve or your peroneal nerve was struck very hard, causing you to faint.'

'I don't – What does that mean?' said Siobhán. 'I mean, what? Is that serious, like?'

'It's not at all unusual,' said the doctor. 'It's sometimes called a vasodepressor response, but it's a physical reaction that not too many people are aware of.'

Siobhán wished that he would lower his mask, because it muffled his voice and apart from that she couldn't clearly follow what he was trying to tell her, and it would have helped if she could have seen the expression on his face. Although he was standing so close to her, he wasn't looking at her directly. His eyes kept darting from side to side as if he were simply reciting this explanation and wasn't particularly interested in her reaction to it.

'Your ulnar nerve is what we commonly call your funny bone, in your elbow. Your peroneal nerve is in your knee. If either of these nerves are struck very hard, it triggers an immediate response. Your body immediately sends a large amount of blood flooding into your legs. This pulls blood away from your major organs like your brain and your heart, and so you lose consciousness.

'That's not too serious if you're sitting down, of course, because all you'll do is slowly slump over. If you're standing up, however, you'll fall over flat, without making any attempt at all to protect yourself, and you can do yourself some serious injury. In your case it appears that one car struck you in the knee, which caused you to faint and fall into the path of another car, which ran over your legs. At the same time, you suffered a very nasty crack on the head, probably from hitting the kerb.

'I've given you morphine to suppress the pain, but I urgently have to check your brain to make sure that you have no internal bleeding. If there is, it could be very debilitating, or even fatal. I also need to look at your legs in case there's still some subcutaneous bleeding there, and to remove any bone fragments, if any. You don't want any impairment of your mental faculties, do you? And you want to be able to walk again, I'd say. You don't want to be some helpless vegetable for the rest of your life.'

'Can I ring my mother, though? I have to ring my mother.'

'You can't do it from this room, I'm afraid, because it's shielded for X-rays and there's no reception. You're not in any condition to be moved yet, either. Quite apart from that, I need to get started on your brain scan as soon as I can.'

Siobhán's mouth turned down and tears slid from both of her eyes. The doctor laid his hand on her shoulder and said, 'There, now, don't be getting yourself all upset. If you give Grainne here your mother's name and number, she'll call her for you and tell her what's happened to you and where you are, and how soon she can come and visit you. How about that?'

Siobhán was still feeling too weak and confused to argue. 'All right, then,' she said. 'But you won't go frightening her, will you? Her name's Mrs Patricia Kilmore, and it's four-three-nine eighty-four eighty-five.'

'And your name is?'

'Siobhán. Siobhán O'Donohue.' She paused to lick her lips, because her mouth was so dry. 'That's on account of my father died and my mother got married again but he went off and left her. Michael Kilmore, I mean.'

'Thanks a million, Siobhán,' said the doctor. 'Grainne, will you go and do that right away?'

'Of course,' said Grainne. 'I won't be long. And I won't alarm her, don't worry.'

As soon as she had left the room, the doctor turned back to Siobhán. 'Now then, I'm going to give you another little injection to put you out for a while. You'd find it unbearable otherwise, the pain. I need to investigate what damage has been done to your legs, to see what I can do to set you right, and unfortunately that means I'll have to do a fair bit of poking around. But don't you worry. We'll soon have you dancing again. It's going to be "eat your heart out, Jean Butler".'

Siobhán looked into the doctor's eyes. They were fixed on her now, very intently, as if he were calculating exactly what he was going to do to her. Because of his mask, though, she still couldn't work out what he was feeling. Pity? Anxiety? Or was it something else altogether? His mask was sucked in and out as he breathed, and she noticed that he was breathing much quicker now, which strangely reminded her of Tadgh when they were in bed together, and he was close to his vinegar stroke. Surely he wasn't *excited*?

He disappeared from her view, but he returned a few moments later pushing a small metal trolley with bottles tinkling together and a metal kidney bowl. He lifted the sleeve of her nightgown and wiped her upper arm with a cold medicated tissue. Then he pierced one of the bottles with the needle of a hypodermic syringe, held it up to the light, and tapped it.

'There,' he said. 'Only a little sting, nothing worse than a gnat-bite, and you'll be in dreamland. When you wake up, Siobhán, I can promise you this, my dear, you won't know yourself.'

Five

As she drove through the drizzle into the city, Katie's iPhone pinged every few seconds with messages and emails, and when she reached her office she found a stack of messages and files waiting for her on her desk. The red light on her phone was flashing.

She was still shaking out her wet raincoat when Detective Dooley knocked at her door. He was looking exceptionally smart this afternoon, in a tight navy-blue suit. He had trimmed his beard and his hair was brushed flat, too, instead of vertical, as it usually was. Most of the time he wore skinny jeans and sloppy Aran sweaters and could easily be taken for a college student. That was why Katie frequently sent him to Cork's dance clubs and discos to check up on the peddlers of MDMA and other recreational drugs.

'I'm in court this afternoon,' he told her, before she could even ask him. 'That Shalom Park rape.'

'Serious?' said Katie. 'I didn't think they were hearing that until the middle of next month.'

'It's only a preliminary hearing. One of the defendants changed his plea to guilty last night and he's prepared to shop the other three. I did text you about it.'

'I'm sorry. I've had a rake of messages this morning and I haven't had a chance to check them all yet. Well, that's good news. I thought it was going to be touch-and-go, getting a conviction for that one. Which defendant was it?'

'Bryan Neeley, the youngest. The GAA player.'

'What changed his mind, do you know?'

'It's only hearsay, like, but I think the girl's father might have got a message through to him. Something along the lines of, "If the court doesn't punish you, then me and my friends will, some dark night when you least expect it, and I don't suppose you want to be spending the rest of your life singing like a Bee Gee."'

'I've gone deaf all of a sudden and I didn't hear that,' said Katie. 'But fingers crossed for a good result, anyhow. Was there something else you wanted to see me about?'

'Oh, yes. This shooting at Ballinroe East. Detective Sergeant Begley went down there again this morning, like, to see how the Bandon cops are getting on with it.'

'And?'

'They let the kennel owner go home about lunchtime, but he's given them an inventory of all his dogs that were taken. I've already circulated all of the pet shops and all of the breeders I know of. I've also passed a copy to Inspector O'Rourke, so that he can contact all of the Travellers he's pally with, in case any of the dogs get offered for racing. I've been in touch with C and E at Ringaskiddy, too, warning them to keep an eye out for any dogs being exported. I know it's too early to expect any kind of response, but you know what these Spaniel Snatchers are like. Once they've lifted a dog, it's spirited away before you can say Brandy Traditional Meat Loaf.'

'We still haven't identified the victim?'

'Not so far. His body's been sent off to CUH, and the technical experts are taking DNA and blood samples. We won't be able to circulate pictures to the media, though, because he doesn't have what you might describe as a face.'

Katie sat down at her desk. On the top of the stack of papers in front of her was a confidential security report on the Cork Islamic community, which numbered about five thousand, and in particular the school that was being set up in the new Muslim cultural centre at Turners Cross. She lifted the cover and read the first page and then let the cover drop back. As if her life wasn't under enough pressure already.

'All right, Robert, thanks. I'll ring Inspector O'Brien and see what the latest is. There isn't too much we can do, though, until we put a name to this dead dognapper. I can't afford to send you all out hunting for missing dogs, as you very well know. I simply don't have the manpower available, or the budget.'

Once Detective Dooley had left, she shuffled through all of the paperwork on her desk to see if there was anything that required her urgent attention. At the same time she listened to the voicemail messages on her phone and checked her texts and her emails. She had taken only one morning off and already she felt that she was being buried under a blizzard of paperwork.

The most pressing message had been sent by Inspector Noonan. Somebody had deliberately started a fire at the new €5 million housing estate built at St Anthony's Park to rehouse the Travellers who had previously lived on the halting site at Knocknaheeny. The Travellers had moved to their smart new houses only under protest, partly because they had wanted financial compensation but mostly because they hadn't been allowed to take their horses with them. Several of them had threatened to vandalise the estate, and now it looked as if one of them might have carried out his threat. At least the city fire brigade had quickly contained the blaze and nobody had been injured.

Katie knew that it would take more than detective work to solve this problem. If it turned out that a Traveller had started the fire, she would have to meet with the Traveller Visibility Group to see if something could be done to settle the Romas' outstanding grievances. Then again, it could have been set by a disgruntled local resident who objected to so many Travellers moving in nearby.

Her phone rang. It was Inspector O'Brien, calling from Bandon.

'Oh, Terry,' she said. 'Thanks a million for ringing. You saved me from ringing you, as a matter of fact. What's the story on this shooting?'

'We're more than slightly puggalised, to tell you the truth,' said Inspector O'Brien.

'Why's that? From the sound of it, it was pretty straightforward.'

'On the face of it, yes. A gang of dognappers breaks into a boarding kennels in the early hours of the morning and starts making off with the dogs, so the owner comes out and takes a potshot at them.'

'So what's the mystery?'

'On closer consideration there's a couple of things that don't exactly fit, like, do you know what I mean? The victim wasn't armed but there was a hurley lying on the ground next to him, as if he'd dropped it when he was shot. The technical experts used a scanner right then and there for fingerprints and the victim had definitely been holding the hurley himself prior to having his brains blown out. However there were scores more prints all over it – handle and bas both – and these all matched the kennel owner, Eoin Cassidy.'

'So the hurley was probably his? Eoin Cassidy's?'

Inspector O'Brien said, 'That's right, and when we questioned him back at Weir Street he admitted it was. First of all he tried to make out that he'd been carrying the hurley along with his shotgun, and that the victim had snatched it from him, but we pointed out to him how unlikely this was. It would have been fierce awkward for him to be carrying a shotgun in one hand and a hurley in the other. Not only that – even if he really *was* carrying the both of them, why did he allow the victim to get close enough to snatch the hurley, when he was also holding a shotgun? And how did the victim manage to get so far away with it before he shot him, and how come the victim was facing him when he fired?'

'What did he say to all of that?' asked Katie.

'He retracted his first explanation, and said that he was under such stress that he was confused, and that maybe he hadn't been carrying the hurley after all. When we asked him again how the victim had managed to lay his hands on it, he said he plain couldn't remember.'

'How about you, Terry?' asked Katie. 'Do you have any theories?'

'I don't have a bull's notion, ma'am, to be honest with you,' said Inspector O'Brien. 'But Sergeant Doherty talked to Cassidy's wife, and *he* came away with the very strong impression that Cassidy wasn't telling us the truth. Not the whole truth, any road.'

'Why's that?'

'She was totally in pieces, that's what he said.'

'Come on, that's understandable, surely. Her husband had just killed a man, and all of their valuable dogs had been stolen. I think I'd be more than a little upset, too, if I was her.'

'I don't know – Doherty reckoned there was more to it than that. She was crying and shaking so much that she could hardly get a word out, and her face was bruised, too, although she kept trying to hide it from him with her hands. He didn't want to push her any further, like, because she was so distressed, and he didn't want to be accused of harassment. But I'd say she needs talking to again, preferably by a woman officer.'

'I see,' said Katie. She sat back in her chair, thinking hard. Then she said, 'Did anybody else get a sconce at these dognappers? I mean, apart from the Cassidys?'

'Nobody,' said Inspector O'Brien. 'Well, that was hardly surprising at four o'clock in the morning, right out there in back of leap. We've checked all the CCTV cameras on the main roads between Kinsale and Clon, but there's no trace of a white van or a Range Rover, which is what Eoin Cassidy said they were driving, so they must have come and gone by some back route. That's always assuming he wasn't lying to us.'

Katie said: 'All right, Terry. Detective Dooley's put out feelers about the dogs around the city. You know, to pet-shops and breeders and vets. I have to say that dognapping doesn't rank very high on my list of priorities, just at the moment. If there wasn't such a strong chance that it could help us to identify our victim I'd put the dogs under "file and forget". But I think you're right. It sounds like there's more to this than meets the eye. For all we know, there may have been something personal between him and this Eoin Cassidy, and this dognapping story is just a blind.'

A new message text popped up on her computer screen from Inspector Noonan. She paused to read it, and then she said, 'Listen, Terry, I'll tell you what, I'll come down to Ballinroe East myself and talk to Cassidy's wife.'

'You mean yourself in person, like?'

'Yes, me in person. Apart from anything else, I'd like to take a sconce at where this shooting took place. What's the time now? I can be down there with you by half-past four.'

'Are you sure about that, ma'am?'

'You said yourself she needed a woman to talk to her. I'll bring Detective Scanlan with me, too. She has a very sympathetic way with her, and it'll be good experience for her.'

'All right, then, that's grand,' said Inspector O'Brien. 'I'll meet you outside the kennels there in – what? – forty-five minutes, give or take. Maybe an hour.'

Katie put down the phone. She didn't really have to go down to Sceolan Boarding Kennels herself. She could have sent Detective Scanlan down on her own to interview Mrs Cassidy, or detailed Detective O'Mara to ride shotgun with her if there was any risk of Eoin Cassidy giving them trouble. But after what Inspector O'Brien had told her, she sensed that there was something unusual about this case which might be worth looking into, and she seriously didn't feel like spending the rest of the afternoon ploughing through her 'in' tray. She could make a start on that first thing tomorrow morning.

There was another reason she was tempted to drive down to Ballinroe East. Even though she didn't like to admit it to herself she wasn't in any great hurry to get back home to John. In fact the very thought of it filled her with a feeling that was close to dread. He had suffered so much, and the rest of his life was going to be one horrendous struggle, both physical and mental. How could she tell him to his face that she didn't love him any more, and that he was going to be nothing but a burden to her?

She shrugged on her raincoat again and went along the corridor to Chief Superintendent MacCostagáin's office. She knocked at his door and he called out, 'Come along in!' although when she went inside he was talking on the phone.

She sat opposite him while he finished his conversation. He seemed bothered about something, and he kept turning a pencil end over end and tapping it on to his desk. He always looked as if he were chewing a wasp, even when he was pleased, but now he was obviously angry, too.

'No, I'm not at all happy about the way you've been dragging this out! Sergeant Lynch handled that situation perfectly correctly, and you need to inform him officially that he wasn't guilty of any wrongdoing! The next thing I know, he's going to be doing a Michael Galvin on us, and committing suicide because he thinks that his career's over and he's going to end up in prison!'

He paused to listen and then he snapped, 'No! Absolutely not! Sort it out and then get back to me directly and let me *know* that you've sorted it out! Today! Yes, *today*!'

He banged down the phone and looked across his desk at Katie with his nostrils flaring.

'Who was that? The Ombudsman?' she asked him.

He nodded, still so angry that he was finding it difficult to speak. 'They've already established that Sergeant Lynch committed no misdemeanour whatsoever. As you know, he wrote in his report that he'd seen Mrs Shelley standing on the pavement when he passed her by on the way to that hit-and-run on Grand Parade, but the CCTV showed her standing in the road.

'He only glimpsed her out of the corner of his eye, for God's sake, and she was less than three feet away from where he said she was. And it certainly wasn't *his* fault that a taxi ran her over. I can't imagine why the GSOC thought that was even worth investigating!'

'And they haven't yet told Lynch that he's in the clear?'

'No. But I shall do myself, right now. Holy Saint Joseph and all the carpenters – as if we don't have enough accusations to put up with, without nitpicking inquiries like this!'

He paused to compose himself, and then he said, 'I thought you were taking the day off, Katie. Weren't you supposed to be meeting that poor fellow of yours, the one who lost his legs?'

'Yes, sir, I was, and I did. John came home this morning. I was going to stay home with him for the rest of the day myself but Begley called me about this shooting down at Ballinroe East.'

'Oh, the dognapper.'

'Well, we're not one hundred per cent sure that he *was* a dognapper yet. The kennel owner claims he was – the fellow who shot him. But we won't know for sure until we have a positive ID. I'm going down to Ballinroe myself to have a word with the kennel owner, and also the kennel owner's wife.'

'What about your legless fellow?'

'He has a nurse who's going to be taking care of him whenever I'm away.'

Chief Superintendent MacCostagáin pressed his hand over his mouth and looked at her narrowly. Then he said, 'Katie – you're sure you haven't taken too much on yourself? You're already up the walls here at the station, especially with all of these new budget cuts. Fair play, your fellow has a nurse. But I remember my sister looking after my old Da when he went doolally. She had a carer to help her out but Mother of God, it almost killed her.'

'John's not demented, sir. He's just disabled. It'll get much easier once they fit him with his prosthetic legs and he can start to walk again.'

'And how long will that take?'

'I don't know. Six months, maybe a year.'

Chief Superintendent MacCostagáin stood up and came around his desk. He stood very close to her, saying nothing for a few seconds.

'I'd better make tracks,' said Katie. 'I've arranged to meet Inspector O'Brien at the kennels, and it's getting dark already.'

'I, ah – well, take care of yourself, won't you?' said Chief Superintendent MacCostagáin. 'If you start to feel that the pressure's too much for you, come and talk to me. It's what I'm here for. You've been pushing yourself to the limit lately, I've seen that, especially with all these drugs flooding into the city.

I don't want you falling apart. Remember what happened to Liam Fennessy.'

Katie said nothing. Inspector Fennessy's personal life had fallen apart, and then he had started taking cocaine, and accepting bribes, and in the end he had shot himself.

'No, sir, nothing like that is going to happen to me. To be honest with you, I don't have the time to fall apart.'

Six

Once they had passed Cork airport, the rain began to ease off and the pillowy grey clouds opened up, so that the pale lemon-coloured light of day could shine through. The hedgerows glittered and the road surface up ahead of them was dazzling.

'How's it going with the drugs programme?' asked Katie. 'Did you manage to have that meeting with the HSE at last?'

'This morning,' said Detective Scanlan. 'Moira Kennedy from HSE and two women from Cuan Mhuire and a fellow from Matt Talbot Services and Jim Geoghegan from Merchants Quay, too. I haven't had the time to write it up for you yet.'

'Not a bother. I wouldn't have had the time to read it, even if you had. What was the general gist of what they had to tell you? They must all be feeling the effects of this drug tsunami too.'

Detective Scanlan said, 'You're not joking. Cork's awash with heroin, that was how Jim Geoghegan described it. By his estimate, there's at least five hundred hard-core heroin addicts in the city centre alone, and he wouldn't be surprised if it's half of that again on top of it. The trouble is, he can only count the number of addicts who come to Merchants Quay to use their free needle exchange.'

'It's getting mental,' said Katie. 'Think of how many peddlers we've lifted in the past two months – not only how many numerically but how much stuff we've found on each one of them. And look at those petty crime statistics we've just had in. They're up seven-and-a-half per cent since the last quarter, and almost all of them are drug-related in one way or another.'

Katie had been aware since the end of the summer that more hard drugs were being peddled in the city than ever before. Not only *more* drugs, but much purer drugs too, so that new users were becoming dependent much more rapidly. Her narcotics squad had reported that heroin was even being sold in broad daylight, in mid-afternoon, in some of the shopping malls. One dealer had been caught right outside Champions Sports in the Savoy Centre, offering free sample packets of heroin to young lads going in to buy runners.

'Moira Kennedy from the HSE said that the hospitals are dealing with at least half-a-dozen near-fatal overdoses every week,' said Detective Scanlan. 'Last year twelve people altogether died of heroin overdoses in Cork city alone, and if things carry on like this, she reckons that this year it will probably be more than twenty.'

'But she hasn't picked up any hint at all where it's coming from, all this heroin? Nor Jim Geoghegan, neither, nor Cuan Mhuire? Because, let's face it, *we're* still totally in the dark, too. The street dealers are mostly the same old scummers as always, but the quantity they're selling now, and the quality of it. There's no question at all that there's somebody new in the business, and they're incredibly well organised. But who is it?'

'I talked to Declan Murphy from the Real IRA yesterday morning,' said Detective Scanlan. 'Even *he* doesn't know who it is, or makes out he doesn't, anyhow, and if anybody should know, it's him. But I'm working on a couple of new contacts at the moment. I think one of them has a half an idea who's behind it, but he's too jibber to tell me.'

'Well, keep on nagging him,' Katie told her.

'I will. Besides, I think he fancies me something rotten, so I might get lucky.'

Katie gave her a quick sideways smile. Detective Scanlan was just twenty-four – tall and thin as a model, with a wave of shoulder-length brunette hair. She was very unusual-looking: she had a long pointed nose, but her huge violet eyes and her pouting pink lips gave her an almost magical appearance, as if she were an *aes sidh*, a fairy who had decided to join the mortal police force.

Over the past few weeks, Katie had become increasingly pleased by the progress she was making. Pádraigin Scanlan was one of a team of four young detectives whom Katie had selected to give special guidance and encouragement. 'Katie's Kids', Detective O'Donovan called them, although he didn't mean it entirely as a compliment. But what these four lacked in street experience they more than made up for in other ways. They were attractive and bright and computer-literate and all of them looked young for their age, which meant that they could mingle with college and university students and infiltrate Cork's thriving club scene. Detective O'Donovan was approaching forty. He was putting on weight and his hair was starting to turn grey. As canny and as hardened as he was, he would have found it impossible to pass himself off as a raver at Rearden's or Cyprus Avenue.

'You *have* eaten something today?' Katie asked Detective Scanlan. 'I don't want you fainting on me in mid-interview.'

'Oh, I'm grand altogether,' said Detective Scanlan. 'I had a cheese and bacon burger at Coqbull for lunch, with the chorizo fries. I'm full as an egg.'

'Holy Mary, I don't know where you put it all,' Katie told her. 'You must have extra-efficient metabolism.'

She looked again at Detective Scanlan in her skin-tight jeans with the belt done up to the very last hole and wondered if she had been as thin at that age. Probably, although she had been much more bosomy. When they had first got together, her late husband Paul had almost been able to close both of his hands around her waist.

'You should eat more,' Paul used to say to her. 'Don't want you snapping in half, like, do we?'

* * *

It was dark by the time they reached the harbour town of Kinsale, but the restaurants and bars were all lit up and the pavements were crowded.

'Jesus, I could do with a drink,' said Katie, as they passed the scarlet-painted front of Max's Wine Bar, on Main Street.

'Serious?' said Detective Scanlan.

'Not really. I don't want to keep Inspector O'Brien waiting. But maybe we'll stop for one on the way back.'

Once they had driven through the busy town centre, the darkness closed in again, and they were on their own. They crossed the long concrete bridge that spanned the last wide bend in the River Bandon. Apart from the roadway ahead of them, flatly illuminated by their headlamps, all they could see now was the black glittering water of the estuary, and a sprinkling of lights from the houses that were perched high on the hills all around them.

In this landscape – although she had Detective Scanlan with her – Katie suddenly felt a pang of loneliness. When she had first told her father that she was thinking of joining An Garda Siochána, he had taken hold of her hands and said to her, 'Think on this, Katie. From the moment you become a guard, no matter how many friends you have, no matter who loves you, people will always be wary of you. You'll have made yourself an outsider, for the rest of your life.'

They turned down the R604 and arrived at last at the entrance to Sceolan Boarding Kennels. Inspector O'Brien was already sitting in his black Mondeo by the side of the road, along with a uniformed sergeant. Katie flashed her lights and they climbed out to meet her.

'What's the story, Terry?' said Katie. 'I hope we haven't kept you waiting too long.'

'No bother at all, ma'am,' said Inspector O'Brien. 'Gave us a chance to have a much-needed hang sandwidge.'

Inspector O'Brien was a stubby little bull of a man with very blue eyes and thinning, combed-over hair. Katie thought that if he put on a long striped apron he would look just like a butcher from the English Market.

'This is Detective Scanlan,' Katie told him. 'I brought her along because she has a way of persuading women to confess to things that they wouldn't even tell their best friend.'

'Sounds exactly like my moth,' said Inspector O'Brien. 'She knows everybody's business before they find it out themselves. This here is Sergeant Doherty. It was Sergeant Doherty who talked to Mrs Cassidy this morning, but like I told you, she was very unforthcoming, and pure distressed, so he considered it wiser to terminate the interview and question her later, when she'd had some time to calm down and reflect, like.'

'Very sensible, sergeant,' said Katie. 'I gather she has some bruising on her face, too.'

'She does, yes, desperate,' said Sergeant Doherty. He was tall and stockily built, with a large bony head, and curled-up ears. In his yellow high-viz jacket he looked even more padded than he actually was, as if he wouldn't be able to run more than a hundred metres before being puffed out. 'I never got around to asking her how she came by them, all them bruises – whether she was the victim of domestic violence or whether she'd had some kind of an accident in inverted commas. You know – tripped and banged her face on the washing-machine like most of these battered wives do. She gave me the feeling that even if I did ask her, she wouldn't tell me.'

'Well, I think you did the right thing by cutting the interview short,' said Katie. 'She only would have retreated into her shell even more if you'd kept on pressing her. You didn't warn the Cassidys that we were going to pay them a visit now, did you, inspector?'

Inspector O'Brien shook his head. 'No, but I've advised Eoin Cassidy that even if he doesn't get formally charged for shooting your man, we'll be requiring his co-operation for quite some time to come. We still need to ask him a rake of questions, and the technical experts haven't yet finished taking prints and fibres from all of the kennels. There's any amount of wire fencing where somebody's sweater or jacket could have got snagged.'

'What about identikit pictures?'

'Those, too. I've told him that we'll be using his description of the victim to prepare some 3-D facial approximations – you know, with the ZBrush software, like. I know they're more generic than your hand-drawn re-creations, but that's all we can stretch to, at the moment. Bill Phinner has a forensic artist on his team, doesn't he? But he told me that she's not available right now.'

'You mean Eithne O'Neill,' said Katie. 'Yes, she's very good. In fact she's brilliant. But she's off on compassionate leave at the moment. Her sister's dying of cancer, sad to say.'

'Oh. I didn't know that. I'm sorry to hear it. And there was me grumbling to Bill because I can't afford a freelance artist. Not on my budget.'

'Well, let's just see how this all plays out,' said Katie. 'Let's go and take a look at the scene of the shooting, shall we, and then Detective Scanlan and I can have a few words with Mrs Cassidy.'

'Her name's Cleona, by the way,' put in Sergeant Doherty. 'And go easy on her when you ask her about the dogs. You'd think she'd lost her children, the way she's talking.'

They returned to their cars and drove up the sloping driveway towards the two rows of kennels. Every individual bay had a light on, even the empty ones; and the two main wall lamps were shining too, so that the tarmac courtyard in between the two rows of kennels was starkly illuminated, like a deserted film set. A blue vinyl forensic tent was pitched right in the middle of it, surrounded by blue-and-white garda tape, and a Garda patrol car was parked beside the house.

After they had climbed out of their cars, Inspector O'Brien came across to Katie and said, 'I did recommend to the Cassidys that they move away for a while, in case any of the gang decided to come back and retaliate. But they insisted that they couldn't leave the dogs that were left behind. There's still thirteen of them all told, and they wouldn't hear of the CSPCA taking them in, even temporary-like.

'That's why I've posted two armed officers here twenty-four hours a day – at least until we've put a name to our victim, and we know exactly who we're looking for.'

'Have they given you a full list of the dogs that were taken?'

Sergeant Doherty held up a folded sheet of paper. 'Twenty-six of them altogether. Mostly they went for the big dogs. Two German

Shepherds, three bull terriers, a Vizsla, two boxers, one mastiff... but there's a Samoyed here and that's worth nearly eight-and-a-half thousand euros, according to Eoin Cassidy.'

They walked towards the house. In one of the kennels, a Labrador was mournfully and repetitively barking, while a wire-haired fox terrier was jumping up and down and yapping in excited bursts.

Inspector O'Brien knocked at the front door and one of the gardaí opened it, almost at once. He must have been expecting them, even if the Cassidys weren't.

'All right, sir?' said the garda. 'Everything's quiet.' He jerked his head towards the kennels. 'Well, except for the effing dogs, like, do you know what I mean?'

They went into the living-room. Eoin Cassidy was hunched on the end of the couch, watching *Today with Maura and Daithi* on the television. The second garda was sitting with his arms folded in a straight-backed wooden chair against the wall, looking infinitely bored. A crumpled copy of *The Sun* was lying on the floor at his feet, where he had obviously dropped it after finishing with the sports pages. He stood up when Katie and Inspector O'Brien came into the room, but Eoin remained where he was, staring unblinkingly at the television, and didn't even turn his head.

'Mr Cassidy?' said Inspector O'Brien. 'Mr Cassidy – this is Detective Superintendent Maguire from Cork City Divisional Headquarters.'

Eoin still didn't look around, so Inspector O'Brien raised his voice. 'DS Maguire has a special interest in your case, Mr Cassidy. She's been investigating a gang of dognappers in the city division for quite some time now, and she believes your man may have been one of them.'

After a long pause, Eoin switched off the television's sound with his remote, and turned around. His face was unshaven with a pale and greasy sheen like linseed putty, and his eyes were so puffy from lack of sleep that it looked as if he could barely see out of them. He was wearing a beige shawl-collared cardigan with nothing underneath but a stained white vest, green-striped pyjama trousers and odd socks, one brown and one blue.

'Jesus and Mary and the Wain,' he said, and he sounded exhausted. 'If I've told you once what happened, Inspector O'Brien, I've told you ten times over. What more do you want me to say?'

'I know that, Mr Cassidy. But DS Maguire hasn't heard it. Not from the horse's mouth, so to speak.'

Eoin took a deep breath. Without looking up at Katie, he recited what he must have told Inspector O'Brien at Bandon Garda Station.

'Cleona woke me up to say that the dogs were going doolally. I took my shotgun and went outside to see what they were so het up about. There was a gang of maybe eight fellers taking our dogs out of their kennels and loading them into a van. I shouted at them to stop but they came for me, and I was afeard they were going to give me a beating, or worse. I fired the one shot up in the air, but they took no notice and kept on coming, so I fired again, and I hit the feller in the head. That's all.'

'All right, Mr Cassidy, thank you,' said Katie. 'I completely understand how traumatic this has been for you, so I don't blame you for being reluctant to go over it yet again. Is your wife at home? Cleona?'

'She didn't have nothing to do with this at all. I made her stay upstairs.'

'All the same, I'd like to have a word with her.'

'What's the point of that? All she heard was the dogs barking. She didn't see nothing. Nothing at all.'

'Where is she, Mr Cassidy?' Katie asked him.

'I don't want her upset, not any more than she is already. She's devastated.'

'We'll do everything we can not to distress her, I promise you.'

Eoin Cassidy hesitated for a moment, his lips moving around as if he were chewing on a lump of gristle and couldn't decide whether to swallow it. Then he said, 'Okay, then. I'll fetch her down.'

'We'd prefer to talk to her on her own, if that's all right with you.'

'All right. I'll take her through to the kitchen. But like I say, she won't be able to tell you nothing. She was here in the house the whole time.'

He stood up and left the living-room. When they had heard him going upstairs, Katie turned to the two gardaí who had been watching over him. 'How's he been? Has he talked to you at all about what happened?'

Both gardaí shook their heads. One of them said, 'He hasn't uttered a single word, like, except to tell us that we could make ourselves a cup of tea. I'd say the feller was in post-dramatic stress disorder, do you know what I mean?'

'Traumatic,' said Detective Scanlan.

'You're right,' said the garda. 'It must have been.'

'Now I come to think of it, we *did* hear him say one thing,' the second garda put in. 'After we'd first come into the house, his missus come halfway down the stairs, wanting to know who we were. She was kind of whispering and screaming both at the same time, if you know what I mean, like she was panicking but she didn't want us to hear. But any road your man pushes her back upstairs and says, "It's all right, love, it's only the guards – it's not them other fellers come back." So she goes back upstairs. But that's all he said. He comes back in and sits right down and switches on the telly and doesn't look at us and you wouldn't even think we was even there, like.'

'Are you quite sure that's exactly what he said?' Katie asked him. '"*It's not them other fellers come back*"?'

'Well, words to that effect,' said the garda.

Katie turned to the first garda. 'And you heard him say that, too?'

The garda pulled a face and shrugged. 'It was something like that, yes. Or, "It's not them again" – something of that nature.'

'But Mr Cassidy was clearly telling her that you were guards, so she had nothing to worry about, and that you weren't somebody else – somebody that she was scared of?'

'When you put it that way, yes, I would say that's a pretty fair interprematation.'

Katie looked at Inspector O'Brien and said, 'The hurley stick. That could explain it.'

She could tell that Inspector O'Brien was thinking along the same lines, because he raised one finger as if he were going to add to what she had just said. Before he could open his mouth, though, Eoin Cassidy appeared in the living-room doorway and said, 'Cleona's waiting on you in the kitchen, but for the love of God go easy on her, will you?'

'I promise,' said Katie. She beckoned to Detective Scanlan and the two of them went along the hallway to the kitchen.

Cleona was sitting at a Formica-topped table next to the right-hand wall. The kitchen was narrow and cramped and looked as if it had last been fitted out in the 1970s, when rustic pine was fashionable. A calendar from the Irish Kennel Club was pinned on the wall next to Cleona, and Katie noticed that yesterday's date had been marked with nothing but a red felt-tip exclamation mark. There was a window over the sink but the blind was still raised and all Katie could see out of it was blackness, and their own reflections, as if three other women were having a ghostly conversation, out in the night.

'Cleona?' said Katie, with a smile. 'My name's Kathleen Maguire and I'm a detective superintendent from Cork city. This is Pádraigin Scanlan. She's one of my team.'

Cleona looked even more devastated than Eoin. She was wrapped in a rose-pink velveteen dressing-gown with the collar turned up. She had applied natural matt foundation all over her face but it did little to cover the bruises on her cheeks and the left-hand side of her jaw, and both of her eyes were swollen. Her hair was like a nest of snakes, as though she had washed it but hadn't bothered to brush it.

Katie sat down next to her and Detective Scanlan sat at the opposite end of the table.

'We're not here to give either you or Eoin a hard time,' said Katie. 'We're only here to clear up what exactly happened.'

Cleona nodded but said nothing.

Katie said, 'So what *did* happen, Cleona?'

Cleona sniffed and took a crumpled tissue out of her dressing-gown pocket so that she could wipe her nose. 'The dogs woke me up. They were barking like you wouldn't believe. Going mad they were. So Eoin went outside to see what was disturbing them. I heard a shot and that was all. Then Eoin came back in and said that a gang of dognappers had been stealing the dogs, and that he'd shot one of them, and killed him.'

'You heard a shot? Just the one shot?'

Cleona nodded.

Katie leaned forward a little. As gently as she could, she said, 'The problem is, Cleona, that there's one or two details that don't exactly fit. You heard only the one shot, but Eoin says he fired two. A warning shot first, and then the shot that killed the dognapper.'

'Well, it could well have been two,' said Cleona. 'I couldn't say for definite. It was all fierce confusing, like, and I was scared half to death. I get terrible nervous at night, right out here in the middle of nowhere at all, especially in the winter, you know.'

'You have your husband to protect you, though,' put in Detective Scanlan.

'Oh, yes. And Eoin's very security-conscious. He always makes sure the kennels are locked and the alarms are set.'

'The alarms didn't go off this time, though, did they?' Katie asked her.

'No. Eoin says that he must have forgot, just for once.'

'That's what he told the officers at Bandon. Do you think he did? Forget, I mean.'

'I don't understand you.'

'Do you genuinely think he forgot or do you think the dognappers knew how to switch the alarms off?'

'How could they?' asked Cleona. She was blinking furiously now and she had to dab at her eyes with her tissue.

'I don't know. I was just wondering if you had any ideas.'

'He said he forgot and of course I believe him. Why wouldn't I?'

Detective Scanlan said, 'It wasn't Eoin who hit you, though, was it?'

Cleona pressed her left hand against her cheek. 'Nobody hit me. I fell, that's all. I tripped over a broomstick in the yard and I fell against the kitchen step.'

'I used to have a boyfriend who hit me,' said Detective Scanlan. 'I was always telling my friends that I'd fallen over. And what was the other excuse? Oh, I know. I'd stood up suddenly in the kitchen and banged my head on a cupboard door that I'd been stupid enough to leave open.'

'Eoin has never laid a hand on me,' Cleona insisted. 'Not once in all our nine years of marriage.'

'You've had your arguments, though?'

'We have of course. Which couple doesn't? But all Eoin does when he flips the lid is take some of the dogs out for a walk.'

'One of the dognappers hit you, didn't he?' said Detective Scanlan. She said it so softly that Cleona could hardly hear her, but when she realised what Detective Scanlan had said, she slowly stiffened in her kitchen chair and pulled her dressing-gown tighter across her chest.

'They came into the house, didn't they, Cleona?' said Katie.

'I told you. I tripped over a broomstick in the yard and I fell against the kitchen step.'

'You don't have to make up a story about it, not for us,' said Detective Scanlan. 'I've seen my own face in the mirror often enough with bruises exactly like yours, and unless you have a pure quare kitchen step with five fingers and a signet ring, it was some feller who hit you, and more than once.'

Cleona took a deep breath, and then another. Katie could see that she was trying desperately hard to compose herself, so that she could stick to her story that she had fallen over, and back up Eoin's story that she had never set eyes on the dognappers.

But Detective Scanlan said, 'Cleona, sweetheart, we're not accusing you of doing anything wrong, neither you nor Eoin. But we can see that you've been badly hurt and how frightened you are. All we need is for you to tell us what really happened, so that we can clear this all up and find the men who did this to you and stole your dogs.'

Katie reached out and laid her hand on Cleona's arm, and squeezed it. 'You won't get into any trouble, Cleona. I promise you. But we have to clear this up.'

Cleona burst into tears. She let out a high-pitched whinny, followed by a deep, lung-wrenching sob. Katie stood up and put her arm around her shoulders, and held her tight. It was over a minute before Cleona was able to stop shaking and wipe her eyes.

'Why did they beat you, Cleona?' asked Detective Scanlan.

'There were two of them. They came into the house. One of them hit Eoin with his hurley stick and knocked him to the floor. The other one—'

She started sobbing again, so Katie and Detective Scanlan had to wait until she was able to continue. They exchanged looks, though, and they both had a strong suspicion what Cleona was going to say next.

'The other one – *what*, sweetheart?'

'The other one did it to me – had his way. I tried everything I could to stop him but he hit me and hit me and hit me, and there was nothing I could do.'

'He raped you?' said Katie.

Cleona nodded. 'I tried to stop him, I swear to God I did. But he was too strong.'

'Can you describe him?' asked Detective Scanlan.

Cleona shook her head. 'The both of them had scarves over their faces. They were rough types, though. They both smelled of cigarettes and drink. But the one who did it to me, the other one called him Keeno.'

'Keeno? You're sure?'

'He called him that more than once. He told him to get off me because they were leaving. "Will you beat on, Keeno," that's what he said exactly, and that was when he got off me.'

Katie sat down again and took hold of both of Cleona's hands. 'Cleona, we'll have to ask you some more questions, but before we do that it's very important that we take you to the hospital for a check-up. You've washed yourself since this happened?'

Cleona nodded. 'I have, yes. I couldn't stand the smell of him on me. He didn't – finish off, though, if you know what I mean.'

'Even if he didn't, and even if you've washed, there's a possibility that there might be some trace left of his DNA. More than that, though, it's vital that you're checked for any sexually transmitted disease. You never know what this Keeno could have been carrying.'

'Eoin told me to do that, too – go to the hospital.'

'Really? So why didn't you?'

'I told him that if I went to the hospital the nurses would have to report what that Keeno had done to me. I mean, like, the way I've been beaten, I couldn't just pretend that I'd had some one-night stand with some fellow and I was worried that he might have given me a dose of something. And if the nurses reported it, Eoin could be in desperate trouble for chasing after those men after they'd already left and shooting one of them out of revenge. After all, they were leaving. He could have just let them go.'

She looked into Katie's eyes with a searching expression that Katie had seen many times before when she was interviewing suspects. It was an expression that said, *You do believe me, don't you?*

Detective Scanlan must have read the same meaning into it, because she said, 'That's true, Cleona. If Eoin didn't shoot your man in self-defence, he could face a charge of manslaughter. But why didn't you simply back up his story, and say that those fellows were attacking him, and that he only pulled the trigger as a last resort?'

'I suppose,' said Cleona. 'But that wouldn't have been the truth, would it?'

'To begin with, Cleona, you denied that those fellows were ever in the house, and *that* wasn't the truth, was it?'

'I didn't want to say what had happened to me. I was mortally ashamed of it, if you really want to know.'

'You didn't *have* to tell us that you'd been raped,' Katie told her. 'It was important that you did, and I'm very thankful that you've had the strength to come out with it, but if you hadn't have told us, we would never have known.'

'No, but you would have asked me why those fellers beat me, wouldn't you? And knowing myself I would have come out and told you anyhow. Well, I have now, haven't I? I thought I could pretend to myself that it never happened, but I can't think about anything else. The feel of that monster. The stink of him. The worst thing was, he kept telling the other fellow how much I was loving it.'

'But what was the *real* reason you didn't want to go to the hospital?' asked Detective Scanlan, very gently. *Mother of God, Pádraigin*, thought Katie, *you're the sharp one.*

Cleona took her hands away from Katie's and clasped them tightly together, leaning forward slightly as if she were in church, and in prayer. After a while she looked up at Katie, and then at Detective Scanlan, and said, 'If I tell you, will you swear on the Holy Bible that you won't tell Eoin?'

Katie had a strong idea now of what she was going to tell them, and so she said, simply, 'Yes, Cleona. I promise you.'

Cleona looked across at Detective Scanlan, and Detective Scanlan gave her a reassuring smile and said, 'Me too.'

'The reason I didn't want to go to the hospital to be examined was that I'm expecting,' said Cleona. She hesitated for a moment longer, and then she said, 'I'm three months gone, and the baby – it isn't Eoin's.'

Seven

Siobhán woke up in a panic, feeling that she was choking. She tried to sit up but she was strapped tightly to the bed with her arms by her sides and all she could do was lift her head up a little. She felt as if she had been trying to swallow a whole handful of thistles and they had got caught in her windpipe.

Her eyes were wide open and yet the room was pitch dark. She couldn't even see a light under the door. She struggled to free her arms but she was fastened to the bed too securely, and after a while she realised that she could do nothing but lie back and call for somebody to help her.

She took in a deep breath and tried to cry out, but all she could manage was a whistling noise, like the tin whistle her younger brother used to play to annoy her. She took another breath and tried again, but that thin reedy sound was all she could manage, with a desperate squeak on the end of it.

She paused for a while, her chest rising and falling as if she had been swimming. Where was she, and why was it so *dark*? She could hear rain sprinkling against the window, and the shushing of a tree, so it must be windy outside. She could hear traffic, too, and voices, and after three or four minutes a door slammed, and she heard footsteps.

She felt woozy, as if she had been drinking too much, and she remembered all the Jägerbombs that she had been tipping back at the Eclipse. But that must have been *hours* ago, so surely she would have sobered up by now? And what had happened since then, and where was she now? She remembered the gingery-haired woman and the tall man wearing a surgical mask, but they must have been characters in a dream, surely? Perhaps she was still dreaming now. That was it: she would wake up at any moment and find that she was lying in her own bed, with Pookie her pink teddy-bear lying on the pillow next to her with his usual stupid smile on his face.

She closed her eyes. She waited, to see if she would wake up, and then she opened them again, but it was equally dark with her eyes open as it was with her eyes closed. What time was it? From the noises outside, and the voices, and the doors slamming, it sounded like daytime. Yet the darkness was seamless and absolute. It didn't make her feel claustrophobic, as if she were shut in a press. She had no idea where she was, so it seemed unnervingly vast and empty, like being in space, but with no stars at all.

Her throat still felt as if it were crammed with thistles, and so she cried out again for somebody to come and help her. Again, she could only manage that barely audible *pheep* sound, and when she tried to cry out louder, she hissed and bubbled like her father bleeding her bedroom radiator.

She tried to calm herself. There must be a reason why her throat was so sore and why she couldn't call out. There must be a reason why this room was so dark. Yet she felt so strange and alone, and her throat hurt so much, that she couldn't stop the tears from filling up her eyes and sliding down into her ears.

It seemed as if an hour at least went by. She thought she could hear a clock chiming in the distance, but it was too indistinct for her to be able to count what time it was. Then there were more voices, and more doors slamming, and more footsteps.

After a few minutes, the door of her own room opened, although it remained totally dark. Siobhán heard somebody approaching her bed, and standing beside her. She could hear them breathing, whoever they were, and she was sure that she could smell coffee on their breath. She didn't attempt to ask them who they were, though, because she knew that it would be hopeless, and that she would simply whistle, or hiss.

'You've been crying,' said a man's voice. 'I'm sorry if I've made you cry.'

Siobhán thought he sounded like the man who had been wearing the surgical mask, but he wasn't at all muffled now. Although she couldn't see him, perhaps he had taken his mask off. But why couldn't she see him? Had he covered her eyes with a blindfold? She couldn't feel a blindfold.

She still didn't try to say anything, mostly because she didn't think she could. The man came right up to her bedside and laid his fingertips on her forehead, as if he were giving her a benediction. His fingertips were cool and very soft, but he exerted enough pressure on her temples to give her an indication that he was very strong, too. She felt that he was silently telling her: *I am an artist. I am infinitely skilful. But beware, because I am powerful enough to kill you if I decide to.*

'Your operations all went very smoothly,' he told her. 'I regret that you'll be permanently paralysed from the waist downward for the rest of your life. There's no chance that you'll ever be able to walk again, but on the bright side you've no infection.'

Siobhán was sure now that this was a nightmare. It had to be. But why couldn't she wake up? She was panting with stress, and whistling soft and off-key with every breath.

'As well as being permanently paralysed, of course, you're permanently blinded, although I expect you've noticed that already. But it's not all bad news. Look at that Stevie Wonder, he does all right, doesn't he? And I've arranged for you to have a bit of assistance getting about.'

Blind? she thought. *Blind in both eyes? So it isn't dark at all – it's daytime. And I'm not asleep. This is real. I'm really here, strapped to this bed, unable to see, unable to speak, unable to walk. I can't even ask this invisible man where I am, or who he is, or why he did this to me.*

'There's one thing more,' said the man, but just as he was about to tell her his iPhone rang, a traditional jangling old-telephone ring.

'Yes?' he said. 'Oh, fantastic, he's here! And does he have the – ?

He does! That's grand! No, no, you can fetch him up here by all means. No, that's fine. She's awake now but of course she's more than a little devastated. Yes, absolutely. I'm sure that will help.'

When he spoke again, Siobhán wasn't sure if he was talking to her or still talking on the phone.

'I'm sorry about that,' he said. 'But I'm expecting a visitor for you – one which I'm sure you'll appreciate no end. Now, where was I? Oh, yes. The eyesight. Or rather, the *lack* of eyesight. The total and permanent lack of eyesight. That happens when both of your optic nerves are severed. I'll admit there have been cases where the optic nerve has been severed in an accident, for instance, and the casing has grown back again, so that the patient has had some limited vision restored. In your case, however, that won't be possible, even if a surgeon who had the skill to do it had a shot at it, and I don't know of any surgeon in Ireland who has.'

Siobhán was sobbing now, her throat choked up so that she could hardly breathe and her spine clenched with pain. All she wanted was for this man to go away and leave her alone, and stop giving her this heartless litany of how she had been mutilated. All she wanted to do was wake up, and if she couldn't wake up, then all she wanted was not to be here. She would rather be nowhere at all than here. She would rather not exist.

But the man didn't go away. In fact she heard him drag a chair over to the side of the bed so that he could sit down close to her, and so that his coffee breath smelled even stronger and she could feel the prickles of his intimate spit against her cheek.

'You're probably wondering too why you're finding it so difficult to speak,' he continued. 'That's because I've given you a laryngectomy and now you have no vocal cords. You can't talk any more. Of course there are ways in which people can overcome this, too. There are plenty of artificial speech devices. There's even a new one which can more or less replicate your own voice. But you won't be getting one of those. You won't be getting *any* of those. You're blind, my love, and you're silent, and that's the way you're going to stay.'

Siobhán sobbed and sobbed until saliva came spluttering out of her mouth and she was sure that she was going to suffocate. She heard the man tugging a tissue out of a box, and then she felt him dabbing at her mouth, but she turned her head away. She would rather choke than have him touch her.

'Are you all right now?' the man asked her.

She kept her head turned away. Even if she was blind and couldn't see him, she wanted him to know that she didn't want to face him.

The man paused for a while, and then he said, 'There's a good reason I carried out all of these operations on you, Siobhán. The thing of it is, I need you to work for me. You're some attractive young woman, you know that, don't you, and wherever you go you'll be given a heap of sympathy because of what you've suffered, a pretty young beour like you. That's important in my business. It puts people off their guard – distracts them, do you know what I mean?

'If you work for me, though, it's critical that you don't know who I am or what I look like, and that you're unable to tell anybody what I'm up to. It's also important that you can't run off, and that's why we broke your legs. Yes, I'm sorry to have to tell you what really happened to you, but I wouldn't want to lie. You weren't involved in a traffic accident at all. Well, you were, in a way. The fellows who picked you up knocked you unconscious and then ran over your knees. That will give you some idea of how much I wanted you.'

Siobhán could hear him continuing to talk to her, and yet now she refused to listen to him any more, or to try to make any sense out of what he was saying. If this were all real – if it weren't all some terrible nightmare, then he must be playing some kind of monstrous practical joke on her. He couldn't *really* have blinded her, and cut her vocal cords, and crippled her. Why would anybody do that? Surely after a while he would peel the black sticky-tape off her eyelids, so that she could see again, and snip away the thick gauze padding from her throat, so that she could speak, and then unwrap the bandages around her knees, and help her back on to her feet. Until he did that, though, she wasn't going to pay any attention to him.

'Ah, here's himself,' said the man. 'And would you look at what he's brought with him – well, sorry, no, you can't, of course. But if you *could*, Siobhán, I promise you that you'd be delighted.'

Although she was doing everything she could to ignore him, Siobhán heard somebody else come into the room, as well as a quick, shallow panting, and the patter of what sounded like paws on the carpet. The panting came closer, and then she felt a dog's wet nose snuffling against her bare right forearm, and its rough tongue licking her. She twisted her arm away, and let out a thin wheeze of disgust.

'There, now, there's nothing at all to get freaked about!' said another man's voice. He had a similar accent to the first man, as if he had been brought up in Cavan but taught himself Dartspeak, the upper-class accent of Dublin 4.

'Here, come on, girl, behave yourself,' the second man said. Then, leaning over Siobhán, 'I've named her Smiley, after the song, like, "When Irish Eyes are Smiling", because she's going to be your eyes from now on, now that you can't see any more.'

Siobhán was still trying her best not to listen, but she couldn't cover her ears, and the man's words made her feel as if she were dropping down a deep dark bottomless well. Warm tears slid down the side of her face, but without her vocal cords she couldn't manage to sob.

'From now on, of course, you'll be needing a wheelchair or a mobility scooter to get about,' said the first man, in a practical tone of voice, and at the same time Siobhán could hear him snapping off a pair of latex gloves. 'But, don't let it bother you, do you know what I mean? Smiley here will be able to guide you around so that you don't end up tipping yourself over the edge of Tivoli Docks, or crossing the road in front of the 208 bus.'

He leaned over her again, much closer, and now he spoke very softly, which Siobhán found so threatening that she shivered. 'Let me give you one word of warning, though, darling. You'll never be able to see again, and you'll never be able to talk, or walk, and did I forget to mention that I've cut the tendons in your wrists so that you can't write any sneaky messages asking anyone for help?'

Siobhán let out another wheeze, and attempted a cough, but it hurt so much that she suppressed another one, even though it made her feel that she couldn't breathe.

'If you give me any trouble at all,' the man whispered, 'it will be a matter of only a few moments for me to puncture your eardrums, and then you'll not only be blind, and dumb, and paralysed, you'll be deaf as well. It makes very little difference to me.'

Siobhán thought: *Why don't you kill me now, and get it over with?* But she couldn't even tell him that. She could only lie there silently weeping while the two men talked to each other and Smiley let out two sharp barks, as if she were asking to be taken out for a walk.

Eight

It was after eleven before Katie returned home. It had been too late to stop off for a drink in Kinsale, but on her way back from Ballinroe East she had called in at Anglesea Street to drop off Detective Scanlan and also to collect a report on pornography fraud which Detective Ó Doibhilin had prepared for her.

When she let herself in, she saw that Bridie was sitting in the living-room watching television with Barney's head in her lap, so the two of them had obviously made friends.

'Sorry I'm so late,' said Katie, as she hung up her coat. 'One thing just led to another.'

'Not a bother,' said Bridie. 'That's what I'm here for. You can come home as late as you like.'

'How's John?' Katie asked her.

'I put him to bed about nine, because his antibiotics and his painkillers make him so sleepy. He was disappointed that he didn't get to see you before I tucked him in, but otherwise he's no worse than you could expect.'

Katie glanced towards the spare bedroom door. The way in which Bridie said that she had 'put him to bed' and 'tucked him in' struck her as sadly ironic, considering that the spare bedroom used to be the nursery, where little Seamus had slept. Even though it had been so long now since that morning when she had walked in and found Seamus cold and lifeless in his cot, she still thought of it as *his* room, and she still felt that his spirit was there.

Bridie had left the door a few inches ajar, in case John woke up and called out for her.

'You don't have to come in too early tomorrow morning,' said Katie. 'I won't be leaving until about nine.'

Bridie patted Barney's head and stood up. 'That's no bother at all. As you know I'm only in Roche's Row. Doesn't take me even ten minutes to get here.'

Katie and Barney followed Bridie into the hallway and Katie opened the front door for her.

'John's putting on a brave face,' said Bridie, as she turned to go. 'Don't let that fool you, though, Katie. Losing an arm or a leg, like, that's almost as bad as being widowed. He's grieving, do you know what I mean? And in some ways it's worse than being widowed, because he can still feel his legs, even though they're not there any more.'

Katie didn't answer that, but smiled tiredly and said, 'Good night, Bridie. We'll see you tomorrow.'

She went back into the living-room, crossed over to the drinks table and poured herself a large glass of Smirnoff vodka. She had been cutting down on her alcohol consumption lately, but right now she felt that she needed a drink to help her unwind. On the television, the chat show presenter Claire Byrne was having a lively conversation with her audience, but the sound was mute, and after watching her for a while, Katie switched the television off. She didn't feel like listening to other people arguing.

Barney made that odd sound in the back of his throat as if he were asking her what was wrong. She scuffled his ears and said, 'I'm grand altogether, Barns, don't worry,' and then went through to her bedroom.

She knew that she would have to talk to Cleona Cassidy again. Cleona had admitted that the baby she was carrying wasn't her husband Eoin's, but she had been willing only to say that the father was 'some feller' that she had met in Kinsale. 'Some feller's' identity was probably irrelevant, but all the same several key questions remained unanswered about the break-in at Sceolan Kennels and about Cleona's alleged rape and the fatal shooting of the dognapper. Whether 'some feller's' identity was irrelevant or not, Katie was always insistent that she knew the complete story before she was prepared to consider a case closed and put together a Book of Evidence.

After they had interviewed Cleona, she and Detective Scanlan had talked again to Eoin Cassidy, but he had stubbornly repeated his original story, word for word, and not a word more. The dognapper had come for him, he had fired a warning shot, and then he had shot the dognapper in self-defence. When Katie had put it to him that he had witnessed Cleona being raped and had shot the dognapper out of revenge, he had simply shaken his head and said nothing.

Katie had also failed to persuade Cleona to go to the Sexual Assault Treatment Unit at Victoria University Hospital, so that she could be intimately examined and DNA samples taken. Gently, she had made it clear to Cleona that if she refused to agree to forensic medical tests, the Garda would be unable to proceed with a prosecution through the courts, even if they managed to find and arrest 'Keeno'.

Cleona had kept her eyes fixed on the kitchen table in front of her and said, 'I'm still alive, and the baby's not hurt, thank the Lord, and isn't that all that matters in the grand scheme of things?'

* * *

Katie undressed and took a long warm shower. When she stepped out of the shower cubicle and looked at herself in the steamed-up bathroom mirror, she thought that she had lost even more weight. She knew that she needed to take a holiday, preferably somewhere sunny like Gran Canaria, but she was snowed under with half-completed cases and reports, and apart from that she had nobody to go with her. What would be the point of going to Gran Canaria on her own? She couldn't take John, and equally she couldn't leave him here.

Maybe she should just take a day off and spend it at the Susan Ryan Beauty Clinic, having a deep massage and a waxing and a manicure.

She tugged on her pink brushed-cotton nightshirt and sat with her feet up on her bed to finish her vodka and read through the report that Detective Ó Doibhilin had given her.

'Porn fraud' was a new on-line phenomenon in Cork. Twenty-three young Cork girls had reported that their photographs had been lifted from their Facebook pages and pasted on to a pornographic site called *Quadruple-X*, with obscene comments about them, or degrading sexual fantasies about what men claimed to have done with them. The site said, 'Look at these sluts! And there's plenty more in Cork where these came from!' In several cases the girls' pictures had been posted showing erect penises up against their lips, or with semen spattered across their faces.

Detective Ó Doibhilin had been trying to trace where the *Quadruple-X* site originated, especially since it featured so many Cork girls. 'We have a few promising leads,' he had written at the end of his report. 'I've also brought in Patrick Kirwan, from the Cork Training Centre, who's an expert hacker. Even if we can't ID the offender and prosecute him, I'm v. confident that Patrick can at least close the site down.'

A fat lot of good that *will do*, thought Katie. *The second you close it down, they'll open it up somewhere else, under another address, like www.Sextuple-X.*

When she had finished her drink, she went back into the bathroom to brush her teeth. As she switched on the light in the hallway, John called out, 'Bridie?' He sounded groggy, as if he were talking in his sleep.

Katie hesitated for a moment and then pushed open the nursery door. John was lying in the single bed beside the window. His hair was tousled and his face was shiny with sweat. The dark brown blanket that was covering his legs was humped up by a metal cage, which kept the weight off his stumps.

He frowned at her as she switched on the bedside lamp and dragged over the small hessian-covered armchair in which she used to sit at night and breast-feed Seamus.

'Katie, you're back,' he said, thickly. 'What time is it?'

'Midnight, nearly. I got back about an hour ago.'

He tried to lift his head off the pillow, but then let it fall back again. 'Mother of God, I feel like shit. I don't know what they put in those pills they gave me. Rohypnol, most like.'

Katie laid her hand on his shoulder. 'John, it's going to take you a long time to recover from this, but you will. You'll just have to be very patient.'

He raised his eyebrows and attempted a smile. 'At least I have you. If I didn't have you, I think I'd take an overdose.'

'You shouldn't talk like that. Look at all the people who have lost their legs like you, and still have full and happy lives.'

He lifted the blanket and looked down at himself. 'Do you know what the worst thing is?'

'You can still feel your legs, even though they're gone? That's what Bridie said, anyway.'

'Well, yes, that's bad enough. I can even wiggle my toes, can you believe that? But that's not it. That's not the worst thing of all.'

Katie waited for him to tell her. She kept her hand on his shoulder and she could feel how tense he was. His muscles were so taut that she felt almost as if he could catapult clear into the air, lifting all his blankets with him, and then crash back down on the bed.

Instead, though, he started to cry. His eyes filled with tears and his mouth was dragged down like a miserable child.

'Oh God,' he said, shaking his head from side to side. 'Oh Jesus and Mary.'

'John,' said Katie, and stroked his sweat-beaded forehead. 'You'll get better and better as the time goes by. It's going to take a while, darling, like I say, but one day you'll be walking again. Who knows, you could even be running, and you'll wonder why you ever felt so desperate.'

'But I'll never be like a man again,' he sobbed, wiping the tears from his face with the sleeve of his pyjamas. 'I'll always be short, like a freak, or a dwarf, or a small kid who never grew up. What difference will it make if I have prosthetic legs, or blades, or whatever? I could have stilts that make me a foot taller than everybody else around me. But that's all I'll be. A freak, or a dwarf, or a small kid on stilts. And don't tell me that everybody else won't secretly feel the same way.'

'They won't, John. People don't treat amputees like that. None of the people that I know.'

But John continued to weep and shake his head, and he gripped Katie's hands so tightly that her rings were pressed painfully into her fingers.

She gradually levered her hands free and then patted his shoulder, although she was aware that she was treating him more like Barney than her one-time lover. 'John, I swear on the Bible that you'll get over this, and that you'll feel like more of a man again. Garda O'Leary lost a leg in a car crash three years ago, and you should see him now. He runs a football coaching course for Rebel Óg.'

John gave a last heaving sob and then he wiped his face with his sleeves again and said, 'You're right, Katie. You're totally right. I know I shouldn't be feeling so damned sorry for myself. And I should be much more appreciative of what you're doing for me. Believe me, darling, I don't take your love for granted.'

'Yes, well,' said Katie. 'Don't you think it's time you got yourself some sleep? Is there anything you need? A fresh glass of water? How about a pee?'

'Do you know what I'd really like?' John told her, still wiping the tears from his eyelashes.

Katie was already halfway out of her chair. He folded back the blanket and said, 'If you could just hold me. If you could just prove to me that I'm still in working order.'

He raised the blanket higher but Katie continued to keep her eyes on his face and didn't look down.

'I love you, Katie, you know that, in spite of everything that's happened. As soon as I landed back at SFX I realised that I shouldn't have walked out on you. There's never going to be anybody else for me, ever. Only you. Hair like rubies, eyes like the sea.'

He kept the blanket lifted but still Katie didn't look down and still she made no move to sit down again. She was desperately trying to think of words to say to him that wouldn't crush him, and that wouldn't rip *her* apart from head to foot with guilt.

'John,' she said, gently, and she prayed that her smile wasn't too patronising. 'You're still very sick. You're up to your ears in drugs. If I started to mess around like that, God alone knows what strain it could put on your stitches. What would your doctors say to me if we had to rush you back into hospital because – well, because of that?'

John slowly lowered the blanket. 'Okay,' he said, although she couldn't tell from his expression or his tone of voice whether he believed her or not. Did he realise that she was making an excuse not to masturbate him because she was no longer sure that she loved him? She bent over and kissed him very lightly on the lips, but stood up straight again before he could put his arm around her shoulders and pull her down closer.

'Goodnight, John,' she said, blowing him another kiss with her fingertips. 'Sleep well. Don't think of yourself ever as being small. You were never small before and you never will be now. You're a giant.'

John gave her a shrug, but he didn't look convinced. She switched off his bedside lamp and went to the door.

'I'll leave the door open in case you need anything. Bridie will be here at nine.'

'I love you, Katie Maguire,' he said, out of the darkness. His voice sounded hollow, like a hermit in a cave.

Nine

John was still asleep by the time Bridie arrived the following morning.

'How's he been?' she asked, heaving off her bulging navy-blue back-pack and smacking the raindrops off it. 'Not too much bother, I hope?'

'No, no bother at all,' Katie told her. She was about to say that he had slept like a baby, but then she thought of Seamus and she stopped herself. She looked across at the clock on the mantelpiece and said, 'I have to go now, but I shouldn't be back too late so.'

'John has an appointment with Doctor Kashani tomorrow morning at eleven-thirty,' Bridie reminded her. 'That's to see if he's ready yet for the next stage of his prosthetics. I'll take him there myself of course but you might want to meet us there.'

'I'm up the walls with work at the moment, but I'll try.'

'It's just in case you want to ask Doctor Kashani direct about John's long-term treatment. You know – when he might expect to start walking again, and what medication he's going to have to take, and for how long, and such, do you know what I mean?'

'Like I say, Bridie, I'll do my best.'

'And of course there's the psychological side to it. Some of the amputees I've taken care of, they've taken a brave few years to get used to losing their arms or their legs or whatever. And it's quare, you know, the fitter they were before their ampumatation, the more depressed they are about it. They keep staring at the place where their leg or their arm was, as if they can force it to grow back again by willpower.'

'I can understand that, yes, after talking to John,' said Katie. 'I don't think he's finding it at all easy to deal with.'

Bridie was struggling to reach behind her hips and fasten her apron. 'He has *you*, at least. You know how much he's relying on you, don't you?'

Katie didn't answer that but said, 'Here,' and tied up the strings for her. 'Tell John I'll try to get back home as early as I can.'

'I will of course.'

* * *

It was raining as she drove into the city on the N25 – not torrentially, but fine silvery cloaks of drizzle that drifted across the city like a procession of ghosts, and softly rattled against the side windows of her car as if they were trying to attract her attention. *Don't you remember us, Katie? We remember you.*

She had received at least a dozen messages, and she listened to them as she drove. Detective O'Donovan needed to talk to her about a District Court case against a Romanian pimp which had collapsed for lack of credible witnesses, and Detective Ó Doibhilin had traced the origin of one of the porn fraud sites. Inspector O'Brien from Bandon said that he had a possible ID on the 'feller' with whom Cleona Cassidy had been having an affair, and Detective Dooley thought that he might have a lead on two of the most valuable dogs that had been stolen from Sceolan Boarding Kennels.

The last message surprised her most of all, though. It was delivered in the dry, emotionless tones of Assistant Commissioner Jimmy O'Reilly.

'Katie, if you would be so good as to come by my office as soon as you get in, there's a matter I have to discuss with you. Something pure confidential.'

Katie was so taken aback by this message that she played it again, twice. The relationship between her and Jimmy O'Reilly had always been unpleasantly abrasive, right from the very start. He was one of the old-school golf-playing stonecutters, and he had made no secret of his annoyance when Katie had been promoted over the heads of several senior male inspectors, even though she was equally experienced and – in some instances – much more qualified. Her appointment as detective superintendent had been part of An Garda Siochána's drive to show that they gave just as much opportunity to women officers as they did to men, but Jimmy O'Reilly had seemed to consider her promotion a personal affront. As far as he was concerned, female gardaí were good only for making tea and comforting battered wives and seeing primary school children across the road.

What had finally brought him to the point where he would barely even speak to Katie was her discovery that he had been passing confidential Garda information to a Cork thug called Bobby Quilty, in return for substantial unsecured loans. He had been borrowing the money to give to one of his young personal assistants, James Elvin, to pay off his gambling debts. James Elvin was not only his personal assistant, but his lover.

So what was this 'pure confidential' matter that Jimmy O'Reilly wanted to discuss with her? Katie had found out that he had been tipping off Bobby Quilty about imminent Garda raids on his properties, but she had still failed to come up with enough incriminating evidence to take to the Commissioner and the Garda Ombudsman, and finish his career. That was why the last few months between them had been characterised by such a hostile deadlock.

After she had hung up her plum-coloured raincoat in her own office she put her head around the door and said good morning to Moirin, her new assistant. Moirin was small and chubby with a pale heart-shaped face and red heart-shaped lips and black bouffant hair, like Disney's Snow White. If Katie hadn't known that she was twenty-six years old and a single mother, she would have guessed that she had only just left secondary school.

'Assistant Commissioner O'Reilly was asking after you, ma'am.'

'Yes, Moirin, I picked up his message on my mobile. I'm heading along to see him now, once I get myself a coffee. But don't be surprised if I come back with two black eyes.'

Moirin gave a hesitant little '*Stop!*' but said nothing else. She had been working here at Anglesea Street for only five weeks and she wasn't yet sure whom it was safe to talk about sarcastically, and whom she should treat with respect.

Katie went to the canteen for a take-away cappuccino and carried it along the corridor to Jimmy O'Reilly's office, pinching the lid between finger and thumb because it was so hot. She knocked and he immediately barked out, '*Come!*'

He was standing by the window with his back to her, looking out at the rain. He was wearing his navy-blue full dress uniform, with his medals and his Sam Browne belt, and she remembered that he was attending a memorial service today for one of his predecessors, Martin Duggan.

'I heard your message,' she said.

He paused for a long moment and then he turned around. He was very thin, with a gaunt, cadaverous face, and a concave chest, and eyes that had as much expression as two stones picked up off the beach. His silvery hair was greased straight back from his forehead and half of his left earlobe was missing, although he had always refused to explain how and when he had lost it. Detective Dooley reckoned that a Rottweiler had mistaken him for a bone.

'Ah, Katie,' he said. 'Sit down for a moment will you.'

Katie sat, placing her coffee cup down on his blotter. He stared at it, his nostrils widening with every breath, as if he were going to tell her to take it off immediately, but then he obviously decided that life was too short and that the relationship between them was strained enough already.

He sat down himself, and tilted himself back in his black leather chair, his hands steepled in front of him, his eyes narrowed towards the window, and not at her.

'You and I are both adults, Katie,' he said. 'I'm not going to pretend that things between us are remotely what you might call amicable. However, we have a job to do and that job is more important than any ill-feeling that we might harbour towards each other.'

'I've no personal ill-feeling towards you, sir,' said Katie. 'I'm perfectly well aware of what situation you found yourself in, and I fully understand why you did what you did.'

'Oh, is that so?'

'Yes. You know full well yourself that when you passed on information to Bobby Quilty, you placed me and three people that I cared about in danger of their lives, and I find that professionally unforgivable. I've said this to you before and I don't mind saying it again: how do you think I can trust you now? How do you think I can take your word for anything?'

Jimmy O'Reilly sucked in his cheeks, and his nostrils flared even wider. Katie sensed that he was right on the brink of jumping up and barking at her, but he restrained himself, and continued breathing steadily, and carried on talking to her in that dry, expressionless monotone.

'As I said, we have a job to do and the job comes first. Especially when it comes to protecting the public at large. I simply want to pass on to you some information which was sent to me late yesterday by the Special Detective Unit.' He paused, and then he added, still without looking at her, 'You can trust *them*, I imagine?'

'The SDU? I would hope so.'

'It's highly classified, this intelligence, Katie, and before I share it with you, I have to warn you that you're not to divulge even a whisper of it to anybody outside of this room. Not yet, anyway. Not until you've satisfied yourself – and *me*, of course – that it's one hundred and ten per cent accurate. Not until you're confident that you're ready to act on it, and make arrests that will lead to certain convictions. You'll understand why when I tell you where it came from.'

Katie said, 'Why can't the SDU act on it themselves?'

'Because they're still unable to verify what they've been told, not to the point where they can justify a search warrant. Whereas *you*, Katie – you're just about the only person in Cork who could do that for them.'

'Why me?'

'The source of their information declines to talk to anybody else, that's why. She says she can't trust any other Garda officer but you, because you came up with the evidence that saved her brother from prosecution.'

'I think I know who you're talking about,' said Katie. 'Maureen Callahan. Is that right?'

'That's right. I don't exactly know the full details of what you did for her brother, but apparently she was adamant that she was only going to share her information with you.'

'Well... I've always had the feeling that Maureen's not altogether happy being a member of the Callahan family,' Katie told him. 'Not an *active* member, anyway. But those three sisters of hers – they're enough to scare the sheet off a ghost. I don't think she ever dares to step out of line.'

Katie knew Maureen Callahan well, and couldn't help herself from liking her, because she was pretty and funny with brassy blonde hair and very smart. The problem was that she was the youngest member of one of Cork's most violent crime families. The Callahans were involved in protection rackets and heroin dealing in the city's nightclubs, but most of their money came from gun-running. They had made a fortune smuggling in automatic weapons and pistols and even rocket launchers from eastern Europe and supplying them to the Authentic IRA and the drug gangs of south-west Dublin.

Like several other criminal gangs in southern Ireland, the Callahans had survived and prospered for so long because they were run by women. Instead of having lethal feuds with their rivals, the way their menfolk did, they gritted their teeth and co-operated with them, no matter how much they despised them. They paid their fathers and sons and brothers to stay in the pub all day and not to interfere with business.

'So what's the story between you and Maureen Callahan, then?' asked Jimmy O'Reilly.

'It was on Paddy's Day last year. There was a fight in the street outside Cubin's and Maureen's brother Padraig was arrested for stabbing a member of the O'Flynn family. The O'Flynn fellow wasn't killed, but he lost three fingers and a lot of blood. The next day two alleged eye-witnesses picked out Padraig, but they were so sure of themselves that I thought that there had to be something suspicious about them. No "ums" or "ahs" or "it might have been him, like, but then maybe it wasn't". That was in spite of the fact that it was pitch dark and everybody involved was either high or langers or both.

'I had my team go through all of the CCTV footage in the city that night, and sure enough there was Padraig Callahan at the exact time of the stabbing, coming out of The Pav.'

Jimmy O'Reilly waited expectantly for Katie to continue, but she didn't tell him what her suspicions had been: that the two eye-witnesses had been bribed by Acting Chief Superintendent Bryan Molloy to identify Padraig Callahan. During the course of his career, Molloy had earned himself a formidable track record for crushing criminal gangs, especially the warring families who used to dominate Limerick's underworld, but he had frequently falsified evidence to make sure that he got the convictions that he wanted. He had retired now, but Katie knew that he still bore her a volcanic grudge, and that was why she never spoke about him, in case word got back to him, and he lodged a formal complaint with the Garda Ombudsman.

When he realised that Katie wasn't going to add any more, Jimmy O'Reilly said, 'Any road, Maureen Callahan approached an SDU detective over the weekend. He was plainclothes, of course, and she didn't know who he was, but for some reason he told her that a friend of his was a guard. She told him that she had some major information about her family that we'd be interested in.'

'Information about what?'

'She wouldn't tell him, but it's a fair bet that it's either about drugs or guns, and even though she'd had a fair few scoops the detective had the feeling that she wasn't messing. Since she wouldn't speak to him, he suggested that she give us a ring here at Anglesea Street, even if she did it anonymous-like. It was then that she mentioned your name, and told him that you were the only Garda officer she felt she could confide in. So – I'd say you need to meet up with her, and as soon as you can arrange it.'

'How can I get in touch with her?'

'Here, take this down,' said Jimmy O'Reilly, opening up a folder on his desk. 'This is her mobile.' Katie took out her iPhone and prodded out the number that he read to her. 'She'll be free sometime after five, so she said, but not to try and get in touch before then because she'll be home with her sisters, and of course she doesn't want *them* to know that she's talking to the guards. If you ring her or text her then you can arrange somewhere discreet to meet her.'

'Can you give me *his* name, the SDU officer? I'd like to speak to him in person.'

'Well, yes, of course I know who he is, but I'm not allowed to tell anybody else, Katie, even you. You know how secretive they are, the SDU. All of this information came direct from Detective Superintendent O'Malley at Harcourt Street.'

'And you have no idea why Maureen Callahan wants to rat out her own family? Surely she'd be risking her life, wouldn't she? Those Callahans, they did for Fergal Ó Brion, I'm sure of it.'

Jimmy O'Reilly gave her a minimal shake of his head. 'You'll have to ask her that yourself, won't you?'

Katie waited for a moment, looking at the young woman's name and number on her iPhone. Something about this didn't quite fit, although she couldn't decide what it was. It was like looking at one of those pictures of a hundred cartoon snowmen, and having to spot the single penguin among them. She knew it was there, but she couldn't see it yet.

'Something wrong?' asked Jimmy O'Reilly. 'You're looking suspicious.'

'That's because I have no reason to trust you about anything whatsoever.'

He shrugged. 'You don't have to trust me. You can talk to Maureen Callahan and make up your own mind about whatever it is that she tells you. If you don't believe her, fair play to you. Don't forget your coffee.'

Katie picked up her cup. Before she left, though, she looked around Jimmy O'Reilly's office and said, 'I haven't seen James Elvin in a while.'

'That's because he doesn't work here any more. Not for over a week now.'

'You're not getting any threats about his debts, are you? None of the casinos have been after you?'

'I'd say that's totally none of your business.'

'Of course it's my business. You're the Assistant Commissioner and I'm the Detective Superintendent and if you're being maced for money I need to know about it.'

Jimmy O'Reilly stood up and walked around his desk so that he could open his office door wide and keep it open. Detectives Roche and Ó Connail were walking past and they stared at them, because it was common knowledge in the station how frosty their relationship was, although nobody knew exactly why.

When they were out of earshot, Jimmy O'Reilly said, 'Listen, Katie, why don't we continue to work together on a purely professional basis and keep our snouts out of each other's personal problems? I'm sure you have plenty of your own to take care of.'

'All I'm saying, sir, is that it would be fierce bad publicity for the force if some casino bouncer was to catch you in the street one night and give you the mother and father of all clatters. Come to that, I don't think *you'd* enjoy it much, either.'

Jimmy O'Reilly closed his eyes for a moment, as if he were praying that when he opened them again Katie would have disappeared, or better still, never existed.

'Joseph and Mary and all the saints, Katie, will you forever stop vexing me and the sun splitting the rocks. I can tell you this for nothing—'

He stopped himself abruptly, and jerked his head towards the corridor, indicating that Katie should leave.

'Go on,' said Katie. '*What* can you tell me for nothing?'

'Nothing,' said Jimmy O'Reilly. 'I'd appreciate if you'd let me know when you've arranged to meet Maureen Callahan, if that won't be too much of a bother for you.'

'Are you *sure* you don't have something you want to tell me?'

He didn't answer. Katie looked at the expression on his face and realised that he couldn't answer, because he couldn't trust himself. His lips were tightly pursed and the muscles in his cheeks were flexing, as if he were grinding his teeth.

'Right then,' she said. 'I'll be away. *Slainté.*'

She lifted her coffee cup as if she were toasting his health. She knew that it was petty, and vindictive, but if it hadn't been for him, John wouldn't have lost his legs, and she wouldn't be feeling so bitter, and confused, and she wouldn't be sick to her stomach with such agonising guilt.

Ten

Detective Dooley was waiting for her outside her office, leaning against the open door and talking to Moirin. They were laughing about last night's *Naked Camera*, in which one of the actors had gone for a haircut but then told the unsuspecting stylist that he was pathologically afraid of scissors.

'How's the form, ma'am?' he smiled, as Katie sat down at her desk and opened her coffee. 'You got my message about the dogs okay?'

'I did, yes. Any more progress since then?'

Detective Dooley checked his watch. 'I'm just heading on to see this feen who's advertising two pedigree dogs online. He only posted them this morning, and they fit the description of two of the dogs that were buged from the Cassidys' kennels.'

'What breed are they?'

Detective Dooley flipped open his notebook. 'One's a German Shepherd and the other's a Vizsla. Both pedigree. He's asking a thousand yoyos for the German Shepherd and seven hundred for the other one.'

'That's a little on the dear side, I'd say, but – you know – not totally outrageous, if they really are pedigree.'

'His name's Mulvaney and he has a kennels down at Riverstick. He calls it a boarding kennels but that's just a front. He's a fence for stolen dogs, and he specialises in top-class pedigree animals, although he'd find a scratty mongrel for you if you really wanted one. He sells most of them on his website but he exports them, too, mostly to some other dodgy dog dealers in the UK. The Brits pay way over the odds for quality dogs.'

'Mulvaney? Gerry Mulvaney? I think I heard his name mentioned before, when all those rough collie puppies were stolen last Easter from Ballygarvan,' said Katie. 'We've never charged him, though, have we?'

Detective Dooley shook his head. 'He always swears blind that he comes by his dogs legitimate. I don't exactly know the science of it, but the registration details on their microchips always tally, or else they don't scan at all, so we've never been able to prove that the dogs are not his. I'm sure Bill Phinner or one of his technical experts can tell you how it's done.'

Katie said, 'It's not so much the dogs themselves that I'm interested in. What I want to know is who gave them to him.'

'I don't think for a moment that Mulvaney will tell me. Even if he *does* give me a name, the odds are that he'll give me a false one, and I know what he'll say. "I swear on the Holy Book that was the name that was given to me by the feller who sold me the dogs and I never saw him before so how was I to know that it wasn't kosher?" But, you know, it's worth having a shot at it.'

'When are you heading on?'

'In about ten minutes. I'm taking Scanlan along with me. I just have to wait until she's finished talking to those Travellers who were driving their horses down McSwiney's Villas.'

'Oh, stop. Serious? I haven't heard about that.'

'The Travellers said it was a protest, like, but two of the horses ended up in a cycle shop, right down the bottom of Blarney Road, and apart from the damage, three four-hundred-euro mountain bikes mysteriously went missing.'

'Mother of God,' said Katie. 'You couldn't make it up, could you? I suppose they're making out that the horses rode off on them.'

She thought for a moment, and then she said, 'I might come with you to Riverstick. I have a pure strange feeling about this dognapping and this feen who got his head shot off. I have to ring Inspector O'Brien at Bandon but I'll be ready to leave after that.'

'Okay, then, ma'am,' said Detective Dooley, although he didn't look particularly thrilled at the prospect of taking Katie along with them. Maybe he had been looking forward to some time alone with Pádraigin Scanlan. 'I'll see you in a few minutes so.'

Katie's iPhone had been pinging incessantly, and there was a stack of unread files on her desk that urgently needed her attention. Not only that, she was due to make an appearance in the District Court shortly after lunch, and at 5:30 pm she had a strategy meeting with Chief Superintendent MacCostagáin and Superintendent Pearse. But a visit to Mulvaney's kennels took priority, as far as she was concerned. These two dogs being offered for sale online were the only serious lead they had so far to the possible identity of the gang who had raided Sceolan Kennels, but there was almost no chance that Gerry Mulvaney would willingly tell Detective Dooley and Detective Scanlan where the dogs had come from. If he could scan the animals' microchips and show that they now legally belonged to him, the two detectives would have no way of putting any pressure on him, but Katie reasoned that the presence of a Garda officer with a little more seniority might impress him enough to co-operate. She could threaten him with a forensic tax audit by the Revenue Commissioners, or an ISPCA inspection, with possible closure on health grounds.

Maybe another reason she wanted to go was because she wanted to get out of the station for a few hours, and keep her mind occupied with anything but paperwork, and Assistant Commissioner Jimmy O'Reilly, and John.

Moirin tapped on her door and said, 'Would you care for another a cup of coffee in your hand, ma'am?'

'Thanks, Moirin, but I won't have time to drink it. I'm going to be flat till the mat all day.'

'I've finished all the filing now, including the Gerrety case. If you like I can go through all of these folders for you, and sort out which ones need answering and which ones are information only. I've nothing else to do.'

'That would be such a blessing, Moirin, believe me. I swear you must have been sent by the Lord God Himself.'

'Well, I was Judge McDonagh's secretary for two-and-a-half

years, as you know, and *he* believed that he was the Lord God Himself, even if nobody else did.'

Once Moirin had taken all the folders away, Katie picked up the phone and called Inspector O'Brien in Bandon. He took a long time to answer and when he did he sounded out of breath.

'Terry? DS Maguire. Are you okay?'

'Oh. Sorry. I've been doing my press-ups. The doctor warned me that my circulation's sluggish. It's sitting at this desk all day that does it.'

'I have your message about Cleona Cassidy. Have you found out who's put her in the family way?'

'Not for definite. But my officers have been taking a picture of Mrs Cassidy around and about Bandon, into all the local pubs and restaurants and so forth. The owner of the Beglan Inn on Kilbeglan Hill reckons she's stayed there twice at least overnight with some fellow he took to be her husband. At least he was seventy-five per cent sure it was her.'

'When was this that they stayed there?' Katie asked him.

'Once in mid-July and then again at the end of August.'

'Did he give a name, this supposed husband?'

'Killick, he thinks, or Cullip. He paid in cash so there's no credit card record.'

'Doesn't the owner have a register?'

'My officer asked him that of course but he said that he's running a sports pub with a couple of bed-and-breakfast rooms upstairs, not the Munster Arms Hotel.'

'Could he describe your man at all?'

'That was why I called you. He said he remembered what the fellow looked like because his barmaid called him the Grey Man. He had grey hair and a grey suit and even his shoes were grey. He said he looked the bulb off that actor Peter O'Toole. Even had the same poofy way of flapping his arms around, do you know what I mean?'

'Yes,' said Katie. 'But the owner hasn't seen him again since August, either with or without Mrs Cassidy?'

'He said he saw him once sitting in a car outside the Watergate bar on Watergate Street and the only reason he noticed him was because the fellow was puffing away at a fag so hard and blowing the smoke out of the window and he thought at first the car was on fire.'

'He didn't remember what type of car it was?'

'No. He thought that it might have been green. But I'd say there's a reasonable possibility that the fellow's local. You wouldn't be likely to go to the Watergate unless you were.'

'All right, Terry. Is that all you have so far?'

'So far, yes. But we'll carry on showing Mrs Cassidy's picture around the town for a while, and we'll also be taking it around Ballinspittle and Kinsale. We might even try as far as Halfway. The pair of them might well have gone further afield for a bit of the jiggery-pokery, where nobody was likely to know them, do you know what I mean, like? But now that we have at least one description, I'm quietly confident we're going to track down this fellow. It's true that he may not have been involved in any way with this dognapping, but at least we'll be able to tick him off the list of suspects.'

Katie said, 'Yes – but think about it, Terry. The alarms at the kennels didn't go off, did they? And I don't believe Eoin Cassidy forgot to set them. Cleona said that he was religious about it, setting the alarms. Somebody might well have found out how to switch them off, and I would be pure interested to know if they did – and if so, *how* they did, and who they were.'

'I'll be in touch with you, ma'am, any road,' said Inspector O'Brien. 'Meanwhile we're still keeping the Sceolan Kennels under twenty-four-hour surveillance, just in case the dognappers come back looking to even the score.'

'Okay, Terry,' Katie told him. 'Although to be honest with you I'm beginning to wonder who has the strongest motive for revenge, and against who. The dognappers, or Eoin Cassidy.'

She was buttoning up her raincoat when Detective Sergeant Begley knocked at her door.

'What's the story, Sean?'

'The dead dognapper,' said Detective Sergeant Begley, holding up a print-out. 'Doctor Kelley's completed her post mortem. She's just emailed me through her interim report.'

'Go on. The primary cause of death wasn't too hard to miss, I imagine.'

'Well, no, I'd say not. "A shotgun wound to the upper section of the deceased's face, resulting in the explosive disintegration of his skull and the forcible expulsion of almost his entire brain, leading not unexpectedly to instantaneous death."'

'Anything else of interest?'

'"Deceased was a white Caucasian male, 1.78 metres in height when his head was intact, weighing just under 81 kilograms. He was a heavy cigarette smoker and he was suffering from hepatic steatosis, or fatty liver. This was almost certainly caused by years of excessive alcohol consumption. His blood tested 93 milligrams per 100 millilitres for alcohol, 43 milligrams over the legal limit for driving, which indicated that he had been drinking for some hours before his death. Apart from alcohol, his stomach contained the half-digested remains of a cheeseburger and fries. His forearms and his chest bear a number of historic criss-cross scars, thirteen altogether, and these strongly suggested that he might have been attacked in one or more knife fights sometime when he was younger. Also the tip of his left index finger was missing. His arms, chest and back are heavily tattooed but all of these tattoos are quite faded and appear to have been done at least ten years ago, depending on the deceased's exposure over the years to sunlight."'

'Faded or not, they could be a fierce help in putting a name to him,' said Katie. 'What are they of?'

'They're not new, like Doctor Kelley said. There's Jesus, and Saint Patrick, but one of them's Val Doonican, believe it or not. The Technical Bureau have forwarded the jpgs to us so you can see them on your PC, and I left a print-out on your desk.'

'I'm sorry, I haven't seen it yet,' said Katie. 'I've been running about a day-and-a-half behind, to tell you the truth.'

'Not to bother. We're already checking them against tattoo patterns online and I've also sent out Markey and O'Mara to canvas the tattoo parlours in case any of their needle jockeys recognises them.'

'Any other progress?'

'Early days yet, but the technical experts have sampled just about everything except his earwax and they're running their tests right now. They've taken all of his clothes too, even his shoes, in case they can work out what kind of mud he's been walking in, so they can tell what part of Cork he came from. I'll tell you, it wouldn't surprise me if they *have* taken a sample of his earwax, so that they can find out who's been talking to him, and what they said.'

'Thanks, Sean,' said Katie. 'I'll call Bill Phinner when I come back if he doesn't call me first. Right now I'm going out with Dooley and Scanlan to look at these dogs.'

'You're going out yourself?'

'You can see a painting in a book, Sean, but sometimes you can only really understand what it's all about if you go to the gallery in person and look at it hanging on the wall in front of you, in the flesh, so to speak.'

Detective Sergeant Begley gave her a bemused little smile but she could tell that he had no idea what she was talking about.

'I'll see you after,' he said. 'There's a girl been reported missing and I have to go and see what *that*'s all about.'

'What age?' Katie asked him.

'Nineteen. So far as I know she went out clubbing on Hallowe'en and hasn't been seen since. There'll be a note on your PC about that, too.'

'Thanks, Sean. I have a whole rake of catching up to do. I'm beginning to think I never will.'

'That's the story of my life,' said Detective Sergeant Begley. 'Just ask the one I married.'

Eleven

It was still raining so Garret brought the ambulance round to the front of the clinic and reversed it right up to the porch. Milo and Grainne and the doctor were already waiting for him inside the oak-panelled lobby. Another man stood close behind them, grey-haired and nearly as tall as the doctor, tightly holding a Labrador cross in a guide-dog harness.

Between them, Siobhán lay strapped on a trolley. She was wrapped in a pale blue honeycomb blanket with her bandaged arms folded across her stomach. Both of her eyes were covered with white gauze pads, held in place by a shiny black plastic sleep mask. Her throat, too, was thickly bound with surgical gauze, under a medicine-pink neck collar. She was unconscious, although every now and then she gave a little jump, and her hands twitched, as if she were dreaming.

Garret opened the rear doors of the ambulance and then helped Milo to push the trolley up to the steps, fold up its wheels, and lift it inside. Both of them were wearing dark green trousers and dark green zip-up jackets, which gave them the appearance of paramedics.

'How are we doing for time?' asked the doctor, looking at his Rolex.

'Oh, we're grand,' said Milo, with a sniff. 'In fact we're probably too early. But at least we'll be able to stop in Waterford for a nosebag.'

'No drinking, though,' the doctor warned him. 'The customs have only to catch the faintest whiff of alcohol on you.'

'Don't you be worrying about that, sir. We'll be making Father Mathew proud, believe me.'

'Just make sure you do,' said the doctor. Then he turned around and snapped, 'What's taking Dermot so long? What a dodderer! I swear to God that man thinks 'punctual' is a hole in your bicycle tyre.'

He went back into the lobby and called out, 'Dermot! What in the name of all that's unholy is keeping you back now?' but almost as soon as he had done so, a squat bald man in a white surgical jacket appeared, pushing a wheelchair. He looked more like a potato-peeler in a restaurant kitchen than a nurse.

Sitting in the wheelchair was an emaciated young man in his early twenties, startlingly pale, wearing red-striped pyjamas and a beige dressing-gown and slippers. His eyeballs were milked over and his light brown hair was patchy, and his head lolled from side to side. He was limply holding up his arms as if he were a puppeteer with two invisible marionettes dancing in his lap.

'Fiontán needed a piss, like,' said Dermot. 'You know he can't get started if I don't whistle a few tunes to him, and even then it's fits and starts.'

'All right, Dermot, I don't need a blow-by-blow account,' said the doctor, impatiently. 'Get him stowed aboard and the lads can get going.'

Milo helped Dermot to lift the wheelchair into the back of the ambulance, and then to lock it into place next to the trolley where Siobhán was lying. Fiontán continued to nod and dip his head, and to flap his hands up and down. Dermot said to him, 'There you are, boy. Have a safe journey and don't you go messing with any of those English brassers! You wouldn't want to be catching one of them sociable diseases!'

Fiontán made a strange froglike sound deep in his larynx that could have been a laugh or could have been a cry of utter hopelessness. There was no way of telling.

Grainne climbed into the ambulance and sat herself in the high-backed chair immediately in front of the trolley, so that she could keep an eye on both Siobhán and Fiontán. There was always a risk that one or other of them might start choking or suffer some kind of a seizure, and the last thing they wanted on a trip like this was to have a dead body to dispose of. Grainne was wearing a dark green overall so that she, too, could be taken for a certified paramedic.

'All right there, girl?' Milo asked her, before he closed the doors.

Grainne reached into her large woven bag and held up a dog-eared paperback. 'I'll be grand altogether, Milo, don't you worry. I'm halfway through the *Fifty Shades of Grey*.'

'Jesus! So long as you don't try and jump on me when we get to Waterford. I've a bad back, like, and my front's no better, and I never did fancy that M and M.'

'S and M, you gom.'

'Well, whatever.' He walked around and opened the passenger door, but before he could climb in, the doctor came up to him and said, 'Milo – just remember what I told you. Take this one very, very easy. If the customs stop you, you know nothing about nothing. Remember what happened to Vogelaar and the rest of those Dutchmen.'

Milo nodded, and tugged an imaginary zip-fastener across his lips.

'Mind you,' said the doctor, 'Vogelaar would never have been caught if he hadn't made that one stupid mistake, and that's one stupid mistake that *we're* not going to be making, and that's for sure.'

'Well, Vogelaar was a mog all right,' said Milo. 'The shades may be on the slow side, some of them, but the one thing they're not is totally thick.'

Once Milo had climbed in, and Garret had started up the engine, the doctor stood back, admiring the ambulance. It was a Mercedes-Benz Sprinter 316 CDI, which he had bought second-hand from a van dealer in Corracunna. It had originally been yellow, with the green chequered Battenberg squares of the HSE emergency services, but he had arranged for it to be resprayed white. Now it carried the lettering *St Giles Clinic Montenotte Cork* on the sides in dark blue italics, and a mediaeval-style picture of Saint Giles holding a wounded hind with an arrow sticking out of its back.

Both classy and pious, he thought, *and which customs officer would have the effrontery to challenge an ambulance that looked so classy and pious?* Not only that, but an ambulance which was carrying two young people with such overwhelming incapacities? There was no way that anybody could think that Siobhán and Fiontán were feigning their blindness, or their inability to speak, or walk, or even stand up on their own.

The grey-haired man handed the Labrador's leash to Dermot and came up behind the doctor, laying one hand on his shoulder. 'Wardy's just sent me a text. He'll have the rest of the stuff by midday tomorrow but it'll probably take six or seven hours to stow it all away and he doesn't want to rush it and make a hames of it. We'll be staying overnight in Basildon and coming back on the morning ferry on Thursday.'

'Take as long as you need,' said the doctor. 'You know how much is involved here. And make sure that Grainne takes good care of young Siobhán, won't you? She's still in recovery, and I don't want her picking up some infection, or having a clonic tonic seizure. I gave her a thorough check-up this morning and I'm sure she's going to be grand. I wouldn't have let her go, else. But it's better to be wide than sitting in Portlaoise for fifteen years with a crowd of smelly old Provos.'

'Sure I know that,' said the grey-haired man. 'If everything goes to plan, though, we're going to need at least a dozen more like her, aren't we? Did you hear from Michael about those other two ambulances?'

'He's calling me later. He says he might have a third one, too, a Fiat Scudo. It seats five but I reckon that might be too small, capacity-wise, if you know what I mean.'

'All right, then,' said the grey-haired man. 'I'll see you late Thursday so, unless there's any problems. Tell Dermot not to give Smiley any chocolate. You can fecking kill a dog, giving it chocolate, and that bitch is worth nearly a grand-and-a-half.'

'Don't worry about it.'

The grey-haired man turned up the collar of his jacket and hurried out into the rain. The same shiny black Opel Insignia in which Milo and Garret had picked up Siobhán was parked close to the dripping wet laurel hedge, and he climbed into it, brushed the raindrops off his sleeves, and started up the engine. As he came round to the front of the clinic, he gave Garret a blip on his horn, and the ambulance started off down the driveway, and he followed it. They turned left, down the steep narrow slope of Lover's Walk, heading for Tivoli, and the N25, which would take them east.

* * *

They had been driving for an hour when the grey-haired man felt his iPhone buzzing in his jacket pocket. They had passed the seaside town of Youghal now, and crossed over the estuary of the River Blackwater. The rain had eased off altogether, and the sky was clear, although there were still some black clouds scowling in the distance up ahead of them.

'It's Milo,' said Milo.

'I know,' said the grey-haired man. 'What's the story, Milo?'

'We've about a third of a tank of petrol left. Like eh, we could make it to Rosslare no bother at all but Garret reckons that if we stop and fill up here that would take us all the way to Essex and the petrol here is a whole lot cheaper than it is in England, especially on the motorway.'

'I suppose that makes sense. But he should have stopped and filled up when we went through Youghal, shouldn't he? I'm not turning around now and going all the way back.'

'No we won't have to. Like there's a pump outside Michael O'Brien's store in Grange, not too far up ahead.'

'Go on, then. I could use some more steamers any road.'

They continued to drive across the wide green upland and there was nothing in sight except for a few distant farmhouses and some hazy purple hills. A few kilometres further on, however, they came to Grange. On the opposite side of the road there was a single-storey shop and post office. Behind it stood a small grey limestone church, Our Lady of the Assumption, with a graveyard populated by white marble angels and a pensive-looking figure of the Virgin Mary, as if she had forgotten where she had left the baby Jesus.

Garret pulled the ambulance up to the single petrol pump outside the store, while the grey-haired man parked close behind him and went into the store to buy himself some cigarettes. A thin chilly wind was blowing, which made the grass by the roadside sizzle softly, but apart from the low groaning of the petrol pump and the cars and trucks which went whizzing past in both directions, there was no other sound out here at all.

'Right, boy, let's get on,' said the grey-haired man, standing outside the store and lighting a cigarette. 'I'd like to be in Waterford in time for something to eat. They serve up a deadly steak and onion rings at McLeary's.'

Milo was counting out the cash to pay for the petrol. From the other side of the ambulance Garret called out, 'Grainne says could you buy her one of them Tayto chocolate bars with the cheese-and-onion crisps in it?'

'Mother of God, have you ever tasted one of them? It's like being sick, backwards.'

'Oh, yeah, and a bottle of Tanora, too.'

'Jesus.'

When Milo had paid and given Grainne her chocolate bar and her drink, they climbed back into their vehicles and started up their engines again. Garret waited for a huge timber lorry to pass, heading west, and then he pulled out sharply across the road. What he failed to see was that a silvery-blue Subaru sports car was speeding up behind him at over 80 kph, and its driver had to brake so hard to stop it from rear-ending the ambulance that there was a shrill scream of rubber, like a Wagnerian chorus, and clouds of black smoke poured out from its tyres.

The Subaru driver blasted his horn, and then he swerved out

to overtake the ambulance and went speeding off.

Garret hesitated for a few seconds, and then carried on driving. The grey-haired man pulled out after him, twisting around in his seat to make sure that no other vehicles were approaching from behind him.

Milo phoned him and said, 'Holy Saint Joseph, did you see that? I don't know what speed he was doing, that feller, but I reckon that *all* of us would have needed this fecking ambulance if he'd hit us, like, do you know what I mean? What a fecking nutjob!'

'Forget it,' said the grey-haired man. 'We don't want any trouble at all on this run, and especially not some road traffic accident.'

'Sure, but what a fecking header!'

They had driven only another kilometre when the ambulance suddenly slowed down and came to a stop. Garret switched on its hazard lights, and the grey-haired man could see that he had opened his door and was climbing out on to the road. He drew his car to a stop and switched on his own hazard lights.

As he got out of the driver's seat, Milo rang again.

'It's that same fecking nutjob. He's parked himself right in front of us, like. I mean, what the feck's he playing at?'

The grey-haired man quietly closed his car door and walked with a measured pace to the front of the ambulance, buttoning up his jacket as he did so. He saw that the driver of the silvery-blue Subaru had stopped right in the middle of the eastbound lane, positioning his car at an angle so it would be even more difficult for the ambulance to get past him. Several cars sped past in the opposite direction, so that the grey-haired man's lanky fringe flapped up with every one that went past.

The Subaru's driver was still sitting behind the wheel. Garret was standing beside the driver's door, but as the grey-haired man came up to him, all he could do was shrug.

'What's the form, Gar?'

'I've told him we have two fierce sick people on board and I have to rush them to a hospital.'

'And what did he say?'

'He said if that's the way I drive I shouldn't be driving nobody nowhere.'

'And what did you say to that?'

'Nothing. Nothing at all. I'm more than minded to smash his fecking window, like, but you told us not to stir the shit so I'm keeping my bake shut and my ball-pein hammer to myself.'

'Go back to the ambulance, Gar,' said the grey-haired man, quietly, half-closing his eyes in the manner of a man used to speaking with authority.

Garret hesitated for a moment, and then walked back to the ambulance and climbed up into the driver's seat. The grey-haired man could see that the Subaru driver was watching him out of the corner of his eye, but he stayed in his seat, his lower lip sticking out in a stubborn pout. He was bulky and broad-shouldered, with his hair close-shaved, and although he was wearing a khaki windcheater, a tattooed dragon's claw was visible at the side of his neck, just underneath his right ear.

The grey-haired man tapped sharply on the driver's window with his heavy signet ring.

'Open up there, will you, sham? I'd like a word.'

The driver ignored him, but grasped his steering-wheel tightly in both hands, clearly enraged by the grey-haired man tapping on his window so hard.

'I said open up there. There's something I need to discuss with you. Besides which, you're blocking up the whole N25. The guards will be here in a couple of minutes, boy, and you'll be hauled in for obstruction.'

Still the driver refused to acknowledge him. The grey-haired man waited for a few seconds, and then stood up straight and turned around, as if he were giving up his attempts to talk to the driver and intended to walk away and let him sit there and sulk for as long as he liked. As he turned, though, he swung his right leg forward and then kicked behind him like a horse, so hard that there was a loud bang and the side of the Subaru was dented with a crescent shape.

He turned back and kicked the car again, with his toecap, and this time the driver wrenched open his door and came rearing out of his seat with his fist raised and his eyes piggy with rage.

'What in the name of feck do you think you're doing? Look at me fecking car you fecking lunatic! Come here and I'll beat the mask off ya! Come here! Look what you've done! Look at them dings! That's going to cost me a fecking fortune to get that fixed!'

The grey-haired man took three or four steps back. Even out here with the wind blowing across the road he could smell that the driver reeked of drink.

'I'll tell you what you'd best be doing,' he said, raising his right hand with his palm held outwards, like a priest giving a benediction. 'You'd best be getting back in that yoke of yours and making tracks, like, as fast as you can, and forget this ever happened.'

'Come here to me?' the driver screamed at him. '*Come here to me?* Look what you've done to me fecking car!'

He took three shambling steps nearer. He was at least four inches taller than the grey-haired man, and probably weighed half as much again. Underneath his khaki windcheater he was wearing a faded maroon T-shirt which left his pale hairy belly hanging out, and a pair of light green tracksuit pants, with a damp patch on them.

'I'm telling you, sham, the best thing you can do is get the hell out of here,' said the grey-haired man. 'Better still, find yourself a layby and conk out for an hour or two. You're totally wrecked.'

'Oh, and I suppose conking out is going to fix these fecking dings in my door, is it?' slurred the driver. 'You fecking gobdaw.'

He staggered forward another two steps, with both fists raised. 'Come on,' he challenged the grey-haired man. 'I'll box the fecking head off ya.'

Milo and Garret were watching this confrontation from the front seats of the ambulance. Garret started to open his door again, as if he were going to get out and give the grey-haired man some support, but Milo said something and he closed it.

Although the driver was looming over him now, and was easily close enough to hit him, the grey-haired man held his ground. He stared up into the driver's bloodshot eyes with a strange detachment, as if he were thinking about some other encounter altogether, with somebody else altogether, long ago.

The driver was confused for a few seconds, and swayed, and almost lost his balance.

'You fecking – sh—' he began, and he failed to see the grey-haired man reach into his jacket and slide out a knife. It was double-edged, and pointed, and its blade was about thirteen centimetres long. Without any hesitation, the grey-haired man positioned it between the driver's thighs and jabbed it upward, directly into the damp patch on his tracksuit pants.

The driver yelped, and hopped, and reached down between his legs, because he didn't understand at first what was happening to him. But the grey-haired man gripped the driver's shoulder in his left hand, to give himself more leverage, and rammed the knife right up into the driver's scrotum, between his testicles, and higher up still, piercing his perineal membrane and cutting into the suspensory ligament that supported his penis.

'*Jesus! Holy Jesus!*' screamed the driver. He tried to pull himself away, but the grey-haired man kept his left hand clamped on his shoulder, and forced his knife in right up to the hilt.

'I told you to get out of here, didn't I, you big mullocker?' he said, between teeth that were clenched with effort. 'I told you to go and sleep it off. But no, not you. You had to be fucky the ninth.'

The driver could only stare back at him and shudder. He couldn't fall backwards or sideways or twist himself free because the knife was buried too deeply between his legs. Not only that, he couldn't really understand what was happening to him, because he was drunk, and his entire body was in a quivering state of shock. Five or six cars passed them by, heading west, and almost as many overtook them, heading east, but none of their occupants would have realised why these two men were standing close together, face to face. One of the men had his hand on the other man's shoulder, and they looked as if they were doing nothing more than having a friendly conversation.

'Please,' said the driver, at last. His eyes were closed now and there were two runnels of clear snot dripping from his nose.

'Please, *what*?' asked the grey-haired man.

'Please, will you take it out of me. Please.'

The grey-haired man said nothing for a while, but the driver was beginning to sag now, and so he was supporting almost all of his body-weight with the knife between his legs. The damp patch on his tracksuit pants had been overwhelmed by a widening patch of blood, and the grey-haired man could feel warm blood dripping from his fingers.

'If that's what you want, sham,' he said. 'I thought you might have been enjoying it, like.'

Before he withdrew the knife, though, he twisted the handle around and around, three times, so that the double-sided blade cut with a soft but audible crunching through muscle and membrane and spongy erectile tissue. Blood began to gush out more copiously now, and the grey-haired man's right hand was smothered in it. He tugged out the knife and gave the driver a hard push backward. The driver fell heavily against the side of his car and then dropped on to the road, knocking the back of his head against the tarmac.

The grey-haired man took out a crumpled green handkerchief and wiped his hand and his knife-blade. He looked around, his eyes narrowed, but there were no cars in sight in either direction. Then he bent over, picked up the driver's left arm, and yanked off his gold-plated Rotary wristwatch. In the front pockets of his windcheater he found his brown leather wallet and his mobile phone, and he took them both.

The driver's eyes flickered open for a moment, and he muttered something like, '*Moira?*' but then he lapsed back into unconsciousness.

The grey-haired man walked back to the ambulance. Garret put down his window and whistled and said, 'Feck me pink you sorted *him* all right!'

'His own fault. He shouldn't have been acting the flute.'

'What's the plan now?'

'We keep on going,' said the grey-haired man. 'I've hobbled his watch and his phone and his wallet so the shades will assume that he was mugged by knackers, most likely, and I doubt he'll be making any sense at all, even if he can remember what happened. What's he going to tell them, like? "I was langers and this ambulance pissed me off so I parked myself dead in the middle of the N25 to stop it?" I'm sure he will... more-e-ya!'

Milo lifted himself up in his seat so that he could get a better look at the driver lying in the road. 'You haven't, like, you know, *done* for him, like?'

'No, I expect he'll recover all right, although I don't think he'll be pleasing the ladies so much any more. Come on, let's hit the bricks before anybody sees him there and thinks to ask themselves why there's an ambulance here but no paramedics doing nothing to help him.'

The grey-haired man returned to his car. The ambulance drove away and he followed it, leaving the Subaru and its driver behind them. He glanced in his rear-view mirror to make sure that there were no other vehicles approaching from the west, but once he was satisfied that this stretch of the N25 was otherwise deserted, he didn't look again.

* * *

Less than five minutes later, the Subaru driver opened his eyes again. His head was pounding with every beat of his heart and his groin was on fire, as if somebody had maliciously tipped a shovelful of red-hot coals into his pants. He was in so much agony that he burst into tears, and let out a thin self-pitying whine. He lifted his head to try and work out where he was, but all he could see was an empty grey sky, and a few stunted trees, waving and rustling in the wind. He didn't even realise that he was lying in the middle of the road.

'*Oh Jesus oh Jesus oh Jesus*,' he whispered. He could feel that he was wet between his legs but he didn't want to put his hand down there to find out why because the burning was too painful. He had never known that anything could hurt so much. He took several quivering breaths, and then he lifted his head again and tried to roll himself over on to his side. He managed it, but when his thighs pressed together he shrieked like a horrified woman.

He lay there for a while, panting. He realised now that he was lying with his cheek against gritty grey asphalt, and he could see grass and weeds on the opposite verge, and a telegraph pole. The pain was so great that his thoughts kept jumbling up. He needed help. He remembered the ambulance. That fecking ambulance that had pulled right out in front of him and he'd nearly rammed into. But it was still an ambulance. Surely an ambulance crew wasn't going to leave him lying here with his groin on fire like this.

'Help,' he said. Then, a little louder, 'Help me, somebody, please, in the name of Jesus!'

Nobody answered. The road remained empty and silent, although he thought that he could hear traffic far, far away. He listened harder. Maybe it wasn't traffic at all. It could be nothing but the wind. Maybe he wasn't lying in the road at all, but floating on the sea. Maybe a witch had turned the water into asphalt, like the legend of Deirdre that his Ma used to read him.

He decided that he had to get up, or he would die. He couldn't lie here any longer. It was already cold, and it would be growing dark very soon, and he would be freezing as well as burning.

Whimpering, he rolled himself over on to his stomach, and then he managed to push himself up on to his knees. He tried three or four times to lift his left leg, but his crotch was too painful and he knew that he wouldn't be able to stand up and walk. He would have to drag himself over to the side of the road. Once he had managed that, though, he could use the telegraph pole to heave himself on to his feet, and he could stand there and wave to any passing vehicles for help.

He started to crawl on his hands and knees. *Where was Ma? Why wasn't she here to pick him up and take him upstairs to bed?* But then he remembered standing in church with his mother's coffin right in front of him and thinking how tiny it was. It was like a child's coffin. How could that be his mother in that tiny coffin, his dearest Ma, the same mother who used to carry him upstairs to bed?

'Come on, Martin, boy, you can make it,' he told himself, under his breath. Two long strings of transparent snot were swinging from his nostrils as he crawled, and he stopped to wipe them on his sleeve.

When he did so, he heard a soft, deep rumbling sound, like approaching thunder, and the wind seemed to be rising in a sibilant whistle.

Oh dear God, please don't let it start raining on me, not on top of everything else, he thought, as the thunder came closer. *I'm cold, I'm burning, I couldn't stand to be wringing wet as well.*

If he had turned his head to the left, he would have realised that a Paddy's Whiskey truck was speeding towards him around the long left-hand curve towards Grange. As it did so, its driver's attention was caught by the stationary Subaru on the opposite side of the road, with its hazard lights flashing. What the driver didn't see was the man kneeling right in front of him, as if he were a humble penitent praying to Saint John Licci, the patron saint of road accident victims.

There was a deep, pillowy thump, and for a split second the man was thrown up against the truck driver's windscreen, his eyes bulging, his mouth stretched open, his arms spread wide. The truck driver stamped on his brake pedal and the man went cartwheeling down the road in front of him, like a circus acrobat. He flew for more than fifty metres before he flopped on to his back, his arms and legs spread wide, but even so the truck's front wheels came to a shuddering halt less than half a metre away from his head.

The truck driver climbed down from his cab, so shocked that he lost his footing and stumbled. He stared down at the man lying in front of his truck, and saw that his tracksuit pants were soaked almost black with blood. Not only that, his head was skewed sideways at an impossible angle, as if he were trying to look over his shoulder at the road surface underneath him.

The truck driver took out his iPhone and shakily prodded out 112.

'*Emergency. Which service?*' asked the call-taker. All the truck driver could manage to croak out was, 'Ambulance.'

Twelve

Before she went to join Detectives Dooley and Scanlan, Katie rang home to see how John was feeling.

'He's taken some tomato soup,' Bridie told her. 'He's sleeping again now. He was complaining that his feet were aching even though he has no feet but all the same I gave him a sedative to take away the pain. It's the phantom pain the doctors call it. If you like I can ask him to call you when he wakes up.'

'No, you're grand, thanks, Bridie. I'm going to be up the walls for most of the rest of the day. I'll give him a call myself when I have a breather.'

'He was telling me that you used to dance together of an evening, him and you. Put some music on the CD player and dance around the lounge, like. *Days Like This*, by Van Morrison, that was your favourite, that's what he told me.'

'Yes,' said Katie, and for a brief moment she had a *tocht* in her throat. *When it's not always raining there'll be days like this.* It was so hard to think of those times when John had been tall and muscular and curly-dark-haired and could lift her up in his arms after they had been dancing and carry her into the bedroom. *When there's no-one complaining there'll be days like this.*

She unlocked her desk drawer and took out her Smith & Wesson .38 Airweight revolver. She was wearing her russet tweed suit today, with a burnt-orange roll-neck sweater underneath, which was long enough and loose enough to cover the holster in her belt. Besides, the Airweight was very small and flat and fitted snugly in its holster against her left hip.

She shrugged on her raincoat and then she walked along to the squad room to meet with Detectives Dooley and Scanlan. They were standing by Detective Dooley's desk, deep in conversation. Pádraigin Scanlan's head was very close to Robert Dooley's, and Katie could see from the brightness in her eyes that their rapport was more than professional. She was always wary about intimate relationships developing between her detectives. If and when relationships went wrong – and they almost always *did* go wrong – they could have a very disruptive effect on their professional judgement. Detectives couldn't investigate crimes objectively when they were angry at the world for leaving them loveless.

They turned around as she approached them. They were both wearing long olive-green trenchcoats with their collars turned up so they could have been mistaken for brother and sister.

'Are we out the gap, then?' Katie asked them.

Detective Dooley said, 'I've just had a call from a snout of mine in Tipp. He does voluntary work for the South Tipperary Rural Travellers' Project.'

He paused, and then he added, 'I used to play seven-a-side Super Touch Hurling with his brother,' as if it mattered to Katie how he got to know him.

'Okay,' said Katie. 'And what did he have to say for himself?'

'He said the rumour's going around the halting site at Ballyknock that there's going to be a major dogfight coming up soon. There's been some new dogs just brought in for training, seven or eight of them from what he'd heard.'

'Did he know what breeds they are?'

'Not all of them, but the fellow who gave him the information said that there were two bulldogs, a mastiff and a Great Dane, and all of them are listed as missing breeds from the Sceolan Kennels.'

'And did he have any idea when this dogfight is going to be held?'

'Sure it depends on the dogs, like. All of those breeds are used as fighting dogs, but if they've been well-fed and cosseted, do you know what I mean, it's going to take a month at least to get them up to gameness.'

'Who are the fighters?' asked Katie. 'Did he give you any names?'

'No, he couldn't – or *wouldn't*, more likely. But I'm going to be getting in touch with Sergeant Kehoe at Tipperary Town and ask him if he has any ideas. I don't know if Guzz Eye McManus is still organising the dogfights up there in Ballyknock but I haven't heard any different.'

'Well, let's get going and have a word with Gerry Mulvaney,' said Katie. 'Sooner or later we're going to get a name out of somebody, so we might as well start with him.'

* * *

Riverstick was a small cluster of houses and farms sixteen kilometres due south of Cork, where the main road crossed the River Stick. Katie had passed through it with Detective Scanlan only yesterday afternoon, on their way to Kinsale. By the time they reached it today, the rain had passed. The sky was still grey but it was bright as a migraine.

They turned off the main road by the Babbling Brook pub and drove up a narrow road with tangled hedges on each side. About a kilometre further on, they turned right up an unmarked lane. At the end of the lane was a wide semi-circular yard, paved in asphalt, with a ramshackle collection of sheds and outbuildings and kennels all around it. Behind the outbuildings stood a two-storey house with a grey slate roof and a tall smoking chimney. It had once been painted primrose yellow but now its paint was faded and its east wall was overgrown with reddish ivy.

'Welcome to Gerry Mulvaney's High Class Boarding Kennels,' said Detective Dooley. 'If you look up his website, you'll see that he's "internationally renowned for the care and training of pedigree canines of all breeds". I don't know about internationally renowned but they know him well enough in Liverpool which is where he sells on most of his stolen animals.'

He parked and they climbed out of the car. They could smell peat smoke from the chimney and hear three or four dogs endlessly barking from one of the outbuildings. They started to walk towards the house, but before they were halfway across the yard, the front door opened abruptly and a man appeared, stalking briskly up to intercept them. He was small and bow-legged, like a retired jockey, and he was wearing a frayed tweed cap and a tweed jacket with sagging pockets, with a yellow Tattersall check waistcoat underneath it.

'Gerry Mulvaney?' Detective Dooley called out. 'Detective Dooley, from Anglesea Street Garda Station.'

'I know who you are, boy,' said Gerry Mulvaney, as he came up to them. His cheeks were scarlet, with very rough skin, as if they had been sandpapered, and his eyes were pale shiny blue like glassy allies. 'I seen you before all right, and I could smell bacon even before you got here. I have a nose as sharp as my dogs here.'

'This is Detective Superintendent Maguire and Detective Scanlan.'

'Oh, the top brass, is it? So what have I done to deserve such an honour?'

'I won't beat around the bush, Gerry,' said Detective Dooley. 'This morning you put up two new dogs for sale on your website, Gerry. A German Shepherd and a what's-its-name, a Viszla.'

Gerry Mulvaney sniffed, and wiped under his nose with the back of his hand. 'It's what I do, boy. I buy and sell dogs, and they're both legitimate, those two. Their chips are sound – you can check them for yourself – and I have all the paperwork.'

'Can we see them?' said Katie.

'Why's that, girl? You think I've invented them? You think I'm selling imaginary dogs? Sure and they'd be cheaper to feed, like.'

'I'd just like to see them,' Katie repeated.

'Well, all right,' said Gerry Mulvaney. 'I suppose it's your job, isn't it, being a nosey-parker?'

He turned around and started to walk across the yard towards the largest of the outbuildings, which was built out of whitewashed breezeblocks. There were three rickety wooden steps up to the door, and the door itself had a heavy padlock hanging on it. Gerry Mulvaney dug a huge bunch of keys out of his jacket pocket, and took what seemed like an interminable time sorting out the right one.

Eventually he opened the door and went inside without inviting them in, but they followed him all the same. Although there were barred windows along either side of the building, so that the building wasn't totally dark inside, he switched on the fluorescent lights on the ceiling, which pinged and flickered into life.

There was an overwhelming stench of stale dog urine, and even though Katie was used to the smell of her own Irish setter Barney, she had to take out the Estée Lauder-soaked handkerchief she always carried in her pocket and breathe it in for a moment.

'Mother of God,' said Detective Dooley, and Detective Scanlan coughed and pressed her hand over her nose.

'Sorry about the fierce smell of benjy in here,' said Gerry Mulvaney. 'They haven't invented an underleg deodorant for dogs yet.'

On the left side, the building was screened off floor to ceiling with wire mesh, and behind the wire mesh it was further divided into eight separate stalls. There were dogs in six of the stalls, and a shaggy black Irish water spaniel jumped up as soon as they came in and started wuffing and flapping its tail. All the others were listless and lay on the floor, staring up at their visitors with mournful eyes, as if they had given up hope altogether.

Gerry Mulvaney led them along to the last two stalls, where a German Shepherd and a caramel-coloured Vizsla were lying. Katie was no expert, although her family had always owned dogs since she was little, but she could see that these two animals were both handsome and well-proportioned and both in beautiful condition. The Cassidys had clearly fed and groomed them well and exercised them every day.

'There,' said Gerry Mulvaney. 'I doubt they'll be here for long, though. I've had two offers for the Vizsla already.'

Katie bent down and peered at both dogs closely. The German Shepherd stood up when she approached his stall, and stared at her, as if he were trying to beg her telepathically, *Please, rescue us. Please get us out of here.*

'And you say they're both chipped and registered with the IKC?' asked Katie.

'Spot on. One hundred and ninety-nine per cent legal and legitimate.'

'So who sold them to you?'

Gerry Mulvaney sucked in his breath. 'Well, it was a private arrangement, like. I wouldn't really be at liberty to tell you that.'

'Who sold them to you, Gerry?'

'They wasn't exactly *sold* to me. It's more like I was asked to see if I could find a good home for them – me having the website and all.'

'All right. You were asked to find a buyer for them. But who by?'

'I can't really answer that one. It wasn't a formal sales transaction, so there's no actual documentation as such.'

'I thought you said you had all the paperwork.'

'Well, let's put it this way, if there *was* paperwork, I'd have it for sure. But it was more like a favour and as you can see I haven't sold the dogs yet. No money has changed hands so nothing of what you might call a commercial nature has actually taken place.'

'Who was it, Gerry? I'm not asking you again. If you don't tell me, I'm going to have to take you in for questioning.'

'You can't do that. On suspicion of what would that be? A feller asked me to find a home for his dogs, if I could, and I told him I'd try. What's criminal about that?'

Katie took a deep breath, but the stench in the building was so rancid that she wished she hadn't.

'What's criminal about it, Gerry, is that we have good reason to believe that these two dogs are stolen property, and if you've agreed to try and sell them, you're aiding and abetting an indictable offence.'

'Oh stop. I can't believe they're stolen. The feller who gave them to me, he's straight as an arrow so far as I know. Besides, he gave them to me, and now like I say they're both legitimately registered to me, and you can't prove otherwise.'

'So if and when you sell them, you're not going to give your man any money?'

'I don't know. I might buy him a drink, like. But until they're sold, it's me who has to go to all the expense of feeding them and taking care of them.'

'You're asking over fifteen hundred euros for the two of them,' Detective Dooley put in. 'That's more than enough to buy you all the dog food you're going to need, wouldn't you say?'

'Oh yeah, and what if one of them gets sick?' said Gerry Mulvaney. 'Canine parvo or the demodectic mange? Have you seen what vets are charging these days? You have to take out a mortgage just to cut your dog's toenails.'

Katie turned to Detective Dooley and Detective Scanlan and said, 'Do you believe any of this story? An anonymous fellow asks Gerry here to find a home for these two expensive pedigree dogs, but he's so *flaithiúlach*, this anonymous fellow, that he doesn't expect even a dooshie percentage of the money that Gerry makes from selling them through his website? Oh – maybe Gerry's going to stand him a pint of Murphy's, if he's lucky.'

'Sounds like cat's malogian to me,' said Detective Dooley.

'Me too, ma'am,' said Detective Scanlan.

Katie turned back to Gerry Mulvaney and said, 'Who gave you these dogs, Gerry? You have one last chance to tell me.'

'I'm not telling you nothing, girl,' Gerry Mulvaney retorted. He was looking angry now, but his bluster gave Katie the feeling that he was frightened, as well as angry.

'You're sure? In that case, I'm going to take you in for questioning. Not only that, I'm going to call the ISPCA, and I'm going to suggest that they conduct a full and thorough inspection of your kennels here, with a view to closing them down on the grounds that they're insanitary, and a threat to the health and wellbeing of the animals you have here.'

'Call them. See if I give a shite.'

'Oh, I will. And on top of that, I'm going to suggest to the tax commissioners that they aggressively audit your accounts for the past five years. You must have made a fair profit out of all these dogs that these anonymous people have been giving you to find a home for. I wonder what's happened to all that money? Did you declare it?'

Gerry Mulvaney said, 'Listen to me, Detective Superintendent Missus-Whatever-The-Feck-You-Call-Yourself. You don't scare me one iota. I've been running these kennels for fifteen years and the ISPCA have never given me a single ounce of bother once, and nor neither have the Revenue. So get up the yard, will you, and take your two wains with you.'

Katie looked at him with a very serious expression on her face. 'You do realise that I'm giving you one last opportunity to tell me who gave you these dogs?'

'And you do realise that I'm giving you one last opportunity to get the feck away from here?' Gerry Mulvaney retorted.

Katie went up to the Vizsla's stall and slid back the bolt on the wire-mesh door.

'Hey now, stall the ball,' said Gerry Mulvaney, stepping forward to stop her. 'This is private property and you don't have a warrant so you can't fecking touch nothing at all. And don't be thinking you can take those dogs away with you, because they both belong to me now and like I said I can prove it.'

Katie ignored him and swung the door open. The Vizsla stood up and came up to her, sniffing at the hem of her russet tweed skirt.

Gerry Mulvaney reached out to pull Katie back, but Detective Dooley grabbed his sleeve.

'Come on, Gerry, boy, you don't want to be done for assaulting a garda, do you?'

Katie had guessed that a stand-off like this might arise, which was one of the reasons why she had decided to come along with Detectives Dooley and Scanlan, and why she had armed herself. Her greatest concern had been that they might be threatened with a shotgun. It had happened to her before when she was a Garda

Sergeant in Crosshaven, and she had been sent to investigate three stolen cows, and shot at by an irate farmer, who had narrowly missed her. But now she had seen how fearful Gerry Mulvaney was, and how she could exploit that fear.

She lifted her sweater and took her revolver out of its holster.

'What in the name of *feck*?' said Gerry Mulvaney.

Katie took hold of the Vizsla's collar and pointed the revolver directly between its agate-coloured eyes. The dog's expression was so appealing and sad that she was glad that it couldn't understand what she was doing.

She turned to Gerry Mulvaney and said, very calmly, 'Mr Mulvaney – I shall have to report to my chief superintendent that we came here to ask you some questions about two dogs that you've advertised for sale on the internet – dogs which we had good reason to believe might have been stolen.'

'What are you playing at, girl?' Gerry Mulvaney demanded. 'What the feck's that gun for?'

'You grudgingly took us to see the dogs, but you were pure aggressive about it,' Katie told him. 'The dogs picked up on your aggression. They became highly agitated and attacked us. I had no alternative but to put them both down.'

'*What?* You're not going to *shoot* them?'

'I'm sorry, I didn't have any alternative. It was self-defence. Detectives Dooley and Scanlan here will back me up.'

'That's right,' said Detective Dooley, picking up on Katie's cue. 'I mean, Jesus, they could have torn our throats out.'

'What in the name of God are you talking about? They're just fecking standing there, good as gold! You can't fecking shoot them!'

'That's not the way I see it,' said Katie. 'The way I see it, these two dogs had to be destroyed. It was a fierce pity, that, because it meant that you weren't able to sell them, and because of that, you had to tell your *flaithiúlach* friend that you wouldn't be able to stand him a pint of Murphy's after all. But what did he care? A generous fellow like that?'

Although Gerry Mulvaney's cheeks remained as two scarlet

spots, the rest of his face turned white, and his pale blue eyes darted from side to side like a cornered rabbit.

'You can't do that! Of course he'll fecking care! *Care?* He'll be raging!'

'So what you were saying... that wasn't exactly true?'

'Not exactly, no, I admit it. But that was because I thought it was none of your business. I'm supposed to sell the dogs and give him the proceeds and I'll take my cut. That's the way it works. But if you shoot the dogs and I can't pay him, he'll fecking *murder* me. I mean that. He'll genuinely fecking murder me, in real life.'

'Well... there is a way that you can stop me from shooting them,' said Katie. The Vizsla was trying to sniff at the muzzle of her revolver now. 'Tell me who gave them to you. Give me a name.'

Gerry Mulvaney's chest rose and fell under his Tattersall waistcoat. At last he said, 'You have to swear to God that you won't let him find out that it was me that told you. Otherwise he'll murder me just the same, either him or his gang.'

'Just tell me the name, Gerry.'

'He calls himself Keeno. That's the only name he goes by. I've done business with him a fair few times before. He rings me and says that he has dogs for sale and he fetches them here and I sell them for him.'

'Keeno?' Katie repeated. She gave him no indication that she had heard that name before. 'Can you describe him?'

Gerry Mulvaney shrugged. 'I don't know, like. Mid-forties I'd say, maybe a little older, black hair. Kind of sleepy-eyed, like, and with a busted nose, too. Tell you who he puts me in mind of – that Sylvester Stallone fellow in the Rocky fillums.'

'What kind of an accent does he have?' asked Detective Scanlan.

Gerry Mulvaney looked hesitant, but Katie kept her revolver pointed between the Vizsla's eyes and nodded suggestively down at it as if she were quite prepared to pull the trigger at any moment.

'West Cork, Kerry maybe. He speaks real quick, like, and kind of slurs what he says. But he never says much. Only "Here's the dogs, like, and we'll be waiting on the grade."'

'Do you have any idea who his gang are? Have you seen any more of them?'

'No. He's the only I've ever seen. Look – you're not really going to shoot them dogs, are you?'

'What kind of a vehicle does he drive?'

'The last time, when he dropped these two off, just some van. Ford Transit, I'd say. Silver, no lettering on it. There must be hundreds of them.'

'How do you pay him?' asked Katie.

'Cash. I ring him up to tell him I have it ready and then he comes to collect it.'

'All right,' said Katie. Usually, she would have been deeply suspicious about everything that he had told her, but he had given her the name 'Keeno'. Even if he had been lying about everything else – even if his dog supplier looked more like John Goodman in reality than Sylvester Stallone, and even if he drove a red Fiat Ducato instead of a silver Ford Transit, Gerry Mulvaney had still made the connection that she was looking for.

She tucked away her revolver, pulled down her sweater and patted the Vizsla on the head. The Vizsla wagged his tail and licked his lips as if he were expecting a treat.

'I'll tell you what we're going to do, Gerry,' she said. 'We're going to take these two dogs as evidence. We're going to give you the money for them, cash, and you're going to tell Keeno that you've sold them, and that you've been paid.'

'Then – then what?' said Gerry Mulvaney, and his left eye was twitching.

'When Keeno comes to collect his money, we'll be waiting to have a word with him. It's as simple as that.'

'But you can't do that! Jesus Christ Almighty, the rest of the gang they'll know it was me who ratted him out and they'll fecking kill me!'

'Your choice, Gerry. If you co-operate with us and help us to detain Keeno, the court should go easy on you. If necessary we can also give you protective custody and relocate you to a safe house. However, if you *don't* co-operate, I'll arrest you now and we'll announce through the media that we're looking for Keeno, so his gang will still know that it was you who gave us his name. If that's what you decide, I wouldn't like to be in your shoes, I can tell you that.'

She looked around the building and said, 'Either way, it's the end for Gerry Mulvaney's High Class Kennels.'

Gerry Mulvaney took a dented cigarette case out of his inside pocket, opened it, and took out a half-smoked cigarette. He lit it with a pink plastic lighter and blew a long stream of smoke out of his nostrils.

'Go on, then,' he said, without looking at Katie. 'Take the fecking dogs. I'm tired of running this fecking business any road. Just make sure that none of Keeno's pals ever finds me, that's all.'

Katie turned to Detectives Dooley and Scanlan and said, 'Can you contact the dog support unit and ask them to shoot down here asap, to pick up these two? And can you arrange with Bandon for Eoin Cassidy to be fetched up here to take a look at them, to see if they're his? I'll talk to Chief Superintendent MacCostagáin and arrange for the cash to be raised to pay this Keeno, and I'll also ask Superintendent Pearse to set up surveillance.'

'Do you know who I feel like?' said Gerry Mulvaney, blowing out more smoke. 'I feel like Michael Collins when he signed that fecking treaty with the Brits, that's who I fecking feel like.'

'What? That you've signed your own death warrant?' said Katie. 'Don't worry, Gerry. We've a whole rake of witnesses under protection – you wouldn't even believe how many – and no harm's come to any of them yet.'

Gerry Mulvaney shook his head and couldn't stop shaking it. 'You know what you are, Detective Superintendent What's-Your-Face? You're a fecking *dearg-due*, that's what you are. A fecking blood-sucking witch. You never were going to shoot those dogs, were you, not in a million years? But you got inside my head. And now look at me. Totally fecking botched.'

Thirteen

Katie had been waiting at the Circuit Court for over half an hour when she heard an ambulance siren outside, and doors slamming, and the sound of running feet. A man's voice shouted, 'Here, this way, and make a bust will you!' and a woman called out, 'Where is she?'

Katie was sitting in the office that the state solicitor used on court days. It was a small stuffy side room with a desk and a green leather couch and shelves crammed with books on case law and family law, as well as *The Irish Constitution of 1937* and the *Acts of the Oireachtas*.

She stood up and went over to the high window that overlooked Cross Street but although she could see the ambulance's flashing lights reflected in the windows of the Washington Inn opposite, she couldn't see the ambulance itself.

She was about to go out and find out what was going on when Finola McFerren the state solicitor came in, looking flustered. She was holding her wig in her hand as if it were a dead rat that she had found in the corridor outside.

'I'm *so* sorry, detective superintendent,' she said. She was a tall woman, almost unnaturally thin, with black-framed glasses that were always perched halfway down her long curved nose. 'Abidemi Nduka has failed to show up. I wasn't so concerned about that. As you know yourself, her testimony wasn't exactly going to be critical. But would you believe that Rosaleen Dunnihy has gone into labour?'

'Stop! So that's what the white van's for?'

'I'm afraid so. Her waters broke, right there in the witnesses' waiting room. It was a blessing it didn't happen while she was on the stand giving evidence.'

'So what now?'

'Judge O'Connell has postponed the hearing *sine die*, and he's said that if it's a boy he wants it named after him.'

Katie wasn't amused. She picked up her briefcase from the couch and said, 'If she was that close to giving birth, like, why did you call her? I've just wasted nearly an hour and I've fierce more important matters to be taking care of.'

'Well, as I've said, I'm sorry. I'll get back to you about it as soon as it's rescheduled, of course, but I shouldn't imagine that will be for several months now.'

'All right. Fair play to you. At least Michael Gerrety will be staying on Rathmore Road where he belongs.'

Michael Gerrety was Cork's wealthiest and most notorious pimp, and he had lodged an appeal against his sentence for conspiracy to drown a teenage prostitute. Katie had been obliged to attend the hearing because his appeal was based on the grounds that she had harboured a long-term personal grudge against him – mostly because of her repeated failure to convict him for living off immoral earnings. He also claimed that she had persuaded the principal witness against him to give false evidence. His appeal was a farce, as far as Katie was concerned, and she knew that he had lodged it for the sole purpose of irritating her and wasting her time.

On her way back to Anglesea Street, Detective Scanlan called her from Riverstick and told her that the Dog Support Unit had arrived and collected the German Shepherd and the Vizsla. Eoin Cassidy would be driven up from Bandon tomorrow morning at 10:00 to see if he could identify them.

Detective Scanlan also told her that Superintendent Pearse had sent down two gardaí with the cash for 'Keeno' to collect, accompanied by four more armed officers from the Regional Support Unit.

'It's all set up now, ma'am. All we're waiting on now is Keeno.'

'Let's hope he shows up sooner rather than later. And keep your eyes open for anybody who might be with him. Bring *them* in too, whatever they say.'

It was nearly five by the time Katie returned to her desk. Moirin went to fetch her a cup of coffee and then quickly ran over the paperwork that she had sorted out for her. She leaned over Katie's desk so that Katie could see into her cleavage. She smelled faintly of Rose's Olde Irish Cough Drops.

'There's three invitations for you to meet different community groups. I'd say the most pressing of these is Irish Rural Link. They're asking for an urgent meeting about Garda station closures. They say in their letter here that the burglary situation in some of the country areas is getting desperate. They reckon that south of the city there's been almost a twofold increase in aggravated break-ins, although a lot of them don't get reported because the victims don't ever think they'll get their property back, or else they're afeared of reprisals.

'It's probably worth meeting with them because they have very good media connections, do you know what I mean, and if you didn't agree to meet them they might crib to the *Echo* about it.'

'I see,' said Katie. 'Let's email them, then, and ask them to suggest a date.'

Moirin jotted that down, and then she said, 'Oh – and you and a partner of your choice have been invited to the Cork Simon Ball next year. I know it's not until April but it's always sold out months before. I'd like to go myself but my Barry's not at all sociable and when he dances you'd think he'd been struck by lightning the way he hops about.'

Katie gave her a tight smile. She couldn't take John as 'a partner of her choice' because it was questionable if he would even be capable of walking by April, let alone waltzing. But the ball was in a good cause, helping Cork's homeless, and it would be good public relations for her to show her face there.

'Okay,' she said. 'Put me down for two tickets. And put an ad in the paper for a man who doesn't dance like a duck.'

It was a quarter past five already, and she was acutely aware that she would now be able to call Maureen Callahan. Apart from that, she had her strategy meeting with Chief Superintendent MacCostagáin and Superintendent Pearse in only fifteen minutes.

'Let's leave the rest of this until later,' she said. 'There's a phone call I have to make and I'm running out of time as usual. But thanks, Moirin. You've taken a ton of pressure off me.'

As soon as Moirin had left her office, Katie picked up her iPhone and called the number that Assistant Commissioner Jimmy O'Reilly had given her. It was answered almost at once, as if Maureen Callahan had been jiggling her phone in her hand, waiting impatiently for her to ring.

'Maureen?' she said.

'Hallo, yes, this is Maureen. Is that who I think it is?'

'It is, yes. Are you able to talk to me, Maureen?'

'I can. I'm on my own at the moment. My sister's gone out for the messages. She won't be too long, though. She's only gone up to Dunne's at Ballyvolane.'

'I've been told that you might have some information for me. Something that you don't want to tell anybody else.'

'Well, that's right, that's right. Sorry to be so skittery. I don't know if I ought to be talking to you like this or not.'

'Try and calm yourself down a little,' said Katie. 'Let me hear what you have to say, and then we can decide what to do about it, if anything. There's no need for you to be frightened, let me promise you that. Nobody else is going to know that you spoke to me – and I mean *nobody*, and not only nobody, but *never*.'

'It's only because I trust you,' said Maureen Callahan. 'I mean I was going to tell that detective feller Dermot and I think I probably could have trusted him, like, but then I wasn't totally sure, do you know what I mean? I thought I could trust my own sisters, like you would, wouldn't you, your own sisters? But could I feck.

After what *they* did I don't think I'm ever going to trust nobody, never again. I mean, Jesus.'

Maureen Callahan spoke in a high-pitched northside gabble, and she kept punctuating her speech with little puffing noises, so Katie guessed that she was smoking at the same time, and just as rapidly as she was speaking. Although she had said that she was nervous, Katie could tell from experience that she was working herself up to saying something that she was determined to get off her chest.

'So why don't you trust your sisters any more?'

'Would *you*? Would you trust anybody who did what they did?'

'I don't know, Maureen. It depends what they did. One of my sisters borrowed my best angora sweater once without asking and burned a hole in it.'

'You're fecking joking, aren't you? A hole in a fecking sweater, I wish! I'll tell you what my sisters did. I was secretly doing a line with Branán O'Flynn, like. You know Branán?'

'Of course. I know all the O'Flynns. I think I've arrested all of them, at one time or another.'

'Well, me and Branán, we'd known each other ever since we was in bunscoil together and he was always flirting around with me even then, when we was kids. But of course we grew up and I was Callahan and he was O'Flynn and we couldn't go on being friends because our families were always at each other's throats. It was Kieran O'Flynn who shot my cousin Alan, not that nobody could ever prove it.'

'Yes, I know about that,' said Katie. 'But, tell me – you and Branán O'Flynn started seeing each other, without anybody knowing?'

'Nobody knew. Not his family, and nor mine neither. We were doing a line, like, for more than six months before anybody found out. I don't know who it was who sneaked on us. It could have been one of the barmen at Jurys Hotel on the Western Road, because we used to go there to spend the night together, like. But somebody sneaked on us for sure.'

'So what happened, Maureen?' asked Katie. Maureen was gabbling and puffing even more furiously, and then she started sobbing, too, although her sobs were more like a seal honking.

'One day two weeks ago I go to meet Branán at the Oval Bar – you know, on South Main Street. We used to go there for a scoop sometimes because we could sit right in the back and nobody would reck us. Branán's not there, but I can't believe my eyes because my Da's there of all people and so is my older sister Bree. My *Da*! And *Bree*! Would you fecking believe it? They grab hold of me and they take me outside and they push me into the car, like. My Da's having a rabbie about me doing a line with Branán but my sister Bree – Mother of God, I tell you, she goes off like a fecking Haitch-bomb. She's allergic to those O'Flynns like I never saw nobody allergic to nobody.'

Maureen puffed and honked and sniffed and honked again.

'Go on,' Katie coaxed her.

'We're driving back home and I go, "What about Branán? You know, "Did you see him, like, and warn him off, or what?" And Bree goes, "Don't you bother yourself about Branán, Mo, because you're never going to see Branán, never again, not so long as you live, and neither is anybody else, neither." So I go, "What do you mean, like, you haven't, like, hurt him or nothing?"

'It's then my Da turns around and goes, "No, pet, we didn't hurt him. He didn't feel a thing."'

'Are you trying to tell me they shot him?'

Maureen let out a long, keening wail, which ended in another sob.

'They only fecking murdered him! They murdered my Branán! The love of my life he was! He and me, we was talking all the time about running away from Cork together and getting married. And they *murdered* him! My own flesh and blood! My own Da, my very own Da, and my own sister Bree! Can you believe it?'

Katie let her sob and puff for a while, and then said, 'Do you know what they did with his body?'

'No. They won't tell me. I've asked them again and again but they say it's better if I never know. More than likely they probably buried him in a bog somewhere, like the O'Flynns was supposed to have done with my cousin Alan.'

'If Branán's disappeared, why haven't the O'Flynns reported him missing?'

'Oh, come on. The O'Flynns wouldn't tell the guards if somebody broke into their toilet and stole their shit.'

'Maureen – are you prepared to make a formal statement about this and testify in court?'

'No, I am not,' said Maureen. 'No way.' Then, 'Stall it for a moment,' and she loudly blew her nose.

When she had finished, she said, 'If you try to make out that I told you all of this, I'll say I didn't. I'll say you must have been dreaming.'

Katie waited for a moment, and then she said, 'I don't understand this, Maureen. If you're not prepared to help me arrest your father and your sister for murdering Branán, then why did you want me to call you? Without your testimony, there's nothing I can do. Your father will deny it and your sister will deny it and we have no idea of where Branán's body might be or where he was killed or how, so we'll have no forensic evidence, either. Don't you want to see justice done?'

'Oh, believe you me, DS Maguire, believe you me – I want justice done. I want *more* than justice done! They've ruined my life – I want to see *them* ruined, too, the whole Callahan family, not just my Da and Bree. I want to see them *all* locked up!'

'All right. You want revenge. But if you won't give me a statement, how do you propose to make that happen?'

'I can't tell you over the phone.'

'Why not?'

'I'll bet you're recording this, aren't you?'

'Of course, yes. All Garda conversations are recorded. But that won't be much use if you come out later and say that nothing of what you've told me is true. Especially if we can't find Branán O'Flynn's body.'

'I'll meet you somewhere tomorrow morning where nobody can see us and nobody can record what I'm telling you,' said Maureen. Her voice was lower now, and slower, and she sounded more guarded than distressed. 'But if you ever come out and say that you met me, and that's where you got your tip-off from, I'll say that you're a liar.'

'So where are you thinking of meeting me?' asked Katie. 'And when?'

'How are you fixed tomorrow morning about eleven? That's about the only time I can get away.'

'I can do that, yes. Where?'

'If you're coming from the city and you go past Blackrock Castle there's a car park for the castle. Do you know it? A short distance past that, though, there's another car park, for people who want to walk by the river. I'll be there at eleven so.'

'Okay,' said Katie. 'I'll be there, too.'

'But no cheating on me, like. No hidden microphone or nothing like that. This has to be confidential.'

'I promise you. No hidden microphone.'

Maureen Callahan hung up without saying anything else. Katie was left staring at her phone indecisively. She couldn't make up her mind if Maureen had been genuinely grieving or whether she had another motive for getting her own back on her sisters. All that sobbing had certainly been dramatic, but maybe it had been a little *too* dramatic. It's fierce hard to tell these days, she thought, now that people weep and wail and build shrines out of flowers and teddy-bears whenever a rock star or a famous actor passes away, as if they had known them personally.

She dialled Detective Ó Doibhilin's number.

'Yes, ma'am?'

'Michael, you know Branán O'Flynn, don't you?'

'Branán O'Flynn? That chancer? Of course. I lifted him only in April I think it was. Selling Krokodil at the late and unlamented Catwalk Club.'

'Would you go round to his house and check if he's there, and if he's not, go round to his usual haunts and find out if anybody's seen him in the past two weeks. But do it dead discreet, like, you know. If nobody's seen him, don't push it and ask what's happened to him. Just say okay and that you'll try to catch up with him later.'

'What's the reason?' asked Detective Ó Doibhilin. 'He's still on bail for that, isn't he? Has he gone on the hop or something?'

'I can't tell you at the moment, Michael, sorry. But if you could do that this evening for me, I'd really appreciate it.'

'Of course, ma'am. No bother at all. There's only that *Operation Transformation* on the telly tonight. I'd rather be out working than watching a bunch of fat eejits trying to turn themselves into thin eejits.'

'Thanks,' said Katie. 'And there's something I need you to do for me tomorrow morning, too. I can't explain why, not at the moment, but I'll tell you what it's all about later. Let's just say that it's kind of insurance. One of those things that may turn out to be a waste of time, but if it doesn't, then you're fierce relieved that you did it.'

'Okay, then,' said Detective Ó Doibhilin, and listened carefully while she explained what she wanted.

When she had hung up, Katie went into Moirin's office and said, 'I'm going into my strategy meeting now, Moirin. I don't know what time we'll be finished so you can go home now if you like. I'll see you in the morning so. And thanks again for all the work you've done today.'

She picked up the folder of rural crime statistics that she was going to take into the meeting. As she did so she remembered that she had arranged to meet Maureen Callahan at the same time as John's appointment at the hospital with Doctor Kashani to discuss his prosthetic legs.

She could hardly ring Maureen Callahan back and change the time of their rendezvous. Maybe she could manage to alter the time of John's appointment. Maybe her life was becoming too complicated altogether.

Fourteen

It was nearly 10:30 by the time she arrived home, and it was raining hard. Bridie must have seen her car headlights as she turned into the driveway because she opened the front door for her as she came hurrying up to the porch with her briefcase held over her head.

'Holy Mother of God, it's bucketing!' said Bridie. 'I left my houseplants out to be watered but they're going to be washed out to sea if it goes on like this!'

Katie gave Barney an affectionate pat on the head and tugged at his ears. 'You've been a good boy for Auntie Bridie, have you?'

'Oh, he's the best-trained dog I ever came across,' said Bridie. 'If he could get up on his hind legs, and if he had hands instead of paws, I swear to God he'd make a cup of tea for me and bring it in on a tray. With biscuits.'

Katie nodded towards the nursery. 'And how's himself? Sleeping, is he?'

'I put him to bed about an hour ago. He's still suffering fierce pain in those imaginary feet of his. He said it's so bad that if they hadn't been ampumatated already, he'd have them cut off.'

Katie went through into the living-room. She was tempted to pour herself a drink but she decided to wait until Bridie had gone home. She didn't want her gossiping around Cobh that she was an alcoholic.

'Listen, Bridie,' she said. 'Something has come up at work. Something important which I really can't get out of. I won't be able to come with you to the hospital tomorrow morning. If you could just make a note for me of what the doctor says about John's progress, I'd be more than grateful.'

'Oh, dear, that's scalding,' said Bridie, as she raised the hood on her raincoat. 'John will be pure disappointed. Like he talks about almost nothing else all day but you, and how excited he is that you're both back together again. He says he can't wait for the day when he's able to walk down the street arm-in-arm with you, and nobody will know that he has the prosthetic legs. All they'll be thinking is, "Would you look at that handsome couple"?'

'He's been saying that to you?' asked Katie.

'Over and over. Never stops. Once he has his prosthetic legs, he said, he's going to ask you to marry him. Maybe I shouldn't have told you that, but that's what keeps his spirits up. He's even talking about the children that you're going to be having together, and what you're going to call them.'

Katie started to smile but then found that she couldn't. She opened the front door and outside the rain was still clattering down from an overflowing gutter.

'I'll see you tomorrow morning, Bridie. Take good care driving home.'

Once Bridie had gone, Katie went back into the living-room. She stood there for a while, with Barney looking up at her and wagging his tail very slowly as if he could sense that she was thinking and wasn't in the mood for play.

'What am I going to do, Barns?' she asked him. 'Jesus. If anybody ever made a rod for their own back.'

She went across to the drinks table and poured herself a large glass of vodka, and then she went into the kitchen, opened the fridge, and topped it up with tonic water. Three bottles of John's medicines were in the fridge, too, as well as three slices of leftover pizza. She bit her lip with frustration and guilt and exhaustion. It stopped her eyes from filling with tears.

Back in the living-room, she sat down and switched on the television so that she could watch the late news. She caught the last few seconds of an item about the new shopping centre that was being built on the site of Cork's old Capitol Cinema, and then a picture of a smiling young dark-haired girl came on to the screen.

'Cork City Garda are appealing for anybody who knows of the whereabouts of nineteen-year-old Siobhán O'Donohue to contact them as soon as possible. Siobhán has not been seen since leaving the Eclipse Club on Oliver Plunkett Street on Hallowe'en night. Her friends say that she had a disagreement with her boyfriend before leaving the club and may be deliberately hiding in order to worry him. However Superintendent Michael Pearse said that after three days her family were deeply concerned about her wellbeing, and she would not be in any trouble if she were to contact the Garda to reassure them that she is safe and has come to no harm.'

Katie made a mental note to talk to Superintendent Pearse tomorrow about this girl. There had only been three abductions in the city in the past eighteen months, mostly because women were being more careful when they went out at night, and in each case the victims had been found alive, although two of them had been raped and one had been badly beaten.

She was listening to a breaking news report about gang warfare between the Kinahans and the Hutches in Dublin when she heard a bell tinkling. It took her a moment to remember that Bridie had told her that she would bring in a bell for John to ring when he needed to go to the toilet, or other assistance. The bell tinkled again, more plaintive than urgent.

She pressed *mute* on the TV's remote and went across to the nursery. The door was already slightly ajar but she pushed it open wider. John had switched on his bedside lamp and he was sitting almost upright in bed, propped up by three large pillows. He smelled strongly of the Boss aftershave that she had given him, as if he had sprayed it on only a few seconds ago.

'Hi, darling,' he smiled, and held out his hand to her. She went over and kissed his cheek and then sat on the bed beside him and took hold of his hand. His fingers were very cold, even though the room was warm, and Katie thought that he was looking very white, like an over-exposed photograph of himself.

'How was your day?' he asked her.

'Oh, the usual mixture of scummers and bureaucrats. How was yours?'

'Bridie took me out for a push, when the showers eased off. We went as far as the Rushbrooke Commercial Park but then it started to rain again so we came back. I had the waterproof cover on so I managed to stay dry until we got home and Barney shook himself all over me.'

'How's the pain?'

'It was bad this morning but Bridie gave me enough oxycodone to fell an army.'

'Listen – tomorrow, when you have your appointment with Doctor Kashani – I'm afraid I won't be able to come with you.'

'Oh.'

'I'm truly sorry, John, believe me, but I have to go and meet somebody about a serious case. I would have postponed it if I could, but I simply can't.'

John shrugged and said, 'Okay. I know you have your priorities. Bridie and me will manage, I'm sure.'

Katie gave his hand a quick squeeze and then stood up. 'I'm going to take a shower. Is there anything I can get you?'

'No, no thanks. Bridie fed me earlier – sausages and colcannon. I'm stuffed.'

Katie went to her own bedroom and undressed. In her wardrobe mirror she thought she had an accusing frown on her face, as if there were another woman on the other side of the mirror who disapproved of the way she was treating John.

Do you love him or not? If you don't love him any more, you shouldn't let him keep his hopes up, just because you feel so guilty. The longer you leave it, the more pain he's going to feel when you finally tell him that it's over. In comparison with your ditching him, the pain he feels in his missing feet is going to be nothing at all.

She couldn't help thinking of the way the Vizsla had looked at her when she had pointed her revolver at its head, not realising that she could end its life with one squeeze of the double-action trigger. John had looked at her in the same trusting way.

She took a long hot shower, as if that could wash away her tiredness and her indecision, and when she stepped out and dried herself and wrapped herself up in her pink towelling bathrobe, she did feel a little better. Her father had always said that it was no coincidence that 'crime' rhymed with 'grime'. 'I'll tell you, Katie – after I'd been rubbing shoulders with sublas all day, I couldn't wait to get into the bath and scrub myself all their muck off me.'

Katie was combing back her wet hair in the steamed-up mirror when John's bell rang.

'*Coming!*' she called out. She couldn't decide if she wanted to grow her hair longer or have it cut very short. She liked the crimson streaks that her hair stylist had given her. Her hair was dark red naturally, but these gave it more depth. She was still thinking about it when John's bell rang again.

She went into the nursery. 'Sorry, John,' she smiled. 'I was just getting myself dry. Is there something I can bring you? Cup of tea, maybe?'

John's eyes were oddly unfocused. She had the feeling that he was remembering the way they were when they had first got together, when he had been tall and muscular and he hadn't been dependent on her.

'Katie...' he said. 'I just want *you*.'

'I'm here. What do you want to do? Talk? We can go into the living-room and watch TV together if you like. Or play some music.'

'I want to see you,' he said, with a slight catch in his throat. 'It's been so long since I've seen you.'

Katie opened out her arms. 'Here I am. I'm not going away. I live here.'

John's eyes still looked unfocused. Katie could almost have believed that he was hypnotised. Maybe it was all the painkillers that Bridie given him. Oxycodone was almost as powerful as morphine.

'Can you—' he began, and gestured with his hands as if he were taking off his pyjama jacket. 'Can I see you without your bathrobe?'

Katie didn't know how to react to that. What was she going to say? *No*? They had been lovers for months, until he had left her to start a new job in San Francisco. Passionate lovers – always hungry for each other. They had made love in her back garden on warm summer nights. They had made love in the woods when they had stayed at the Parknasilla hotel in Kerry. They had even made love in her office, in Anglesea Street. And now she wasn't even going to let him see her without her bathrobe?

'You know how much I adore you, don't you, Katie?' said John. 'You're everything I ever could have wished for.'

Katie loosened her tie-belt. She pushed her bathrobe off her shoulders, although she hesitated for a moment before she let it drop to the floor. When she did, there was silence between them. She simply stood there, naked, with her arms by her sides, while John stared at her.

At last, he said, 'Let me feel you, Katie. I haven't felt you for so long.'

She approached his bed, and stood close enough for him to touch her. She didn't know if she ought to be doing this or not. In one way she felt as if he were treating her like a goddess. In another way, she felt as if he were treating her like a slave-girl, or a slut. Did she want to show herself off to him? Did she want him to touch her? Was there something about this that excited her, or did she simply feel that she owed it to him, because of him losing his legs?

For a split-second she felt like turning away, picking up her bathrobe and leaving the room. But then he reached up and cupped her right breast, gently weighing it in the palm of his hand, and rotating the ball of his thumb around her nipple. He had always been a very strong lover, and even though his hand was cold now, she found that coldness arousing.

He caressed her left nipple, too, between finger and thumb, until it stiffened, and her areola crinkled. She closed her eyes for a moment, but when she opened them again John still had that strange detached expression, as if he were thinking about the way they used to be, rather than the way they were now, tonight, in what had once been the nursery.

He lightly ran his fingers down her sides, right down to her hips, and that made her shiver. Then he stroked the smooth mound of her vulva, and slid his fingertip between her lips, stroking her clitoris. She was wet now, and she could not only feel her wetness but hear it, as her lips faintly clicked.

It was then that he pulled back the bedcover. His penis was sticking out of his pyjamas, purple-headed and hard and already glistening with juice. He didn't say anything, but reached with his right hand around the small of Katie's back and pulled her even closer, so that she nearly overbalanced and fell on top of him.

'Climb on to me,' he panted. 'Climb on to me, I'll be all right.'

But Katie suddenly thought: *This is madness. What am I doing? I'm frustrated and I'm guilty but John's drugged up to the eyeballs with painkillers and God alone knows what this could do to his stumps. He's only a few weeks out of surgery. What if one of his femoral arteries burst and he bled to death?*

Much more than that – you simply don't have the same feelings for him any more.

She looked down at John's face and she was sure now that she didn't love him. She might be responsible for the mutilated state he was in, but he was too weak and too needy and he was expecting too much from her, and she realised now that he always had expected too much. Perhaps she was being callous, but it was almost impossible to serve in the Garda for as long as she had, and not become callous, or thick-skinned, at least. Certainly it had made her self-protective.

She took hold of his right arm and carefully levered it away from her back.

'What?' he said.

She stepped away from the side of the bed. 'We can't do this, John. I appreciate how you feel but you're not ready yet. This could kill you.'

'What are you talking about? *Kill* me? Of course it wouldn't. Besides – you think I'd want to die any other way? Please, Katie. I need you. Look at me. I'm dreaming about you every night and daydreaming about you every day.'

'John, you're not ready. Not physically, and not emotionally, either. And I'm not either.'

'I don't understand. You wanted me here, didn't you?'

She picked up her bathrobe and put it on again, tying the belt up tight. Then she went back to the bed and folded back the duvet to cover John.

John held on to her arm. 'What do you mean you're not ready?' he asked her. 'You felt as if you were.'

'John – it's not easy for me to come to terms with what's happened to you. You've changed more than you think, and it's not just your legs.'

'How? How I have changed?'

'I don't know exactly. But after what's happened to you, how could you not be different?'

'I still love you. That hasn't changed.'

'Well, maybe it's me, then. I'm finding this too hard to deal with. On top of that, I'm totally stressed out at work. There's a flood of drugs coming into the city and because of that the crime rate's gone up through the roof. We're having a struggle to cope with it, and every day it gets worse.'

'Please, Katie. I'm aching for you.'

'Didn't you hear what I said? I'm up the walls, John. I couldn't give my mind to it.'

'There's nobody else, is there? Some lover you haven't told me about. You're always ranting on about that Jimmy O'Reilly. It's not him, is it?'

Katie tugged her arm free. 'Jimmy O'Reilly wouldn't spit on me if I was on fire. Besides that, he's as gay as Christmas.'

'Katie. Katie, I love you.' His voice cracked as if he were going to cry.

'I know, John,' said Katie. 'I know you do, and I'm sorry. I can't tell you how sorry. I shouldn't have led you on like that. I just thought – well, to be honest with you, I don't know what I thought. I wasn't thinking at all.'

They looked at each other for a long time and neither of them spoke. Both of them knew that it was better to say nothing, in case something was said.

At last Katie said, 'You're sure I can't fetch you anything? Glass of water, maybe?'

John shook his head. 'I think I'll go back to sleep now, if it's all the same to you. If I can't have you for real, at least I can dream about you.'

'Goodnight, then,' said Katie, and left the room.

* * *

In the small hours of the morning, she was woken by the sound of sobbing, and what must have been John beating his fist against his pillow.

'*Oh, God*,' she heard him groaning. '*Why me? Oh God, why me?*'

Fifteen

Siobhán was woken up by the sound of a door banging, and voices. She could sense that she was still in the ambulance, because she could feel it swaying as somebody climbed into it, and approached her.

The trolley on which she was lying was unlocked, and then she felt herself being pushed to the rear of the ambulance, and lifted out. She could smell cigarette breath, and diesel fumes. A man's voice said, 'Watch it, Tommy,' and then Fiontán let out one of his strange froglike croaks, like a bewitched prince out of a fairy-tale.

She felt the trolley being lifted up again, and one side knocked against a doorframe. Then she felt herself being wheeled along a corridor, with the trolley's wheels squeaking. The same man's voice said, 'Take her down the end room for now. It's going to take us five or six hours at least to load up. When's Nick coming over?'

'He said he'd be here by now,' said another man. 'You know him, though. Takes longer to get ready than my old woman.'

The men were obviously English, and working-class. Siobhán recognised their accents from *EastEnders* on the television. She had been drugged and asleep for most of the journey, but she had woken up when she and Fiontán had been taken out of the ambulance for the ferry crossing, and she had been aware of the movement of the deck underneath her. She hadn't heard any other passengers talking, though, so she had assumed that they were shut in their own private cabin.

While they were on board, Grainne had lifted her head for her and helped her to drink a cup of sweet tea, and then fed her with a cheese sandwich and a Kit-Kat. In spite of the fact that Grainne had aided and abetted her being blinded and maimed, or perhaps because she felt remorseful about it, she had been very gentle and motherly towards her, continually asking her if she was comfortable, and if there was anything she needed.

I need my sight, and my voice, and my hands, and my legs. Or if I can't have those, I need to die, because I might as well be dead.

Shortly before the ferry arrived in Fishguard, she had needed desperately to urinate. She had flapped her arms, trying to catch Grainne's attention, and at last Grainne had leaned over her and said, 'What is it? What do you want, Siobhán? Another cup of tea, is it?'

She had shaken her head and pointed between her legs as best as she could.

'Oh, you need to pee, is it, or is it a jobby? Well, don't you bother about that, darling, just do it, because you're wearing a nappy, like, and we can change you after.'

She had flapped her arms again in protest, but Grainne had ignored her. After that, she had held on for as long as she possibly could, but in the end the pressure had been too much to bear, and she had let it go. She felt the warm flood between her legs and she sobbed in misery and embarrassment and helplessness.

'Don't you worry about it, Siobhán,' Grainne had told her, patting her hand. 'Things won't get any worse, I promise you.'

Now she found herself pushed into what sounded like a large empty room. Her trolley was parked beside a wall and she was left there. She could feel a cold draught, so the door must have been left open, and she could also hear shuffling footsteps and banging noises, which made her think there must be a long corridor outside the door.

She heard more footsteps, and a man coughing, and the *snap-snap-snap* of a cigarette lighter that didn't work first time. After a few moments she smelled cigarette smoke.

A man's voice said, 'Where does all this lot come from?' She recognised him from the clinic in Cork. She was sure that he was the man who had brought the dog into her room.

'Schoon sent it from Rotterdam just before he was collared. But don't worry about it. The next shipment's all lined up. We're getting it direct from Engelsbel next time.'

'Schoon was such a fecking eejit.'

'Well, he was and he wasn't. I mean, he was a genius to think of doing this in the first place, you got to give him that. Altogether I reckon he shipped in well over four hundred million quids' worth. I mean, that's pretty fucking impressive, isn't it? You got to give him that.'

The two men must have turned their backs or moved away from the door, because after that Siobhán could still hear them talking together, but much less distinctly, so that she could only catch one or two words. She was beginning to shiver, in the draught, and the wetness between her legs had turned cold and had started to sting. If she had been able to speak she would have called out to one of the men and begged them to come in here and strangle her, or tie a plastic bag over her head so that she suffocated.

After a few more minutes, she heard at least two other men approaching, and because of that they stepped back and now she could hear them clearly again.

'How's the form?' asked the man from the clinic.

'Got about half of it stashed away, mate. There's so much there, I don't think we're going to be able to get it all in, not on this run.'

'How much altogether?'

'Well, what, there's over two hundred kay of coke, seventy-five kay of crack, and seventy-five thousand Es.'

'Holy shit. All right. Pack away as much as you can and we'll pick up the rest next time. Gearoid is buying two more vehicles this week so the fleet's building up. We should have six at least by the end of January. To be honest with you, though, we never thought the business would expand so quick.'

One of the other men coughed. 'It's the kids these days, innit?' he said, in a gravelly voice. 'They can't get enough of it. We could ship in twice what we're shipping in now, easy, – three times as much – and they'd still be crying out for more. In my days it was purple hearts. I remember when they made purple hearts illegal and they went up from sixpence each to ninepence.'

'You can remember the Battle of Waterloo you can, Wardy,' put in another man.

'Listen, I'm not complaining,' said the man from the clinic. 'But just make sure everything's sealed in one hundred per cent airtight. Those sniffer dogs the customs have at Rosslare, they can tell if you're carrying a half-sucked Fisherman's Friend in your pocket.'

'Don't you worry, mate,' said the man called Wardy, and coughed again. 'All the packets are wrapped up tight in your polafeen and all the panels are going to be riveted. That ambulance could be stuffed full of rotten kippers and nobody would smell 'em.'

'It had better not be, boy,' said the man from the clinic, and from the tone of his voice Siobhán sensed that he was only half-joking. From the way they spoke to each other, she could tell that these were men who were doing business together because it suited them, but who didn't trust each other at all.

She heard them walk away. Wardy's spasmodic cough grew fainter as he went off down the corridor. Then she could hear nothing but a faint metallic hammering sound. Then even that stopped, and there was silence.

She had never felt so desperately alone in her life. She thought of saying a prayer, and asking God to take her back in time to that night outside the Eclipse Club. Why hadn't she waited for that Hailo taxi? But she knew that God wouldn't answer her, and that He couldn't or wouldn't give her what she was asking Him for. At some time in her life she must have offended Him dreadfully, although she couldn't think how, but plainly He was punishing her for it, and He wasn't yet ready to forgive her, if He ever would.

So she lay on her trolley in complete darkness, not knowing where she was or when anybody was going to come for her, and the tears slid from her eyes and into her ears. She couldn't stop shaking in the chilly, relentless draught. Somebody had left a door open somewhere, as if to taunt her. *You're not locked in, love. There's a whole world outside. If only you could see where it was, and if only you could walk.*

Sixteen

Bridie arrived at 7:05 the next morning, while Katie was still standing in the kitchen, eating a piece of toast. She had forgotten to buy any fresh bread yesterday, so she had been left with the heel, which she and her sisters used to fight over when they were young. Her coffee was still so hot that she could drink it only in sips.

'Is John awake yet?' asked Bridie, as she hung up her coat.

'Not yet. I don't think he slept very well last night. Help yourself to some coffee. There's plenty in the pot.'

'Oh, I can't drink coffee. It gives me the palpimatations. I'll make myself a cup of tea, though.'

Katie watched her fill the kettle and then she said, 'I'll be straight with you, Bridie. Me and John had a bit of a confrontation last night. I've taken him in because I feel responsible for what happened to him, but he seems to have read too much into that. It's partly my fault, I admit. I thought my feelings for him wouldn't have altered, but I'm afraid they have.'

Bridie puffed out her cheeks. 'Well, I've seen it often enough before. Somebody falling ill, like, or getting some kind of serious injury, like your John. Overnight their partner finds out that they're not a lover any more, they're a carer. It puts a fierce strain on any relationship, no question. The multiple sclerosis, and the motor neurone disease, they're desperate, but I think the dementia is the worst of all. It must be so hard to keep on loving somebody who doesn't even know who you are.'

'I have to confess, Bridie, I really have no idea what to do.'

Bridie went to the cupboard and took out a cup and a saucer. 'I'll talk to Aileen Noonan when I take John to the hospital this morning. She's his therapist. I know she was keen for him to stay here with you, for the sake of his morale, like. But if things aren't working out —'

Katie's iPhone played 'Tá Mo Chleamhnas a Dhéanamh'. She picked it up and it was Detective Dooley.

'Just to let you know, ma'am, we've lifted Keeno. Mulvaney tipped us off that he was on his way to pick up his money, and he showed up about twenty minutes ago.'

'He accepted the money?'

'Oh, yes. We made sure of that. Mulvaney handed him the envelope and he took it, and we have the conversation between them recorded. He specifically asked how much Mulvaney had been paid for each of the dogs, the German Shepherd and the Vizsla, so he can't deny that he didn't know what the money was for, or try to make out it was payment for something else altogether.'

'Was he alone? How was he? Did he put up any resistance?'

'He came by himself, yes, and he put up no kind of a struggle. None at all. He wasn't armed, and there were no weapons of any kind in his car. He came out with a few curse words that I'd never heard before, but that was all. He wouldn't give his name or address or nothing like that, or make any kind of a statement. He wouldn't even admit that his name was Keeno.'

'Doesn't he have any ID on him? A wallet? How about a phone?'

'No wallet, no phone. Only a thick wedge of money. Any road we've arrested him for handling stolen goods and we're bringing him in now, him and Mulvaney, and we'll be able to interview him later.'

'That's grand, Robert. Good man yourself. I'll be in myself in half an hour, traffic willing. Eoin Cassidy's coming in at ten to identify the dogs, so now we can get him to identify Keeno, too.'

'That's what they call killing two birds with one manslaughter suspect, isn't it?'

'Now then, Robert.'

'Sorry, ma'am.'

* * *

Before she left, Katie went in to see John. He was awake, although the curtains were still drawn and the room was gloomy.

'I'm off now,' she said. 'I wanted to wish you good luck at the hospital, that's all. I'm truly sorry I can't come with you.'

John shrugged and gave her a weak smile. 'You said sorry yesterday, Katie. You don't have to apologise twice.'

She stood in the open doorway not knowing what to say next. John lay looking at her with half-closed eyes as if he were allowing himself to slide back into sleep.

'Well, then, good luck, John,' she said at last. 'I'll see you after.'

'I'll win you back!' he called, as she walked out. 'I promise you that, sweetheart! I'll win you back!'

* * *

She watched through the two-way mirror as Keeno was charged and fingerprinted and photographed. She didn't want to make herself known to him yet – not until he had been made to wait for two or three hours. Waiting made arrogant men angry and weak men even more unsure of themselves, and whichever they were, they were always likely to come out with more than they had originally meant to.

Gerry Mulvaney had been right: he did bear a slight resemblance to Sylvester Stallone, although he was stoop-shouldered and pot-bellied, rather than muscular. His hair was tangled and grey and stained ginger at the front from smoking. His eyes were hooded and his nose was twisted into an S-shape. He had thick dry lips and he was continually licking them. He was wearing a grey leather jacket and a black shirt that was open at the neck, with grey-and-white chest hair curling out of it.

'God – if only Mrs Cassidy had consented to a DNA test,' she said to Sergeant Begley, who was standing beside her to see Keeno being processed.

Sergeant Begley shook his head. 'Myself, I reckon there's a whole lot more to this than meets the eye. It was hardly worth a full-scale raid on those kennels for the sake of two thousand euros.'

'We still don't know what's happened to the rest of the dogs,' said Katie. 'Dooley tells me that some of them may have been taken for dogfighting up at Ballyknock.'

'Well, sure, there's plenty of money in dogfighting all right. But not all of the dogs would have been suitable for that, would they? It's no good setting a chihuahua up against a mastiff, is it?'

Katie had to admit to herself that he was right. Even if the two dogs that they had found at Riverstick and the dogs that were supposed to be fighting at Ballyknock had all been stolen from the Sceolan Kennels, what had happened to the rest of them?

Keeno slowly turned his head and stared in their direction. He would have been able to see nothing more than his own reflection, but if he had any experience of being arrested before, he would have guessed that he was being observed from behind the mirror. He gave a slow wink, and stuck out the tip of his tongue.

'Why do I have the feeling that we'll be lucky to get any information at all out of that scummer?' said Sergeant Begley.

'For the same reason that I do,' said Katie. 'It would probably be more than his life's worth to tell us who his gang are.' She paused for a moment, and then she said, 'Any progress with that missing girl?'

'Siobhán O'Donohue? We're still tracking down all of the crowd from the Eclipse Club on Hallowe'en. There was over a hundred and fifty of them, like, so it's taking a bit of time. A few of them saw Siobhán having a bit of a scrap with her boyfriend, and then going to the bar and knocking back three or four of them Jägerbombs. Then she left – bit unsteady on her feet by all accounts.'

'We've interviewed her boyfriend?'

'Of course. A young shamfeen from The Glen called Donal O'Grady. He said that his relationship with Siobhán had been turning sour for a few weeks before Hallowe'en and that night he shifted some other girl just to show her. That was what kicked off the argument.'

'Do you think her boyfriend might have had anything to do with her disappearance?'

'No, he didn't for sure, although he was one of the last people to see her. He said he came out of the club with this new girl of his – Phil, the girl's name is, Philomena. He saw Siobhán standing in the street like she was waiting to have another crack at him. He shifted Phil again right in front of her just to underline the fact that they were finished.'

'And after that?'

'He took Phil home and then went home himself. He didn't see where Siobhán went – whether she walked or got a taxi or what – and so far nobody else saw her, either, although we have a few more witnesses yet to track down.'

'She lives in Knocka, doesn't she?' asked Katie.

'That's right.'

'Most likely then she would have hailed a taxi or called for one, especially if she was langered.'

'Of course. But we've contacted all of the cab companies and none of them have a record of a fare at that specific time of the morning from Oliver Plunkett Street to Killiney Heights.'

'Maybe a taxi driver picked her up but didn't take her home. We've had *that* happen before, as you know yourself. Did she use any particular taxi app? A lot of girls do these days.'

'That's a thought. I'll have Ó Doibhilin ask her boyfriend – her *ex*-boyfriend, anyway. And if *he* doesn't know, I'll tell him to ask her family.'

At that moment Katie's iPhone pinged. Detective Scanlan had texted her to say that Eoin Cassidy was waiting by the front desk.

'Eoin Cassidy's here,' she told Sergeant Begley. 'Now we'll find out for sure where these dogs came from. That's unless he makes out they're his when they're not.'

Sergeant Begley grunted with amusement. 'Do you know what my wife always says? They should stop calling us *An Garda Siochána* and call us *Daoine Nach Bhfuil A Chreideann Aon Duine* – the people who don't believe anybody.'

They went downstairs and met Eoin Cassidy in the reception area by the front desk. He was accompanied by a beefy crimson-faced uniformed garda from Bandon. By contrast, Eoin looked tired and wan and he hadn't shaved this morning. Even his brown tweed jacket looked tired, and his trousers drooped.

'You've found Lili then?' he said, as Katie came up to him. 'And one of the German Shepherds – it'll either be Gus or Bandit. I'm hoping it's Gus. I mean, I won't be upset if it's Bandit, of course not. But Gus is only three and Bandit's seven.'

'We don't know if it's either of them yet, Eoin,' said Katie. 'A handler from the Dog Support Unit has them out in the car park, if you'd like to come and take a look.'

Eoin followed Katie and Sergeant Begley out of the back door. It was cold out there, but there was no wind, and the sun was shining behind a thin haze of cirrus, and at least it wasn't raining. A white dog support van was parked by the entrance, and a handler was waiting with the German Shepherd and the Vizsla from Riverstick.

As soon as he saw them, Eoin hurried over and knelt on the ground between them and put an arm around each of them. When he looked up Katie, his eyes were shining and it was clear that he was close to tears.

'Oh, it's them all right,' he said. 'It's Lili and Gus. No question about it. See, Gus has this saddleback pattern, and this black mask over his face. I've brought photos with me if you want to make comparisons. And Lili, she has this scar on her left hind leg. Oh, this is fantastic! I don't know how to thank you. Their owners are going to be over the moon.'

Katie said, 'I'm pleased for you, Eoin. We'll take a look at your photos, if we may, and we'll be keeping the two dogs here for two or three days for forensic tests. We'll want to check what they've been eating, and if they've been given any drugs, or picked up any infections. We'll also be looking for dust or any other residue caught in their coats. That could give us a clue to where they've been.'

'Of course,' said Eoin. 'I can wait. I'm just so happy out. Now you've found these two it gives me much more hope that we can find the rest of them.'

'Come up to my office,' said Katie. 'There's more I have to talk to you about.'

She turned to his beefy escort and said, 'We'll be a while. Why don't you go to the canteen and treat yourself to a cup of tea? They have home-made barmbrack, too, if you're hungry.'

On their way upstairs, Katie stopped by the squad room and called for Detectives Dooley and Scanlan to come with them. When they reached her office, they all sat down on the oatmeal-coloured couches underneath the window. Eoin appeared to be nervous now, and kept rolling and unrolling his thin brown tie around his fingers.

'You need to know that we have the man known as Keeno in custody,' said Katie. 'You know – Keeno? The man who entered your home on the night when all of your dogs were stolen and raped Cleona.'

Eoin gave a little quiver, as if a goose had walked over his grave, but said nothing, and kept on rolling his tie.

'He's here now, Eoin, downstairs,' Katie told him. 'We need you to come and take a look at him, to see if you recognise him.'

'I've told you over and over what happened that night,' said Eoin. 'I don't have to repeat it, do I?'

'Eoin – it's no use trying to pretend that those two men didn't come into your house and that the one called Keeno didn't sexually assault Cleona. If you won't admit to what really happened, I may have to consider charging you with obstructing our enquiry. I've already arranged to meet with the Director of Public Prosecutions to discuss a charge of manslaughter against you. There's enough evidence to suggest that you weren't acting in self-defence at all and that you shot that intruder in cold blood, whoever he was. The court may take it into account that he invaded your home and was party to stealing your property, but that doesn't mean that they'll let you off completely.'

'Before I say anything else to you, I want to talk to my solicitor,' said Eoin.

'Eoin – listen to me, I'm bending so far over backwards to help you here that my head's almost touching the floor. If you can identify Keeno, we can put a lot of pressure on him to tell us who stole your dogs, and once we know who stole them, we should be able to recover them for you – *all* of them, with any luck.'

'I appreciate your finding Gus and Lili for me, detective superintendent. I'm pure grateful, I can tell you that. But I want to talk to my solicitor.'

'Time's running out, Eoin, even if it hasn't run out already. If we hadn't located them, Gus and Lili would have been sold off by now and you *never* would have got them back. The rest of the dogs are probably being sold off even as we speak. We can find them for you if you help us to track down the gang who took them, but if you won't, then there's very little we can do. I don't have the manpower or the financial resources to go looking for twenty-four missing dogs. I'm sorry, but there it is.'

'Maybe there's another way,' said Eoin.

'I don't understand.'

'Like, maybe you could look at this the other way around.'

'"The other way around". What do you mean?'

'Maybe you could use a pet detective. I mean, if a pet detective could trace where the rest of the dogs have been taken, then you'd be able to discover who stole them.'

'There's only one pet detective in the country that I know of,' said Detective Dooley. 'His name's Robert Kenny and he's based in Dublin. In fact I think he's the only pet detective in Europe. He calls his agency "Happy Tails".'

'Yes… I've heard about him,' said Katie. 'He's helped the Dublin Garda a couple of times to track down stolen dogs. He's very successful, too, so far as I understand it.'

'Actually, there's another pet detective now, in Limerick,' said Eoin. 'He used to be a member of the Limerick and District Canine Club. I met him at their last annual championship dog show. Conor Ó Máille.'

'What qualifications does he have, or is he just an amateur?'

'Oh, no. He took a proper course in pet detection in Fresno, in California, and he's a certified MART.'

'MART? What's a MART when it's at home?'

'Missing Animals Response Technician. Sixth Scents, that's the name of his business – "Scents" like in smells. He's been doing all right, too, so he tells me.'

'"Missing Animals Response Technician",' said Detective Dooley, shaking his head. 'Holy Saint Joseph.'

But Detective Scanlan said, 'I don't know, Robert, maybe we shouldn't mock. I think it might be quite a good idea, bringing in somebody who's an expert in finding lost animals. And like Eoin says, it's looking at this whole enquiry the other way around. The gang who stole those dogs are going to be keeping sketch for *us*, aren't they? Not some lone dog detective. This could totally take them by surprise.'

Katie turned back to Eoin. 'Eoin, I'm asking you one last time if you'll agree to come downstairs now and see if you can identify the suspect we have in custody. If you do, you can save us a heap of time and unnecessary effort, and taxpayers' money, too.'

Eoin said, 'No. I'm sorry. Not until I've had the chance to talk to my solicitor. It's Kevin Cushley, in Bandon.'

Katie took a deep breath. She was tempted to say something cutting to him, but she held her tongue. 'Very well,' she said. 'I'll ask my secretary to phone him for you.' She went to speak to Moirin, and then she beckoned Eoin to come into Moirin's office, so that he could talk to his solicitor in private.

While he was gone, Katie said to Detectives Dooley and Scanlan, 'Well? What's your opinion?'

'I still think it's worth calling in this pet detective,' said Detective Scanlan. 'Supposing he can actually find these dogs, that would be fantastic. If he can't – well, whatever he charges, it can't be much, and at least nobody will be able to say that we were too stick-in-the-mud to try something different.'

Katie looked at her watch. She was due to meet Maureen Callahan in less than forty minutes. She could faintly hear Eoin in Moirin's office saying, '*No*,' and '*No*,' and '*No, well that's what I told them*.'

After a conversation lasting over ten minutes, he came back in.

'So, what did Mr Cushley have to say?' asked Katie. 'Are you coming downstairs to identify Keeno or not?'

'No. I can't identify him because I never saw him.'

'You're still insisting that he didn't come into the house and assault you and your wife?'

'Yes.'

'Even though Cleona says that he did?'

'Yes.'

'So why do you think she said that?'

'I have no idea. You'll have to ask her.'

'I have, and she said that's exactly what happened.'

Eoin pulled a face, as if to say 'Maybe she did, but there's nothing that I can do about it.'

Katie said, 'All right, Eoin. You can go now. But don't forget that you're still on station bail. Robert – could you find the officer who escorted Mr Cassidy, please, and see them out?'

When Detective Dooley had taken Eoin away, Detective Scanlan said, 'Now what?'

'I have to go out for an hour or so,' said Katie, looking at her watch again. 'When I come back we can have a chat with our friend Keeno, although Sergeant Begley doesn't think we'll get anything out of him but bad language and neither do I.'

She paused for a second, thinking, and then she said, 'While I'm gone, Pádraigin, why don't you look up this pet detective? What was his name? Maybe he *could* help us. You never know, like, do you?'

Seventeen

As she drove to Blackrock, Katie was held up by pothole-repairing works at the junction with Beaumont Drive, and that made her five minutes late for her meeting with Maureen Callahan. She hoped that Maureen hadn't thought that she wasn't going to turn up, and already left, but when she turned into the car park she saw that there were only three cars there, and through the tinted windows of a red Audi parked at the very far end she could see the distinctive gleam of Maureen's brassy blonde bob.

She parked her own Focus as far away from the Audi as she could. She was wearing her dark blue duffel-coat and before she got out of the car she tugged up the hood so that even if anybody were watching from a distance they would have difficulty in telling who she was. She walked up to Maureen's car but she went straight past it without stopping and without looking at Maureen. As she made her way to the footpath that ran beside the river, however, she heard a car door slam and knew that Maureen was following her.

She kept walking. The River Lee was wide here, a glittering grey, with a view on the opposite bank of Tivoli industrial estate with all its Lego-coloured shipping containers and the estuary of the Glashaboy River. Maureen had obviously chosen to meet her here because the footpath was screened from the road by thick bushes, and only somebody in a passing boat could have seen them talking together.

After she had walked about a hundred metres, and smiled at an elderly woman who was walking an equally elderly brown poodle, Katie stopped, and turned around, so that Maureen could catch up with her. Not far behind Maureen stood the limestone towers of Blackrock Castle, which looked like a castle out of a fairy story. These days, it was an observatory and a restaurant, and Katie and John had eaten there quite often, but it had originally been built in the reign of Elizabeth I to defend Cork harbour against marauding pirates. Quite appropriate to meet here, thought Katie, considering how the Callahan family made their money, smuggling arms.

Maureen had pulled on a black woolly slouch hat to cover her distinctive blonde hair, and she was wearing a long black overcoat and black high-heeled boots. She was tall, taller than Katie, and easily the prettiest of the Callahan sisters, with an oval face and chocolate-brown eyes and naturally pouting lips, although she had an angry three-pronged scar on the left side of her forehead, as if she had been struck with red-hot fire tongs. As she came close to her, Katie could smell Joy, which had always been one of her own favourite perfumes.

'How's the form, Maureen?' Katie greeted her.

'How do you think? I wish to God that I wasn't meeting you like this, if you want to know the truth, but I'm not going to let them get away with it, do you know what I mean?'

She paused, and then she said, 'You've no microphone?'

Katie unbuttoned her coat and held it wide. 'You can frisk me if you like.'

She turned her pockets inside-out, too. 'And see, look, I've left my phone behind in the car, so I won't be able to record you with that, either.'

'Okay, then, I'll trust you. You saved my brother after all.'

They started walking together. Maureen was very twitchy, and kept turning around to make sure that nobody was following them. After a while, Katie said, 'Are you one hundred per cent sure that your sisters had Branán murdered? They haven't just locked him up in a garage somewhere, or chased him out of Cork and told him never to come back?'

'Oh no, they've done for him all right. Threatening people, that's not their style. If you cross my sisters, that's it, you might as well call for a priest right away, because they'll have you as soon as look at you. No second chances. My Da says if somebody miders you, don't threaten them, because you'll only make an enemy out of them, and one day they could catch you unawares, like, and do for you when you least expect it. So it makes sense to do for them first. After that, you don't have to be looking over your shoulder every five minutes.'

'But if you're not prepared to give evidence against them, how are you going to make sure that they get punished for killing Branán?'

'Because I can get them locked up in jail, that's how. Why do you think I wanted to talk to you?'

'Go on, then. *How* can you get them locked up in jail?'

Maureen glanced around again, and then said, 'They're having a huge shipment of guns and explosives delivered. Like, *huge*. Biggest this year, I'd say. Sometime on Friday night most likely.'

'Where's it coming from, this shipment?' asked Katie.

'The Czech Republic, through Boulogne, that's the usual route. But it's here in the country already.'

'Where?'

'I'm not too sure. Wherever they landed it. It could have been Kinsale or Kilmacsimon Quay up the Bandon River, or further along the coast maybe. It would have depended on the tides, like, and whether they thought that anybody had got wind of it. Maybe even Tralee.'

'Do you know what's in it?'

'Assault rifles, the Czech ones, they're like AK-47s. And Skorpion machine pistols, you can get four thousand euros each for those. And Semtex.'

'So this is all arriving here in Cork on Friday night? Where, exactly?'

Maureen pressed her hand over her mouth and looked out across the river. For a long time she said nothing at all, but then she turned back to Katie and said, 'Even with what they did to Branán, this isn't easy. I mean, it's betrayal, like, isn't it, and that goes against the grain.'

'Maureen, those guns are going to be used to commit crimes, and probably to kill people. The explosives, too. I know that your motive for telling me about them is revenge, rather than saving lives, but think about it. You'll not only be making sure that your sisters get the justice they deserve, you'll be doing something in the public interest, for a change.'

'Well, I suppose you're right,' said Maureen. She thought for a moment, and then she said, 'No, you *are* right, and I'll tell you what I'll do. As soon as the shipment's delivered, I'll ring you to let you know where it is.'

'Can't you tell me now?'

'I can't, no. I wish I could, but there's a score of different places where they store stuff and I don't know where they're going to put this shipment yet. My sisters have been fierce cagey with me lately, do you know what I mean? Like I say, though, the moment I know that it's all been unloaded, and where, I'll ring you. If you can just give me your number?'

Katie told Maureen her number and Maureen put it into her iPhone.

'Right then,' said Katie. 'I'll be waiting to hear from you.'

There was much more that Katie could have said to her. She could have said that even though she was acting as a Garda informant, she might still face historical charges for her own involvement in the arms-trafficking racket. After all, she had been working for the family business ever since she had left school, and over the years the Callahans had handled millions of euros' worth of Semtex, as well as assault rifles, handguns, and even rocket launchers. Indirectly, the Callahans could be blamed for countless deaths and robberies, both south and north of the border. If a politician or a gangster had been shot in Dublin, you could almost be sure that they had been killed by a gun supplied by the Callahans.

A judge might give Maureen a lighter sentence in return for her assistance for putting the rest of the Callahans behind bars, but that could scarcely go unnoticed by her father and her sisters, and she would be at even greater risk if the DPP decided not to prosecute her at all. It wouldn't matter if she had a recording of this conversation or not, her family would immediately realise then who had shopped them; and if what Maureen had told her was true, and nobody who crossed the Callahans was given a second chance, she would have to go into witness protection for the rest of her life.

Katie could have warned her about this, but she didn't, because so far Maureen hadn't given her enough information to make an arrest. She hadn't told her exactly where the shipment of arms had been landed or where it was now, or exactly where in Cork it was going to be stored. That meant that Katie wouldn't be able to set up surveillance on the storage facility before the arms were delivered. She wouldn't be able to see who delivered them, and have the chance to arrest them, too.

It was a typical professional dilemma. She didn't trust Maureen Callahan at all, and yet if she didn't act on what she was telling her, she could miss out on making one of the most spectacular arrests of her whole career.

As they walked back to the car park together, Maureen lit a cigarette, and puffed at it very quickly, almost as if she wasn't used to smoking. They separated without saying goodbye.

Back in her car, Katie looked at herself in the sun-visor mirror to tidy her hair.

If she's not being straight with me, she thought, *why has she gone to such lengths to tell me about Branán O'Flynn being murdered and this huge arms shipment coming in? If only some or none of it is true, what exactly is she after?*

* * *

Keeno was sitting in the interview room looking bored when Katie and Sergeant Begley and Detective Dooley came in. His hands were clasped together behind his head and he was staring at the ceiling and ostentatiously chewing gum. Garda O'Keefe was sitting in the corner looking equally bored. Katie knew Garda O'Keefe well, and she understood why he had been assigned to guard Keeno. He was a member of the Irish Elite Boxing Club and had been Garda welterweight boxing champion two years running.

Katie sat down in front of Keeno and Sergeant Begley and Detective Dooley sat on either side of her.

'No chance of a smoke, I'm guessing?' said Keeno.

Sergeant Begley said nothing but pointed to the *No Smoking* sign next to the door.

'You've been given the leaflet explaining your rights?' asked Katie.

Keeno didn't answer but Detective Dooley said, 'He has, yes, although he didn't read it. He ripped it up into twinchy little bits and tossed them on the floor. But he was given it.'

'You haven't yet told us your name and address,' said Katie. 'Gerry Mulvaney calls you Keeno. What's your full name?'

'Gerry Mulvaney? That arsehole? He can call me whatever he fecking well chooses to.'

'I'm asking *you*, not Gerry Mulvaney. Now that you've been arrested and charged, the law requires you to give us your name and address. If you refuse to do that, you'll be committing a further offence under the Public Order Act.'

'Away to feck. If I tell you my name then you'll know who I am. And if I tell you my address, you'll know where I live.'

'Exactly, that's the whole idea. Who are you? And where *do* you live?'

'Do you think I'm stone mad? I want a solicitor. I want something to eat. I'm thirsty.'

'Tell me your name and address first.'

'I want a solicitor. I want something to eat. I'm thirsty. On the leaflet it says that you have to give me something to eat and drink, and you have to call me a solicitor too. It's my legal right.'

'You tore up that leaflet without even reading it,' said Detective Dooley. 'How do you know all that?'

'No comment.'

'You're entitled to make phone calls, too. Are you aware of that?'

'Oh, yes, and I know what would happen if I made a fecking phone call. You'd only be hacking it to find out who I was calling.'

'What's your name, Keeno?' Katie repeated. 'And what's your address? I'm not asking you again.'

'"Notso", that's my name. "Notso Fecking Thick As You Think I Am." And I live Up The Fat Woman's Arse On Shandon Street.'

'Jesus,' said Sergeant Begley. 'I haven't heard anybody say that since I was in bunscoil.'

Keeno kept on chewing with his mouth open and staring up at the ceiling but Katie could guess why he was being so obstructive. If he told her his name and address, her detectives would quickly be able to put names to the rest of the gang who had stolen the dogs from the Sceolan Kennel, and if the rest of the gang were all tracked down and arrested, they would know that Keeno had been blabbing. His life wouldn't be worth living, either inside jail or out of it.

He might be acting arrogant, but Katie was sure that, behind that arrogance, he was frightened.

'Fair play to you, Notso,' she said, doing her best to sound unperturbed. 'Let's forget about who you are for a moment, and let's talk about some of the things you've done.'

'Like what? I've done nothing, never. I'm a decent law-abiding citizen, that's me. You took my fingerprints, didn't you? You checked them on your computer, don't tell me you didn't. What did you find? Not a tap, that's what you found. If you'd found anything, you wouldn't have to be asking me who I was.'

It was Katie's turn not to answer. Keeno was right, of course. They *had* checked his fingerprints on the AFIS database, but they had failed to come up with a match. And while Detective Dooley had pointed out that he seemed to know all of the civil rights, even though he had torn up the mandatory leaflet that he had been given, that didn't necessarily mean that he had been arrested before. He might have attended a Garda station with a friend who was charged with an offence, and read about his rights there; or maybe he had simply taken the precaution of finding out what his rights were if he ever did happen to be lifted.

'We took a hair sample for DNA as well as fingerprints,' said Katie.

'So?'

'So we didn't expect to find a match on the FSI database. That hasn't been up and running all that long, anyway. But we're more than confident that we'll find a match from Sceolan Boarding Kennels.'

'I don't know what the feck you're talking about,' said Keeno. He kept his head tilted back but he stopped staring at the ceiling and instead he dropped his eyes to stare at Katie, and stare at her very intently. She had seen the same expression in the eyes of men who had been just about to hit her – or try to hit her, anyway.

'I think you know full well what I'm talking about, Keeno,' she told him. 'In fact I'm sure that you do. I'm talking about the wife of the owner of Sceolan Boarding Kennels, Mrs Cleona Cassidy. I'm talking about a home invasion in the early hours of the first of this month. This happened while a gang was carrying out a major robbery there, during the course of which twenty-six pedigree dogs were stolen. *Including*, would you believe, the very same two dogs which you offered for sale to Gerry Mulvaney.'

'No comment,' said Keeno, but he didn't take his eyes off her. Although he hadn't changed his position, with his hands clasped behind his head, Katie could almost feel his mounting tension. She sensed that he could spring out of his chair at any second.

'Two men forcibly entered Mr and Mrs Cassidy's house,' she said. 'One struck Mr Cassidy with his own hurley and knocked him out. The other raped Mrs Cassidy.'

'No comment,' Keeno repeated.

'While she was being assaulted, Mrs Cassidy heard the other man call her rapist by name. He called him "Keeno". That's not a very common name, is it, Keeno? What do you have to say about that?'

'I never told you my name.'

'No, you're quite correct, you didn't. But Gerry Mulvaney called you Keeno. We have your conversation recorded. And the two dogs that you tried to sell him, the German Shepherd and the Vizsla, both of those have been identified by Eoin Cassidy as having been stolen from Sceolan Kennels. It's all adding up, isn't it, Keeno? I mean, a logical person would assume that the Keeno who raped Mrs Cassidy and the Keeno who tried to sell Gerry Mulvaney those dogs, they were one and the same man. And that same logical person would assume that Keeno was you.'

This time, Keeno said nothing, but slowly lowered his arms and sat up straight. Garda O'Keefe sat up straighter, too. In fact he placed both of his hands on his thighs and leaned slightly forward, as if he were ready to jump up at any moment.

Katie lifted up the first page of the sheaf of papers that she had in front of her, to give Keeno the impression that she was reading a report from the Technical Bureau.

'Supposing that the DNA from the hair sample which we took from you earlier – supposing that matched any DNA that we might have taken from Mrs Cassidy after her rape? No matter who you are or what you call yourself – Keeno or Notso or Mr No Comment – supposing I charge you not only with handling stolen property, but with robbery, and with rape. Do you have any idea how long you'd be spending in jail?'

Keeno was too worked up to be listening closely, because he didn't hear the conditional words that Katie had used deliberately – like 'might' and 'supposing' and 'would'.

Instead, he panicked, and thumped his fists on the table, and let out a roar that was almost a scream. He reared up from his chair, knocking it on to the floor behind him. Katie and Sergeant Begley and Detective Dooley started to stand up, too, but he seized the edge of the table and tipped it up, so that all three of them stumbled backward over their chairs.

He started to head for the door, but Garda O'Keefe seized him before he was halfway there, and pinned his arms behind his back. Keeno had obviously been held like this before, however, because he jerked his head back, so that Garda O'Keefe had to jerk back, too, to avoid being hit in the face, and then he dropped to the floor, as abruptly as if his spine had snapped, so that Garda O'Keefe lost his grip on his arms.

He rolled over twice across the carpet, and as Garda O'Keefe bent down to grab him, he arched his back and kicked him in the chin. Garda O'Keefe's jawbone cracked as loudly as a pistol-shot, and he staggered back, one hand held over his mouth.

'You stay down!' Sergeant Begley shouted at Keeno. 'Stay down there on the floor, you scummer!'

But Keeno scrambled to his feet and headed for the door again, and when Sergeant Begley and Detective Dooley went for him, he pushed both of them so hard that they collided with each other. Detective Dooley tried to seize his arm, but Keeno punched him in the left ear, and then punched him again on his cheekbone.

Sergeant Begley forced him up against the wall next to the door. They struggled for a moment, grunting. Sergeant Begley was red in the face, his teeth gritted, while Keeno's eyes were bulging, his head straining forward, his mouth wide open, like a zombie trying to take a bite out of Sergeant Begley's neck.

Katie had lifted the table back on to its feet. She reached over and pressed the alarm button and then she hurried across to Garda O'Keefe, who was sitting on the floor now, holding his jaw.

'I've called for back-up,' she told him. 'They'll be here in a flash, don't worry.'

He nodded to indicate that he had heard her, but she could see behind his hand that Keeno had kicked his jaw sideways, and dislocated it completely. A long string of blood and dribble was hanging from his fingers.

She turned back to Sergeant Begley and Keeno, who were still wrestling with each other by the door. Detective Dooley was trying to join in, but he still looked stunned, and couldn't seem to keep his balance. Keeno was like a bull gone berserk, fuming with rage and fear and almost unstoppable, but at the same time he really knew how to fight. Without any warning at all, he head-butted Sergeant Begley. There was an audible clonk of skulls, and Sergeant Begley took an unsteady step backwards, and then another, half-concussed. Before he could recover, Keeno punched him hard in the belly. Then he turned to Detective Dooley and punched him again, too, a left-handed blow that hit his right cheekbone.

To Katie, all of this struggling seemed to be happening in slow-motion, and although she could hear the alarm beeping, she wondered why it was taking so long for anybody to come and help them. As Sergeant Begley and Detective Dooley stood stunned, Keeno was reaching out for the door-handle, and even though Katie knew that he had no hope of escaping from the station, she called out, '*Stop there! Don't you move a muscle! I said, stop!*'

She thought that her words sounded slurred, and long-drawn-out, and when she started to head towards Keeno, she felt as if the air in the room had become so dense that she could only bound her way across the floor like an astronaut on the moon.

Keeno turned towards her. He had the same blank expression on his face as before. *I don't give a shite if you're a woman, I'm going to hit you all the same. That's your place in life, to do what you're told, and if you don't do what you're told, don't be surprised if you're hit.*

Katie saw him raising his arm. His hand was open, so it looked as if he intended to slap her, rather than punch her. She saw Detective Dooley reaching out, trying to catch his sleeve. She heard Sergeant Begley shout something, although she was concentrating too intently to hear what it was. It just sounded like '*Mmmmwerrrrrrrr!*'

She spun around on the ball of her right foot and kicked Keeno in the chest with her left toecap. Even when she was sparring at her kick-boxing class she had never kicked anybody as hard as she did then.

Keeno crashed back against the door, and then slid down until he was sitting on the floor. His head was tilted to one side and his eyes had rolled up into his head so that only the whites were showing. The palms of both of his hands were upturned and open as if he were making an appeal to heaven.

'Holy Mary Mother of God,' said Sergeant Begley.

Katie recovered her balance, and as she did so, the world seemed to speed up again. She could hear the alarm frantically beeping, and now a garda's face appeared in the window in the door. He was rattling the door handle from the other side and trying to push the door open.

'Okay, hold on!' Katie called out. Between them, Sergeant Begley and Detective Dooley dragged Keeno away from the door and laid him on the floor. Immediately, the door burst open and three uniformed garda pushed their way in.

'What's the story here?' one of them asked. 'Anybody hurt?'

'We had a bit of a scrap with our suspect here,' said Sergeant Begley. 'One of you needs to take O'Keefe to the Mercy. His jaw's been busticated.'

'You look like you've had a fair bashing yourself, sergeant,' said the garda, pointing to his forehead.

'Oh, I'll survive so. I've one devil of a headache, but it's nothing that a couple of Nurofen won't see to.'

Katie was standing over Keeno. His eyes were closed now and he was still unconscious.

'What about your man?' asked the garda.

'DS Maguire gave him a kicking, that's all. He'll probably come round in a minute.'

Another gingery-haired garda knelt down on the floor beside Keeno and bent over to hear if he was still breathing. Then he pressed his fingertips against his carotid artery to check his pulse.

'Yes, he's still with us. But Jesus, you must have given some kick there, ma'am.' He looked up at Katie, impressed.

'Tell me about it,' said Sergeant Begley, ruefully rubbing his stomach where Keeno had punched him. 'Three hefty men in the room, like, and one of them only a boxing champion, and it takes a woman to bring your man down.'

One of the gardaí led Garda O'Keefe away, so that he could

drive him to the Mercy Urgent Care Centre in Gurranbraher; and Katie told Detective Dooley to go to the first-aid room downstairs to have ice packs applied to his bruise. The two remaining gardaí fetched a stretcher, and heaved Keeno up on to it. Keeno's eyes remained closed, although the lids were fluttering as if he were having a fit.

When they had lifted him up, Katie shook his shoulder and said, 'Keeno? Keeno? Can you hear me, Keeno? *Keeno!*'

He didn't respond. Katie shook him again, harder, but still he didn't open his eyes. Maybe he really was concussed, but Katie guessed that he might be feigning unconsciousness because he was humiliated at having been knocked out by a woman, or else he didn't want to answer the charges against him, or both.

'Take him to a holding cell, would you,' said Katie. 'You'd better call Doctor Fitzpatrick, too, to give him a once-over. If he hasn't woken up, make sure you lie him on his side. I don't want him swallowing his tongue or choking on his own vomit. He's probably faking, but I don't want to take the risk, like.'

The two gardaí stretchered Keeno out of the interview room. After they had gone, Katie turned to Sergeant Begley and said, 'As for you, Sean, I'm sending *you* home. Put a cold compress on your forehead, put your feet up, and have yourself a good hot cup of tea. I'll see you tomorrow so.'

'What about Mulvaney?'

'I'll be having a word with him now, although I doubt that he'll tell us much more than he's told us already. Even if he does know who these dognappers are, I think he's far too frightened to give us their names.'

'So what's the plan?'

'I'll probably let him go for now. I don't want to bring him up in front of the court until we have much more evidence against the whole gang. If we prosecute him, they'll only go to ground, and then we'll never find out the whole extent of what they're up to.'

Katie was halfway back to her office when Detective Scanlan came hurrying up the corridor after her.

'Ah, Pádraigin,' she said. 'I was going to be calling for you shortly. We have to go through the formalities with Gerry Mulvaney and Dooley's indisposed, to say the least.'

'I know. Jesus. He came into the squad room and showed me his bruises. How about yourself? You weren't hurt at all?'

'Not a scratch, thank God. Was there something you wanted?'

'Yes...I managed to contact that pet detective. Conor Ó Máille. He's in Kenmare today, looking for somebody's lost greyhound, but he should be able to come up to Cork and see us tomorrow. He'll give me a call when he gets here.'

'All right,' said Katie. 'I've been trying to imagine what a pet detective looks like. Curly brown hair like a poodle, I'll bet, and a wet nose, and a habit of sniffing all the time. Give me a minute now, would you, and we'll go and see if we can get anything sensible out of Gerry Mulvaney if anything, as if.'

Eighteen

She was right, of course. Gerry Mulvaney insisted that he didn't have a clue if Keeno was a member of a dognapping gang, and even if he was, what their names were, or where they came from. So far as he was concerned, Keeno had acquired the dogs legitimately, and his only possible misdemeanour was that he always insisted on being paid in cash, and didn't supply any paperwork.

After twenty minutes of fruitless questioning, during which most of Gerry Mulvaney's responses were shrugs, and scowls, and 'how the feck should I knows', Katie told him he could go. She released him on station bail, without surety, but she set a bail bond of €1,000 for him to appear in front of the District Court in three weeks' time. She was hoping that by then she would have been able to identify the dognappers, and that she might be able to pressure him to turn state's evidence against them, in return for dropping any charges for handling stolen property.

She accompanied him downstairs to the front desk.

'Are you sure there's nothing more you want to tell me?' she asked him, as he crossed the reception area.

'I can give you my old granny's recipe for drisheen,' he told her, zipping up his jacket.

'Thanks, but I think I'll pass on that if it's all the same to you,' said Katie. 'Good luck to you so. I'll see you in three weeks' time, if not before.'

Gerry Mulvaney didn't answer, but pushed his way out of the door. Katie watched him go, and as he went down the front steps of the station, a maroon Honda minicab sped up to the kerb, into one of the spaces reserved for Garda vehicles, as if it had been waiting for him to appear. He hurried over to it, opened one of the rear doors and climbed in. The minicab immediately pulled away.

Katie couldn't see the taxi's licence plate from where she was standing, so she went upstairs to the CCTV viewing room, where two gardaí were sitting in front of the multiple screens that covered almost all of the city centre. She said to the young female garda, 'A Honda taxi just pulled up in front of the station and then shot off again. It was only a couple of minutes ago. Check its number for me, would you?'

'Of course, ma'am. Hold on a second.'

While Katie stood behind her, she played back the recording from the camera on the opposite side of Anglesea Street. Katie saw the taxi speed backwards into the parking space outside the front of the station, and then freeze. She thought the driver looked Asian, and she could just make out the name *Tuohy's Taxis* on the side. The garda jotted down its licence plate number on her notepad, tore it off, and gave it to her.

Katie headed back to her office. On her way there, Chief Superintendent MacCostagáin called her from his open office door.

'*Katie!*' he blurted out, and his mouth sounded full.

She stopped, and he put down the cheese sandwich that he was eating, stood up from his desk and came across to her, still chewing, and wiping his mouth with a tissue.

'I hear you had a pure scrap with your dognapping suspect.'

'You're not joking. He went totally mental.'

'I saw Sean Begley on his way home and he told me all about it – O'Keefe having his jaw dislocated, poor fellow, and Dooley being knocked about like that. Mother of God. And that was some fierce debt on Sean's own forehead.'

'I'll be charging the suspect with assault,' said Katie. 'It's all on CCTV of course, so we won't be lacking in evidence.'

'Sean said that it was you who stopped him. Fantastic – but remind me not to pick a fight with you myself.' He reached out and momentarily squeezed her elbow, the way that friends do.

'It was my dad told me to take up kick-boxing,' said Katie. 'He said he'd seen too many women beaten up – even by men who said that they loved them.'

'I'll be after asking you for a full report on how it all happened, though,' said Chief Superintendent MacCostagáin. 'Sorry about that, but the next thing we know we'll have all of the civil rights groups jumping on top of us. "Police brutality", "the Garda are nothing but trained thugs" – we'll get all of that, you wait and see.'

'Not a bother,' Katie told him. 'I'll try and have a report on your desk by tomorrow afternoon at the latest.'

'How's it going any road, this dognapping inquiry? Did you get anything out of Gerry Mulvaney?'

'Mulvaney? I might as well have been throwing biscuits at a bear. And the whole enquiry's becoming more and more complicated. It's taking up far too much of my time, to tell you the truth. We still haven't been able to identify the man who was shot by Eoin Cassidy, and even if we *do* find out who he was, I can't really see where that's going to take us. Fair play, it might lead us to tracking down the rest of the gang, but you can hardly call it the crime of the century, can you, stealing twenty-six dogs, even pedigree dogs. Look at that fellow in Rathpeacon last year – he hobbled fourteen hundred prize-winning chickens – and what did he get? Three months suspended sentence and two hundred hours mopping the floors in some old people's home.'

'What about the charge against Eoin Cassidy?'

'I can't see that going anywhere, either. I'd wager money that he shot your man out of revenge because his wife had been raped, and he was raging – not because your man was threatening him directly. That's what his wife says, anyway. But she won't testify to that in court and so we don't have any evidence one way or another. We'll be lucky to get a conviction for manslaughter, what with all the mitigating circumstances.'

'Oh well, we can't win them all, can we? And between you and me your man probably deserved to have his head blown off.'

'One thing –' said Katie. 'How's the manpower situation looking in the next couple of days? Saturday in particular?'

'Why's that? Do you have some operation planned?'

'I'm not sure yet. If it goes ahead, though, I'll need twenty uniforms at least, and I'll be calling in the Regional Support Unit too. But it's all a bit up in the air at the moment. I'm still waiting to be given some further information.'

'Well, Michael Pearse told me this morning that he's pretty much up to full strength, in spite of this flu that's been going around. I think there's a rock concert at the Marquee on Saturday evening, Sleep Thieves or somebody, but that won't be starting till seven at the earliest. Michael will give you the exact numbers he has available if you need them. Can you give me some idea of what you have in mind?'

'Not yet, sir. Not really. I've been given what sounds like a good tip-off but so far I'm being very wide about it. I don't want to jump the gun, like, and make a hames of it.'

'Jump the gun,' she thought. *That's fitting, considering we'll be raiding a huge shipment of illegal arms.*

'All right, then, I'll let you get on,' said Chief Superintendent MacCostagáin. 'Wait, though – there was one thing I meant to tell you. That girl – the one who went missing on Hallowe'en – her mother has contacted Search and Recovery. So they'll be scanning the river for her now.'

'Oh, no. That's not good news.'

Katie had called on Cork City Missing Persons Search and Recovery many times in the past – CCMPSR they called themselves. They were a group of twelve volunteers who regularly searched the River Lee with two inflatable boats, looking for the drowned bodies of people who had disappeared. Several of them were the relatives of drowning victims themselves. The River Lee gave the city of Cork its character, but Corkonians drowned in it with depressing frequency – half accidentally and half deliberately. From the latest annual report that Katie had seen, fourteen per cent of all the fatal drownings in Ireland had occurred in Cork, more than any other single location in the whole country.

'I hope to God they don't find her,' she said. 'I mean, I hope to God they don't find her in the river.'

* * *

As she was buttoning up her coat to leave the office, Katie's iPhone pinged. It was a text from Detective Sergeant Kyna Ni Nuallán.

Kyna was taking two weeks' holiday in Gran Canaria before returning to duty. She had fully recovered from a bullet wound to her stomach, and from sustaining a broken nose, and she had sent Katie a selfie, tanned and smiling and holding up a bright orange cocktail beside the swimming pool of the Hotel Riosol.

I thought you might like to know that Ive changed my mind about leaving Cork and going back to Dublin, she had texted. *Ive had time to rest and get my confidence back. After everything that's happened I don't feel afraid anymore.*

There was a pause, and then she texted more.

It's hard to work with you the way I feel about you but I know now that it would be unbearable if I never saw you again. If its all right with you and the powers that be I'll report back to Anglesea Street Dec 1. Im sure we can find a way of making it work.

Another pause, and then a third text.

And being happy XXX.

Katie saw more in Kyna's expression than simple pleasure. Her eyebrows were raised and her lower lip was protruding very slightly as if she were coaxing Katie to say *yes, Kyna, please stay in Cork*. It gave her a surge of mixed feelings. In a way, she had been relieved when Kyna had told her that she was going to ask for a transfer to Dublin. She had known that she would miss her badly, but she had considered that she had enough complications in her life.

Perhaps Kyna was right, though. Perhaps they could work together as friends and colleagues without allowing their attraction for each other to distract them. After all, Kyna had been one of the best young detectives on her team, and she would have been sorry to lose her, professionally as well as emotionally. She had a particular talent for asking questions that caught suspects off guard and got them to admit to their guilt without realising what they were doing.

Oh, Kyna, she thought, *this is all I need.* She stood by the doorway of her office holding up her iPhone and staring at that elfin face, trying to make up her mind what to do. Should she reply to her text and say that she'd be delighted to welcome her back; or should she tell her that in the long run it would be far less painful for both of them if she transferred to Dublin?

Maybe the way she was thinking was skewed by her problems with John. She remembered what it was like to kiss Kyna, and John hadn't kissed her like that since they had first become lovers. Kyna's kisses had been tender and appreciative and almost magical, the sort of kiss that she would have expected from somebody who looked like one of the *Aes Sidh*, the fairy folk. The tip of her tongue had barely slipped between her lips. In the last few months of their relationship, John's kisses had become increasingly few and far between and almost perfunctory. They had only been demanding when they were in bed and making love, and then they had often been too forceful, so that she had felt that she was being smothered.

Apart from that, she had craved his kisses then, whatever they were like, but now she didn't.

Holy Saint Joseph and Mary, she thought, *what am I going to do?* As difficult as she found it to make a decision, she strongly felt the need to have *somebody* holding her, *somebody* kissing her, *somebody* telling her how much they loved her and appreciated her, especially now that her workload was so demanding.

She decided to wait, and think about it some more. She could text Kyna after she had gone home and found out how John was progressing. At the moment, the inside of her brain felt like a kaleidoscope, full of shattered, brightly coloured fragments, and it was hard to think straight.

She was just about to walk out of the door when Kyna texted her again.

BTW this place is black with Cork folk! Ive bumped into 2 or 3 that I know already including Orlaith O Dalaigh you remember that pole dancer I lifted last year. She pretended not to reck me!

Katie couldn't help smiling. It didn't surprise her, though, that Kyna had found Gran Canaria crowded with local people having a winter break. It was one of the few package holiday destinations to which they could fly direct from Cork Airport without having to change planes.

She sent Kyna a smiling emoji and then she switched off her office lights.

* * *

On her way out, she knocked at the door of Assistant Commissioner O'Reilly's office, to see if he had returned yet from his meeting with Commissioner Noirin O'Sullivan in Dublin. She wanted to tell him that she had met Maureen Callahan, and that Maureen had given her a tip-off about an impending arms shipment, as inconclusive as it was. However she had been reluctant to phone or text him about it. She couldn't pin down exactly why it was, but she still felt something about the whole set-up didn't quite fit. If she phoned or texted him about it, there would be a record of what she had said, and at the moment she wanted to avoid that. Besides, more than anything, she wanted to see him face-to-face when she told him. Jimmy O'Reilly might be devious and deceitful, but he always had difficulty in disguising his feelings. She had heard Detective Dooley say that when he was annoyed he had a face like a bulldog eating thistles through a barbed-wire fence.

She was just glad that she had taken at least one precaution to protect herself, if anything went wrong.

Jimmy O'Reilly's office door was opened by one of his civilian assistants, a young man with a brushed-up blond quiff who looked like Tintin's twin brother, even down to the sky-blue sweater with the rolled-up sleeves.

'Ah, DS Maguire. It's himself you were looking for, is it? He won't be back tonight, sorry.'

'He'll be in tomorrow, though?'

'I don't think tomorrow, either. He has a two-day charity golf match at Fota. It's in aid of the meningitis, I think, or the myeloma, I forget which. He'll be off to Dublin directly that's over so he won't be back until Monday morning. He'll be ringing in of course. Shall I tell him you wanted to see him?'

'No thanks, you're grand. I'll call him myself.'

The last call she made before leaving the building was down to the holding cells to check up on Keeno.

The duty garda slid open the safety-glass window in the cell door so that Katie could peer inside. Keeno was lying on the bunk facing the door but his eyes were closed.

'Doctor Fitzpatrick came in to take a look at him?'

'About an hour ago, yes. Your man came to when he was having his blood pressure taken. From the way he was talking it seemed to me like he had a reel in his head but the doctor said his blood pressure was slightly on the high side but otherwise he was grand.'

'What did *he* say?'

The duty garda shook his head. 'I asked him if he wanted anything to eat or drink, and if he wanted to make any phone calls, but he said no, he didn't. Well, that's not exactly what he said, but that was the gist of it.'

'What *exactly* did he say?'

'I don't think there's any necessity to repeat it, ma'am.'

'Go on, tell me. I'm sure I've heard worse.'

The duty garda took a deep breath. 'He said go and eff yourself you tramp's abortion bastard.'

'I see. And is that all?'

'That's all. Then he closed his eyes and fell asleep and he's been asleep ever since, so far as I can tell.'

'Okay, thanks. We'll be interviewing him again in the morning. In the meantime, you'll keep a close eye on him, won't you?'

'Oh, don't you worry, ma'am. I'll watch him like a hungry hawk.'

Katie took one more look at Keeno. He certainly looked as if he were asleep, and not pretending. His mouth was half-open and his lower lip was sagging, and she was sure that if he were awake he wouldn't want to look so gormless.

* * *

John and Bridie were sitting in the living-room watching television and eating pizzas when she arrived home. Barney had been out in the back garden but when he heard her car he started barking at the kitchen door for somebody to let him in.

John was wearing a red sweater and pale yellow pyjama trousers. Up until now he had covered his legs with a blanket, or let his trouser-legs hang down so that it wasn't so obvious that he had no lower limbs. This evening, though, he had rolled his trousers right up to his knees, so that his stumps were showing. His right leg was about two inches longer than his left.

His curly hair was washed and combed and he had shaved, and she could smell his aftershave. When she came in through the door he put aside his plate of pizza and smiled at her and said, 'Katie! You're home good and early for a change!'

'We didn't expect you back so soon,' said Bridie, standing up. 'Sorry we've started our tea without you. I can pop a pizza in the oven for you now, if you like?'

'No thanks, Bridie,' Katie told her. 'I don't have much of an appetite at the moment. So how did it go at the hospital this morning? I must say you're looking very happy out.'

'Don't I get a kiss?' asked John.

Katie crossed over to the couch, leaned over and kissed him on the forehead. He reached up and held her head and kissed her on the mouth. He tried to push his tongue between her lips but she kept them tightly closed.

'Okay,' she said, pulling herself free of him. 'Sorry – it's been a long day. Tell me what Doctor Kahani had to say.'

'It's not just what he said, it's what he did, that's why I'm feeling so cheerful. He said my stumps have healed up brilliantly – not that he calls them "stumps", they're "residual limbs", so far as he's concerned.'

'That's wonderful. Did he say when can you have prosthetic legs fitted?'

'Why do you think I'm smiling? I'll be able to have my first ones within three or four weeks. My stumps have healed so well that he called the prosthetist in, and a very attractive prosthetist she is, too, Niamh McKenna. She made plaster casts of both of my stumps and she'll be sending them off tomorrow to have the sockets made.

'Doctor Kahani said that I can look forward to walking around just like I used to, and being as tall as I used to be. My therapist Aileen said it's like a bereavement when you first lose your legs, but once you have your prosthetic limbs fitted, that really helps you to come to terms with it. You know what I feel like, sweetheart? I feel like I'm going to be a man again.'

He didn't say '*– the same man that you first fell in love with*', but the implication was there.

Bridie had let Barney in, and he came up to her and snuffled around her legs. He seemed to be uncertain of John, now that his stumps were exposed.

Katie said, 'That's fantastic, John. That really is.' *But maybe I shouldn't seem too excited about it, otherwise he'll think that I want us to carry on like we were before.*

She turned to Bridie and said, 'Finish your pizza, Bridie, and take your time. You don't have to hound it. I'll just go and get changed.'

She patted Barney and went towards the door. John said, '*Katie?*'

She stopped. 'What is it?'

'You *are* pleased, aren't you, that I'll be walking again? You don't want me to stay like this, do you?'

'Of course I don't want you stay like that. Why would I? I'm really truly delighted for you, John. I'm a little tired, that's all.'

'What I mean is, I know you like being in charge. And if I stayed like this, you'd *always* be in charge, wouldn't you?'

Katie opened her mouth to say something but then closed it again. She knew that he was getting at her for rejecting him last night. She must have made him feel small and impotent, and this was his way of telling her how much he had resented it.

She thought of what Kyna had texted her. *Im sure we can find a way of making it work. And being happy XXX.*

* * *

Her phone rang. John had gone to bed over an hour ago, and Katie was sitting in her dressing-gown on the couch watching *Bridget and Eamon*. Usually it made her laugh but tonight for some reason it left her unmoved. Perhaps the chain-smoking Bridget frying her husband's breakfast with two hundred grams of lard was too close to reality to be funny.

She picked up the phone and it was Detective Ó Doibhilin, ringing her from outside Charlie's Bar on Union Quay. In the background she could hear drunken shouting and the sound of a siren.

'Apologies for ringing you so late, ma'am, but I've been around the city all evening asking after Bradán O'Flynn. All his usual haunts, the Oval, the Vicarstown, El Fenix. Nobody's seen hide nor hair of him for at least two weeks. Mind you, that was only the people who would speak to me. A fair few of them know who I am and wouldn't say a word, especially the umpa lumpas in Charlie's.'

'Thanks a million, Michael,' said Katie. 'The reason I wanted you to check was that I've been told that somebody had done for him.'

'Serious? Nobody I talked to this evening said anything about that. Jesus. Any idea who it was?'

'I've been given some names but I'm not at all sure yet that my source is reliable. I'm expecting to be told more tomorrow. Once I have the whole picture I'll be giving you a full update one way or the other. To be totally honest with you, I'm hesitant to launch a full enquiry and then find out that I've been led right up the garden path. I can't afford it financially, and after that fiasco with Bobby Quilty, when he was tipped off in advance that we were going to raid him, I can't afford it career-wise, either. Once bitten, twice wide.'

'Oh, yes. The ill-fated Operation Trident.'

'More like Operation Complete And Utter Laughing Stock. Three properties raided simultaneously, wasn't it, and all we found were three dead bodies and no way of proving that it was Bobby Quilty who had them shot. Did I ever tell you that I was sent a stiff note from the commissioner herself about that? "You have to remember that the promotion of female Garda officers to the highest ranks has to be constantly justified by the highest standards of performance."'

'Yes, you did mention that, ma'am, in your debriefing. Twice.'

'Did I? Oh, sorry to repeat myself. It only goes to show how thwarted I felt about it, and I don't want to risk the same thing happening again.'

'Well, that's understandable, I'd say,' said Detective Ó Doibhilin. 'Any road, all I can tell you tonight is that there's no sign at all of Bradán O'Flynn in the city centre and I didn't come across anybody who had seen him for at least a fortnight, either dead or walking around.'

'All right then, Michael. Goodnight, and thanks again.'

Katie switched off the television, shut Barney in the kitchen with a bowl of fresh water and then went to bed. Her bedroom was warm enough for her to sleep naked, which she usually did, but ever since John had been staying here she had been wearing her ankle-length brushed-cotton nightgowns.

As she lay there in the darkness, her eyes still open, staring at the ceiling, she heard a tinkling sound and thought with a sinking feeling that John was ringing his bell for her. Then she realised that a stiff breeze was beginning to blow from the south-west, and that it was only the Tierneys' wind-chimes, next door. She was relieved, but also annoyed, because the wind-chimes always disturbed her sleep. Since the wind was up, it would probably start raining, sometime in the early hours, and that would probably wake her up, too.

So Bradán O'Flynn hadn't been seen around recently. That wasn't watertight proof of Maureen Callahan's story, although it went some way to supporting it. She really needed to discuss what Maureen had told her face-to-face with Assistant Commissioner O'Reilly. If necessary, she could always drive out to Fota Island tomorrow and meet him on the golf course. Before she went to those lengths, however, she decided that she would call Detective Superintendent O'Malley at the SDU headquarters in Harcourt Street, in Dublin, and see if she could arrange to speak to the detective who had first made contact with Maureen. She was interested to know exactly what she had told him, and how sincere he had judged her to be.

Apart from that, she had one more course of action to follow up, although it was still too early to tell where that might lead her, if it led her anywhere at all.

She fell asleep, although she dreamed that she was wandering through a dark, rank-smelling forest and that she was being followed by a shadowy hunchbacked figure with wild curly hair and stumps for legs, ringing a bell like a leper.

Nineteen

Kieran had been standing outside County Hall with his thumb sticking out for only five minutes before a black Opel pulled into the side of the road and waited for him, with its hazard lights flashing. He ran towards it through the driving rain, his khaki windcheater rustling and his knapsack jostling on his back.

When the driver lowered the passenger-side window, Kieran saw that there were two middle-aged men in the car, both wearing formal black overcoats, like undertakers. The man in the passenger seat said, 'Where you heading for, boy?'

Kieran found the look of him quite intimidating. He had short grey scrubbing-brush hair and roughly pitted cheeks that looked as if they had been sandblasted. Kieran himself was plump and pale with blond eyelashes which led to all his fellow students at the University of Cork calling him Porky.

'Like eh, Killarney,' he said. 'But anywhere along the way will be grand.'

The man coughed and said, 'We're going only as far as Macroom. But if that'll suit you.'

Kieran was hesitant, but it was raining so hard now that it would be self-flagellating to turn them down. 'Macroom would be fantastic, thanks.'

'Hop in, then.'

Kieran wrestled his knapsack off his back, opened the rear door and tossed it inside. Then he climbed in after it. As soon as he had closed the door, the driver pulled away from the kerb, so fast that Kieran was tilted over sideways.

'Put your seatbelt on, boy,' said the man in the passenger-seat, turning around. The driver didn't look round but Kieran could see that he was taller, and had a floppy black fringe, which he intermittently swept back with his left hand as he drove.

He was driving very fast, too – so fast that he had set his windscreen wipers to full speed, so that they were flapping wildly from side to side. Carrigohane Road led due westwards from County Hall and ran dead straight for over three-and-a-half kilometres. As they were nearing the Blarney intersection, where the road began to curve southwards, Kieran saw that his speedometer was quivering close to 80 mph.

'Always in a rush, Ger,' said the man with the scrubbing-brush hair, as if he could sense Kieran's alarm. 'I reckon it was his Ma. Whenever she sent him off for the messages, she'd tell him to be back before he got there, and he took it literal-like.'

'You leave my Ma out of this, Milo,' said Ger.

He kept up his speed around the long tree-lined bend through Carrigohane, even though the limit was only 50, but he began to slow down when he reached the roundabout with Model Farm Road. This was a narrow semi-rural road which meandered between fields and nurseries and factories and private bungalows, all the way back into Cork City. Instead of staying on the main road, Ger turned left, and started to drive down it.

'Hey, hey! *Hey!* This isn't the right way!' said Kieran. 'If we go this way, we'll end up exactly where I started from.'

'Ger knows a short cut, don't you, Ger?' said Milo, reaching into his inside coat pocket and taking out a packet of Don Corleone cigarettes.

'I don't understand. How can this be a short cut, when we're practically going in the opposite direction?'

'Saves us going through Ballincollig,' said Ger. 'Traffic's always desperate slow through Ballincollig.'

'Yes, but we don't have to go through Ballincollig. We could have gone straight down to join the N40, and then whack, all the way through to Macroom.'

'Oh, we'll end up on the N40 all right, don't you worry about that,' said Milo. 'Just sit back and relax and enjoy the ride.'

He tucked two cigarettes between his lips, lit them, and then passed one of them to Ger.

Kieran said, 'I'm sorry. I didn't realise that you smoked. I can't stay here in the car with you if you smoke. I have asthma.'

Milo turned around again, blowing a long stream of smoke out of the side of his mouth. 'Asthma? That's *ideal*, boy, ideal! The sicker you are, the better we like you.'

'Listen, I really need to get out,' said Kieran. 'Could you stop the car, please, so that I can get out.'

'That's pure ungrateful of you, wouldn't you say?' said Milo, with smoke leaking out of his nostrils with every word. 'We offer you a free complimentary ride all the way to Macroom, for no charge at all, and what would that have cost you on the bus? And now you're throwing our generosity right back in our faces! What's the problem with young people these days? When I was your age, boy, I had to walk everywhere, whether it was flogging down with rain or not!'

Kieran coughed, and held his hand to his throat. 'It's the smoke. I'm asthmatic, and my inhaler's run out.'

'Why don't you open the window?' said Ger, over his shoulder.

'That won't help,' Kieran protested. 'The smoke will blow straight in my face then, and the rain, too. Please – just stop. I can easy hitch another lift from somebody else.'

'Me and my friend here – supposing we don't *want* you to be hitching a lift from somebody else?' said Milo, looking at Ger now, and not at Kieran, and smiling.

'Will you please just stop! I can hardly breathe back here!'

Ger turned to Milo and said, 'He does sound awful wheezy, like.'

'*Stop and let me out!*'

Kieran shifted himself across the back seat, took hold of Ger's head-rest with both hands, and began to shake it violently, harder and harder.

'Stop and let me out! Stop and let me out!' His voice had risen to a high-pitched, whispery scream.

'Jesus Christ!' shouted Milo, and twisted around in his seat so that he could grip Kieran's wrists and tug him away. But Ger had already had enough: he stamped on the brakes and the car slithered to a stop.

They sat there for a moment, all staring at each other, panting. The car was filled up with cigarette smoke and even Milo had to cough.

'Jesus fecking Christ,' said Milo.

Kieran said, hoarsely, 'Thanks for the lift – not.' He was trying to sound brave but he grabbed his knapsack and opened the car door and scrambled out as quickly as he could, slamming the door after him.

He stood in the teeming rain watching the Opel's red brake lights flare up for a second, and then its orange indicator lights flashing. It pulled away from the kerb and carried on along Model Farm Road – although now it was creeping along very slowly.

Kieran looked around. His heart was beating hard and he wasn't sure what he should do. He had told Milo and Ger that he could 'easy' get a lift from somebody else, but as far as he could see in both directions there was nobody. There was a gateway about two hundred metres further back along the road, but it led only to a derelict house with boarded-up windows. Beyond that he could see a sign for Nangles Garden Centre, and then a row of single-storey houses, but no cars, no tractors, nobody walking along the pavements. Even if a car did come by and stop for him, it was highly unlikely that they would be able to give him the long-distance lift he needed to take him on his way to Killarney. He guessed that he would have a better chance if he walked all the way back to the roundabout on the main road.

He hitched his knapsack on to his shoulders, zipped the collar of his windcheater right up to his chin, and started to trudge west. The rain was blowing directly into his face and he kept coughing. He cursed himself for not bothering to refill his inhaler. His parents had plenty of spares but he had assumed that he would be home in Killarney before he needed it.

He turned around, just to make sure that the black Opel had gone, but he was disturbed to see that it had travelled no more than a hundred metres down the road. He walked on a little further but then he turned around a second time and realised that it had actually stopped. Its rear red lights were shining so it must still be in gear and Ger was keeping his foot on the brake pedal. What were they waiting for? Why didn't they just drive off?

He started to walk faster, and then he broke into a jog. The road ahead of him was still deserted, although he could see a small car reversing out of the driveway of the furthest bungalow. He hoped that it would turn and head towards him, but once it had reversed it headed off in the opposite direction.

He looked around yet again. The black Opel still hadn't driven away. Maybe he was panicking for no reason at all. Maybe they had just stopped to make a phone call. All the same, he kept walking and intermittently jogging as fast as he could, his chest whining and his knapsack slapping *thwack, thwack, thwack* against his back.

He had only managed to cover about a hundred metres when he heard a whinnying sound. He kept jogging, but when he quickly turned his head, he saw that the Opel was reversing towards him with its two nearside wheels on the pavement, and fast.

He gulped in air, and then he started to run. It would be suicidal to try and cross the road, and he couldn't push his way through the bramble-hedge on his right-hand side, because he could see that there was a barbed-wire fence running through it. His only chance was to reach the derelict house, and escape through the metal gate.

He ran as hard as he could manage, his legs and his arms pumping, every breath squealing in his windpipe. He didn't dare to turn around, although the Opel sounded as if it were almost on top of him.

He reached the gate, and pushed it, and it clanged, but it wouldn't open. He saw almost at once that it was padlocked, with a chain. He grasped the top rail, preparing to heave himself over, turning towards the Opel at the same time to see how close it was, but it was then that it caught up with him. It hit him at an angle, at nearly 15 mph, so that his back was crushed against the concrete pillar on the left-hand side of the gate, and both of his knees were bent the wrong way underneath its rear bumper, with a complicated crackle like kindling catching fire.

The Opel drove forward a few metres, and then stopped. Kieran remained where he was, his eyes staring with shock, his jaw hanging open. There was no visible blood. His knapsack had cushioned his spine against the sharp edge of the concrete pillar, but after his legs had disappeared under the car, the rear bumper had split his pelvis in half.

Milo and Ger opened their doors and climbed out. Milo looked around but Model Farm Road was still deserted, and the rain was still dredging down, as heavy as ever. As they walked up to him, Kieran fell sideways, with his head in a puddle. The rain pattered on the hood of his windcheater and dripped off the end of his nose.

Milo squatted down close to him, still sucking on the end of his cigarette, and said, 'Hey! You still with us, boy? Can't have you dying on us now, there's not a priest in sight!'

Kieran let out a groan that ended in a squeak, and a bubble of blood appeared between his lips, and then burst.

Milo stood up. 'You're a right fecking Footy McLoughlin sometimes, Ger, I tell you. You only had to knock the poor bastard off his feet. You didn't have to knacker him completely! I just hope he's still living and breathing by the time we get him back to Saint Giles, or Gearoid's going to do ninety.'

'Ah stop, he'll be okay,' said Ger, flicking his cigarette butt into the road. 'Gearoid can just bend his legs back and he'll be fit as a butcher's dog.'

'It's not his fecking legs I'm worried about. Gearoid wants them with their legs broke as you know full well. Saves him operating on their knees – taking out their nutellas or whatever you call them.'

'Well, it's not doing his health a heap of good lying out here in the wet,' said Ger. 'Let's stow him away and skirt on before anybody sees us.'

He opened the rear door of the Opel. Between them, he and Milo lifted Kieran up and manoeuvred him on to the back seat. His legs were both dangling at such awkward angles that Milo had to twist one of them sharply to get him in through the car door; and when they laid him down they could hear the two sides of his broken pelvis grating against each other, like a broken earthenware basin. He was still alive, though. He was breathing in a high-pitched whistle, and he whimpered when they laid him on his side.

They had just climbed back into their seats when a Garda patrol car slowly drove past. They could see the gardaí looking at them, but the patrol car kept on going. Milo turned to Ger and said, 'There you are. Remember that fortune cookie I had at Panda Mama last week? "*You will have a narrow escape from bad luck.*"'

Ger waited until the patrol car was out of sight and then pulled away from the kerb. 'Yeah – but you remember what mine was? "*You will meet the lover of your dreams.*" That hasn't happened yet, has it?'

Milo took out two more cigarettes. 'Maybe if you stopped drowning yourself in that fecking Lynx aftershave and shaved off that scobe 'tache.'

'Oh yeah? I've never seen the girls falling over you, boy. I've never even seen the sneaky butchers giving you the eye.'

Kieran, in the back, let out a quivering little scream of pain, and then fell silent.

Twenty

Katie had only just sat down at her desk when Detective Scanlan knocked at her door. Pádraigin was wearing a plain long-sleeved dress in charcoal-grey wool and her hair was tied back with a grey satin ribbon, but Katie thought the severity of her appearance made her look unusually attractive, like a sexually repressed bunscoil teacher.

'It took a while, ma'am, but I've found out at last who ordered that taxi that picked up Gerry Mulvaney.'

'Good work. Who was it? Or did he order it himself?'

'No, no, he didn't. It was ordered on account, but the controller at Tuohy's Taxis who took the call was off duty last night when I rang them. He'd left no note about that particular job, and nobody at the taxi office knew where he was – out on the lash, as usual, so they said – so I had to wait until he came in this morning. He told me the taxi was ordered by a woman called Grainne Buckley. It seems like she orders nine or ten taxis a week, sometimes more.'

'Really? Where does she live?'

'Tuohy's always send her invoices care of McMahon's solicitors in South Mall, and they pay them online. But almost every taxi she orders is either *from* or *to* St Giles' Clinic – that's on the Middle Glanmire Road in Montenotte, not too far past Lover's Walk.'

'St Giles' Clinic? I don't think I've ever heard of them.'

'They have a website but it doesn't tell you very much. It says that they're a private care and rehabilitation home for patients with severe disabilities, that's about all. It doesn't list any of the staff or describe exactly what they do.'

'Have you checked them out? Are they registered with the HSE?'

'It says they are, on their website. It also says that they're registered with the UK Department of Health. I haven't yet double-checked that, though.'

Katie prised the lid off her coffee and sat back.

'Why would a private clinic in Montenotte send a taxi to pick up a scumbag of a dog thief from Riverstick?'

'I have no idea,' said Detective Scanlan. 'It's like that Sherlock Holmes story, isn't it, about the dog that didn't bark in the night-time.'

'Well, there was a reason why the dog in the story didn't bark, wasn't there?' said Katie. 'The dog in the story knew the villain, that's why it didn't bark. So – it might sound unlikely – but maybe the people at St Giles' Clinic know Gerry Mulvaney.'

'What's the next step, then?'

'God knows. This dognapping enquiry is taking up more and more time and we already have more on our plate than we can handle. Maybe you and Dooley could shoot up to Montenotte and see if you can find this Grainne Buckley. All you have to do is ask her why she provided a taxi for Gerry Mulvaney and see where it goes from there. It could be that she and him are nothing more than friends, or acquaintances. Maybe he has a relative who's a patient up there. Who knows?'

'All right, we'll do that,' said Detective Scanlan. 'And by the way, Conor Ó Máille will be here at eleven-thirty or thereabouts. The pet detective.'

'Oh Jesus, yes. The pet detective. I just hope it was a good idea, calling him in.'

'You never know. He could take over some of this dognapping enquiry, and give us a bit of a break.'

'I'll believe that when I meet him. He'll probably have a magnifying-glass in one hand and a cat-basket in the other.'

Detective Scanlan said, 'I'll see if Dooley's free now, any road. I should be back here before Conor Ó Máille turns up.'

'Good. Make sure you are. It was your idea, after all, calling him in.'

When Detective Scanlan had gone, Katie asked Moirin to ring the Special Detective Unit in Dublin for her so that she could speak to Superintendent Matthew O'Malley. He answered immediately, and sounded very brisk and attentive. She could picture him: white-haired, bull-necked, strong-chinned, sitting to attention.

'Kathleen, yes, how are you? Last time we met was at that annual superintendents' conference in Naas, wasn't it? What a hoolie that was and no mistake! What can I do for you today?'

'I don't need very much, Matthew, just a little information. It's about that detective of yours who met Maureen Callahan.'

Superintendent O'Malley didn't answer immediately, and she thought that he might not have heard her, so she added: 'The one you told Jimmy O'Reilly about, so that he could tell me.'

'Oh, yes – yes of course,' said Superintendent O'Malley. For some reason he sounded more wary now, as if this was something that he didn't want to talk about.

Katie said, 'Anyway I met Maureen and she told me that her family are due to receive a very large shipment of contraband guns.'

'Well, guns, that's mainly the business they're in, isn't it, the Callahans? But it would be a real bonus to catch them at it, I must say.'

'The shipment's supposed to be arriving in Cork on Friday night, although she couldn't or wouldn't tell me exactly where. She said she'd text me as soon as she found out.'

'I see.'

Katie hesitated for a moment. '*I see*?' Was that all he had to say? If their positions had been reversed, her immediate response would have been '*Why? What earthly reason would Maureen Callahan have for betraying her own family about a shipment of guns? Apart from the treachery of it, breaking the criminal code of silence, doesn't she realise the appalling risk she's taking with her own life?*'

'As soon as Maureen tells me that the weapons have been delivered, and where, I'll obviously set up a raid,' she said. 'Before

I consider mounting *any* kind of operation, though, I really would like to talk to this detective of yours, the one who met Maureen. I'd like to hear what his opinion is.'

'His opinion of what?'

'Well, his opinion of Maureen's motive for giving us incriminating information about her own family, for starters.'

'Did *she* tell you her motive?'

'Yes. She said she was convinced that her family had murdered her boyfriend, Bradán O'Flynn, because they couldn't tolerate a Callahan doing a line with an O'Flynn.'

'That sounds like a strong enough motive to me.'

Again, Katie thought, *How incurious can he be?* He was a senior detective, and yet he hadn't asked what had led Maureen Callahan to believe that Bradán O'Flynn had been murdered. Neither had he asked if *I* had prior knowledge that he might have been killed, or was missing; or when this murder was supposed to have taken place, or how; or if there was a body. All the same, she didn't challenge him. She had seen Superintendent O'Malley in arguments before, and she knew that it was easy to put his back up.

'I'd still like your detective to know what Maureen told me about the arms shipment,' she said. 'He seems to have won the Callahan family's confidence, so he's bound to have some thoughts about it. I mean, he may think that for some unknown reason she's just stringing me along.'

There was a very long silence, and then Superintendent O'Malley said, 'I'm sorry, Kathleen. I can't share his identity with you. As you well know, all SDU detectives operate deep under cover – they have to if we're going to be effective. We can't even tell quite senior officers who they are. Sometimes our investigations involve what you might call transgressions by the Gardaí as well as organised criminals – bribery and blackmail and so forth.'

'Like wiping penalty points off driving licences, you mean?'

'Well, yes, that kind of thing. And worse. So if I told you who our man was, his usefulness in Cork would be totally compromised, and that would mean months if not years of subterfuge going to waste.'

'Oh, you don't trust me, is that it?' said Katie. 'A member of one of Cork's most wanted criminal families trusts me, but you don't?'

'Kathleen, you know that's not the case. But I have to think of our man's personal safety, too. If his cover was blown, you know as well as I do that he'd be floating in the Lee within the hour with a bullet in the back of his head.'

'Does Assistant Commissioner O'Reilly know who he is?'

'I can't answer that, Kathleen. I'm sorry. It's simply a question of security.'

'I'm only asking you if Jimmy O'Reilly knows your man's identity, that's all.'

'Why should that make any difference? But if you really must know, he doesn't. Absolutely not.'

'So you don't even trust *him*?'

'Jimmy O'Reilly and me go back a long way, Kathleen. I trust him implicitly. In this case, though, it was safer for all concerned if he didn't know our operative's name.'

'Very well, Matthew,' said Katie. 'Let's leave it at that, shall we?'

'You'll keep me informed about this arms operation? It could be quite a feather in your cap if you pull it off, couldn't it? I'll promise you this: if you do, I'll buy you lunch at the Greenhouse.'

'We'll see,' said Katie, although she thought, *Jesus, how old-school Gardaí can you get? I'm surprised he doesn't offer me honorary membership of the Masons.*

'Good luck to you Matthew,' she told him, and put down the phone. Then she sat sipping her coffee for a few minutes, thinking, with that blank unblinking stare that her late husband Paul used to call her Sínead O'Connor face. He hadn't dared to disturb her when she looked like that 'in case you jump up and bite my fecking balls off, just because I'm a man'.

She had picked out at least one factual discrepancy in what Matthew O'Malley had told her. He had insisted that Jimmy O'Reilly didn't know the identity of the SDU detective, while Jimmy O'Reilly had said that he did, even though he wasn't allowed to tell her. Not only that, he had responded to all of her questions in the way that many criminal suspects did, strong on bluster but weak on detail, because they were making up their answers as they went along and they were challenging their questioner not to believe them. She could imagine that he had been fiddling with his pen while he spoke to her, and furrowing his eyebrows, and suddenly tilting back in his chair.

Her experience told her that he was lying about something, or at least not telling her the whole truth. But why? He had so much to gain if the Callahans were caught and convicted. It would shut down one of the biggest suppliers of illegal weapons into the country, both to criminals and dissident Republicans, and the SDU could take the credit for making the initial contact with Maureen Callahan.

* * *

She finished her coffee and then she decided it was time to go down to the holding cells to see if Keeno was in any state to be interviewed. When she arrived there, though, she found that there were three gardaí crowded in the corridor outside Keeno's cell, and that his cell door was open.

'What's going on?' she asked.

The gardaí shuffled aside so that she could enter Keeno's cell. Keeno was lying flat on his back on his bunk while a middle-aged female paramedic was kneeling beside him, packing away a defibrillator. A male paramedic was standing in the corner holding up a stretcher. Keeno's eyes were closed and his face was a strange dusty grey, as if somebody had emptied a pepperpot all over it.

'What's happened?' asked Katie.

'SCA,' said the paramedic in the corner. 'His heart's beating normally again now but we're going to take him to the Mercy for observation. You can thank your officers there for saving his life.'

The duty garda said, 'It was real sudden, ma'am. He wasn't too bad this morning although he was complaining about a pain in his chest. I fetched him some toast and a mug of tea and he was right in the middle of drinking his tea when he collapsed. I gave him CPR until Brogan could fetch the defibrillator.'

'Well done the both of you,' said Katie. She looked down at Keeno and said, 'All right, you'd better take him away. At least one officer will have to go with him. Brogan – could you sort that out with Sergeant Kenny?'

Garda Brogan raised his hand in acknowledgement and went off. The paramedics lifted Keeno on to their stretcher and covered him with a blanket. He looked ghastly. If Katie hadn't been able to see his chest rising and falling as he breathed, she would have sworn that he was dead.

'He's in desperate bad shape,' said the female paramedic. 'He has severe bruising to his chest, almost like somebody's hit him with a sledgehammer. That could have been the cause of his arrhythmia. His blood pressure's way up, too. One hundred and forty over ninety.'

'He's going to recover, though?'

'I wouldn't put money on it. The state he's in, he could have another arrest at any time.'

Katie followed the paramedics to the front doors of the station and stood watching as they carried Keeno out and hurried him through the rain to the waiting ambulance. She realised that the consequences of this could be serious. If Keeno died, and it was established by the state pathologist that her kick to his chest was the cause of it, then it was almost certain that she would be suspended pending a full enquiry. It wouldn't matter that she had kicked him while defending herself and her fellow officers. As Chief Superintendent MacCostagáin had warned her, there were plenty of civil rights groups who would immediately jump on what she had done as yet another example of 'Garda brutality'.

She was still standing in the reception area when a taxi drew up outside the station. A tall man in a brown cap and a long brown coat climbed out, carrying a briefcase. He came briskly up the steps, pushed his way in through the doors, and walked across to the front desk.

Katie had been about to return to her office but she stayed where she was for a few moments because the man was extremely good-looking, almost film-star good-looking. After he had lifted off his cap to shake the rain off it, he ran his left hand through his wavy brown hair, which was as dark and shiny as polished mahogany, and Katie had immediately noticed that he was wearing no ring on it. His profile was strong and slightly Nordic, with a straight nose and a prominent jaw, and he had a dark neatly trimmed beard; but what caught Katie's attention more than anything else was the way he was smiling. He seemed to be very relaxed with the world, and very sure of himself, even in a Garda station. He was carrying a brown leather overnight case.

He went up to the desk and spoke to Sergeant Mulligan. Katie was too far away to hear what he was saying, but she saw Sergeant Mulligan shake his head. The man said something else, and then Sergeant Mulligan pointed towards Katie with his biro.

The man turned around, saw Katie, and smiled even more broadly. He came across the reception area and said, 'Detective Superintendent Maguire, is it?'

There wasn't only humour in his smile, there was humour in his eyes, too. They were the same polished-mahogany brown as his hair, and they shone, as if he had just thought of something that really amused him.

Katie nodded, closing her eyelids in a blink that was slightly longer than a normal reflexive blink, even though she knew why she was doing it. It was the long appreciative blink of a woman who likes what she sees, and can't help communicating it.

'That's me, yes. Is there something I can help you with?'

The man kept on smiling. 'I was supposed to be meeting Detective Scanlan, is it? But I'm a little early and I've just been told that she isn't back yet.'

'And you are?'

'Oh, forgive me.' The man put down his case, took out his wallet and handed Katie a business card. 'Conor Ó Máille, Sixth Scents, Pet Detective.'

Twenty-one

Kieran opened his eyes. He could see nothing but a pale green fog, and if it hadn't been so warm he could have believed that he was floating out at sea somewhere. His whole body felt as if he were made of waterlogged sponge, and he was only just managing to keep his face above the surface. He thought that he was dipping up and down, and slowly turning round and round, and after a while the sensation began to make him feel sick.

He seemed to have been floating for over an hour when a face suddenly appeared in front of him. Perhaps he had nearly drowned and somebody had pulled him out of the water. Yet he still felt as if he were dipping up and down, even when the face came nearer, and stared at him intently.

It was a man's face, lean and sharply chiselled, almost starved-looking, with cavernous eyes and hollow cheeks and a complicated nose. His lips were tightly pursed, as if he were sucking a particularly sour lemon drop.

'How do you feel?' the man asked him, after a while. His voice sounded small and far away, as if he were trying to make himself heard from another room. 'Are you feeling any pain?'

Kieran had to open and close his mouth two or three times before he could remember how to speak. He had to think hard about the man's question, too. *Was* he feeling any pain? He was feeling sodden, and nauseous, and no matter how hard he tried, he couldn't quell the sensation that he was bobbing up and down. But was he feeling any pain? He didn't think so, although for some reason he was aware that he *had* been hurt –

devastatingly crushed, and recently, too – but he couldn't clearly recall how. It was like trying to remember what it had been like being born.

'*Mo*,' he managed to enunciate. He had meant to say 'no' but his lips were too bloated.

'Listen to me, Kieran – *are* you feeling pain, or are you not? I need to know, so that I can adjust your morphine dosage correctly. You don't want me to be giving you an overdose, now do you?'

Kieran slowly managed to turn his head to one side, even though his neck-muscles felt stiff and badly bruised. He could see now that he wasn't floating on the ocean at all, or that he was even outdoors. The pale green fog wasn't fog at all, but pale green walls. He turned his head back again, and he could see a fluorescent strip-light on the ceiling, and dark green curtains, and a wallchart, and a picture of trees.

'Do you know where you are?' the man asked him. His voice was becoming louder and more distinct, as if he had entered the room now and was walking towards him.

'*Mo*,' said Kieran.

'I'll apprise you, in that case. I'm a doctor and you're in a clinic. St Giles' Clinic. You've had an accident.'

Kieran tried to take a deep breath but his lungs were too congested and all he could manage was a squeak.

The man leaned even closer. 'Do you remember the accident? Do you remember what happened to you?'

'Mo.'

'Well, I'll tell you. You stepped into the road without looking both ways and you were hit by a passing car. It ran over your legs so I'm sorry to say that your legs are not in very good shape at all. In fact to be honest with you they're a mess. You have other injuries too, even more serious.'

'What? What *im*-juries?'

'You have what we call an "open book" fracture of the pelvis. That means that there was a traumatic external rotation of your hemi-pelvis on the left-hand side. This caused the separation of the left and right halves of your pelvis front and rear. Like a book opening up.'

Kieran stared at the man blankly. He didn't understand what he was talking about at all. In fact he wasn't really listening. He just wished that the bed would stop undulating and that he didn't feel so sick. What was he doing here? He thought he was on his way home to see his parents in Killarney. Maybe he was still in bed and dreaming and it wasn't time to get up yet. He mustn't forget to stop at O'Connor's Newsagents on the way home and buy his mother a box of chocolates. Lily O'Brien's chocolate mint cremes, those were her favourite.

'Fortunately, Kieran, you suffered no major damage to your blood vessels or your internal organs. The disruption of your pelvic ring is the worst of it, and I can fix that for you without invasive surgery. I'll be rigging up an external fixation around your pelvis to keep the halves securely in position while they fuse themselves back together.'

'I have to get up,' said Kieran.

'What?'

'I have to go home. They're expecting me.'

'Kieran, there's no way at all you're going anywhere. You're in no fit condition. Both of your legs are pulverised and your pelvis is cracked apart. You're going to be fixed up with a metal framework screwed into your bones for at least a month, if not longer.'

Kieran tried to move but all he succeeded in doing was making himself feel as if he were wallowing up and down.

'Later today I'll be doing what I can to salvage your legs,' the man told him. 'I'll be taking the measurements, too, for your fixation. All you have to do now is relax and rest and try not to get yourself all worked up. Are you thirsty at all? Would you care for some water?'

'I have to go home. They're expecting me, Mum and Dad. Mum said that she was making her fish pie for me, special. Help me up, will you?'

'Kieran, I told you. You're too badly injured. I'll ring your mum and dad for you and tell them what's happened to you and where you are. How about that?'

'You don't know their number.'

'It's on your mobile. Don't worry, that was recovered after your accident, along with your bag. Like I say, Kieran, all you have to do is rest. You have people here who are going to take the very best care of you, I promise you that.'

Kieran tried one more time to get up, but this time he sicked up about a beakerful of brownish liquid, mixed with orange sludge, which was half-digested baked beans. It ran down the sides of his neck on to the bed.

'Grainne!' called the man. 'I need some cleaning-up here, please! Kieran's just decided to show us what he had for breakfast!'

Twenty-two

'I have to admit that I never met a pet detective before,' said Katie, stirring her coffee.

She and Conor Ó Máille were sitting close together on the oatmeal-coloured couches in her office. Rain was trickling fitfully down the windows, and it was so dark and grey outside that she had switched on the table-lamps.

'You never did? Well, that doesn't surprise me,' said Conor, still smiling at Katie with that winning smile. 'There's not too many of us, to say the least. We could have held an all-Ireland pet detectives' convention in one of those old telephone boxes, and there would still would have been plenty of room for a pole-dancer.'

Katie smiled back at him. 'So, Conor, how did you get into the pet detection business? If you don't mind my saying so, you don't look even in the slightest how I imagined you were going to look.'

'No? And how did you imagine I was going to look?'

'I don't know. Cable-knit sweater. Corduroy trousers. And bald. And smelling faintly of dog.'

Conor laughed. Katie couldn't remember when she had immediately warmed to a man so much.

'I kind of got into it by accident,' he told her. 'About five years ago my sister's Labrador went off chasing deer in the Crone Woods in Wicklow and disappeared. She tramped around the woods all day and whistled and called but she couldn't find it. In the end I contacted Happy Tails in Dublin – they're pretty much the leading pet detective agency. After two days' searching with a tracker dog they found her Labby in a ravine. I was pure impressed with the way they did it.

'About six months later my property development business went to the wall – like almost every other property development company in Ireland. So, overnight, I was out of a job. It was then that I thought about being a pet detective. I've always had a soft spot for animals, dogs especially. You probably know that the name Conor means "hound lover", so my parents christened me very appropriately, wouldn't you say? I also saw that – apart from Happy Tails – there's not much in the way of competition. So I sold my beloved Jaguar and used the money to pay for a training course in America. Now I'm a fully qualified missing animal response technician.'

'So how's business?' asked Katie.

'Brisk, believe me. Mostly in dogs these days – and mostly in stolen dogs, rather than dogs that have just gone wandering off.'

'The last figure I had was a hundred and fifty stolen dogs a week.'

'It's way, way more than that. The trouble is that a lot of owners don't report them as missing. The dognappers call the owners almost as soon as they've taken their dogs, and demand a ransom to have them returned. "Pay up, and don't tell anyone, especially the guards, or you'll never see your dog again." So most of the time they pay up. If they don't, the dognappers can always sell the dog on, so *they* don't lose out, whatever happens. But most of the time people pay. I think I've only known one case where an owner has point-blank refused.'

'How much of a ransom are we talking about, on average?'

'It depends on the dog. If it's a show dog, thousands. Even tens of thousands. But people will pay a very substantial ransom for a family dog, too. Can you imagine a father having to explain to his children that he wasn't prepared to pay to get their beloved Woofy back?'

Katie said, 'We've contacted all of the owners of the twenty-six dogs that were taken from the Sceolan Kennels. Two of the dogs we've managed to retrieve – a German Shepherd and a Viszla. Then there's four that we suspect have been taken for fighting – a Great Dane and a mastiff and two bulldogs. But as for the rest of them – none of the owners have told us that they've been approached to pay a ransom.'

'Do you have a list of their owners?' asked Conor. 'Contact numbers, too, if possible. I'll get in touch with all of them, and I can usually tell when they've been asked for a ransom. People will say things to a pet detective that they wouldn't report to the Garda.'

Katie called out to Moirin and asked her to print out a list of the stolen dogs.

'That'll help me to know where to start looking for them,' said Conor. 'There are six basic reasons why dogs are stolen, but of course it depends on their breed and their age and their pedigree.'

Moirin came in with the list and Conor quickly scanned through it. 'Yes... I'd say that whoever stole these dogs knew exactly what they were doing. The most expensive dogs are usually sold on, mostly to the UK, and at least ten of these look likely candidates. There are two Samoyeds, and you can get at least five thousand euros in the UK for a good Samoyed. Then there's four Rottweilers and three Akitas and two Egyptian Pharaoh Hounds, and one Cavalier King Charles Spaniel. A first-class Cavalier King Charles Spaniel can go for as much as ten thousand, if you can find the right buyer.'

'What about the others?'

It had stopped raining now, and a glimmer of sunlight was breaking through the clouds, so that the raindrops clinging to the window sparkled and danced. The sunlight also showed up a few grey hairs in Conor's beard.

He looked up from the list. 'The two bulldogs and the mastiff and the Great Dane – you suspect they might have been selected for fighting?'

'That's right. We've no definite proof as yet but we've had a tip-off that they may have been taken up to Ballyknock for training.'

'Oh, Guzz Eye McManus.'

'You know him?'

'Mother of God, I should think so. He's always in the market for fighting dogs. I've traced several stolen bulldogs to Guzz Eye McManus but I've never got them back. Either they were dead already or else there was no way at all of retrieving them. I'm a qualified detective but I don't have powers of arrest, like you do. Taking a dog away from Guzz Eye McManus would be the quickest way to get stabbed in the stomach that I can think of.'

Conor paused for a moment, and sipped his coffee. 'Still... it might be worth my sniffing around Ballyknock to see if I can find out who actually has those dogs. That might give you a lead to the rest of the gang.'

'You could do, so long as you don't think it would be too risky,' said Katie. 'I don't want to be the one responsible for getting you gutted by Guzz Eye.'

'I'll be all right provided I keep a low profile, but it could prove to be something of a short cut. If we can identify the gang then you can arrest them and interrogate them and at least one of them is bound to tell you where all of the dogs have been spirited off to. It would be quicker and cheaper than trying to trace each dog individually. I can still do that, certainly – track them down one by one – but it could take months, and I do charge five hundred euros per animal for my Platinum Paws search.'

Katie couldn't help smiling. 'Your Platinum Paws search? What's that?'

'That's when my clients pay for every available search technique, such as DNA analysis to check for blood and hairs; and pet behavioural profiling. It also includes the use of night-vision cameras and listening devices if necessary; as well as area and trail search; and of course poster and flyer distribution. I have some other tricks up my sleeve, too, like humane trapping.'

'I see. Impressive.'

'Well, it works. I find animals. Cats are the most difficult, they can hide themselves almost anywhere, like under a car bonnet, or inside a tumble-dryer. I once found a cat in a microwave. But I find them.'

'There are three greyhounds on that list. I suppose they're used for racing.'

'Probably, and there are two lurchers too. They're always sought-after for the track. But any one of these dogs could have been sold to a breeder. Most of them are young and presumably they're fit and well looked after.'

'There's a beagle, and a Bedlington terrier.'

'A farmer or a pest-control operative or a Traveller will pay you a lot for those, because they're great for lamping – you know, going out at night poaching rabbits and hare. The Bedlington terrier in particular, because they were originally bred for catching vermin, and they're good and scrappy.

'There's one more reason why dogs are stolen, although I can't immediately see any on this list that fit the bill. That's for medical research. Some perfectly respectable hospitals and pharmaceutical companies will pay a considerable sum of money for a suitable animal for vivisection.'

A picture of Barney suddenly came into Katie's mind, bustling up to the front door to greet her every time she came home, his tongue hanging out, his tail slapping against the radiator in the hallway.

She was about to say something to Conor when there was a knock at her office door and Detectives Scanlan and Dooley came in.

'Ah, grand, you're back,' said Katie. 'Here, we have a visitor. This is Conor Ó Máille, our pet detective. Conor – this is Detective Scanlan who first had the idea of calling you in, and this is her partner Detective Dooley.'

Both Detective Scanlan and Detective Dooley looked surprised by Conor's appearance – especially Detective Scanlan, who actually blushed.

'I've already informed Conor that he doesn't look anything like we expected a pet detective to look,' said Katie.

'I thought he'd be the bulb off Jim Carrey, myself,' said Detective Dooley. 'What was that film?'

'*Ace Ventura, Pet Detective*,' smiled Conor. 'Don't worry, I'm always being ribbed about it. It's surprising how much it helps, though, if people don't take me too serious. They tend to let their defences down and tell me things that they would never admit to a garda.'

'We've run through the list of stolen dogs,' said Katie. 'We don't have any hope of getting anything out of Keeno at the moment, so Conor thinks that the next best step would be for him to go up to Ballyknock and see if he can locate those fighting dogs, and find out who took them there.'

'That sounds like a plan, like,' said Detective Dooley. 'I had a call just now from Sergeant Kehoe at Tipperary Town. He said there's two main fellows who train dogs for fighting up there, Bartley Doran and Paddy Barrett.'

'Doran I know,' said Conor. 'Barrett I don't. But at least that narrows it down, doesn't it?'

'Let's hope so,' said Detective Dooley. 'The only thing I'd say, though, is you need to be doggy wide of a fellow called Guzz Eye McManus. If he susses what you're up to, he'll rip your lungs out as soon as look at you.'

'Oh, I'm very familiar with McManus,' said Conor. '*And* his reputation. Don't worry. I think I can mingle with the dog fighters without being rumbled. I've done it before. I make out I'm looking for good fighting dogs to buy, for breeding. If it's okay with you, detective superintendent, I'll go up there first thing tomorrow morning.'

'You live in Limerick, don't you?' said Katie. 'Where are you staying while you're here?'

'Oh, I'll probably check in to the Gabriel House Guesthouse, do you know it? On Summerhill. I like the breakfasts there because they keep their own chickens. Fresh eggs, every morning.'

'What about transport? I saw you came in a taxi.'

'My own car's out of commission just at the moment, being repaired. I had an altercation with a fellow in Mallow who'd stolen his neighbour's dog, and he rammed me, broadside. I was thinking of renting a car while I was here.'

'You don't have to do that. We have a car pool here and you can use one of those. Moirin will take you back down to the front desk and you can ask to speak to Sergeant Browne.'

'Thanks a million. That'll be grand.'

Conor stood up and held out his hand. Katie stood up, too, and took it. They looked into each other's eyes and Katie could see that he was telling her something that he wasn't yet ready to put into words. For a brief moment, he laid his other hand on top of hers, and then he said, 'You have my mobile number, don't you, on my card, and you know where I'll be staying. In any case I'll call you tomorrow morning before I leave for Tipp.'

'You're sure you don't need any back-up? I could send a detective with you, for protection.'

'No, no. It's better if I'm on my own. They're fierce suspicious of strangers, these dog fighters, but they know my face, even if they don't know what I really do for a living.'

She called in Moirin to escort Conor down to the reception area, and then she turned to Detectives Dooley and Scanlan.

'Well?' she said, still with a smile on her face.

'Well, he's not what *I* expected, either,' said Detective Scanlan, fluttering her eyelashes.

'How did you get on at St Giles' Clinic?' Katie asked them.

'That's an awful quare place,' said Detective Dooley. 'We rang the doorbell and it took about five minutes before we got an answer, and then the door was opened up by some short squat fellow who looked like Frankenstein's assistant. We asked for Grainne Buckley and he made us wait in the hall for another ten minutes.'

'It was spooky, that's the only word for it,' Detective Scanlan put in. 'It was dead cold, like, and dark, and every now and then we could hear somebody upstairs making a weird kind of a howling noise. We couldn't decide if it was a human or a dog. I felt like we were in a horror film.'

'But you saw Grainne Buckley?'

'Oh, she came down after we were almost ready to go up and find her, but she was pure tick,' said Detective Dooley. 'I asked her why she had ordered a taxi for Gerry Mulvaney but she came over so offended you'd think I'd asked her what size knickers she wore.

'She swore on the Bible that she'd never heard of anyone called Gerry Mulvaney and since that was the case, why would she have ordered a taxi for him? She said she'd had the same trouble several times before, unauthorised people ordering taxis on the clinic's account. I told her the controller at Tuohy's had been sure that it was her who had rung him, but she totally denied it. It must have been somebody taking her name in vain, that's what she said.'

'What about the taxi driver?'

'Well, of course, as soon as we left the clinic we went down to Tuohy's to find him. As luck would have it, he'd just come in from a job.'

Detective Dooley took out his notebook. 'Uday Malaki, his name is. Iraqi. Been here in Cork for three-and-a-half years now. He said he picked up Gerry Mulvaney from Anglesea Street and took him to Kent Station.'

'So Mulvaney was taking a train somewhere? But who ordered the taxi for him and why did they order it on St Giles' Clinic account?'

'That's the six-million-euro question.'

Katie went over to her desk and activated her computer. 'So what do we know about St Giles' Clinic, besides the fact that it takes care of seriously handicapped people and that it's awful quare?'

She found the clinic's website. It was emblazoned with the picture of St Giles tending to a hart that had been wounded by hunters, with a line of italics underneath it saying *We rehabilitate and care for those with severe disabilities*. Apart from that, though, there was only the scant information that Detective Scanlan had told her about. The clinic's address, its email and telephone numbers, and a line saying that it was registered with the HSE and the UK Department of Health. None of its directors or medical staff was named, and there was no mention of how many patients it cared for, or any details of what specific services it provided.

Detective Dooley said, 'I did notice that they had three ambulances around the back. Two of them were white, and carried that same picture of St Giles, and the lettering St Giles' Clinic, Cork. The third one was an ordinary yellow NAS bus, but it was one of the older Mercedes models and one of its wheels was jacked up. It looked to me like it was being refitted.'

'They have *three* ambulances?' asked Katie. 'Why would a small private clinic need three ambulances?'

'I don't know. There's no law against it, is there? They could have, like, fifty ambulances if they wanted to.'

Katie stared at the picture on the screen of St Giles, feeling both irritated and frustrated. Her previous chief superintendent, Dermot O'Driscoll, had always admired her ability to sniff out cat's malogian. She strongly believed that there was more to Gerry Mulvaney's connection to St Giles' Clinic than a fraudulent call for a taxi. In her experience, anybody who swore anything on the Bible was almost always lying – as was anybody who swore that they were telling the truth on their mother's grave. Invariably, those suspects' mothers were still living and breathing and watching *Fair City* every night.

The trouble was, what would be her justification for investigating the clinic any further? It would take time and money and what had they really done to lead her to suspect them of criminal activity? On top of that, the clinic might lodge a complaint of Garda harassment, which would lead to more paperwork and more time-wasting and more adverse comments in the media. She could see it now – *Cork Garda Bully Home for Incurables.*

'Very well,' she said. 'We'll have to leave it like that for the time being. But keep your eyes and your ears open for any mention of St Giles' Clinic. I'll ask some of my doctor friends about it, too – whether or not they know who runs it, and how it's financed.'

Detectives Dooley and Scanlan left, and Katie switched off the table-lamps and returned to her desk and the neatly sorted files that Moirin had left for her. She had only just started signing letters when Moirin came in with a cup of coffee for her.

'I thought you might be needing a bit of a pick-me-up,' she told her.

'Oh, thanks, Moirin. You're an angel. I'd give you a promotion if there was anything higher you could be promoted to.'

She was about to ask Moirin what she had thought of Conor Ó Máille – strictly from a woman's point of view – when a voice at her office door called out, '*Hello?*'

She looked past Moirin and saw that it was Conor Ó Máille himself.

'Conor,' she said, relieved that she hadn't yet opened her mouth. 'Is everything fixed?'

'Sorry to interrupt you,' he said. 'I have the room booked at the Gabriel House all right but your sergeant downstairs has no spare cars available from the car pool, not until tomorrow morning. But that's not a bother. I wasn't planning on driving up to Ballyknock until mid-morning tomorrow at the earliest. There wouldn't be any of those dog-fighting fellows around, anyhow, not until the afternoon. They don't dislike anything except work and getting out of bed before lunchtime.'

'So what are you going to do now?'

Conor looked at his watch. 'Oh, I have plenty to keep me busy. I have to get some messages, and I also have clients to see here in Cork, as well as a couple of vets. One of them's going to be showing me a new breed identification test. It's a way of telling precisely from a dog's DNA if it's pure bred or if it's a boxatian or a corgollie.'

'Well, I'm finishing early,' said Katie. 'I have some things to sort out at home. So if you're still around at five I could give you a lift up to Summerhill. It's not much out of my way.'

'You're sure? You don't have to. It's only ten minutes and I could always walk it.'

'No, it's no trouble at all. If you come back here at five-thirty I'll be ready to go.'

Conor looked at her, and she looked back at him, and Moirin looked at both of them. There was no mistaking what had just been arranged. Conor said, 'Okay, then, that's very kind of you. I'll see you after.'

Moirin went back to her office. Katie didn't ask her what she had been thinking of asking her. She didn't need another woman's opinion of Conor, not now. She was soon going to find out for herself.

Twenty-three

'What did those gardaí want?' asked the doctor, looking up from his computer screen.

Grainne said, 'They knew that Gerry had been picked up from Anglesea Street by a taxi on the clinic's account.'

'God in Heaven. How did they find *that* out? Don't they ever mind their own business? What did you tell them?'

'I told them I'd never heard of Gerry and I knew nothing at all about it and nobody of that name came here. I said that we'd had a fair number of hobblers recently charging their taxi fares to our account, so it must have been one of them.'

'What if they question the driver?'

'Don't worry about that. It was Uday. He knows better than to tell the guards our business. He wouldn't like his cheap supply cut off, like, would he? If they do ask him, he'll probably tell them he took him off to the airport or somewhere like that. Somewhere they won't get suspicious if he doesn't come back within a day or two.'

'Or *ever*, in his case. Not as the Gerry Mulvaney of old, anyhow. He deserves this, that's all I can say. I mean, how stupid can one man be? If he had two brains he'd be twice as stupid.'

Grainne nodded towards the computer screen, which was displaying a three-dimensional image of a human pelvis. 'What are you planning on doing to him, then?'

'Oh – this isn't for Gerry, this is our friend Kieran. I've just been working out what kind of a patient *he's* going to be. His hips and his legs were badly crushed, but he was lucky that no arteries were ruptured and that there was minimal soft-tissue damage, considering. I'll give him the usual laryngectomy and I think that the legs will have to come off, but I'm pretty sure that I can reconstruct his pelvis so that he'll be able to function as at least two-thirds of a human being.

'What I still can't decide is whether to blind him or not. I know it's safer for security's sake, but it seems a pity that not even one of our patients can see what's happening to them. It's like inviting an audience to the theatre to watch a play and then keeping the curtains closed. This is clever stuff we're doing here. It would be gratifying if some of our patients could appreciate it.'

'Even if he couldn't speak, though, he could blink,' Grainne cautioned him. 'Some quadriplegic patients communicate like that, don't they? One blink for yes, two blinks for no.'

'I don't know how many blinks it would take to say, "*I was run over in the street by two goms in black suits who took me to St Giles' Clinic where my legs were amputated and I can identify the very doctor who did it.*" No – I'm minded to leave him his sight but puncture his eardrums. If he's stone deaf, he won't be able to make much sense of what's going on around him.'

Grainne had been admiring herself in the mirror on the wall behind the doctor's desk, primping her gingery hair with her fingertips. She thought she was looking quite attractive for forty-five, although she wasn't sure about that lavender wool dress.

'He'll still be able to write and draw, though,' she said. 'That's unless you sever his tendons, like the others.'

The doctor turned to her, hawk-faced, with the thinnest of smiles. 'It's sometimes hard to believe that you were Nurse of the Year, Grainne, I'll tell you. No – what I was thinking of doing was amputating both of his arms, too, just below the shoulders. That will leave him two stumps to balance himself with, and to turn himself over from time to time so that he doesn't develop bedsores. But it won't handicap him totally. It's amazing what limbless people are capable of doing with their mouth alone. Look at that Prince Randian, the Human Torso, in *Freaks*. He could shave himself and he could even roll his own cigarettes, just using his lips.'

'I never saw that film and I never wanted to see it. I don't think I'm so much a connoisseur of the grotesque as you are.'

'Now then, Grainne. I'm a doctor. All doctors have to be connoisseurs of the grotesque, as you put it. It's our job.'

'All right. So this Kieran's going to be limbless and deaf. What about Gerry?'

The doctor stood up. He was wearing a grey jacket of herringbone tweed which hung on him as if he had recently lost a lot of weight, or if he had bought it in the 1990s, when shoulders were wider. He looked tired, but satisfied, like a man who has been working too hard, but is beginning to reap the rewards for it. The rose gold Breitling Navitimer watch which he wore loosely on his right wrist had cost over €19,000.

'Let's go and see Gerry, shall we? Let's ask him what his preference is.'

He switched off his computer and he and Grainne walked along the corridor to the wide staircase that dominated the centre of the house. From some of the doors they passed they could hear groaning and sobbing, and the high-pitched flutelike sounds made by men and women who no longer had a larynx but were still desperate to speak.

The doctor felt at last that this clinic was his kingdom, and that he had won back all of the power and the prestige that he had lost three years ago. His humiliation when he had been struck off the medical register had driven him close to suicide, and if it hadn't been for his brother he might well have taken himself down to Tivoli Docks and found a cure for his mortification in the cold grey water of the River Lee. His medical knowledge had also helped to dissuade him. He knew as a doctor that there was nothing romantic about death by drowning: drowning is agonisingly painful, and personally he had very little tolerance for pain.

He and Grainne crossed the gloomy hallway to the reception room where Gerry Mulvaney was waiting for him. The room was huge, with a very high ceiling. Above the red marble fireplace hung a vast mirror, like the mirror in *Alice Through the Looking-*

Glass, which reflected the view through the window of dark green dripping laurel bushes.

Gerry Mulvaney was sitting on one of two enormous leather chesterfields, which made him look as if he had shrunk to the size of a small child. He was leaning forward nervously and smoking, and darting forward every now and then to tap his cigarette into an ashtray which was on a side-table just out of his reach. On the other chesterfield sat Dermot, placidly tapping away at his iPhone, although it was obvious that he wasn't there simply to keep Gerry company.

'Gerry,' said the doctor. 'I thought you'd given up on the smoking. So bad for your lungs.'

Gerry Mulvaney shrugged. 'It's me fecking nerves that bother me, more than me lungs.'

The doctor sat down on the chesterfield close to him, while Grainne sat next to Dermot, her hands in her lap, with a prim smile on her face that Gerry Mulvaney found even more disturbing than the doctor's concern about his health.

'The bottom line is, Gerry, you've messed up good and proper,' said the doctor. 'Keeno's still being held by the guards as far as we can find out, although I'm not too worried that he's going to tell them anything. Keeno wouldn't tell them if they were on fire.'

'Well, I know that for sure,' said Gerry, leaning forward to crush out his cigarette and then taking out a packet of Marlboro to light another one. 'You can always trust Keeno to keep a confidence, like.'

'Not like you, Gerry, I'm sorry to say. It's some hole you've dropped us in here, boy. No mistake about that. You shopped Keeno to the guards and you put the whole operation at risk. It's not just two dogs we're talking about here, Gerry. If it was, well, I'd still be taking a very dim view of it, but we're talking about so much more than that. We're talking about millions of euros, Gerry. *Millions*.'

'What was I supposed to do, like?' asked Gerry. 'There was that fecking Maguire woman, pointing her gun at the dogs' heads and saying she was going to do for them right there and then if I didn't go along with her. Keeno would have been raging if she'd shot them, you know that.'

'And you believed her? Holy Saint Gabriel and all the Archangels, Gerry, you're beyond stupid, you really are. Haven't you read about her in the papers, that DS Maguire? She was the one who got Michael Gerrety put behind bars. Michael Gerrety, the biggest wheeler-dealer since Charlie Haughey, and that must have been about as easy as nailing a jelly to a tree, believe me.'

'All right, fair play to you, she wheeled me. What can I do except say that I'm sorry?'

The doctor leaned back a little. 'There's still a risk, Gerry, and that risk is *you*. If I let you go now, what are the chances that DS Maguire isn't going to pay you another visit at Riverstick and threaten to shoot a few more of your pooches?'

'I wouldn't say a word, not now. You know that. I wouldn't let her wheel me twice. Not with *that* trick, any road.'

The doctor was concentrating on picking a stray speck of dust from his sharply creased black trousers. 'I can't risk it, Gerry,' he said, almost sadly, without looking at him. 'If I can't trust you once, how can you expect me to trust you twice?'

'Because you can, that's why. Because I've learned me lesson.'

'It's all very well you saying that, but how can I be sure that she's not going to try some other scam on you, and you'll be gabbling away to her fifteen to the dozen. You see, it's not only the money that's involved here, it's our liberty. I have no intention of spending any time at all in jail because some clapped-out dog-hobbler couldn't keep his mouth shut.'

He paused, and then he said, 'Besides which, you owe us the cost of two fine pedigree dogs.'

Gerry Mulvaney didn't answer, but continued to puff at his cigarette. He was sure that whatever was said next, it was going to be bad, but he couldn't guess what it was. He shifted on the leather chesterfield like a man who feels a pressing need to go to the toilet.

'St Giles' Clinic is doing better every day,' said the doctor. 'The only problem is, we need more patients. It's a clinic which takes care of people with severe disabilities, as you know, but it's hard to find sufficient numbers of people with severe disabilities to make it profitable.'

'Bit like my business,' said Gerry, uneasily. 'There's never enough good-quality dogs, do you know what I mean, like? Not to make a decent living out of.'

'What I thought was, Gerry, you could help us out, and at the same time compensate us for the two dogs you lost. *And* make amends for Keeno being lifted.'

Gerry Mulvaney was really agitated now. 'Oh, yeah. And how would I do that, like? I'm not exactly *flathúl* to say the least.'

'It's not money I want from you,' the doctor told him. 'I want you to volunteer to be a patient here.'

'What?'

'I said, "I want you to volunteer to be a patient here."'

'But how could I be a patient here? All your patients are total fuck-ups, aren't they? There's nothing wrong with me at all except a twinge of the gout now and again and sometimes I get the sore eye arses.'

'You get the *what*? Oh, you mean "psoriasis". But gout and psoriasis, they're not disabilities. Not the kind you need to be suffering from, if you're going to be a patient here. I'm talking about paralysis, a complete inability to walk or even to sit up unaided. I'm talking about dumbness – or "muteness" if I'm going to be less medically but more politically correct.'

Gerry Mulvaney was staring at him in disbelief. His mouth was open and he wasn't even dragging at his cigarette any more.

'Then of course there's blindness,' said the doctor. 'Blindness combined with paralysis, that's a good one, especially if the patients can't speak to tell you how helpless they feel. Then there's deafness. On top of those, there's a whole variety of amputations. No feet, no legs below the knee, no legs below the pelvis. No genitalia. No fingers, no forearms, no arms at all. You can choose from any combination you like.'

Gerry Mulvaney kept on staring at him, and then he suddenly cracked into a grin and said, 'Jesus! You're right! You made your point there! I *do* get wheeled easy, don't I? You almost had me pissing meself there! Holy Saint Joseph! What a gowl I am!'

He was still shaking his head in amusement when the doctor said, 'Gerry – that wasn't what I was saying to you.'

The doctor's voice was calm and he was sitting back relaxed with his legs crossed, although Grainne had raised her eyebrows and even Dermot had stopped prodding starting prices into his iPhone and looked up, his beady eyes bright with interest.

'You wasn't?' said Gerry Mulvaney. 'Then sorry, you have me totally puggalised here.'

'I was giving you a list of options,' the doctor told him. 'If you're going to become a patient here, you'll have to have a number of severe disabilities, and you can choose any combination you like. My only stipulation is that your combined disabilities must make it impossible for you to escape, or to communicate with anybody in the outside world in any way at all, either by speech or by writing.'

Urine began to run from between Gerry Mulvaney's thighs and drip down the front of the chesterfield on to the carpet. Grainne wrinkled up her nose in disgust and tutted, but the doctor said nothing.

'You're serious, aren't you?' said Gerry Mulvaney, his throat tight with desperation.

'I am serious, yes. But at least I'm giving you a choice, and that's not a privilege that any of my patients are normally offered, believe me.'

'Why don't you just take me outside and put a bullet in my head? I'd rather you did that.'

'I expect you would. But then you'd be dead, wouldn't you, and you'd be no use to me at all. I'm running a clinic here, Gerry, not a funeral parlour. Dead, you'd be nothing but an inconvenience, because I'd have to find somewhere to bury you. Alive, you'll be a lasting asset, because you'll be able to pay me back day after day, month after month, possibly for years.'

'If you think I'm going to choose to have any of those things done to me, you're stone hatchet mad!'

'Some of them will be done to you whether you like it or not. I just thought it would be friendlier to give you a say in which ones they are.'

Gerry Mulvaney looked down at the carpet, breathing heavily. Then he reached across and crushed out his cigarette.

'There's no rush,' said the doctor. 'Have a good think about what would be best for you. Would you prefer to see, or to hear? Would you prefer to have hands, or feet? It's entirely up to you.'

At last Gerry Mulvaney stood up. The crotch of his green corduroy trousers was soaked. He stared at the door as if he were calculating his chances of getting there before he could be stopped. The doctor nodded almost imperceptibly at Dermot and Dermot put down his iPhone and stood up, too, his hands clasped together in the classic pose of bouncers everywhere.

'*When—?*' Gerry Mulvaney began, and his voice was little more than a whinny. 'When were you thinking of doing this? Like, disabling me, like?'

'The sooner the better,' said the doctor. 'Sometime over the weekend, probably. I don't think there's anything in the Holy Book which says you can't amputate on the Sabbath.'

Grainne suppressed a smile. She always enjoyed the doctor's mordant sense of humour, mostly because she was the only one in the clinic who understood it. Milo and Ger never did, even though they were a mordant sense of humour in themselves.

'Right,' said Gerry Mulvaney. He cleared his throat and repeated, 'Right.'

It was then that he spun around and instead of making a dash for the door, he galloped towards the large sash window. He crossed his arms in front of his face and threw himself at the glass, just as Dermot caught up with him and launched himself on top of him. There was a splintering crack that sounded more like a lightning strike than a window breaking, and both of them ended up hanging over the window-frame, half-in and half-out of the room – Gerry Mulvaney face down and Dermot on top of him. Glittering fragments of glass were spread across the floor like a scene from *Frozen*.

Dermot stood up and brushed the shattered fragments from his white surgical jacket. There was a two-centimetre cut on the top of his bald head but otherwise he was unhurt. The doctor helped him to lift up Gerry Mulvaney and sit him down on the floor. Gerry Mulvaney's face was glistening scarlet with blood, like a Hindu demon. His eyelids were drooping but he had suffered a deep diagonal laceration across his lips, so that he was finding it difficult to speak.

'Looks like this feen needs to see a doctor,' said Dermot.

Twenty-four

After lunch, Katie and Detective O'Donovan had to make an appearance in court. They were giving evidence against appeals that were being made against two convictions – one for drug dealing and one for indecent exposure.

Katie was attending in person because both cases were more serious than they looked on the list. The drug dealer was a divisional drugs squad detective who had misreported the number of packets of heroin that had been confiscated during a raid on a house in Kerryhall Road. He had been caught trying to sell the drugs in order to pay off his mortgage arrears.

The flasher was a former TD. He was a candidate for the Dáil who had lost his seat at the last election for Cork South Central – the so-called 'constituency of death' because its four seats had been so hard to win. He was already alcoholic but his dependency on drink had worsened after his defeat. He had exposed himself to a woman at the delicatessen counter of Tesco's at the Paul Street shopping centre, asking her, 'What do you think of this sausage, then?'

In court, the flasher insisted that he had genuinely been drawing the woman's attention to a Clonakilty white pudding on the display counter, and that he had failed to realise that at the same time he was experiencing a 'clothing malfunction'. The bench listened to him patiently, and then Detective O'Donovan showed them new CCTV evidence from Tesco that proved he had flagrantly displayed himself – or, as the state solicitor's counsel had put it, 'actually waved it, like the national flag'.

Both appeals were turned down, although the detective's term of imprisonment was reduced from two years to eighteen months on compassionate grounds and the former TD was spared jail if he agreed to residential treatment for his alcohol addiction.

Katie and Detective O'Donovan shared a large black umbrella as they left the courthouse. The rain was hammering down again so hard that it was dancing like fairies on the surface of Washington Street.

'That poor TD,' said Detective O'Donovan, as he opened the door of Katie's car for her. 'I didn't honestly know whether to laugh or cry.'

'It's still an offence, and a fierce unpleasant one at that,' said Katie. 'I know that he was so drunk that he doesn't even remember doing it. If he'd done it to *me*, though, he'd have remembered it all right. I'd have chopped it off as soon as look at it.'

Detective O'Donovan gave her a sickly grin. 'Remind me not to have a clothing malfunction when *you're* around, ma'am.'

She had just switched on her engine when her iPhone pinged. She had a text message from Dr Kelley the Acting Deputy State Pathologist, who was still working at the morgue at Cork University Hospital.

Dr Kelley had completed her post mortem examination of the alleged dognapper who had been shot by Eoin Cassidy, and as soon as she had done that, the Technical Bureau had created an image of his face with computer software. His likeness had been shown every night for three nights on the RTÉ television news, and published in the *Examiner* and the *Echo*, but so far nobody had come forward to say that they recognised him. Because of that, Bill Phinner the chief technical officer was going to be sending down his forensic artist Eithne O'Neill to draw her own reconstruction of the dognapper's face.

Eithne had been away on compassionate leave, tending to her dying sister. According to Dr Kelley's text, however, her sister had passed away and she desperately wanted to get back to work to take her mind off her grief.

'Jesus,' said Detective O'Donovan, as they drove back through the rain to Anglesea Street. 'Some way of getting over your grief, wouldn't you say, drawing pictures of some scummer with half of his head blown off?'

'Eithne's brilliant, though,' said Katie. 'She has this fantastic feeling for dead people's personalities, as well as the way they must have looked. She draws them like she actually *knew* them. You can never match that with any software.'

She reached the Garda station, and parked, and she was about to climb out of the car when her iPhone pinged again and Dr Kelley sent her another text.

'Stall it for a moment,' she told Detective O'Donovan, laying a hand on his arm. 'Dr Kelley says that she's just started her post mortem on a fellow called Martin Ó Brádaigh. He was the victim of a road traffic accident two days ago on the N25 near Grange. Run over by a truck.

'She says her examination was held up until today because she had to deal urgently with two newborn babies from the maternity ward.'

She paused for a few moments while she read more of Dr Kelley's text.

While she did, Detective O'Donovan said, 'That's right, Martin Ó Brádaigh. I know him myself. He's the owner of Ó Brádaigh's Used Motors on Watercourse Road – or *was*, rather. Sergeant Breen sent us a report from Dungarvan about that accident, Ó Brádaigh being a Corkman and all. Knocked flat by a Paddy's Whiskey lorry, he was. For some reason he'd stopped his car in the middle of the road and was crawling around the carriageway on his hands and knees. The paramedics who picked him up said his body fair reeked of alcohol, what was left of him. He had a record for drunk driving. The demon drink, eh? Makes you show off your sausage and crawl out in front of traffic and all sorts.'

Katie said, 'There's more to it than that. Dr Kelley says that some of his most serious injuries weren't caused by being run down. He has deep gashes in his perineum which look as if they might have been inflicted by a knife or some other sharp instrument.'

'The perineum?' said Detective O'Donovan, frowning. 'Isn't that the bit down between your – Jesus? *Ouch!* The stinky bridge we used to call it at school, if you'll pardon the language.'

'Think about something else,' Katie advised him. 'Think about what kind of sandwich you want for your lunch.'

'Holy Mary Mother of God. I don't think that'll help at all. It'll probably put me off cherry tomatoes for the rest of my life.'

As soon as she had returned to her office, Katie hung up her coat, made a finger-waggling coffee-drinking gesture to Moirin, and then phoned Dr Kelley's number.

Dr Kelley answered almost at once and said, 'Detective Superintendent! Thanks a million for calling. You've read my text, then?'

'I have, yes. Jesus. Your man was *stabbed* before he was hit by that truck? Stabbed between the legs?'

'He was, and very deep. You wouldn't believe the internal trauma. At first guess I'd say a sharp pointed knife, more like a kitchen-knife than a clasp-knife.'

'Would that in itself have proved fatal, if he hadn't received medical attention?'

'He'd lost a fair amount of blood but no major arteries were severed. So, yes, he probably would have survived. The Waterford guards had him fetched in here so that I could carry out a routine post mortem, but mainly to test him for alcohol and drugs. The coroner will be asking why he was wandering around in the middle of a fast main road, after all.'

'Was he drunk, or high?'

'His blood alcohol level was 87 milligrammes, and there were traces of cocaine in his blood and his urine and his saliva. I took a full range of samples as soon as his body arrived – but, like I say, I had to postpone the full post mortem until now. They've had a nasty outbreak of respiratory syncytial virus infection in the maternity ward, with two fatalities, sad to say. It doesn't appear to be the usual strain of virus at all, so they're in something of a panic.'

'I hate to ask you this,' said Katie, 'but why weren't the stab wounds noticed as soon as your man was undressed?'

'One of the garda who brought him in said that the truck which hit him was travelling at eighty kph. The truck wasn't fully loaded but it still would have weighed at least nine thousand kilos. Internally, he was smashed to bits and his entire skin surface is covered in bruises and tears and abrasions. To give you some idea, imagine a man who's been killed in a fight with a bear and then thrown off the top of a cliff on to a whole heap of jagged rocks.'

'How long will it take you to complete your post mortem?'

'It won't be today of course. Mid-morning tomorrow, I'd say.'

'Please call me, if you would. I think I need to come down and take a look. Depending on what you find out, this could be a murder enquiry, or manslaughter at the very least.'

'I will, no bother at all.'

Katie called Detective O'Donovan to bring him up to date on what Dr Kelley had told her. Then she rang Inspector O'Rourke and asked him if he had any news about Keeno.

'The Mercy are keeping me informed, ma'am. They contacted me last about an hour ago. He's still unconscious – no better but no worse. They're keeping him on a respirator to aid his breathing.'

'What about poor Garda O'Keefe?'

'His jaw's been reset but he can take only liquids at the moment. He's in good spirits, though, according to his girlfriend. She says the only thing you mustn't do is make him laugh.'

She didn't need to ring Sergeant Begley. He had called her this morning to say that he had seen his doctor, and he had been signed off work for three days at least.

She went back to her computer screen. She ran through the latest monthly figures for drug seizures and quickly saw that in spite of her new strategy to stem the new flood of narcotics she seemed to be fighting a losing battle. In fact the figures were 6.5 per cent up on last month. What she found hard to understand was that Revenue had reported an ever-increasing success rate in detecting drugs smugglers through Ringaskiddy and Rosslare ferry ports, and both Cork and Shannon airports – Shannon in particular. If they were catching more and more mules, where were all these drugs coming from?

She sat back. She was feeling tired now, and pre-menstrual, and although she was hungry her stomach felt bloated. She wondered when Maureen Callahan would call her to tell her when and where the arms shipment was going to be delivered, and what kind of a raid she would have to set up, and how quickly. She wondered if John would still be awake when she returned home, and what kind of a mood he would be in. His desperate optimism was becoming almost more than she could bear. It made her feel heartless, and uncharitable, and she didn't believe that she was either.

All she had to look forward to this evening was meeting Conor Ó Máille, and she was beginning to regret that she had offered to drive him back to his guest house. She didn't feel attractive at all, and certainly not in the mood for being seductive.

She went into the small bathroom at the side of her office. She was surprised to see that she didn't look nearly as puffy and tired as she felt. After she had brushed her hair and applied some more lipstick she pouted at herself in the mirror, and turned her head coquettishly from side to side, and thought that she scored at least 75 per cent of her usual attractiveness.

'You should always remember that you're looking at men from the inside of your face,' her grandmother had told her. 'They're looking at *you* from the outside, like, and they'll see what they want to see.'

She had never quite understood what that meant, but in a way she thought she did now.

* * *

Conor knocked on her office door dead on 5:30 pm, as if he had been waiting in the corridor outside and counting off the seconds on his watch.

She was handing Moirin the last of the files that she had been reading and the letters that she had signed. She took a last sip of her coffee but it was cold.

'Are you finished?' he asked her, with a smile. 'I can always wait for you, if you're not ready.' He was carrying a large bag from Saville menswear store on Oliver Plunkett Street, as well as his overnight case.

'No, I'm ready,' she said, putting on her raincoat. 'What have you bought?'

'A couple of shirts and a Tommy Hilfiger sweater.' He lifted the sweater out of the bag to show her. It was a strong red colour, and she had always liked red, because it clashed with her dark red hair.

They went downstairs in the lift, facing each other, smiling, but neither of them saying anything. Outside in the car park it was still raining hard, so Katie put up her umbrella. Conor took it from her and held it over their heads as they hurried over to her Focus, and then he opened the driver's door for her.

'Are you hungry?' he asked her, when he had dropped his bags and the wet umbrella behind his seat.

'Starved. But I have a leftover stew at home. I always make far too much.'

'Well, I'm starved, too. I didn't have any breakfast this morning. How about I buy you an early supper before you drive me up to Summerhill?'

'All right,' said Katie. 'But let's go halves on it. This will be a business dinner, not a date. What do you fancy to eat?'

'I could murder a steak. Oh, sorry. That wasn't a very tactful thing to say that to a detective superintendent, was it?'

Katie backed out of the car park and turned into Old Station Road. 'I'll tell you where we'll go then, Isaacs, on McCurtain Street. I haven't been there in donkey's.'

Actually, the last time she had eaten at Isaacs was with John, the night before he had left her and gone to San Francisco. Perhaps if she had supper there with another man, it would do something to erase a memory that still hurt her when she was least expecting it. That evening, John had made her feel that she was letting him down, and that her job was more important than his happiness.

She parked on St Patrick's Quay and took a sneaky short cut on to McCurtain Street through the office building at the back of the car park. She and Conor walked along the street together arm-in-arm, so that they could both hold the umbrella. It was dark now, and the road was glistening with reflected lights.

'By the way,' she said, as they reached the front entrance of Isaacs restaurant and folded the umbrella, and shook it. 'Off duty, you don't have to call me "Detective Superintendent". I'm Katie.'

'All right, then, Katie,' said Conor. 'I like that. And off duty, I'm not "hound lover", I'm Conor. Or Con, if you prefer.'

'What does your mother call you?'

'She used to call me You Little Whelp, but that was a long time ago. Now she calls me Con, or Connie-boy when she wants me to do something for her.'

They went inside. Isaacs was brightly lit, with shiny parquet floors and small tables and bentwood chairs. Some of the walls were rough stone because the restaurant had been converted from an eighteenth-century warehouse. A waitress found them a table in the small room at the back of the restaurant where there was less likelihood of Katie being recognised. It was still early, so only three or four other tables were taken, but Katie knew that it would be crowded later, and it was the kind of restaurant where many of the diners would know who she was.

She could have done with a drink now but she was driving so she ordered only water. Conor asked for a glass of Malbec.

'I'll be absolutely truthful with you, Katie,' said Conor. 'If I had been introduced to you without knowing that you were a senior officer in the Garda, I would have guessed that you were an actor.'

'Oh, yes?' said Katie. 'And what would have made you think that?'

'To start with, you're very confident – very sure of yourself. You don't *um* and *ah* when you speak. Also – you're watching people all the time, which is what actors do. They're forever making a mental note of other people's facial expressions, and the way they carry themselves. I know that because my Uncle Liam was an actor. He even had a part in *Glenroe*.'

The waitress brought their drinks and asked them if they had decided what they wanted to eat, so Conor paused for a moment. When she had gone, he said, 'You're also incredibly attractive.'

Katie said, 'Ha! Lots of female gardaí are incredibly attractive. Look at Noirin O'Sullivan, and she's the Commissioner. You can't say that she's not a handsome woman.'

'I wouldn't. It's just that I think you're handsomer. And, like I say, I would have guessed that you were an actor before I would have guessed that you were a detective. Or maybe a TV news presenter.'

Katie had ordered a warm chicken salad and Conor had asked for the seafood chowder. As she started to eat, Katie said, 'You're flirting with me, then?'

'Yes,' said Conor. 'You don't mind, do you?'

Katie shook her head while she finished her mouthful. Then she said, 'No. I like it.'

As they ate, the restaurant gradually began to fill up, so that by the time Katie was eating a rhubarb and apple crumble, every table around them was taken, and the conversation level was so loud that whenever Conor said anything she had to lean forward and ask him to repeat it. But it didn't matter if she could hear him or not. She knew what he was telling her, and she felt the same way about him.

It was still raining when they left Isaacs shortly after 7:30. This time, as they walked together back to the car, Conor held the umbrella and he and Katie held hands.

As they passed the Everyman Theatre, Conor nodded towards the playbills outside and said, 'There – *Sisters of the Rising*. That would have been just the part for you, if you'd been an actor. Nurse Elizabeth O'Farrell, one of the women who made Ireland what it is today – the same as you have.'

Katie laughed. 'Go on,' she said. 'You can flatter me as much as you like. I don't get too much of it at work, I can tell you.'

They drove up Summerhill until they reached the Gabriel House guest house. It was a large four-storey period building, painted white, with a grey slate roof and window-boxes at every window. Katie pulled up outside and said, 'There. You can take the umbrella if you like. I have plenty more at home.'

Conor looked at her intently and for the first time this evening he wasn't smiling. He took hold of her hand and then he leaned across the car and kissed her – first on the right cheek, then on the left. Then he kissed her on the lips.

Katie closed her eyes. The kiss went on and on, and became deeper and more urgent the longer it went on. Conor's tongue tussled with hers, and then he licked her teeth and pressed his lips against hers until she felt that she was going to suffocate with pleasure.

The kiss ended, and they both sat back with their eyes fixed on each other.

At last Conor said, 'I don't want to borrow your umbrella. I want you to come with me.'

Katie turned her head away and looked up at the lighted windows of Gabriel House. Conor said nothing but waited for her to make up her mind.

After a few seconds she switched off the Focus's engine, released her seatbelt, and opened her door.

Twenty-five

Conor's room was at the very top of the guest house. Katie climbed up the steep white-painted staircase with its blue floral carpet and she could hear Conor right behind her, his shopping bag rustling and knocking against the banisters. She felt as if what was happening to her now was unreal, and that perhaps she *was* an actor, and this was nothing more than a play. Yet she was completely sober, unlike most of the first times that she had been with men. She was climbing these stairs because she wanted him – she wanted Conor, and for no other reason.

He unlocked the door of his room and let her in. Before he switched on the lights she walked over to the windows and looked out. She could see almost all of the city centre, from Kent railway station to St Finbarr's Cathedral, and all the streetlights glittering, and traffic crawling along the quays like fireflies. And of course the River Lee itself, black and black-hearted.

Conor turned on the bedside lamps rather than the main light. The room was comfortably furnished, red-carpeted, with a king-size bed and gilt mirrors and antique-style chairs, and it was warm.

'I have to make one call,' said Katie. 'I have a girl at home who's dog-sitting for me. I have to tell her that I won't be back.'

'Of course,' said Conor. He came over and helped her out of her raincoat, and then he took off his own coat and carried both of them over to the wardrobe. 'We have to take care of our four-legged friends. What is he? Or she?'

'Barney's a boy. An Irish setter. And he's pure smart. I don't think he even realises that he's a dog.'

She rang her home number, and Bridie answered, 'Detective Superintendent Maguire's residence. Bridie Mulligan speaking.'

'Oh, Bridie, this is Katie. How's the form?'

'All quiet, Katie. Nothing to report. Himself had a sleep this afternoon and now he's watching the telly. He's looking forward to you coming home.'

As she was talking, Conor came up behind her and eased her tweed jacket off her shoulders. She changed hands with her iPhone so that he could slide the sleeves off. He took off his own jacket, too, and laid both jackets on the nearby chair.

'That's the thing, Bridie,' said Katie. 'It looks like I won't be able to make it back home tonight. We've had an emergency here and I don't know how long it's going to take to deal with it. Is it all right if I ask you to stay over? You can sleep in my bed if you like, and you'll find a clean nightdress in the press and clean towels on the shelf in the bathroom. I'll make it worth your while.'

'That's no bother at all, Katie. I always fetch my toiletry bag with me, in case I have to stay late.'

Conor lifted Katie's hair and kissed the nape of her neck. The soft brushing of his beard against her bare skin sent a tickling sensation all the way down her spine.

'You don't have to worry about Barney,' she said. 'All you have to do is feed him in the morning and make sure his water bowl's always topped up. Mrs Tierney will come around in the morning to take him on his walk.'

'What about himself? What do you normally give him for his breakfast?'

Now Conor took hold of the hem of her sweater. When he started to lift it, though, he uncovered the holster attached to the waistband of her skirt, and the black synthetic grip of her Smith & Wesson Airweight revolver. He backed away immediately, both hands raised, as if she had caught him in mid-felony.

Katie turned around and smiled at him.

'I'll come quietly,' he whispered.

'A couple of boiled eggs and a cup of tea will do,' she said. 'Maybe some toast and blackcurrant jam if he wants it. Thanks, Bridie. I'll see you tomorrow so. Give him my best wishes, won't you?'

She put down her iPhone and went up to Conor and put her arms around his neck. 'That's that sorted,' she said.

'I've never been out with an armed woman before,' he told her. 'I'm not sure what the protocol is when it comes to undressing. Do I have to have a firearms licence?'

'Well, it's straightforward enough. I take off my holster and you carry on where you left off.'

She unfastened her gun and laid it on the side-table next to her iPhone. 'There.'

'That's a fierce unusual breakfast for a dog,' said Conor, coming up close to her again, and taking hold of her sweater. 'Two boiled eggs, a cup of tea, and some toast if he wants it. With blackcurrant jam? I mean, none of that will do him any harm, but—'

'I told you,' Katie interrupted him. 'Barney doesn't realise that he's a dog. He'd be smoking cigarettes and trying to drive my car if I let him.'

She stood on tiptoe so that she could give him a flurry of little kisses, to distract him. Even though she was wearing her thick-soled lace-up shoes he was six inches taller than her, at least. He kissed her back – a long, slow kiss, with his brown eyes open, looking directly into hers – and at the same time he started to lift up her sweater.

Katie raised both arms so that he could take her sweater off. She was pleased that she had put on one of the new Heidi Klum bras that she had bought last week from Brown Thomas, with fuchsia pink flowers on it, and that she was wearing the matching thong, too. Most of her underwear drawer needed sorting out and throwing out, and she hardly ever managed to wear underwear that matched.

'I love that perfume you're wearing,' said Conor, as he reached around and unfastened her bra, sliding the catch open one-handed.

'Obsession. It's what I wear to work to intimidate my superior officers. The men, anyway.'

He took off her bra and dropped it to the floor. Then he held her breasts in both hands, gently rolling his fingertips around her nipples. They kissed even more deeply, and as her nipples stiffened, Katie began to feel more than just attraction, she felt hunger. She began to kiss him so hard that she was almost eating him. At the same time, she started to unbutton his thick blue mouliné shirt, pulling it off his shoulders. His chest was hard and muscular, with a V-shaped arrow of dark brown hair on it, and his stomach was taut – the stomach of a swimmer, or a man who exercised every day.

Once she had wrestled off his shirt, she unbuckled his tan leather belt and opened his trousers, tugging them down to his knees. He was wearing navy-and-white striped boxer shorts, which did nothing at all to conceal how stiff he was.

'Sit down,' she said. 'Sit on the bed.'

He sat down, prising off his shoes with his feet. Katie knelt on the floor in front of him to drag off his trousers, and then she pulled down his boxer shorts. His penis was huge – much thicker than John's. Its head was swollen to a dark mauve colour, and it was already gaping at her with a glistening drop of fluid. Conor had trimmed the hair around it as neatly as his beard, which told Katie that he was vain about his appearance, but which also suggested that he was aware of what women liked in bed.

She grasped the shaft of his penis tightly and rubbed it slowly up and down. Then she closed her eyes and touched her fingers of her left hand to her forehead like a clairvoyant.

'It's telling me something,' she said.

'What's it telling you?'

'It's telling me that it feels exposed out here, without any trousers on. It needs to find somewhere dark and warm and slippery to hide in.'

She opened her eyes and looked up at him with a mischievous smile on her face and both of them laughed.

'That's amazing,' said Conor. 'Jesus. I won't bother to say a word in future... just let the flute do the talking for me.'

Katie stood up and he unzipped her skirt. She kissed the top of his head while he took off her pantyhose and then her thong. When he had done so, he kissed her between the legs, and gave her a quick lick with the tip of his tongue, too, which made her shiver.

They climbed together on to the bed and kissed and caressed and stroked each other. Katie had made love to only one man since John had left her, and he had been rough and preoccupied with other thoughts, even when he was on top of her. But Conor was giving her all of his attention now, massaging her breasts and running his fingers down to her hips to make her shudder with pleasure.

'You have.... the most extraordinary face,' he told her. 'You look like one of those beautiful women in a mediaeval painting. I've never met a woman who looked so willing and yet so sure of herself, both at the same time.'

'Well, you're not so bad yourself, Mr Hound Lover,' said Katie. 'When I saw you walking into the station there, I thought you looked like one of those Vikings that used to come into Cork in a longboat, looking for a bit of rape and pillage.'

'I promise I won't pillage,' said Conor. 'I don't want to be seduced and arrested, all on the same night.'

Katie reached down and cupped his balls in her hand. They were hard and tightly wrinkled and she gently played with them as if she could tell his fortune from those, too.

'Your breasts are beautiful,' he told her, although he sounded a little breathless because of the way that she was fondling him.

'Too big,' she said.

'They don't look too big from here. It's your perspective. You're closer than I am, so they look too big to you, but they're not.'

Katie couldn't help laughing again. A man had never aroused her so much and yet so amused her at the same time.

'Mother of God,' she said. 'You sound like that episode of *Father Ted*. "Big, near... small, far away."'

With that, she opened her legs wide, and took hold of his penis, and guided the head of it between her lips, so that it nestled there for a moment. She kept a tight grip on it, though, so that he couldn't push himself forward and penetrate her, and she looked up into his eyes and kissed him and said, 'It's talking to me again.'

'What's it saying now?'

'It says it wants me, but the question is, do you?'

'What's the difference?'

'There's a whole rake of difference, Conor. Your cock turns me on all right, but I don't go to bed with cocks. I go to bed with men. What I mean is, once your cock is satisfied, and shrinks away, will you do the same? I'm not asking you for commitment. I'm simply making sure that I'm not just another notch on your bedpost.'

Conor smiled. 'There's only one way to find out, Katie. Try me and see for yourself. And will you tell the flute to shut up for a moment? I want you, the same as he does. In fact, right at this moment, about a hundred times more than he does.'

Katie laughed again, and released her grip on Conor's penis, and he slowly pushed himself into her. She had always been quite tight, but Conor was the first man who had ever made her gasp when he entered her. He felt enormous, as if he were stretching her apart and filling up her whole pelvis. She closed her eyes and clung on to him, digging her fingernails into his back, while he entered her right up to the hilt, and she could feel his neatly clipped hair prickling against the smooth bare lips of her vulva.

Now there was no more laughing. Their lovemaking became powerful and rhythmic, with Conor plunging into her again and again, faster and faster, with both of them panting like a duet.

She was beginning to feel the warm dark tension of an orgasm rising up inside her when Conor suddenly took himself out of her, and sat up on the bed with his back straight.

'Let me be true to my name,' he breathed.

'What? What do you mean?' Katie asked him.

'Turn over,' he said.

'What?'

'Turn over. I'm a Hound Lover, let me love you like a hound loves his bitch.'

Katie turned over and knelt up on her knees and elbows. Conor parted the cheeks of her bottom with both hands and gently entered her vagina from behind, sliding all the way in. He then began to make love to her again, not as quickly as before, but very deep – so deep that he kept touching the neck of her womb and making her flinch.

She couldn't remember when she had last felt a sensation like this. She stared down at the pillow and all she could think of was the ever-increasing tightness between her legs, and Conor's penis slowly but relentlessly pushing its way into her body. She felt her muscles ripple inside her, and then the darkness rose to overwhelm her and she was quaking and quaking and crying out loud, and even though she was crying out loud Conor kept pushing his penis into her again and again until she thought that she was going to go mad with the ecstasy of it. *Stop, oh God, don't stop!*

But Conor did stop, although he was still inside her. He gripped her hips, and she could hear him breathing very quickly, as if he were trying to stop himself from sneezing. Then he climaxed, and she could feel the warmth of his semen flooding her vagina. It was such a relieving, satisfying sensation that she dropped her face forward on to the pillow and felt that she could have stayed like that for ever.

At last, though, his penis subsided and he took himself out of her, and she could feel his wetness running down the inside of her thighs. She eased herself over on to her side, and held out her arms for him, and they hugged and kissed each other, and stroked each other's faces and shoulders and backs as if they had both discovered something magical that nobody else in the world had ever discovered before.

Now, they hardly spoke, although they both continued to smile at each other. There was nothing they needed to say, not yet. Katie felt as if her life had suddenly been brought into perspective. All of the pressures that she had been facing at work and all of the guilt that she had been feeling about John still seemed important, but she saw now that she could cope with them. Even if she and Conor never slept together again, she knew that she was strong and attractive and her life had much more to offer than pompous senior officers and Knocknaheeny scumbags and a crippled former lover who was only staying with her because he had nowhere else to go and nobody else to take care of him.

Conor at last looked at his watch and said, 'Look – it's still early. Let's go out for one last drink, shall we? It'll only take us a couple of minutes to walk up to Henchy's so you won't have to drive.'

'All right,' said Katie. 'But when we get back, I think the flute will be asking for an encore.'

Conor gently touched her forehead, and brushed her hair out of her eyes. 'He won't be the only one.'

* * *

They walked up Summerhill arm-in-arm to St Luke's Cross and went into Henchy's, with its black-painted front and its windows engraved with lettering. They sat in the same corner seats next to the front door that she had sat in with Kyna the last time she had been in here, and she thought of Kyna and wondered how she was and what she would think of Conor. Would she be jealous?

They shared a bottle of chardonnay that wasn't quite cold enough. Conor talked about some of the pets that he had managed to find, including a bull terrier that had almost bitten his fingers off when he had tried to tug it out from underneath a snooker table. An elderly man at the bar was telling a long and incomprehensible joke about goats being thrown down a well, which he could hardly finish because he was wheezing with laughter.

'What time are you driving up to Tipp tomorrow?' Katie asked him.

'It'll take about an hour and three-quarters, traffic willing, so I reckon about twelve.'

'I'm coming with you.'

'Really?' said Conor. She had an inkling that he had nearly said '*No, you're not*,' before remembering that she was a senior Garda officer and that she was employing him to do a job for her.

'Yes, really. I want to see these dog fighters for myself.'

She didn't say how strongly protective she felt towards him, now that they had made love. She wanted to make sure that if some hard case like Guzz Eye McManus found out tomorrow who he really was, and what he was doing in Ballyknock, he wouldn't end up in a shed somewhere in Ballingarry North with his skull smashed in.

* * *

It was still raining as they walked back down the hill to the guest house. Back in Conor's room, they undressed and took a shower together, soaping each other and kissing and enjoying the slippery wet feeling of each other's bodies.

When they had towelled themselves dry, they lay on the bed together, naked, just looking at each other. Katie stroked Conor's damp beard and said, 'I have to leave pure early tomorrow. I have to go back home first and then to the hospital and God alone knows what else will have come up for me to deal with. I'll pick you up at twelve.'

'I think you work too hard.'

'So do I.'

She reached across and started to fondle his penis, which quickly stiffened. 'This is one of those nights that I wish would go on for ever,' she said.

'It's only a pup. We have plenty of time.'

'That's what I'm always telling myself. But it isn't true.'

She got up on to her knees and grasped his penis in her hand and took him into her mouth. She felt that it was like sucking a large glossy plum, and she was almost tempted to bite into it. He laid one hand on her thigh and let his head drop back on the pillow and let out a soft, contented sigh.

'This,' he said. 'This is a preview of Heaven.'

She swirled her tongue around and around him, and probed him with the tip of it. She was aroused by the feeling that she was both subservient and in control, slave and mistress at the same time. She took him in deeper, as deep as she could without choking herself, and with her right hand she rubbed him more and more briskly until she felt his leg-muscles tightening up.

'Oh dear God,' he whispered, and climaxed. The first spurt Katie swallowed, but then she took him out and he spurted again, and his semen shot up the side of her cheek and across the bridge of her nose.

She sat up straight and reached for the pillow so that she could use the pillow-case to wipe her cheek. Then she leaned over and gave Conor a long, lascivious kiss.

'Thank the Lord the brassers down on Union Quay couldn't see me like that. They'd have said that I had a face like a painter's radio.'

She laughed and Conor laughed and they held each other close. She hadn't felt so much like herself for years. Every day since she had first joined An Garda Siochána she had been aware that she was responsible for the care and protection of other people, and so she had always been restrained in what she said and how she behaved, and she had always tried to set a moral example. Tonight she felt free to be rude and relaxed and slutty and do whatever she liked. Her late Uncle Sean always used to say that 'inside every garda there's an anarchist bursting to get out – look at your father'.

In the very small hours of the morning, in darkness, they started to make love again, but gave up halfway through, laughing, because they were both too tired. The next time Katie opened her eyes it was 5:55. It was still dark outside but it was morning and she knew that it was time for her to get up and go.

When she was dressed she kissed Conor's bare shoulder and whispered, 'I'll see you after, Mr Hound Lover.' Then she left the room and quietly closed the door behind her.

It was still raining, and the streets were still glistening and black. As she drove along the Lower Glanmire Road, beside the

River Lee, the radio was playing 'My Love Took Me Down to the River to Silence Me' by Little Green Cars. It was a song about a girl being abandoned, but Katie sang along with it, in a very high voice, feeling happier and sillier than she could remember.

Twenty-six

'He's out so,' said Dermot, lifting the mask off Gerry Mulvaney's face. He flicked the tip of Gerry's nose with his finger just to make sure.

'It's a fierce pity in a way, that they have to be anaesthetised,' said the doctor, methodically pushing down the fingers of his surgical gloves, one after the other. 'It would be interesting to see how much each procedure hurt, and what reaction you'd get. Maybe if I gave them a hefty dose of meldonium. Rugby players take that, so that they can carry on playing even when they're badly injured. It could work with surgical patients too, don't you think?'

'What are you planning to do to him, like?' asked Dermot, although he sounded more interested in going outside for a cigarette than learning how the doctor intended to mutilate Gerry Mulvaney.

'Well – I considered leaving him his eyesight, because he knows who we are already, and I thought what difference would it make? But maybe Grainne's right and he could communicate by blinking; and if he still had his eyesight he could see where we were taking him and how much stuff we were shifting, and all kinds of incriminating details, even if we were careful. So the eyes have to go.'

'Poor old Gerry,' said Dermot. 'If he wasn't such an eejit I'd almost feel sorry for him.'

'Then of course we'll have to stop him from speaking, so it's the laryngectomy, just like the others. On the other hand, I may try a glossectomy, which means taking out his tongue, although he still might be able to speak in a gargled sort of a way. But then

I was trying to think of a new way to stop him from writing, and to stop him from running off. What I'm going to try is, removing his radius and his ulna from his forearms, as well his carpals and metacarpals and phalanges from his hands.'

'Come here to me?'

'Dermot, the love of God, haven't I taught you all of this? How do you think you're going to become a fully qualified surgical assistant if you can't remember the simplest human anatomy? They're all bones, Dermot – *bones*.'

'Oh, well, sorry, like. Bones. You should have said so.'

'I did. I simply gave them their proper names. Like your gluteus maximus and your gluteus medius muscles constitute your arse.'

'All right, I have you. I'll remember that in future.'

'I'll also remove his tibia and his fibula from his lower legs, as well as the tarsals and metatarsals and phalanges from his feet.'

'That's more bones you're talking about, is it?'

The doctor nodded, closing his eyes briefly to indicate how long-suffering he was. A highly respected surgeon who used to mingle with TDs and media celebrities like Pat Kenny. One single misjudgement had reduced him to the company of criminals like Gerry Mulvaney and fools like Dermot. And who could blame him for that misjudgement? It had been moral, rather than surgical. His superior skill had never been in question.

'Let's get started, shall we?' he said, and Dermot lifted off the green surgical sheet that had been covering Gerry Mulvaney up to his neck. Under the stark overhead lights, he looked pitifully emaciated, with dead-white skin and wiry grey body hair. The doctor could see a diagonal scar under his right rib-cage, where he must have had his gall-bladder removed.

At this point, Grainne came into the room, tying up a surgical apron around her waist.

'Lend us a hand here, Grainne,' said the doctor. 'He needs to be face-down.'

Between the three of them they turned Gerry Mulvaney over, angling his head to the right so that Dermot could keep an eye on his breathing. Between his shoulder-blades there was a full-colour life-size tattoo of the face of Jesus, with long auburn curls and a crown of thorns, which gave the doctor the uncomfortable feeling that the Son of God was watching him.

Grainne sponged the back of Gerry Mulvaney's leg with water and then smeared on Chloraprep antiseptic with a white plastic applicator.

The doctor waited for a minute for the Chloraprep to dry, humming to himself. Then he said, 'Number twenty-two, please, Grainne,' holding out his hand but without taking his eyes off Jesus. Grainne passed him the scalpel and he held it in a fingertip grip before starting to make a slide incision down Gerry Mulvaney's calf-muscle. There was very little blood. The incision opened up to reveal fat and flesh, all the way down to his bones.

'So, when you've done this, like –' said Dermot, '– when you've taken out his bones, he's going to be kind of floppy, isn't he?'

The doctor was carefully slicing around the cartilage where the tibia joined the patella. 'That's exactly it, Dermot. Not the medical word for it, but yes – *floppy*. Floppy legs so that he won't be able to walk, and floppy arms so that he won't be able to write, or draw, or do anything at all except wave his floppy hands around. He'll be blind and dumb and have no more rigidity in him than a raggy doll.'

Today, the doctor was going to remove only the bones from Gerry Mulvaney's right leg and foot. He would start on the left leg and foot tomorrow morning, and possibly one of his forearms, if he had time. There was no need for him to rush. He was sending an ambulance on Sunday afternoon to catch the evening ferry to Fishguard, but he could use Siobhán again for that trip, and one of the first patients that Milo and Ger had picked up for him, a homeless teenage boy called Fearghal. At least they had assumed Fearghal was homeless, because they had found no address on him, and his disappearance had never been mentioned in the media. The doctor had amputated his right leg and his left arm, so that he was asymmetrical, and would never be able to balance himself, and then he had blinded him by spraying oven cleaner into his eyes.

The doctor was well aware that some people would regard him as cruel, but as far as he was concerned, he was doing his patients a considerable favour. Once he had operated on them, they had some purpose in this world, which is more than they had ever had before.

* * *

It took him over three-and-a-half hours to complete his surgery on Gerry Mulvaney, and then suture and dress his incision. Gerry Mulvaney's two leg bones lay in a plastic washing-up bowl on the side-table, as well as his ankle and toe bones, like a scattering of fivestones.

Gerry was beginning to regain consciousness, because he was muttering and groaning and his right hand kept twitching.

The doctor snapped off his surgical gloves and said to Grainne, 'I'll leave you and Dermot to take care of him now, will I? Lorcan should be here by now. Give him the morphine to keep him quiet. The usual dose.'

He took off his bloodstained green apron, bundled it up, and dropped it into the dirty clothes basket beside the door. He felt quite pleased with what he had decided to do to Gerry. He could be sitting in the ambulance, with his arms neatly folded over his blanket, and yet he would be incapable of doing anything with them except to flap them. He wouldn't be able to see and he wouldn't be able to speak, so no matter how frantic it was, a bit of flapping would communicate nothing to the customs officers at Rosslare.

Before he went downstairs, the doctor crossed the corridor to check up on Kieran. Since his operations, Kieran had been running a high temperature, well up to 38 degrees C, and the doctor was more than a little concerned about post-operative fever. He had measured Kieran for his fixation, the metal framework which he would use to re-set his broken pelvis, and sent off the specifications to GS medical supplies in Dublin. However he didn't expect to receive the parts for at least another two days, and he was concerned that Kieran might succumb to infection or lung collapse before they arrived. That would face him not only with the problem of disposing of Kieran's body, but paying for the fixation too, for no profit whatsoever. He could hardly charge it as a business expense.

He stood over Kieran, who was deeply sedated now, his plump face white and glistening with sweat, like a glossy death-mask fashioned out of lard. His breathing was shallow and quick, and it wouldn't have surprised the doctor if he had stopped breathing altogether while he stood there. He wished to God that Ger hadn't run him down with such enthusiasm. He had needed only to knock him over, and break a leg if possible, not crush him.

He stayed for a little longer, but when he was satisfied that Kieran was reasonably stable, he left the room and went downstairs.

The grey-haired man was waiting for him in the reception room. He was standing in front of the fireplace and looking at himself in the mirror, smoking. He was wearing a grey tweed suit with a black waistcoat and his hair was lank and straggly, as if he had been caught in the rain but hadn't bothered to comb it since.

On the chesterfield next to him there was a large green tartan holdall, with its handles fastened together with brown parcel tape.

The grey-haired man blew smoke and then nodded towards the window, which was boarded up with plywood.

'What's the story about that then?'

'Gerry was trying to leave us in a hurry. Collins will be coming round tomorrow morning with replacement glass.'

'I always told you that fellow was trouble. He's one of life's incompetents.'

'He certainly is now. I'm taking out his leg bones below the knee and his forearm bones below the elbow, and I'll be blinding him so.'

The grey-haired man raised his eyebrows. 'Nobody could ever accuse you of not being inventive, Gearoid, I'll give you that.'

'Huh,' said the doctor, as if he didn't take that as much of a compliment. Then, 'How much do you have there?'

'Eleven thousand seven hundred and ninety,' said the grey-haired man. 'And that's just for the five of them. That woman in Belgooly gave me four-and-a-half grand to get her Samoyed back, which was about what she paid for it in the first place.'

The doctor ripped off the parcel tape and opened the bag. He rummaged inside and took out two packets of brand-new €500 notes. He sniffed them as if he were making sure that they were fresh and then dropped them back into the bag.

'I imagine you advised her what would happen if she notified the guards?'

The grey-haired man nodded. 'I told her that Samoyeds with no heads win very few best-of-breed prizes in dog shows, and I believe she took the hint.'

'When do you think you'll have the rest sorted?'

'Hard to say. Most of the owners are out of the country which of course was why their dogs were in the kennels in the first place, and I haven't been able to contact them yet. But Aileen's working on them for me. It shouldn't take longer than a week or so.'

'Okay, if that's the best you can do. I have enough to pay Ward for this weekend's shipment, but O'Driscoll hasn't stopped pestering me for more, and Vasilescu says he can't keep up with demand. I mean, holy Saint Joseph, the amount they're selling, you'd think the entire population of Cork was sniffing or smoking or shooting up.'

'They're paying you, though, aren't they? O'Driscoll and the others?'

'Of course. Holy Mother of God, Lorcan, I'd soon cut them off if they didn't. It's the delay, that's all, while the cash gets laundered. I have no intention of being caught out by the Criminal Assets Bureau – not like that Patrick Duggan, with all those empty beer kegs full of euros buried under his farmyard. It's not only that, though – we need to expand the business much faster if we're going to dominate the market, and that means converting at least three more ambulances, and doing it soon. We're going to need more patients, too.'

The grey-haired man crushed out his cigarette and blew out a last stream of smoke. 'There's a breeding kennels in Mullingar that has twenty or thirty pedigree Akitas that we could go after. They're fetching very decent prices in the UK just at the moment, Akitas, and we can sell them for fighting, too. The Pakis in Manchester will always pay well over the odds for Akitas.'

'What about those fighting dogs? What's happening with them?'

'Bartley took them up to Ballyknock. He's handed them over to some friend of McManus to train them. We could be looking at a hundred grand out of them if we're lucky.'

The doctor said, 'I have no belief in luck, Lorcan, you know that. There's no such thing. There's only winning or losing, and the only difference between winning and losing is forward planning. Like the father used to say, the road to ruin is signposted with spontaneity.'

The grey-haired man said nothing to that. They both knew that the doctor had acted spontaneously just once in his career, and that had been the finish of him.

'I'll get this dealt with,' said the doctor, picking up the holdall. 'Are you still okay for Sunday? It'll be Siobhán again, and Fearghal. Fiontán's not too fit at the moment.'

'That's the whole fecking point, isn't it?' grinned the grey-haired man. 'None of them are supposed to be fit. The unfitter, the better, that's what I thought.'

Twenty-seven

Katie was home by a quarter to seven and quietly let herself in. The nursery door was closed but the kitchen door was open and Barney came snuffling out to greet her. Bridie was up already, and boiling the kettle to make a pot of tea.

'Thank you so much for staying over, Bridie,' smiled Katie. 'You don't know what a blessing that was.'

'Oh, it was no bother at all,' Bridie told her. 'In fact it was fantastic to get a quiet night's sleep for a change. My neighbours upstairs have a new wain and it's forever bawling its head off and of course they're forever getting up and down to feed it, or change it , or walk up and down trying to get it back to sleep. It's like having the army upstairs, I tell you.'

'John still sleeping?'

'He was complaining about the phantom pain again after I gave him his supper so I gave him some of the codeine linctus and he's been in dreamland ever since. I hate to say it but you look fair done yourself. What kind of an emergency was it?'

'Bit of a scrap,' said Katie. 'All sorted now, though. I'll just go and take a shower and change.'

'A cup of tea will crown you, and how about something to eat? I'm famous for my French toast if you could fancy that.'

Katie smiled and nodded. She was suddenly beginning to feel very tired.

* * *

John still hadn't woken up by the time she had to leave, so she sat down in the living-room to write him a note. Barney came and stood protectively beside her, with his tongue hanging out.

'Dearest John, sorry that Cork's criminal fraternity keep calling me away! Bridie told me that you were suffering pain again, I hope I'm not making it worse for you. I'll be back home this evening at about—'

She heard the nursery door open, and her pen froze, because Bridie was still clattering about in the kitchen, so she couldn't have opened it. Then she heard a soft stomping sound, followed by a pause, and then another, and another. Gradually, awkwardly, the sounds came towards the living-room door.

Katie put down her pad and turned around. The door was open but there was nobody there. She waited, and listened, and Barney listened too, and made that mewling noise in the back of his throat – the noise he made when he suspected that the postman was outside, or that there was a rabbit in the garden.

It was then that John appeared, and quickly made a grab for the sides of the doorframe to support himself. He was wearing a blue pyjama jacket and rolled-up pyjama trousers, and his stumps were covered in thick white surgical socks. His hair was tousled and his face was very pale. He was gritting his teeth in an effort to grin.

'John!' said Katie. 'For the love of Jesus!' She stood up immediately and went across to help him.

He raised one hand and said, 'I'm okay! I'm fine! Look at me, I can walk!'

'Are you sure you're okay? Come and sit down.'

'I'm grand. I really am. My therapist said I should try to walk as soon as possible. I started yesterday and I was hoping to show you last night when you came home.'

'I'm sorry. We had a crisis at the station and I had to stay there all night. Are you sure I can't give you a hand?'

John said, 'No, no – I can manage. It's a question of balance, that's all.'

He hesitated for a moment, and then he released his grip on the doorframe and made a jerky, hurried rush towards the couch. Katie held out her hands in case he stumbled and fell, but he reached the couch and stood there, panting and not grinning any more, but plainly triumphant.

'There! And you wait until my legs are ready! You won't be able to tell that's it not the old me!'

Katie said, 'That's pure fantastic, John! Well done.'

She couldn't tell him how unnerving it was to see him standing up. Apart from the fact that the trauma of losing his legs had turned his hair grey and etched deep lines into his cheeks, he was now six inches shorter than she was, instead of six inches taller. She felt as if she were dreaming, and talking to some extraordinary dwarf.

She picked up the piece of paper on which she had been writing and tore it in half. 'I was just leaving you a note to tell you that I should be back this evening. I can't say what time because I have to go to Tipperary. I'll be off now. Do you need a hand getting back to bed, or are you going to stay here?'

'I'll stay here for a while. Give us a kiss before you go.'

Katie bent forward and kissed him. His lips were very dry and his breath smelled faintly of garlic. He reached up and laid his hand on her shoulder and tried to kiss her more deeply, but she pulled away and said, 'Really, John, I have to go. I'm late already.'

As she turned to leave, he took two unbalanced steps towards her, reaching out for the flap of her jacket, but Barney nudged him with his nose as if he were warning him not to touch her.

''Bye, Bridie!' Katie called out. 'I'll see you after! Probably about eight!'

Bridie came to the kitchen door, wiping her hands on her apron. 'You don't have to hurry, Katie! If you can't manage to come back at all, it won't bother me! I can have another good night's sleep!'

* * *

She stopped at Anglesea Street to see if she had any messages or letters that needed her attention, and to tell Moirin that she would be driving up to Tipperary.

Detective Ó Doibhilin met her in the corridor as she was leaving. He was eating a hand pie which he kept behind his back while he talked to her.

'Nothing to report of any note, ma'am,' he told her, wiping the crumbs from his mouth with the back of his hand. 'She went to the Douglas Village shopping centre yesterday evening and parked in the multi-storey for two hours, but that's all. The rest of the time she's been at home.'

'Well, who knows? We may see her heading somewhere interesting tomorrow,' said Katie. 'Good man, keep your eye on her.'

'Don't worry about that, ma'am. She won't be going anywhere unless I know about it. Where are you heading on to now – the Wilton Hilton?'

Katie drove to the University Hospital. She didn't mind that it was still raining because the rain seemed different today – fresh rain, washing away the past. Dr Kelley was already in the mortuary, sitting in front of her computer; and Eithne O'Neill was there, too, standing beside the body of the dead dognapper, with a small sketchbook. Eithne was a slim, pretty girl, but this morning her hair was tied back severely and she was wearing no make-up and there were dark smudges under her eyes as if she hadn't been sleeping.

Katie raised a hand in salute to Dr Kelley but went across to talk to Eithne first. She tried not to look at the dognapper with the top half of his face blown off and his dark red sinus cavities exposed, but it was horribly fascinating and she found it very hard not to. She couldn't help thinking: *The inside of my head looks like this, too.*

'I heard about your sister, Eithne,' she said. 'I'm so sad for you. I really am.'

Eithne gave her a fleeting smile. 'Thanks for that, ma'am. At least it was quick. She only found out two months ago that she had the liver cancer. The first time she went to the doctor he told her she was pregnant. She was so happy, until she found out what it really was.'

'That's tragic. I'm surprised you want to come back to doing this. So soon, anyway.'

'I've seen enough dead people to know that life doesn't last for ever. And you never know when it's going to be your turn. Like this fellow here. I'll bet he wouldn't have bothered to eat any supper that evening if somebody had told him that he was going to have his head blown off before he had the chance to eat tomorrow's breakfast.'

Katie looked at Eithne's preliminary sketches. She had already created an image of a man with a triangular face, with a prominent nose and a weak, receding chin.

'The ZBrush image didn't show his forehead wide enough, in my opinion,' said Eithne. 'I reassembled all of the pieces of his skull that we'd been able to salvage from the crime scene, and I'd definitely say that he had a dome-shaped forehead. I should have a finished image by later today, or maybe tomorrow.'

'I'm not too sure I like the way he's staring at me,' said Katie.

'That's because people with this kind of physiognomy tend to keep their chins down and look up at you, rather than straight and level, and that gives them the appearance of being disapproving or suspicious. It can also make them appear to be shy, even if they're not shy at all. That's one thing I've learned about facial reconstruction. Don't think about the way a deceased person looked to the outside world, think about the way *they* thought they looked.'

Dr Kelley came across. She was a small, tubby woman with heavy-rimmed glasses and bushy eyebrows. Katie had always thought that with a pair of tweezers and a little blusher she could have made herself quite attractive, in a Russian doll-like way.

'I've been watching this young lady at work and she's amazing,' said Dr Kelley. 'But why don't you come over and take a look at our stabbing victim?'

Katie gave Eithne a brief, consoling hug, and then said, 'What was your sister's name?'

'Aoife. But our mother called her Féileacán, because she was always running around flapping her arms like a little butterfly.'

'Féileacán, that's pretty. I'll say a prayer for her tonight, I promise.'

She followed Dr Kelley to the other side of the mortuary, where Martin Ó Brádaigh's body was lying on a stainless-steel autopsy table – naked, with only a folded green sheet over him to cover his genitals. His chest and his forearms were tattooed with snakes and demons and naked girls, although he was covered in so many bruises and contusions that some of the images had been scraped off or blotted out. His head was still violently angled to one side, as if he were straining to see himself reflected in the table underneath him.

'Almost all of his injuries are consistent with him having been hit by a speeding truck,' said Dr Kelley. 'There's even a diagonal dent across his forehead which exactly matches the driver's side windscreen wiper.'

'Was there any chance at all that he could have survived?'

Dr Kelley shook her head. 'Not a hope. His internal injuries are so catastrophic that it's going to take me ten minutes at least in the coroner's court just to read them all out. Nobody could have been hit by a vehicle of that mass at that speed and not been instantly killed. The total momentum was approximately one hundred and ninety-eight thousand metres per second.'

'But the stab wound?'

'Like I say, it must have been inflicted before he was knocked down. It was fresh, though. From his condition I would estimate that he was stabbed no more than thirty minutes or so before the truck hit him.'

She lifted the sheet that was covering Martin Ó Brádaigh's midriff. His penis and his scrotum had been lifted up and stuck to his stomach with surgical tape so that his perineum was exposed. Between his testicles and his anus there was a ragged, star-shaped laceration, although Katie could see by the wider slices at the side of the star where the knife must have first been pushed into him.

'Mother of God, that must have been agony,' she said. 'And whoever did that, they must have wanted to cause him the maximum pain possible.'

'I've taken an X-ray and a CT scan,' said Dr Kelley. 'What I'm going to do now is feed the scan into a 3-D printer so that I can give you a plastic replica of the knife that was used to stab him. Every knife-blade has its tiny imperfections so if you can find the original knife you'll be able to compare it and prove that it was the actual weapon involved.'

'That's a start anyway,' said Katie, although she didn't like to say that her chances of finding the original knife were almost nil. What she really needed were eye-witnesses to the stabbing. If it happened out in the open, right in the middle of the N25, in daylight, somebody must have seen it, surely? One witness had come forward to say that he had actually seen the Paddy's Whiskey truck hitting Martin Ó Brádaigh when he was crawling across the road, and two more witnesses had seen his body shortly afterwards, when the truck driver was calling for an ambulance. But he had stopped his Subaru right in the middle of the eastbound carriageway, and that was presumably when he was attacked. She found it hard to believe that not a single passing driver could remember his car obstructing the road, or have seen any other vehicles parked nearby. His attacker must have had some means of getting there and getting away afterwards, unless he had run off over the fields, which didn't seem likely.

Katie thanked Dr Kelley and said goodbye to Eithne and then she drove back to Anglesea Street. As soon as she got back into her office she called Mathew McElvey in the press office to come up and see her. He was in the canteen but he came up immediately, carrying a half-finished cup of coffee.

'Mathew, I want you to put out a witness appeal for this fellow Martin Ó Brádaigh who was run down on the N25 just past Grange.'

She explained how Ó Brádaigh had stopped his car in the middle of the road, leaving his door open, and that it was likely that he had been assaulted shortly after.

'To anybody driving past, it may not have been apparent that he was being attacked, which may be the reason why nobody's come forward.'

'Where exactly did this happen? And when?'

'One of the sergeants at Dungarvan has all the details,' said Katie. 'I have his name here, yes – ask for a Sergeant Breen. He should be able to email you a picture of the car, too, and that might jog somebody's memory.'

'When do you want this to go out?' asked Mathew.

'I'm leaving for Tipp in about an hour and a half, and I'll be gone for most of the afternoon, so if you can have it ready for me to see before then. Ideally, I'd like it go out in time for the *Six-One News* this evening, and tomorrow morning's *Examiner*.'

'Oh, right. And if any of the media want to talk to you about it?'

'Put them through to Inspector O'Rourke. I'll brief him all about it before I go.'

After Mathew McElvey had gone, Katie sat at her desk for a few moments, looking at the letters and folders that Moirin had left for her. She thought about Conor and she couldn't help smiling to herself. She had never wondered before what it might be like to resign from An Garda Siochána and live like an ordinary wife. Even when she was married to Paul it had never entered her mind, and she had certainly never considered it with John. But now, with Conor?

She even wondered what it might be like to have another child. Or children even. A little boy and a little girl. Nothing would bring her little Seamus back, even if she wept all day and all night for the rest of her life. But she was still young enough to have more.

Moirin came in, with half an egg-and-tomato sandwich on a plate.

'Do you fancy this, ma'am? I'm as full as a goose. I think the eyes overestimated the stomach, like, do you know what I mean?'

'No, thanks, Moirin,' said Katie. She was too churned up inside to feel hungry, too excited. 'Detective O'Donovan will probably do it justice, though. He'd eat the Lamb of God that one, and come back for the ewe.'

Twenty-eight

She hardly recognised Conor when he arrived at the station just after 12:00. He was wearing a black baseball cap and a puffy bronze windcheater and black jeans, and dirty runners. His eyes were hidden behind RayBans.

'State of you la,' she said, smiling.

'Oh come on, this is my dog fighter's disguise. I couldn't blend in with the likes of Guzz Eye McManus if I was too sartorial.'

'How about me? Do you think I'm too dressed up?' asked Katie. She had put on her black raincoat with the pointed hood, the one that John said made her look like a witch, and shiny black leather boots.

'No, you're perfect. You look like my girlfriend would look, if you were my girlfriend, but that's how I'll have to introduce you.'

She reached up and took off his sunglasses. The desk sergeant noticed her doing it, and stared at her intently for a moment before going back to the report he was filling in. She looked directly into Conor's eyes and said, 'Fair play. I don't mind being your girlfriend.'

They took a black Mercedes E-Class saloon from the station's car pool – and not only because it suited Conor's alias as a disreputable dog breeder more than Katie's Focus. If Guzz McManus got a hacker to search through the RSA computer records, they would find that the Mercedes had belonged for the past three years to Redmond O'Dea of North Tipperary, whose address was Firmount Kennels, Carrigahorig.

The rain eased off as they drove northwards on the M8 past Watergrasshill, although the clouds were still oppressively low, as if God were trying to suffocate them under a thick grey duvet. Katie tuned the car's radio to 96FM for some quiet background music. She couldn't stop staring at Conor as he drove, and from time to time he glanced back at her and smiled. She found him fascinating to watch, and if anything she thought that he was even more good-looking than when he had first walked into the station. She laid her hand on his left thigh, and he briefly laid his hand on top of hers.

'Don't forget that your name's "Redmond", will you?' she reminded him. 'I hope to heaven that I don't. And my name's Sinéad.'

'I'll remember that all right,' he told her. 'I once went out with a girl called Sinéad, and she had the same hair colour as you. She wasn't so pretty, though.'

'Flatterer. Go on, though, I like it.'

Conor said, 'First of all we have to find out who has these dogs. We'll try Bartley Doran first, and then this Paddy Barrett. It wouldn't surprise me at all, though, if it's Doran. He's like the Billy Walsh of fighting-dog trainers, and if these are real high-quality dogs, I'm pretty sure that McManus will have passed them on to him.'

After an hour and a half, Conor left the M8 at Garranmore and then drove down through Ballymackane to Palmer's Hill, a narrow hedge-lined road which crossed back over the motorway. On the far side of the motorway, on top of a hill, and almost completely hidden by trees and fencing, was the Ballyknock Halting Site.

He turned into the site, and parked the Mercedes behind a battered blue horsebox. Seven or eight children were playing nearby, and they all stopped running and skipping and slowly came up to the car to stare at Katie and Conor as if they were aliens. The youngest boy was frowning at them with undisguised hostility and elaborately picking his nose at the same time.

'Well, well – a welcoming committee,' said Katie. 'Except they don't look too welcoming, do they?'

'Don't worry,' said Conor. He had obviously been expecting this. As he climbed out of the car he reached into the pocket of his windcheater and took out a paper bag. Then he called out, '*All-a-bah!*' and tossed a handful of Caffrey's rhubarb-and-custards into the air. The children instantly scattered, shouting and pushing each other as they snatched up the sweets from the muddy pathway.

'That's not too hygienic,' said Katie, as she came round the car to join him.

'Don't fret about it. These kids were brought up on a diet of mud. Mud and manriklo.'

'Oh, that's not true. The Pavee have the cleanest kitchens I've ever seen. And they won't eat any animal that licks its own behind.'

Conor took hold of her arm and laughed. 'Only joking, girlfriend.'

All along the opposite side of the pathway there was a row of white-painted mobile homes, with plant pots outside them. Further along, a group of women were standing around in front of one of the homes, smoking, and they too turned to stare at Katie and Conor.

Conor waved and shouted at them in a strong north Tipperary accent. 'Well! How are ye?'

None of them answered, and they all turned their backs. Conor shrugged and led Katie across to the second mobile home in the line. A spotty teenage boy in a grey hoodie was standing on the step outside the door, playing a game on his mobile phone.

'How are ye?' said Conor. 'Is The Guzz in?'

The boy reached behind him and knocked on the door with his knuckles. 'Guzz! There's some feen out here axing after ye!'

After a few moments the door was opened and a sallow young woman with braided hair and huge gold earrings came out, smoking. She stared at Katie and Conor suspiciously.

'Well,' said Conor. 'It's Taunisha, isn't it? How's your granny for turf? You remember me, don't you? Redmond. I was here in the spring, looking for breeding dogs to buy.'

'Oh yeah, so you was. This your wife, is it?'

'Girlfriend. Sinéad.'

'*Girlfriend?*' Taunisha raised one perfectly arched eyebrow. *She must regard me as far too ancient to be single*, thought Katie. If a Pavee girl wasn't married by the time she was twenty she was considered to be on the shelf.

'I'd like a chat with The Guzz, if that's okay,' said Conor.

'All right. You'd best come in.'

Katie and Conor climbed the steps and entered the mobile home. Taunisha turned left and ushered them into the living-room, which was foggy with cigar and cigarette smoke. It was furnished with overstuffed crimson velvet chairs and gilt-fringed cushions, and the windows were framed by crimson velvet curtains, drawn back in swags. Against the wall stood a dresser that was cluttered with silver-framed photographs of mastiffs and bull terriers, as well as shining silver cups and shields, and stacks of cigar boxes. Katie felt as if she had stepped into a miniature palace, and in a way she had, because the king himself, Guzz Eye McManus, was sitting on a chair that looked more like a throne.

He was short and squat, The Guzz, with a huge belly. He was totally bald, and he had no eyebrows, which probably meant that had suffered from alopecia. He looked to Katie like a statue of Buddha, except that he was a grumpy Buddha, and his left eye was turned at forty-five degrees to the left, while his right eye was looking straight at her. He was wearing a tight red T-shirt with a fancy red-and-black waistcoat over it, and black tracksuit pants, although his thighs were so swollen that they looked like two giant-sized black puddings. In contrast, his feet were tiny, a child's feet, in white Nike runners that couldn't have been larger than size 4.

He had a half-smoked cigar between his thick rubbery lips, and when Katie and Conor came in, he sucked at it so that the tip glowed orange, and then took it out, and blew a steady stream of blue smoke at them.

Sitting beside him was a thin, dark-skinned man with his jet-black hair pulled back into a man-bun. His forearms were covered in curly tattoos and he was wearing four or five gold bracelets on both of his wrists. A deck of cards was splayed out on the coffee table between them, so it looked as if they were halfway through a game of ten-card rummy.

'Guzz,' said Conor. '*Yoordjeele's soonee-in munya...* good to see you. And you're well, I hope?'

'Redmond,' said The Guzz. 'What's the craic, boy? I thought I might have seen you at Clonlong this summer. There was some deadly fights that day, feen, I can tell you.'

'I heard, but I was in the UK – Rotherham, for my sins – selling off half-a-dozen bull terriers.'

'Who's this you've fetched with you? Not the same beour as last time. Or is it just some sly lack?'

'No, this is Sinéad. Say hello to The Guzz, Sinéad. The lord of the dog-fighting rings.'

Katie said, 'Good to meet you, Guzz,' but The Guzz completely ignored her. Instead he said to Conor, 'What are you after, then, Redmond? Or do you have some dogs for sale?'

Katie knew that this was going to be a critical moment, and she inwardly prayed that Conor could pull this off without arousing The Guzz's suspicions.

'Just something a little bird told me,' said Conor. 'I heard that somebody fetched some first-rate animals up here to Ballyknock within the past few days, for training up to gameness.'

'Did you now?' said The Guzz, puffing at his cigar again.

'I was told there was seven or eight of them, all pedigree. Two bulldogs and a mastiff among them, and a Great Dane, too. I'm fierce interested in the Great Dane for breeding, because I have a Great Dane bitch up at Carrigahorig, and she's just gone into proestrus.'

The Guzz said nothing for a while, but looked Katie up and down with his one good eye, and smoked. Taunisha came back into the living-room and said, 'Guzz, I've put on the kettle. Do you fancy a cup of weed?'

The Guzz didn't answer her, either. Without turning to Conor, he said, 'Who's your "little bird", then, Redmond?'

'Ah, Guzz, you know what the dog business is like as well as I do. You can't take a chihuahua for a shit in the middle of the Gortavoher Forest without somebody grassing on you.'

The Guzz seemed to be content that Conor wasn't going to give away the name of his informant, because all he said next was, 'All right. Fair fucks to you. What's in it for me, then?'

'I'll make it worth your while, Guzz. Put me in touch with whoever has the dog for training – then, if they allow me to lend a borrow of it so that I can breed it, I'll pay you five hundred euros commission – and say, five per cent of whatever I make from the pups when they grow up.'

'A thousand commission, and ten per cent for each pup,' said The Guzz, picking a shred of tobacco-leaf from his lower lip and holding it up in front of his left eye, so that he could examine it more closely.

Conor lifted his chin and thoughtfully stroked his beard with the back of his hand. 'Whoo... that's more than twice what I've ever paid before. How about seven hundred and fifty, and seven-and-a-half per cent?'

'A thousand, and ten. Take it or leave it. It don't make a scrap of difference to me, boy.'

Katie thought: *Take it, Conor, for the love of God. I can charge the thousand-euro commission to operational expenses, and you're not really going to be breeding that Great Dane, anyway, so there won't be any pups.*

'All right, you're on,' said Conor. He spat into the palm of his hand and held it out, and The Guzz shook it.

'You'll be in fierce trouble if you don't pay up, though,' said The Guzz. 'My lads will be up to Carrigahorig before you know it, and your kennels will be accidentally burning down to the ground, with you in them, if you're not wide.'

'You'll get your grade, don't you worry,' said Conor. 'They don't call me Redmond the Reliable for nothing.'

Normally, Katie would have laughed at that, but her nerves were as tense as a tightly wound clock. 'Redmond the Reliable'.

She would have to tease him about that later. More like 'Conor the Conman'.

'Doran has them, Bartley Doran,' said The Guzz. 'You know where his place is, don't you? Down the road here, about a kilometre short of Cashel, and off to the left. He's training them up for the next big fight we'll be holding here.'

'When's that, Guzz?' asked Conor. 'Bartley's going to want him back well before then, isn't he, so that he can get him up to gameness.'

'It won't be for a couple of months or so. I'll let you know nearer the day. I don't want anybody tipping off the shades.'

'Thanks, Guzz. I'll go and talk to Bartley and then I'll go into Cashel and get your grade for you. I'll drop it in after.'

The Guzz was giving all his attention to crushing out his cigar. There was so much smoke curling around him that he looked like a magician performing a disappearing act. As Katie and Conor turned to leave, though, he said, 'I'll give you one thing, Redmond. You've great taste in women. Fetch her here when you've finished with her.'

They left the mobile home and walked back to their car. The children ran up to Conor and said, 'Any more sweeties, mister?'

'Not at the moment, kids. But I'm going into town and I'll fetch you some back with me. What's your favourite?'

'Peggy's Legs!' piped up one of the girls, jumping up and down. 'Fetch us some Peggy's Legs!'

They climbed into the car, turned around, and drove out of the halting site and back on to Palmer's Hill. As they drove they could see for twenty or thirty kilometres all around them – green fields and farms and distant mauve mountains.

'"Redmond the Reliable",' said Katie, slapping Conor playfully on the shoulder. 'If you hadn't made it up, I would have said that you couldn't make it up.'

'You can't complain, girlfriend! I got what we came for, didn't I?'

'Yes, you did. But I'll tell you this. That man scares me, that Guzz Eye McManus. There's not many men who scare me, but he does. When he said he would burn your kennels down, with you in them, I believed him. Thank God you don't really own a kennels.'

* * *

Bartley Doran's farm was at the end of a long lane with overgrown bushes on either side. The further they drove down, the narrower it became, until the brambles were scraping and squeaking against the wings of their Mercedes on both sides.

'Sergeant Browne's not going to be pleased,' said Katie. 'These cars are like his children.'

They reached a rusty five-bar metal gate with a padlock and chain on it, and Conor stopped. 'Let's hope we don't have to leave in a hurry,' he said. 'I don't relish driving all the way back to the main road in reverse.'

On the other side of the gate there was a muddy concrete yard, and a large green-painted house that looked as if it had been extended again and again, with each extension uglier and more out of proportion than the last. Behind the house there was a large steel barn, also painted green, although the paint was flaking; and a row of three wooden sheds.

Katie was about to climb out of the car when her iPhone pinged. She had a message from Detective Dooley. She had asked him to keep her up to date on Keeno's condition in the Mercy. *Keeno no change*, he had texted. Katie closed her eyes for a moment and said a silent prayer to St John of God the patron saint of heart sufferers to keep Keeno alive. She despised the man, but if he died it would cause her more grief than he was worth.

As they left the car and approached the gate, a cheerful-looking man in a tweed cap and a khaki anorak came limping briskly across the yard towards them, lifting a blackthorn stick in greeting. He called out, 'Hold on there folks and I'll unlock it for ye!'

As he came nearer, Katie saw that he had tangled sandy eyebrows and pale green eyes, almost colourless. His nose was squashed and puglike, so that Katie could see up his nostrils, and his cheeks were scarlet and laced with broken veins, as if he spent most of his life standing in a field in a cold north-westerly wind – either that, or drinking a bottle of whiskey every night.

Katie noticed that his anorak was bulked out on the left-hand side, and its collar gaped to the left, and she guessed that he could be wearing a shoulder-holster underneath it.

'It's Redmond, isn't it?' he said, as he reached the gate, although he didn't hold out his hand. 'The Guzz rang me and told me that ye was heading down here. Ye was after that Akita, weren't you, the last time ye was here. When was that?'

'April,' said Conor.

'April, was it? Jesus, the way time flies. Well, I'm fierce sorry that I couldn't let ye borrow him for breeding, but it was far too close to the fights, like. It's the Great Dane you're after this time, isn't it, that's what The Guzz told me. I think we might be able to come to some mutually profitable arrangement with that feller. Look – bring your motor into the yard and then I'll take ye to see him.'

He unlocked the gate, dragging off the chain, while Conor went back to the car.

'And what's *your* name, darling?' he asked Katie.

'Sinéad,' said Katie, and gave him a silly simpering smile, trying to look as if she didn't have a brain in her head.

'I'm Bartley,' said Bartley. 'Bartley Doran. I'll expect Redmond's told ye all about me.'

'Only that you're the best dogfight trainer in the whole of Ireland.'

'Ireland? The whole fecking world, darling. The whole entire planet.'

Conor brought the Mercedes into the yard and swung it around so that it was facing back towards the gate. Katie was glad he had done that. When you were dealing with men like Bartley Doran, you never knew when you might have to leave at very short notice.

Bartley led them around the side of the house to the row of wooden sheds. He opened the door of the first shed and beckoned them inside. Instantly, they were met with a barrage of ferocious barking, and the clanging of dogs throwing themselves up against the sides of their cages.

'Holy Mother of God,' said Katie, but Bartley continued to beckon them in.

'There's nothing to be afraid of, girl. They can't get at ye.'

The shed was divided into six wire cages, much like the cages where Gerry Mulvaney had kept his dogs, except that the dogs in these cages had no bowls of food or water. The smell of urine and faeces was overwhelming, and when Katie stepped inside it brought tears to her eyes and made her retch.

'Sorry about the hong,' said Bartley.

Only three of the dogs were jumping up against the sides of their cages. Two bull mastiffs had heavy steel chains wrapped around their necks instead of collars, and they were too weighed down to jump, although they were barking so hysterically that they sounded as if they were screaming.

The Great Dane was down at the end of the shed, and he was barking, too, but it sounded to Katie as if he were frightened and hungry rather than aggressive. He was full-grown, at least 85 centimetres in height, with a glossy black coat.

Conor went right up to his cage and said, 'Here, boy, here boy. I'm not going to hurt you,' but the Great Dane backed away as far as he could and continued to bark.

'How long would ye be wanting him for?' asked Bartley.

'About a week I'd say. The Great Dane bitch I have at the kennels has just gone into heat. When would you need him back?'

'Ye can take him for two weeks if you like. It depends what we're talking about moneywise.'

Katie couldn't stop herself from retching again, behind her hand. She was so glad that she had said no to Moirin's club sandwich this morning.

'Two grand,' said Conor.

'Three,' said Bartley.

'How about two-and-a-half?'

'Three.'

'Okay, then. Three it is. I'm going into town right now and I'll bring the cash right back for you.'

Before they left the shed, Katie stopped by the bull mastiff's cages. Both of them came right up to the wire and barked at her as if they were ripping the lining out of their throats.

'What are the chains for?' she shouted at Bartley, above the barking. 'They must be desperate heavy for them.'

'That's the whole point, darling,' said Bartley. 'Carrying the weight of them chains, day and night, that builds up their neck and their upper body strength. I have some extra weights, too, which I hang on to their chains when I take them out for a run.'

They stepped outside. As he shut the door of the shed, Bartley said, 'If you're so interested, darling, why don't ye come and take a gander at how I train the dogs up to gameness. I was all ready to do a little baiting when The Guzz rang me.'

Katie already knew that dogfight trainers used extreme cruelty to prepare their animals for a match, and she was aware of what baiting involved. She would have given anything to arrest Bartley Doran there and then, but she knew that it would be far too dangerous without back-up. Apart from that, she would need lengthy and careful surveillance of what he was doing, and independent evidence from witnesses. What was she going to tell the court? 'I saw dogs with no food and nothing to drink and heavy chains round their necks'? The judge would want to know why she hadn't simply reported Bartley to the ISPCA. Case dismissed.

Limping, Bartley led them back towards the large steel barn. As they came nearer, Katie could hear several dogs barking from inside there, too.

'So what's your line of business, darling?' Bartley asked her. 'Or are you a lady of leisure? Or pleasure?'

'I'm a hair stylist,' said Katie.

'Oh, yeah? Where's that, then?'

'Gerrardines, on Liberty Square, in Thurles,' Katie told him, without hesitation. She had done over half an hour's homework for her role as 'Sinéad'.

'Oh! Hair stylist! Maybe I can persuade ye to pop down here now and again and give us a trim,' said Bartley. 'I have to keep me ginger curls in order, if ye know what I mean, wink, wink.'

Katie simply blinked at him as if she didn't have any idea what he was talking about. He opened up one of the barn doors for them and they went inside.

The floor of the barn was thinly covered in sawdust. On the right-hand side a circle of wooden crates formed a makeshift dog-fighting ring, and three bored-looking young men were sitting on the crates, each of them holding a dog tightly on a leash – two bull mastiffs and a Staffordshire bull terrier. Katie thought the young men looked like members of an unsuccessful heavy metal band – all three of them were wearing black T-shirts and their arms were blue with tattoos right up to the elbows. They had silver studs through their cheeks and hair that was shaved at the sides but grown long on top and tied back with elastic bands.

The dogs were barking and snarling and trying to lunge at each other, and Katie could see that it was taking all of the young men's strength to hold them back.

Another dog was tied up by itself to one of the crates – a chocolate-brown poodle. The poodle was in very poor condition – its coat obviously hadn't been clipped in months and it had wood-shavings and twigs and dried leaves clinging to it. It wasn't joining in the cacophony of barking – it was simply standing where it was tethered, shivering.

'All right, lads?' Bartley said to the three young men. 'We'll get started on the baiting directly so. I'm just giving these good people the guided tour.'

'This bastard's only shit on me runner,' said one of the young men, in a slurred Kerry accent.

Bartley laughed. 'Ha! I hope you gave him a fierce good kicking for it!'

'He did that all right,' another of the young men put in, with a cackle. 'Right in the mebs. Never saw a dog jump so high in the whole of me life.'

On the left-hand side of the barn stood several large pieces of equipment that looked as if they had been stolen from a children's playground. There was a tall metal pole with six arms jutting out from the top of it, like a helicopter propeller. From each of these arms a chain was dangling, with a collar on the end of it.

'This is the jenny, or the catmill some folks call it,' said Bartley, limping up to it. 'We chain the dogs up, one dog to each beam, like, except for one beam, which has a bait animal chained up to it, like a cat or a pup or a rabbit maybe, or another dog that's not been showing too much fighting spirit. Of course the dogs try to chase after the bait, and sometimes they go round and round for fecking hours. Once the exercise session's over, we take off their collars and throw them the bait, as a reward, like. If we do that, though, that's the only food we'll give them all day, and that makes them fight each other all the more fiercer for it. A dog will always fight better if he's hungry. And thirsty. And hurt.'

Next to the catmill there was another metal pole, with a powerful spring hanging down from the top of it. Attached to the spring was a ragged piece of brown-and-white cowhide, about the size of a hand-towel, which was torn and pitted with scores of teeth-marks.

'This is the jump pole,' Bartley explained. 'The dogs jump up and bite the leather, and they hang there for as long as they can. It's great for strengthening their jaw-muscles, and the back legs, too, because they keep on jumping up until they've got a good grip.'

'But why do they want to do that?' asked Katie.

'Because they're starving,' said Conor. 'You've heard of shipwrecked sailors eating their own shoes. This is the same.'

'You see that birdcage, darling, down on the floor there?' said Bartley. 'Now and then we'll shut up a cat in it, or a pup, or a chicken, and we'll hang that from the spring instead of the leather. I tell you, once those dogs have got their delph into that cage they'll hang there till hell freezes over. Like Redmond says, they're starving.'

Next to the jump pole there were two professional-size treadmills that Katie could well imagine had been stolen from some gym.

Both of them had chains and collars fastened to them and both of them reeked of dog urine.

'Well, they speak for themselves, these do,' said Bartley. 'We can chain a dog up to one of these and make it run for hours. Great for its heart, like, and its stamina. If it collapses, we leave the treadmill running so it gets battered about, so it soon learns to stay on its feet, even when it's flah'd out.'

'Sounds like me at Gerrardine's, after a long day,' said Katie. 'You wouldn't believe how tiring it is, doing highlights, and having to listen to some auld wan rabbiting on about the cruise she took to Ma-*jork*-ah!'

Pretending to be Sinéad helped her to suppress her rage. The last time she had felt as angry as this was when she had arrested a 41-year-old father in Togher for sexually abusing his own three-year-old daughter.

'We also give the dogs a rake of vitamins and drugs to condition them and stir them up to fight,' said Bartley. 'Testosterone, and weight-gain supplements, and steroids, as well as speed and cocaine. It works out expensive, for sure, but we make so much profit out of each fight that it's nothing at all by comparison. That last fight at Clonlong, like, we netted over three hundred thousand.'

Conor said, 'That's fantastic,' although Katie pretended that she hadn't heard, or wasn't interested even if she had. But she was beginning to see the raid on Sceolan Kennels in a new and very different light. Once the twenty-six stolen dogs had been sold, or ransomed, or trained for dogfights, the dognappers could easily clear three-quarters of a million euros out of it. That meant that it could have been far more profitable than an armed bank robbery or a major drugs deal.

'What's that, up against the wall there, that pole?' asked Conor.

'That?' said Bartley. 'That's what we call a flirtpole. It's hand-held, the flirtpole, for when we're exercising only your single dog. We fix a lure to the end of it like a piece of meat or a dead cat or something and then we drag the lure around us in a circle, and the dog goes chasing after it.'

He laid his hand on Katie's shoulder and gave it a squeeze. 'I'll tell ye this, darling, people say that dogs are intelligent, but if dogs had any fecking sense at all they'd come up to us when we're dragging the flirtpole around and say, "Come here to me, feen, there's no way I'm running around and around after that lump of meat like some kind of four-legged eejit. Take it off the end of that fecking pole and feed it to me right now or I'll bite your fecking ankles."'

'If a dog said that to me, I'd be amazed,' said Conor. 'I haven't yet met a dog that could even say "Give me a slice of Clonakilty black pudding, fried on both sides."'

Katie was about to laugh, as Sinéad would have done, but Bartley turned to Conor and his tone was unmistakably aggressive. 'Don't ye try taking the piss out of me, Redmond, boy. I don't think your beour here would want to see ye ending up as dog bait – would you, darling?'

'Only codding you, Bartley,' said Conor, giving Katie a quick, cautionary look. In spite of his smiling and his over-familiarity, there was nothing pleasant or forgiving about Bartley Doran, and now Katie had seen how quickly he could turn.

Bartley limped back to the dogfight arena. 'Right, let's get this show started, shall we? Dylan – you want to put the bait in the ring, boy?'

Katie moved close to Conor and said, under her breath, 'Mother of God. I know what's going to happen and I don't really want to watch.'

Bartley turned around and beckoned them to come closer. 'C'mere!' he called them, over the ceaseless barking of the three fighting dogs. 'Ye'll like this, I promise ye!'

Dylan handed the leash of his bull mastiff to the young man sitting beside him. He walked around the ring to where the poodle was tethered, and untied it. Then he picked it up and threw it bodily into the middle of the ring, as carelessly as a baggage handler throwing a bag. It fell on to its side, rolled over, and then scrambled unsteadily back on to its feet, still shivering.

The three fighting dogs went berserk. Their barking rose to a harsh and frenzied yammer, more like pneumatic drills than dogs, and they strained at their leads so hard that the two young men who were holding them were pulled unwillingly on to their feet. Terrified, the poodle backed away to the opposite side of the ring, limping like Bartley, and Katie could see that one of its legs was sticking out at an awkward angle, and was probably fractured. When it reached the wooden crates it tried to jump up, but the crates were too high and it could manage only an awkward series of ineffectual little hops.

'Oh Jesus Christ,' said Katie. It was taking every ounce of her self-discipline not to take out her gun and stop this horror immediately.

Bartley raised his left arm in the air. He kept it raised for four or five seconds, for dramatic effect, and then he shouted 'Let 'em go, lads!' and brought it down as if he were starting a race.

The three young men unclipped the fighting dogs' collars. The dogs instantly stopped barking and shot across the ring. The poodle made a last desperate effort to jump over the crates, but it couldn't summon up enough strength, and the fighting dogs tore into it as if they hadn't been fed for days. Katie guessed that Bartley had starved them on purpose, just for this.

One of the bull mastiffs bit into the side of the poodle's neck, while the Staffie crunched into its spine. The other bull mastiff went for its belly, tearing away curls of brown hair and triangular flaps of skin. The poodle screamed like a badly injured child, and so the first bull mastiff clamped its jaws into its face, shaking its head violently from side to side. It ripped off the poodle's nose and most of the flesh from its cheek, and dragged out its left eye on a string of optic nerve.

Bartley whacked his blackthorn stick on top of the crates in delight. 'What do ye think of that, then? There's a sight for sore eyes, wouldn't you say? There's a fecking sight for sore eyes!'

The three young men were whooping and laughing and whistling to the fighting dogs to encourage them. 'Come on, Tyson, bite his fecking head off!'

Blood was spraying around the dogs as if they were being attacked by a swarm of angry red wasps. Their assault on the poodle was relentless, and Katie had to close her eyes. Even with her eyes closed, though, she could still hear snapping and wrenching noises, and the sound of the fighting dogs snarling and guzzling and growling as they ripped the poodle apart. But still, somehow, the poodle kept on screaming.

Conor put his arm around her shoulders and spoke quietly into her ear. 'I know how much this disgusts you, Sinéad, but Bartley has his eye on you and you have to look like you're enjoying it.'

Katie knew that he was right. She opened her eyes and looked across at Bartley and gave him a thumbs-up and grinned. Bartley had obviously been watching her, because his expression changed from suspicious to satisfied, and he lifted his stick in acknowledgement.

The poodle made one last effort to escape from its tormentors. Half-blind, with its sides hanging in shreds, it twisted itself free from them and managed to hump its way to the middle of the ring. Its belly had been torn open and it was dragging its glistening intestines through the sawdust. Again, Katie felt an almost irresistible urge to pull out her revolver, if only to shoot the poodle and save it any more agony.

Conor must have sensed her despair, because he squeezed her arm. She knew that he adored dogs, too, and that it was just as painful for him to witness this baiting as it was for her.

The poodle stood still, ruined, with its head bowed and one ear hanging loose. The three fighting dogs jumped on it again, and it dropped sideways on to the floor. All Katie could see after that was their wrestling blood-spattered bodies and their stumpy tails sticking up as if they were sexually excited.

Bartley let them ravage the poodle for a minute or two longer, but then he pushed aside one of the crates and limped into the ring. 'That's enough, now!' he shouted at them. 'Fecking get off out of it! Ye've had your fill of fun, ye greedy bastards!'

The fighting dogs took no notice of him, so he lifted his

blackthorn stick and started to beat them on their backs, so hard that they were yowling in pain and backing away from him.

'Come on, lads,' Bartley said to the three young men. 'Get their leads on and lock them back up in their cages.'

He turned to Katie and Conor and said, 'They didn't do bad at all, did they? Except they shouldn't have let up like that and give the bait a chance to get away. When they're in a real fight, that could be fecking fatal, I tell ye. Still – a couple more sessions like this and they'll be up to gameness, I'd say.'

The three young men clipped the dogs' leashes back on and dragged them away. After they had gone, Bartley took Katie and Conor back outside. As they left the barn, Katie looked back at the grisly remains of the poodle and wished that she were able to take a photograph of it. Even if she never managed to arrest Bartley for handling stolen animals and dog fighting, a least the ISPCA could try to prosecute him for cruelty.

Conor zipped up his windcheater and said, 'Thanks for the show, Bartley. That was ten times better than anything that's been on the telly.'

'True that,' said Katie. 'Made my hair stand on end, I'll tell you, and I'm a professional stylist.' She couldn't think of anything to say that was stupider than that.

'Like, most people are far too fecking soft on their dogs,' said Bartley, as he accompanied them back to their car. 'The Lord specifically created dogs for the service of man, and that's all there is to it. Why, even the Lord's name is "dog" spelled backwards. Dogs are for sniffing out rats and racing and fighting and guiding blind feckers across the road. They're not for eating you out of house and home and then dossing down on your couch and farting like the Uillean pipes.'

'Well, we're heading into Cashel now to fetch your grade for you,' said Conor. 'It won't take us long. I'm pure pleased to have found a Great Dane as fine as that one. Who'd you get him from, by the way? I wouldn't mind seeing if they have any more as good as that.'

Katie took out her iPhone and held it up in front of her face so that she could pretend to primp her hair, as if she wasn't at all interested in how Bartley was going to answer that question. But having that one question answered was the only reason they had driven all the way up here to Ballyknock, and braved a face-to-face meeting with Guzz Eye McManus, and witnessed Bartley's gruesome dog baiting. She was so tense waiting to hear what Bartley was going to say that she stopped tweaking her hair and held her breath.

'Oh, sure, yeah,' said Bartley. 'Ye have only to ask him and he'll find ye whatever breed you want. He doesn't come cheap, mind, and he doesn't expect ye to be asking him any nosey-parker questions about where he gets them from, the dogs.'

'Maybe I know him already,' said Conor.

'Well, happen ye do, but he doesn't advertise himself on the interweb or anything like that.'

'So?' said Conor.

'So, like, what?'

'So what's his name?'

'Oh. Didn't I say? Lorcan Fitzgerald. That's your man.'

'So how can I contact him, this Lorcan Fitzgerald?'

'Hold on,' said Bartley, taking his mobile phone out of his pocket. 'I have a number for him here. What you do is, you ring this number and tell him who you are and what you're after, and if he likes the sound of you, he'll ring you back.'

'And if he doesn't like the sound of you?'

'Then he won't ring you back. Simple as that.'

* * *

They drove back down the narrow claustrophobic lane to Palmer's Hill and then into the town of Cashel. Neither of them spoke for a while, although Conor reached across and laid his hand on top of Katie's hand, just for a moment. It was almost like a benediction.

They parked outside the large grey AIB Bank in Cashel's Main Street, but before they climbed out of the car, Katie said, 'Holy

Mother of God, Conor. I've seen some vile things done to innocent animals in my life, but *that*.'

'I know, it's beyond horrible, but it's happening all the time,' Conor told her. 'These dog fighters go to animal shelters and make out they want to adopt a dog, or a cat. Either that, or they'll look online for people advertising unwanted animals "free to good home". Of course all they really want them for is bait.'

Katie said, 'That Bartley. I swear to God I could have shot him.'

'I know. But I think you showed amazing restraint. Jesus, you even managed to *smile* at the fellow, and that must have taken some effort. The problem is, he trains dogs for dog fighting because it makes him a fortune, all tax-free, and he knows he's going to get away with it. Like you told me yourself, the Garda don't have the time or the budget to go chasing after people like him who are mistreating dogs. And what we saw today, that's only the tip of the iceberg. If a bait animal is fit enough to fight back, Bartley will wrap its snout with duct tape, so that it can't bite one of his precious fighting dogs. Either that, or he'll yank out all of its teeth with a pair of pliers. No anaesthetic. And even if it manages to survive a baiting, he'll throw it to his dogs to kill afterwards.'

'I don't think I want to hear any more. Let's go in and get those two scumbags their money.'

They went into the bank and Katie asked to see the manager. He was young and bald and bespectacled and very obliging. She showed him her ID, and he confirmed it by ringing Chief Superintendent MacCostagáin at Anglesea Street and the manager of AIB in South Mall, where the Cork Garda and Katie herself both had accounts. Within less than twenty minutes, Katie and Conor walked out of the bank with four thousand euros in cash in a Tesco bag.

Katie saw a maroon-painted pub on the opposite side of the street, Pat Fox's Bar. She really could have done with a drink right then, but she knew that they were pressed for time, and even as 'Sinéad', she didn't think it was a good idea to go back to Bartley Doran and Guzz Eye McManus with vodka on her breath.

Before they got into the car, though, she said, 'Don't forget the Peggy's Legs. You don't want those Pavee kids letting our tyres down.'

They crossed the road, went into SuperValu and bought twelve Peggy's Legs – sticks of hard caramel-flavoured rock with the slogan *Peggy's Leg that never wore a garter* on the label.

'I used to love them when I was a kid but I've almost forgotten what they taste like,' said Conor, as they drove back along Palmer's Hill. 'I should have bought a few for myself.'

'Just as well you didn't,' said Katie. 'They're murder on the teeth.'

* * *

While they had been away in Cashel, Bartley had dosed up the Great Dane with Zylkene tranquilliser tablets. It was so dopey that it could barely walk, and it took all three of Bartley's young assistants to heave its huge haunches into the back of their Mercedes. Once it was inside, it sprawled out on the seats and fell asleep.

'I gave him double the recommended dose,' said Bartley, as he fastidiously counted his money, licking his thumb every now and then as he turned over the new €100 notes. 'He's a hell of a big beast, though, and you've a way to go back to Carrigahorig, haven't ye, an hour and a half at least. Make sure ye give him plenty of water when he wakes up. He'll be dehydrated, like, and confused, too. I don't suppose he'll feel like shagging much for a day or two, till his head's cleared.'

They left Bartley's place and drove back to the Ballyknock Halting Site. The children ran over as soon as they saw them, and Conor called out, '*All-a-bah!*' again and tossed the Peggy's Legs into the air. Normally, Katie would have been amused to see the children scrambling after them, because it reminded her so much of her own childhood, playing rats-and-rabbits and shadows in the alley at the back of her parents' house, but she was still tense and sick to her stomach after watching the poodle being torn apart.

Guzz Eye McManus took his commission without even bothering to count it, as if it were a long-overdue debt that Conor was giving him, and if it were short, Conor would live to regret it.

'You have the Great Dane then, Mr O'Dea?' he said, puffing at the stub of his cigar. From the way that he called Conor 'Mr O'Dea', Katie guessed that he had checked up on the Mercedes' number plate while they were away.

'He's in the back of the car, Guzz. Dreaming about bones, probably.'

'Make sure you fetch him back to Bartley within three weeks so. He's going to need at least a month to train him up.'

Still Katie said nothing, but between them, Bartley and The Guzz had given her a rough idea of when the next dogfight was going to be held.

When they left Ballyknock, Katie told Conor to drive northwards for a while, as if they were really going back to Carrigahorig. She kept turning around in her seat to make sure that they weren't being followed by one of Guzz Eye McManus's men, but the road behind them was empty, and when they reached the intersection with the M8 at Garranmore, they joined the motorway and headed south.

'You can step on it now,' said Katie. 'If you get caught for speeding, I'll make sure that the penalty points are wiped off your licence.' It was a joke, but a bitter one, considering the scandal of wiped-off penalty points that had led to the resignation of the previous Garda Commissioner, Martin Callinan.

Conor said, 'Serious?' and when she nodded he put his foot down and they sped back to Cork city at over 120 kph, with the Great Dane snoring stentoriously in the back. Katie felt wrung out, but she didn't want to close her eyes because she knew what would happen if she did: she would see the gory remains of that poodle, as vividly as if she had managed to take a photograph of it.

Her iPhone pinged. It was another text from Detective Dooley: KEENO STILL OUT. That was one relief, anyway.

It had been dark for over an hour by the time they arrived back at Anglesea Street. The Great Dane was still sleeping but he had stopped snoring and was making little wuffling noises, as if he were gradually returning to consciousness. Katie had phoned ahead to Sergeant Nolan of the Dog Support Unit, who was waiting for them in the car park with a van, ready to take the Great Dane to the unit's kennels.

Like the German Shepherd and the Viszla that they had recovered from Gerry Mulvaney, the Great Dane would be thoroughly checked by a vet, and treated for any illnesses or injuries or drug abuse, but he would not be returned to his owners. Katie had stipulated that none of the dogs' owners should have their pets returned to them yet, or even be notified that they had been found. She didn't want the dognappers to get any inkling of how far they had progressed in their investigation, and in particular she didn't want Guzz Eye McManus or Bartley Doran to realise that they had been duped by 'Redmond' and 'Sinéad'.

Sergeant Browne came waddling up to them in his yellow high-viz jacket as they parked the Mercedes. He saw at once that its sides were badly scratched.

'Jesus,' he said. 'You didn't go driving it through a barbed-wire fence, did you?'

'Sorry about that, sergeant,' said Katie. 'Collateral damage.'

'That's going to need a full respray, like,' said Sergeant Browne, running his fingertips along the scratches. Then he opened the back door of the car and said, 'God Almighty! I don't believe it! That hound's pissed all over the seats!'

Katie and Conor left him to fuss over his scratched and soiled Mercedes and went inside the station. They stood in the reception area facing each other. Although it was still so early in the evening, a very drunk man was having his details taken at the desk, with a uniformed garda to support him on either side. He was singing the chorus from 'The Fields of Athenry', over and over.

'*Our love was on the wing, we had dreams and songs to sing, it's so lonely round the fields of Athenry.*'

Conor said to Katie, 'What are you doing now? Do you want to have something to eat, and then come back to the guest house with me?'

She was tempted to reach up and stroke his beard, and kiss him, but instead she said, 'Not tonight, Conor. I have to get my team started on tracking down this Lorcan Fitzgerald. Then I have to take myself home. I do have other people in my life I have to take care of.'

She didn't say that after today's experience at Bartley's she had no appetite at all, and that she was feeling too stressed and hormonal to think about making love to him.

'Okay,' he said. 'I think I'll walk back to Summerhill. I could use some fresh air and some thinking time. I won't kiss you, not here in front of your fellow officers, but consider yourself kissed.'

'You too,' smiled Katie. 'I'll call you later so, when I'm home.'

'*Low lie the fields... of Athenry... where once we watched the small free birds fly...*' sang the drunk, and then fell over backwards.

Twenty-nine

John was delighted to have her home so early, and he couldn't resist giving her a demonstration of how well he could make his way around the house on his stumps. Before she had even had the chance to take off her raincoat, he had shown her how he could walk in and out of the nursery and into the kitchen.

He had combed his hair and shaved and he was wearing the paprika-coloured sweater that she had bought him for his birthday last year, and neatly rolled-up pyjama trousers.

'And now –' he said, triumphantly, '– now I'm going to pour you a well-deserved drink. Sit down, make yourself comfortable. I'm not an invalid any more. I'm your partner again, fully mobile.'

Katie hung up her coat and sat down on the couch. Barney sat close to her, and she tugged at his ears and stroked him and couldn't help thinking about the poodle at Bartley's place.

John poured her a large Smirnoff Black Label with a slice of lime in it and brought it over for her, although he was still unsteady and halfway across the room he staggered and nearly spilled it.

'I should be having my first prosthetic fitting by the end of next week,' he told her, lifting himself up on to the couch next to her. 'When's your next weekend off? We could drive down to the Ring of Kerry maybe and have lunch at that lobster restaurant you like.'

Bridie appeared in the doorway and said, 'I'll be away now, Katie. I defrosted that chicken pie like you asked me. I'll see you tomorrow so.'

'Thanks a million, Bridie. Goodnight.'

Katie sipped at her drink but it didn't relax her in the way that it usually did, and for some reason it tasted bitter. Maybe the lime was off. She put it down on the coffee table and sat up very straight, clasping her hands tightly together.

John laid his hand on her shoulder and said, 'How was Tipperary? You look like you've had a hard day.'

'You could say that, yes. It wasn't easy.'

'How about I put that chicken pie in the oven? You'll feel better once you've had something to eat.'

'Yes, put it in the oven. You have some. I'm not at all hungry.'

'I'm not going to eat if you're not going to eat. I know how hard your job is, Katie, but you mustn't allow it to stress you out so much. You have to take better care of yourself.'

Katie turned to him and snapped, 'I *can't* take better care of myself! How do you expect me to take better care of myself when I have to take care of so many other people? I have to take care of the whole of Cork, for the love of God – and *you*, on top of that.'

John took his hand away. 'I'm sorry. I didn't realise I was that much of a burden.'

'You're not. No more than anybody else. I've had a traumatic day, that's all.'

'Then let me help you get over it. Come on, Katie, I'm your partner. I'm your lover.'

Katie took a deep breath. There were a thousand hurtful things she could have said to him then, but she was too tired to start an argument. All she wanted was for John not to be there any more, but where could he go? She couldn't throw him out of the house.

'I'm going to take a shower,' she said, standing up.

'Katie—'

'Heat that pie up, John. I'll talk to you after.'

She went into her bedroom, closed the door, and stood with her fists and her forehead pressed against the door panel, her teeth clenched with anger. She wasn't angry with John. She was angry at herself for not having the courage to tell him how she really felt. As soon as he had been delivered to her door, she had realised that she no longer loved him, but now that she had met Conor, she didn't even *like* him any more.

She undressed and put on her dressing-gown, and she was about to go to the bathroom when her iPhone played 'Tá Mo Chleamhnas a Dhéanamh'. It was Detective Dooley. She had given him Lorcan Fitzgerald's number before she left the station, to see if he could trace him.

'It's a stealth phone number, ma'am, so we haven't been able to get a fix on it. One of those Nokia 5000-D2s I shouldn't wonder.'

'Well, that doesn't entirely surprise me. Is there any record of him on Pulse? There must be a good chance that he's had previous convictions.'

'There's Lorcan Fitzgerald the footballer who plays for Bohemians in Dublin, but I can't imagine for a moment that he's into dognapping. Altogether in the whole country there's two hundred and eight more Lorcan Fitzgeralds. About a third of them we can eliminate because of their age or where they live or their professions – you know, if they're a priest, like, or somebody whose job wouldn't allow them the time to go dognapping, like a doctor or a firefighter or a publican maybe, or a chef. I have Scanlan and Markey checking through the rest.'

'We can ring him,' said Katie, 'but let's leave that until tomorrow morning. I'll have the pet detective do it, because he knows all the ins and outs of the dognapping business and he'll sound more believable than any of us.'

'You trust him, this pet detective?'

'Trust him? Oh, yes, Robert. I trust him.'

* * *

Katie showered and washed her hair and then put on her pale blue nightgown and went into the living-room to talk to John. He was no longer there, although she hadn't heard him clumping down the hallway. He wasn't in the kitchen, either, and when she looked in the fridge she saw that he hadn't taken out the chicken pie.

She went to the nursery door, and gently knocked. There was

no answer, so after a few seconds she opened it. John was lying on the bed, his eyes closed, still wearing his paprika sweater and his rolled-up pyjama trousers. She went across and bent over him to make sure that he was breathing. Although she didn't think that he was suicidal, his painkillers and sedatives were very strong and he might accidentally have taken an overdose.

As she was leaning over him, he opened his eyes and stared at her.

'John?' she said. 'Mother of God, you made my heart go sideways there for a second!'

He didn't answer, but continued to stare at her, unblinking. Then he closed his eyes again.

'*John?*' she repeated, but he still didn't answer. Either he was asleep, and his eyes had opened as an unconscious response to her coming so close to him, or else he was awake and he was deliberately ignoring her.

She waited for a while to see if he would open them again, but he continued to lie motionless, breathing steadily, until she had to assume that he really was sleeping.

Very quietly, she tiptoed out of the nursery, but she left the door about ten centimetres open, in case he called out for her during the night.

* * *

As exhausted as she was, she found it impossible to get to sleep herself. She was still awake when the clock in the hallway chimed midnight, and so she switched on her bedside light again and lay there listening to the rain pattering against the window. She couldn't get the picture of the dismembered poodle out of her mind, and she was also wondering when Maureen Callahan was going to call her and tell her that the arms shipment had been delivered.

She had roughed out a plan for a raid, but until she knew where the weapons and explosives were going to be stored, it was almost impossible for her to work out how many officers she was going to need. She would certainly have to call on the Regional

Support Unit for armed officers, and bomb disposal experts from Collins Barracks. But there could be all kinds of tactical problems, depending on the building they were raiding – whether it was located in a residential area where civilians might be put at risk, or out in the countryside where the Callahans would be able to see them coming from a distance.

On top of that, she was still deeply suspicious of Maureen Callahan, and the way in which she had been put in touch with her. Maybe she would have been more trusting if the contact hadn't been arranged through Jimmy O'Reilly. In his early days in the Gardaí, Jimmy O'Reilly had been an outstanding officer, promoted rapidly through the ranks until he had been appointed Chief Superintendent of the Wexford Division and then Assistant Commissioner of the Southern Region. But Katie had discovered that he had been borrowing money from the gang leader Bobby Quilty to pay off his boyfriend's gambling debts, and now she wouldn't trust him to fetch her a cup of coffee from the canteen without spitting in it.

She felt equally wary of Detective Superintendent O'Malley, of the SDU. She was prepared to accept that she was being paranoid, especially with all of the stress that she was facing at work and at home, but her father had often told her, 'Trust your nose, Kathleen – more than your eyes, and more than your ears. Somebody may look like Saint Dionysus, and they may sound pure plausible, but if what they're telling you doesn't *smell* right, then it won't be right.'

Eventually, she switched off the light, turned over in bed, and managed to drop off to sleep. She was woken just after 4:20 by John clumping down the hallway to use the toilet, but then she dozed for another two hours. She had a vivid dream that she was walking very quickly along Lavitt's Quay. The sky was grey and a strong wind was blowing. She was trying to catch up with her late husband Paul, who was hurrying ahead of her with his head bowed and his coat flapping. She wanted to tell him about Bartley Doran and how horrible the dog-baiting had been, but even when she called out to him he wouldn't slow down. He disappeared around the corner of St Paul's Avenue and when she turned the corner after him he was gone.

Of course he's gone, she told herself, in her dream. *He's dead.*

Thirty

To Katie's relief, Bridie came early and so she was able to leave the house while John was still asleep. She wouldn't have known what to say to him, or how to act. Should she say sorry, or should she pretend that last night hadn't happened, and be smiley and bright? And should she mention that he had opened his eyes and stared at her, when he was sleeping?

She reached her office at ten minutes to eight, but she still hadn't heard from Maureen Callahan about the arms shipment. Maureen had told her that it would probably be delivered sometime during the night, but it was possible that there had been some delay, and it hadn't yet arrived.

Today was Moirin's day off, but she had left Katie some letters to sign and this month's financial report. Katie didn't open the financial report immediately. She knew that she had seriously overspent, mostly on overtime, because of the extra hours that her drugs team had been putting in. In a way, her investment had paid off: they had made over thirty per cent more arrests for drug offences this October than they had in October last year, but she still felt that she was swimming against the tide.

Detective Ó Doibhilin knocked at her door. His hair was sticking up and his tie was askew and one of his shirt tails was hanging out.

'Good morning to you, ma'am,' he said. 'Glad you're in early.'

'State of you, Michael,' said Katie. 'You haven't been in a scrap, have you?'

Detective Ó Doibhilin hastily tucked in his shirt tail. 'It's been a bit of a night, that's all. There were six students taken into the Mercy, just after two o'clock. They were having a house party in Greenmount and according to their pals they'd been hounding N-Bombs like they were sweets.'

'What kind of a condition are they in?'

'Vomiting and heart arrhythmia mostly. Two of them had to be given CPR. They're all going to survive, but it was touch and go for one of them.'

'Jesus. Those N-Bombs can give you permanent brain damage if you're not careful. Did you find out who supplied them?'

'We have, yes, and I'm dead sound about that. He's downstairs right now. White male, mid-twenties by the look of him. We caught up with him on Oliver Plunkett Street, right in the middle of trying to sell more stuff. He had a satchel bulging with N-Bombs and Smiles and Cimbi-5 and Solaris. I'll be handing them over to the Technical Bureau as soon as they get in, for analysis.'

'Good work, Michael. The rest of the kids at the party – were they all students?'

'About thirty of them, most of them from UCC. They told us that the campus has been flooded with psychedelic drugs in the past couple of months, and they reckoned that at least eighty per cent of their friends have been taking them.'

'I think I'll have to have a word with Dr Murphy about this, although I don't think there's much that he can do about it. I mean, he's the president of UCC, but he can't exactly go searching through his students' pockets, can he? Do the kids have any notion at all where all these uppers are coming from?'

'No, they don't. But they were so devastated about these six almost dying on them that I'm pretty sure they would have told us if they'd known. They didn't hesitate to give us a good description of the fellow who was dishing out the N-Bombs at the party. They didn't know his real name. They only called him Boxty. He has red hair sticking up like a bog-brush and a yellow leather coat so it wasn't too hard for us to catch up with him, especially since he was out on Oliver Plunkett Street, flogging his stuff outside the Old Oak.'

'Thanks, Michael. Let me know when you've interviewed him, won't you? It might be a good idea to have Scanlan with you, too. She has a knack of winkling incriminating evidence out of suspects without them even realising what they're telling her.'

'I will, sure,' said Detective Ó Doibhilin. 'Oh – and by the way – no movement from herself.'

'Okay. Keep your eye on her, though, won't you?'

Detective Ó Doibhilin gave Katie a military-style salute and left her office. Katie went back to signing her letters, but only a few seconds after he had gone there was another knock at her door. She looked up and to her surprise and delight Kyna Ni Nuallán came in, her arms stretched out wide, suntanned and laughing.

Katie pushed her chair back and stood up, and the two of them hugged each other and kissed – on each cheek at first, and then slowly and tenderly, on the lips.

Kyna had grown her blonde hair long, but had tied it back with a red-and-yellow scarf. She was wearing a dark red pea-coat and tight blue jeans and boots. Because of her suntan, she looked less like one of the fairy-folk and more like a fashion model. Her nose had been broken by one of Bobby Quilty's thugs, which was why she had been away on sick leave, but it had now healed perfectly straight.

'You don't know how pleased I am to see you,' said Katie. She had to wipe tears from her eyes with her fingertips.

'It was so good to get away like that. It helped me to sort my head out, like, do you know what I mean? I think I was suffering from post-traumatic stress, I really do. It was the helplessness, like, being abducted like that. That was the first and only time I ever felt helpless in the whole of my life.'

'And?' said Katie. 'You still want to come back here to Anglesea Street?'

Kyna smiled. 'Yes, I still do.'

'And what about us? What about you and me? We have to be realistic.'

'I know. But inside the station we can be Detective Superintendent and Detective Sergeant, and when we're outside of it we can be just good friends.'

'You're sure?'

Kyna nodded. 'How's John?' she asked. 'Have they fixed him up with his artificial legs yet?'

Katie closed the financial report and put it away in a drawer. 'Come and have a coffee and I'll bring you up to speed.'

* * *

They went into the Market Tavern across the road and sat down by the window.

'So sad they closed the Honeycomb Café,' said Kyna, as the barman brought them two cups of coffee. The Honeycomb had been a favourite with the gardaí and the firefighters from the fire station next door, but the building had been sold and it was now a Japanese restaurant called Sakura.

'How far do you think your average guard can run after a criminal when he's had nothing to eat but noodles and sushi? He'd be puffed out after two hundred yards and the feen in the tracksuit would be laughing his head off at him. But you give that same guard a bacon-and-sausage sandwich and a strong cup of tea and he'd be sprinting along like the Terminator. Unstoppable.'

She poured three sachets of brown sugar into her coffee and noisily stirred it. 'Anyway,' she said, 'what's the latest?'

Katie told her that John was waiting to have his prosthetic legs fitted, but no more than that. She didn't tell her that her love for him, once so passionate, had completely turned to ashes. After that, she brought her up to date on the dognapping from Sceolan Kennels, and how she had kick-boxed Keeno. Then she described her trip with Conor Ó Máille up to Ballyknock yesterday, and the baiting of the poodle. She explained that she had brought in Conor to help them find out who the dognappers were, but she made no mention of spending the night with him in the Gabriel Guest House, nor how she felt about him.

Kyna looked at her keenly, holding her coffee cup in both hands. 'You *like* him, don't you, this pet detective? I can tell.'

Katie could feel herself blushing, but there was nothing she could do about it. 'He's good-looking, there's no question about that.'

'And you like him?'

'Yes. I'd be lying to you if I said I didn't.'

'So what does John think about him?'

'John doesn't know he exists.'

'Aha. And you're not going to tell him about him, are you?'

'Do you know something, Kyna, you were always a good interrogator. Young Pádraigin Scanlan, she's good, too. I've always said that women can get much more out of suspects than men.'

'But you're not a suspect. Or are you? Something's happened between you and this Conor Ó Máille, hasn't it?'

'I've told you I like him. Let's leave it at that, shall we? How was Gran Canaria? I can't believe how well you're looking, and you're not even wearing any make-up.'

Kyna reached into her bag and took out her mobile phone. 'Here – let me show you some pictures. Like I told you, the hotel was wall-to-wall with holidaymakers from Cork, so I didn't have any trouble with the language, except for one fellow from Knocknaheeny who kept trying to chat me up. I couldn't understand a single word that he was saying so I asked him to speak slower, and do you know what he said? "*Let's... go... halves... on... a... bastard.*"'

She came and sat close to Katie so that she could flick through her holiday pictures with her. As usual, she smelled of Miracle, by Lancôme. Katie briefly wondered what it would be like, to have her as a partner, instead of a man. Spending all of their time together, going on holidays together, sleeping together.

Kyna showed her selfies taken by the hotel pool, and pictures of the meals that she had eaten, including ceviche and sea-scorpion. There was a selfie of her by the sea, wearing a wide-brimmed straw hat and a tiny black bikini. The last two pictures showed her at Las Palmas Airport, late last night, waiting to catch her flight home. She was holding up a bright orange cocktail in the bar, as if she were drinking a toast.

Katie said, 'Stall it a moment. Let me look at those again.'

Kyna handed her the mobile phone and Katie flicked back to the bar pictures and enlarged them. Sitting close behind Kyna at the bar, with his own mobile phone pressed to his ear, was a young man in a black leather jacket. His black hair was shaved so short that he looked almost bald, and he had a snub nose and a distinctive pattern of moles on his right cheek, like a star chart of Cassiopeia. Katie recognised him at once.

'Do you know who that is? That fellow you're sitting next to?'

Kyna frowned at the picture and then shook her head. 'Haven't a notion. Never seen him before in my life. Don't even remember seeing him then.'

'That's Branán O'Flynn. One of the O'Flynn crime family.'

'Well? Even criminals have to take a break, now and again. And they can probably afford to, unlike the rest of us.'

'Branán O'Flynn is supposed to have been shot dead by the Callahan family.'

'He doesn't look very shot dead to me. He's talking on the phone and he's laughing.'

Katie handed the phone back to her. 'You're not going to believe this,' she said, and she told her all about the message from the SDU that Jimmy O'Reilly was supposed to have passed on to her, and her conversation on the phone with Maureen Callahan, and how she had met her at Blackrock Castle to be told about the arms shipment, and why Maureen wanted to take revenge on her father and her sisters.

Kyna sat listening and slowly shaking her head. When Katie told her that she was waiting even now for Maureen Callahan to ring her and tell her where and when the guns were delivered, she put down her coffee cup and said, '*Dia ár sábháil*. God save us. It's a set-up, isn't it? I'd give you odds on it. It's that Jimmy O'Reilly, setting you up. You were right to be so suspicious.'

'I had a quare feeling about it right from the beginning,' Katie told her. 'When you think about it, somebody like Maureen Callahan would *never* come to the guards to get her revenge. Not in a million years. If Branán O'Flynn really was her boyfriend, and if her sisters really had arranged for him to be shot, she would pay some shamfeen to burn their houses down, or shoot their pets, or even shoot *them*.'

'So you don't believe there's any arms shipment at all?'

'I doubt it. If there was – and we seized it because of Maureen Callahan's tip-off – her life wouldn't be worth a thrawneen, would it? She's anything but stupid, so she knows that. That's what I've been thinking in the back of my mind all along.'

'But what if you *had* believed her? Or what if you simply hadn't been able to find any evidence that she wasn't telling you the truth? You would have *had* to set up a raid, wouldn't you?'

'I wouldn't have had any choice,' said Katie.

'Spot on. Like – supposing there really *was* an arms shipment, but you didn't take any action to confiscate it, even though Maureen Callahan had tipped you off? You'd be right in the shite, excuse my language. But supposing there *wasn't*, and you spent thousands of euros mounting a raid that came to nothing at all? You'd *still* be in the shite. So you couldn't win, like, could you, either way.'

Katie said, 'True that, Kyna. After the hames I made of those three raids in Operation Trident, I would probably find myself reprimanded, or suspended, or even sacked.'

'There you are – that's the set-up. Any money you wouldn't find Maureen Callahan supporting your story. Even if she did, she doesn't exactly have a glowing reputation for public service, does she?'

'I bet she would swear that she never spoke to me on the phone, or met me, either,' said Katie. She was growing quite angry now that she had seen that picture of Branán O'Flynn. 'I *also* bet that Superintendent O'Malley would deny that she ever spoke to any undercover SDU officer, and so he couldn't have passed on a message about her to Jimmy O'Reilly. And I *further* bet that Jimmy

O'Reilly would say that he never passed on any such message to me. He would probably say that I'm just out to undermine his authority, like I did with Acting Chief Superintendent Bryan Molloy. Except that Jimmy O'Reilly deserves to be undermined, just like Molloy deserved it.'

'So what are you going to do?' Kyna asked her.

'Wait and see. Maureen Callahan doesn't know that we have a picture that proves that she was lying. Neither does Jimmy O'Reilly. And I've taken some precautions to protect myself.'

'Such as?'

'When I went to meet Maureen Callahan at Blackrock Castle, I asked Michael Ó Doibhilin to follow me and attach a GPS tracker to her car, one of those mini ones. We've been keeping an eye on her movements ever since – not that she's done anything very exciting, except to visit her sisters and go to Douglas Village for the messages.'

They finished their coffee and then they went back across the road to the station. As she walked back along the corridor to her office, Katie received a text message from Detective Dooley that Keeno was still comatose. Almost immediately afterwards she had another text from Dr Kelley, saying that she had printed several 3-D versions of the knife that had been used to stab Martin Ó Brádaigh and that she would be bringing them over before she took the train back to Dublin.

Chief Superintendent MacCostagáin was away for the weekend, but Katie promised Kyna that she would talk to him on Monday about her rejoining her team.

'I can't see that there's going to be any problem,' she smiled. 'Denis MacCostagáin loves you nearly as much as I do.'

'I'll head on then,' said Kyna. 'I have a fridge full of empty food so I need to go to Tesco. Are you around tomorrow?'

'I don't know. It depends what happens today. Can you just email me that picture of you and Branán O'Flynn before you go?'

When Kyna had left, she went to the window of her office and stood there for a while, thinking. It was a windy day, as windy as it had been in her dream about Paul, and the clouds were clearing away, so that the Elysian, the tallest building in Ireland, was shining pale green.

It was 9:00 am now, so Conor would probably be up and showered and have had his freshly laid eggs for breakfast. She needed to ring him and ask him to come down to the station so that he could make a call to Lorcan Fitzgerald. He could see if Fitzgerald was interested in some pedigree Shar-peis or Akitas for fighting, and arrange to meet. If Conor actually brought the dogs with him, and Fitzgerald agreed to buy them, he could be arrested and brought in for questioning.

She was about to call Sergeant Nolan of the Dog Support Unit to see what dogs he could rustle up for her when her iPhone rang. It was Maureen Callahan and as before she sounded breathless, as if she were smoking, or in a panic, or both.

'DS Maguire? It's Maureen. They arrived about an hour ago, the guns. They had some kind of a hold-up, I don't know what it was. But any road it's all been delivered and stored away. My father and my sisters are going up there at half-past three to look it all over, and also to meet some fellows from Armagh who've told us they're interested in making them an offer for the Skorpions.'

'Half-past three,' said Katie, trying to sound calm. 'I see. And what's the location?'

'Sarsfield Court Industrial Estate. It's the second warehouse on the left when you drive in. It's painted green and it has a sign on it saying Boyle Power Tools but they've gone out of business now and my family rents it.'

'I have you,' said Katie. At the same time she had clicked on to Google Maps and was checking the street view of Sarsfield Court Industrial Estate to see if Maureen was giving her an accurate description. There it was – a small green warehouse signposted Boyle Power Tools. It had a wide forecourt and it also looked as if there was clear access all around it, so if she had wanted to launch a raid, she could have organised it so that gardaí burst into the building from all sides simultaneously, and nobody inside would be able to escape.

'Where will you be?' she asked Maureen.

'I'll be far, far away, don't you worry. I don't want Bree or my father to get the idea that I had anything to do with this.'

'Fair play, Maureen. You can ring me later if you like, to see how it went. Mind you, you'll probably see it on the news.'

'You won't be mentioning my name, will you? Not to the news people.'

'Maureen, this is strictly between you and me. Nobody else will ever find out where we got our information from, even when this comes to court.'

'Thank you, DS Maguire, and bless you. You're the only guard that I've ever liked, or ever trusted. All I can wish for after today is that my sisters tell me where Branán's body is buried, so that I can give him the proper funeral that he deserves, and lay flowers on his grave.'

'That's very touching, Maureen,' said Katie. 'I won't let you down, believe me.'

Maureen hung up without saying anything else. Katie sat at her desk staring at her phone for a few moments. In spite of what she now believed, there was still a remote possibility that Maureen had been telling her the truth as she saw it. What if she really had been doing a line with Branán O'Flynn, but instead of killing him, her father and sisters had paid him to stay away from Cork for a week or three, just to scare her, and teach her a lesson?

What if the warehouse at Sarsfield Court Industrial Estate really was crammed with automatic weapons, and she did nothing about it? Every innocent person who was shot by one of those guns would be on her conscience, for ever.

She called Detective Ó Doibhilin. 'How's it going with your N-Bomb salesman?'

'It's not going at all at the moment. He's asked for his lawyer and his lawyer won't be able to get here until four o'clock at the earliest.'

'He's an N-Bomb pusher and he has his own lawyer?'

'Not a cheap one either. Charles Cathal from Cathal and Brogan.'

'Now, that *is* interesting. Charles Cathal mainly deals with cases of medical malpractice. Why would he take on a drug-pushing scummer like this – what's-his-name – Boxty?'

'Search me. But Cathal usually charges anything up to two hundred and sixty-five euros an hour. He must feel sure that Boxty's going to be able to settle his bill.'

'Maybe he knows that whoever employs Boxty is going to be able to settle his bill for him.'

'That could be more like it, sure. But I'll call you anyway when Cathal gets here.'

'You should be clocking off by then, shouldn't you? You've been up for most of the night.'

'I've had a shower and a bite of breakfast and I'll be having a day off tomorrow. I'd like to see this one through.'

'All right. Just this once I'll approve your overtime. But don't make a habit of being too conscientious. I can't afford it. Right now, though, would you keep a fierce close eye on Maureen Callahan for me? I may be totally mistaken, but I have the feeling that she'll be making a move soon.'

'I will of course.'

Katie checked the map on her computer screen. Sarsfield Court Industrial Estate was only about twenty minutes' drive to the north of Cork City, past White's Cross and Upper Glanmire, and not too far from Fairy Hill, but it was surrounded by nothing but farms and fields. 'Right in front of your nose but right in the back of nowhere in particular,' as her Grannie used to say.

To mount a raid, or not to mount a raid? That was the question. She almost felt like tossing a coin. The trouble was, her whole career would depend on that toss, and she always preferred judgement to chance.

She called Superintendent Pearse. 'Michael, it's Katie. Can you spare me two of your men as back-up this afternoon? Only the two, yes – but tooled up, please, the both of them, although I'm not expecting any armed resistance. Sarsfield Court Industrial Estate. Yes. About half-past three. But I'll come down anyway at half-past two to give them a briefing.'

That's decided then, she told herself. *You know you've made the right decision. Well – you* hope *you've made the right decision. And if you haven't, and you get sacked, you could always marry Conor and live happily ever after as a housewife. Four out of six of your sisters have done it, why shouldn't you? I could quite fancy the name Katie Ó Máille, and I would love to have children. Two boys, and two girls. And another dog.*

Conor's phone was engaged the first time she rang, and still engaged ten minutes later. She left him a voice message and after another five minutes he rang her back.

'How's the form, girlfriend?' he asked her.

'Now then, let's keep this strictly professional, shall we?'

'I'm sorry. How's the form, Detective Superintendent? Did you have any joy with Lorcan Fitzgerald?'

'That's why I was ringing you. We haven't been able to trace him yet. He doesn't appear to have any previous convictions, not under that name anyway, and he's not listed on any electoral register. I thought I might be able to get some information about him out of Gerry Mulvaney, but Gerry Mulvaney seems to have disappeared off the face of the earth, and Keeno's still in a coma.'

'So what do you want me to do?'

'I'd like you to call him on the number that Bartley Doran gave us. Tell him you have some fantastic fighting dogs and would he be interested in buying them off you.'

'Okay. As soon as I'm dressed I'll come down to the station.'

'You're not dressed yet?'

'No. I'm standing here stark naked in front of the mirror admiring myself.'

'Oh stop. I never felt jealous of a mirror before but I do now.'

* * *

Conor arrived at Anglesea Street half an hour later, and a female garda from reception brought him up to Katie's office, all smiles. When the garda had gone, he took Katie in his arms and kissed her. His beard was neatly trimmed and he smelled of some woodsy spicy shower-gel.

'I missed you last night,' he told her, in a very soft voice.

Katie said nothing, but shrugged and twiddled with the button on his coat.

'So you want me to call this Lorcan Fitzgerald?' he said. 'And – what – offer him some fighting dogs?'

'That's right. Tell him what dogs you have and arrange to meet up with him.'

'What dogs *do* I have?'

'So far Sergeant Nolan can get me a Neapolitan mastiff and two bull terriers. He may be able to borrow an Akita too. I have all their details... age, height, weight, vaccinations, whether they're microchipped or not.'

'What if Fitzgerald's not interested?'

'Then do your pet detective bit and try to get some clues out of him about his location, at the very least, and how you can contact him again. Tell him you can get him more dogs if he wants them.'

'And what if he *does* want to meet?'

'Sergeant Nolan will fetch you the dogs to take with you. Then – when you meet Fitzgerald – try and engage him in conversation about the way he does business. Ask him as many questions as you can about the dogs he supplied to Guzz Eye McManus and where he got them from. If you can get him to admit that he hobbled them from the Sceolan Kennels, that would be fantastic, although I doubt that he will. Anyway you'll be wearing a wire so whatever he says will be recorded.'

'All right, then. When do you want me to ring him?'

'Right now, if you're up for it. I'll just call Dooley and Scanlan. They can bring us up a phone which can't be traced, so Fitzgerald won't be able to check up on you. They can also listen in – well, if and when Fitzgerald rings back.'

'I'm beginning to enjoy this,' said Conor. 'Maybe I should have been a Garda detective rather than a pet detective.'

'There's not as much money in it,' Katie told him. 'You'd be earning less than thirty thousand, even after three years' service.'

'Yes, but what a beour I'd have for a boss.'

Thirty-one

Detective Ó Doibhilin was sitting in front of his PC, pecking out a report on last night's N-Bomb incident, when he heard a *beep!* from his iPad. He picked it up and saw that Maureen Callahan's car was on the move.

He watched it for a while, swigging the last of his can of warm Pepsi-Cola, trying to see if he could judge where it was heading. The car left Douglas Lawn, where Maureen Callahan lived, and joined the eastbound lane of the main N40. Its signal temporarily disappeared while it drove through the Jack Lynch Tunnel, but then it reappeared on the other side of the river, and turned east again when it reached the intersection with the N25.

It was only then that he called Katie.

'Maureen Callahan's on the move, ma'am. She's on the main Cork Road heading east. Just passing the Euro Business Park. She's driving like she stole it, too, the speed she's going.'

'Thanks, Michael, and listen – get yourself ready to go after her. If she's going where I think she might be going, I want you to be there, to see what she does, and who she meets.'

'No bother, ma'am. My jacket's hanging ready on the back of my chair.'

Detective Ó Doubhilin kept watching the progress of Maureen Callahan's car as it crossed over Harper's Island and reached the roundabout at Cobh Cross. It left the main Cork Road then and turned due south towards Fota Island.

He called Katie again. 'She's heading towards Fota. She's slowing down. She's turning into the Golf Club.'

'Go after her, Michael. *Now!* And fast.'

Detective Ó Doibhilin pushed back his chair, picked up his jacket and his iPad, and hurried out of the squad room. He passed Detective Markey as he clattered down the stairs, and Detective Markey said, 'Jesus, Michael! You got the runs, boy?'

He ran across the car park, unlocking his dark green Astra as he ran. He climbed into it, slammed the door, and screeched out on to Old Station Road, almost colliding with a laundry van. His Astra had flashing blue lights concealed behind the front grille, and a siren, and he switched them both on as he weaved through the traffic on Albert Street and crossed over the Eamon De Valera Bridge.

Once he was clear of the city centre and heading east on the Lower Glanmire Road, he put his foot down until he was speeding along by the river at over 90 kph. Once he was past Tivoli and the road became a dual carriageway, he sped up even more, to 140 kph. He reached Cobh Cross in less than fifteen minutes, and turned south towards Fota Island.

When he drove into the Fota Golf Club, he saw Maureen Callahan's red Audi on the right-hand side of the car park, close to the main entrance. There was no sign of Maureen Callahan herself.

He called Katie. 'I'm here at the golf club. Her car's here all right, but she's not in it.'

'Why don't you go inside and look for her? She doesn't know you by sight, does she?'

'I shouldn't think so. I've only seen her once myself and that was when she was up in the District Court.'

'That's good. But keep sketch for Assistant Commissioner O'Reilly. He'll reck you for sure, and that could mess up everything.'

'I have you,' said Detective Ó Doibhilin, although he didn't ask her to explain what 'everything' was, or how 'everything' could be messed up by Assistant Commissioner O'Reilly recognising him. 'The sun's almost nearly on the verge of shining so I'll put my shades on.'

The Fota golf clubhouse was made up of a collection of old limestone farm buildings. It looked grim and grey from the outside, but inside it had been expensively renovated and it was airy and light with the atmosphere of a five-star hotel. It was crowded this morning because of the three-day charity tournament, and it was nearly lunchtime. Detective Ó Doibhilin carefully manoeuvred his way between circles of red-faced men in tweeds and Aran sweaters, braying loudly to each other about birdies and eagles and how they had nearly come unstuck at the newly designed Par 38th hole on the Barryscourt Course.

He went from one reception room to the next, looking for Maureen Callahan. At last he caught sight of her sitting on a stool in the Spike Bar, drinking a glass of white wine and chatting to the barman. She was wearing a smart grey suit and very high heels, and her blonde bob was shining. The barman said something to her and she threw back her head, laughing.

Almost all of the tables and chairs in the bar were occupied, but Detective Ó Doibhilin managed to find a leather armchair in the corner which afforded him a view of the bar. He sat down and texted Katie to tell her that he had found Maureen Callahan and that he was keeping her under observation. He even took a surreptitious photograph of her and emailed it as a follow-up to his text.

So far there was no sign of Assistant Commissioner O'Reilly, but the bar was packed and it was difficult for him to see everybody from where he was sitting. He caught the barman staring at him as if he were wondering why he hadn't bought a drink, but then a large gingery man came up to the bar to bellow out an order for another round, and the barman turned away.

Katie texted him to ask *Any developments??* but he had to text back with a thumbs-down emoji.

He had only just sent that, though, when a very thin man with grey brushed-back hair stood up from a table by the window, turned around, and came walking across to the bar. Detective Ó Doibhilin half-covered his face with his hand, and pretended to be concentrating on his mobile phone. The man was Assistant Commissioner O'Reilly, wearing a dark brown three-piece suit of Donegal tweed and carrying a brown leather briefcase. He stood close to Maureen Callahan, although he didn't appear to acknowledge her in any way. He didn't even turn to look at her. Instead he snapped his fingers for the barman and the barman brought over his bill.

Detective Ó Doibhilin texted: *J O'R's here. He's signed his bill. Now he's leaving. Didn't say word one to MC.*

He had to keep his head right down as Assistant Commissioner O'Reilly passed him by, so close that he could have stuck out his foot and tripped him up. When he was able to look up again, he saw that Maureen Callahan was still joking with the barman. But he saw something else, too: when Assistant Commissioner O'Reilly had been signing his bill, he had set his briefcase down on the floor, next to the legs of Maureen Callahan's barstool, and his briefcase was still there.

Detective Ó Doibhilin couldn't really pick it up himself and run after him and say, 'Stall the ball, sir, you forgot this!' Assistant Commissioner O'Reilly would demand to know what the hell he was doing here, in the Fota clubhouse, and in any case Detective Superintendent Maguire had told him that it would mess up 'everything'.

He quickly texted Katie and told her about the briefcase, sending her a picture of it, too. Katie texted him back. *If MC picks it up & walks out with it follow her. If she doesn't hand it in or return it to J O'R lift her for theft. Don't open it in case it's a bomb.*

Detective Ó Doibhilin waited another ten minutes while Maureen Callahan finished her glass of wine. During all of that time she didn't look down at the briefcase once, and he began to wonder if she had even noticed that Assistant Commissioner O'Reilly had left it behind. Eventually, though, she blew the barman a kiss and slipped down from the barstool, and without hesitating she picked up the briefcase and walked out of the bar with it.

Detective Ó Doibhilin followed her as she made her way out of the clubhouse and into the car park. She went straight over to her Audi, lifted the boot, and dropped the briefcase inside. As soon as she had slammed it shut, and opened the driver's door, Detective Ó Doibhilin went up to her and held out his ID.

'Detective Garda Michael Ó Doibhilin,' he told her. 'Would you please tell me your name?'

Maureen Callahan blinked at him in surprise, as if he had magically appeared out of thin air. 'Maureen Callahan. What's it to you?'

'Well, I'll tell you what it is to me. Maureen Callahan, I am arresting you under section four of the Theft and Fraud Act, 2001, for appropriating property with the intention of permanently depriving its owner of it, namely a briefcase that a fellow left behind in the Spike Bar and you have just hobbled. You are not obliged to say anything unless you wish to do so, but whatever you say will be taken down in writing and may be given in evidence.'

'C'mere to me?' said Maureen Callahan. 'What in the name of God are you talking about, boy? The briefcase belongs to me anyway. Your man was taking care of it for me, that's all, and when he left he gave it back to me.'

'Do you know who your man happened to be?'

'I don't know. Just an obliging fellow, that's all. I didn't want to have the briefcase down at my feet while I was sitting at the bar in case somebody tripped over it.'

'Would your man corroborate this?'

'Would he what?'

'Would your man back you up and say that you were telling me the truth?'

'Of course he would, if only I knew who he was.'

'You must think I came up the River Lee in a bubble,' said Detective Ó Doibhilin. 'I know who he is, and *you* know who he is, and you must know that I know who he is. And I know that he knows who *you* are, and I know him well enough to know that he'd be the last person on the Planet Earth to mind a briefcase for any member of the Callahan family.'

Maureen Callahan blinked at him again, as if she hadn't understood a word that he had said. 'I'm saying nothing,' she snapped.

'What's inside the briefcase?'

'I told you. I'm saying nothing.'

'Right. I'm taking you in to Anglesea Street Garda Station, where you'll be formally charged. Will you open up the boot for me, please, so that I can take out the briefcase.'

Maureen Callahan stayed where she was for a few seconds, breathing deeply, as if her patience with the world was just about exhausted. Then she went round and opened the Audi's boot. Detective Ó Doibhilin took a forensic glove out of his pocket, snapped it on, and lifted the briefcase out.

'You muppet,' said Maureen Callahan. 'I can promise you this, boy – there's a fair few people who's going to be fierce sorry about this by the end of the day, and I can promise you this, too – one of those people won't be me.'

Thirty-two

Detective Dooley dialled Lorcan Fitzgerald's number and then passed the handset to Conor. They were sitting on the couches in Katie's office – Katie and Conor and Detectives Dooley and Scanlan – and they could all hear the ring tones on her conference phone.

After only three rings, a recorded voice said, 'Lorcan speaking. Tell me what's on your mind and leave me your number and I'll get back to you. Or not, as the case may be. If I don't get back to you, don't ring again. *Slán go fóil.*'

Putting on a strong Tipperary accent, Conor said, 'Lorcan? This is Redmond O'Dea from the Firmount Kennels in Carrigahorig. It was Bartley Doran give me your number. I have some grand dogs suitable for training up to gameness. A Neapolitan mastiff, he's the star of the show. I'm not codding you, he's a beast of a yoke. And a couple of bull terriers, too. They're real aggressive. They'd bite the leg off of an ironing-board. Any road, this is my number. Looking forward to hearing from you.'

'That was perfect,' said Katie. 'Now all we have to do is wait.'

'I think he'll call back all right,' said Detective Dooley. 'It's the Neapolitan mastiff that'll swing it. They're fecking *yuge*, those dogs. My brother had one once and when it was fully grown it was bigger than him, and my brother's not what you'd call a midget.'

Detective Ó Doibhilin knocked at her open door. 'I'm back now, ma'am, and I have Maureen Callahan down in the interview room. I have the briefcase, too. I took it over to the Technical Bureau and they've X-rayed it. There's no explosives inside of it.'

'I didn't think there would be,' said Katie. 'It's better to be sure than have yourself blown into five thousand pieces. I'll come down now and have a chat with Ms Callahan.'

She stood up. 'I shouldn't be long, but if Lorcan Fitzgerald rings back while I'm away, be sure to page me, won't you?'

When she and Detective Ó Doibhilin went downstairs to the interview room, they found Maureen Callahan sitting with her arms crossed, scowling. Detective Scanlan was sitting at the end of the table, while Sergeant Daley was sitting directly opposite, laboriously filling out the charge sheet against her, his thick-rimmed glasses on the end of his nose and his tongue clenched between his teeth. The brown leather briefcase, still unopened, lay on the table between them.

'Well now, Maureen, here's a contradictory situation,' said Katie, pulling out a chair and sitting down next to Sergeant Daley. 'One minute you're helping us out with a valuable tip-off, and the next you're stroking our Assistant Commissioner's briefcase.'

'I'm saying nothing,' said Maureen.

'You told Detective Ó Doibhilin here that the briefcase belongs to you. Is that true?'

'I'm saying nothing until I can ring my solicitor, and then I'm saying nothing. The law gives me the right to say nothing.'

'It does, yes, Maureen. But if you choose to say nothing when you could have said something to prove your innocence, the court will take a fierce dim view of that, I can tell you. They don't care to have their time wasted, and neither do I.'

'I'm saying nothing.'

'Let's see what's inside this briefcase, shall we?'

'You'd have to be having a warrant for that.'

'If it's not your briefcase, why should you care? In any event, we can search you and your personal property without a warrant if we have reasonable suspicion that an offence has been committed.'

Maureen said nothing, but continued to scowl. Katie stood up, took a pair of black forensic gloves out of her jacket pocket, and tugged them on. Then she flicked the catches on the briefcase and opened it up. Inside, under several layers of bubble-wrap, it was packed with bundles of €20 notes. She lifted up the bubble-wrap, picked up one of the bundles of notes and looked at what was printed on the label – €1,000.

There were twenty bundles altogether. She checked all of them, flicking through the notes to make sure they were all genuine, and not just bundles of paper with €20 notes top and bottom.

'So you were sitting in the bar at Fota Golf Club with twenty thousand euros in small-denomination notes in your briefcase, but because you were frightened that somebody might trip over it, you gave it to a total stranger to look after? Is that your story?'

'I'm saying nothing.'

'You might be saying nothing, but I'm saying that these twenty thousand euros are a pay-off to you from Assistant Commissioner O'Reilly to meet me and give me information about an illegal arms shipment.'

'You can say what you like, girl,' Maureen retorted. 'How are you going to prove it, that's the thing?'

'I shall ask Assistant Commissioner O'Reilly, right to his face. And I shall also be sending this briefcase back to our technical experts to check it minutely for fingerprints and DNA. If there's any forensic evidence at all that Assistant Commissioner O'Reilly left any trace of himself inside of it – if he handled this money or this bubble-wrap, then you're going to be in deep, deep trouble, and so is he.'

'Away to feck, DS Maguire. You're only saying that to scare me. Well you won't scare me, I can tell you that. Nothing scares me, girl – nothing!'

Katie closed the briefcase and sat down again.

'You can refuse to answer if you like, Maureen, but let me ask you this – there's no arms shipment, is there?'

'I want to make a phone call. I'm entitled to make three phone calls.'

'You can make all the phone calls you want to, but later. There *is* no arms shipment, is there? You were helping Assistant

Commissioner O'Reilly to set me up, and that's why he's given you twenty thousand euros.'

'You're dreaming, girl – you're dreaming. All I can say is, dream on.'

Katie leaned forward and said, 'If you admit this now, Maureen, the law will be very light on you. In fact you'll probably get off scot-free for being co-operative.'

'I'm saying nothing.'

'But you did tell me about this arms shipment, didn't you? All these AK-47s and Skorpion machine pistols and Semtex? That was how you were going to get your revenge on your father and your sister Bree?'

'That's right. They told me all of these arms were coming in, but if they didn't, that's not my fault. That's what they told me, that's all. You can't blame me for believing something that I was told.'

'They told you they'd murdered Branán O'Flynn, didn't they? And you believed that, too, did you? Although you could have checked if they really *had* murdered him, just by ringing him?'

Now Maureen was beginning to realise that Katie was talking her into a corner, and she said nothing.

Katie took out her iPhone, found the photograph of Kyna sitting at the bar in Las Palmas Airport, with Branán O'Flynn sitting directly behind her, and held it up in front of Maureen's face. Maureen glanced at it, and flinched, and then looked away.

'That's your dearly beloved Branán sitting there, isn't it, chatting away on his mobile? Can you guess when that picture was taken, Maureen? And where?'

'I have no idea,' said Maureen. 'You're heartless, you are. I'm grieving for him.'

'That picture was taken yesterday evening in Gran Canaria. If your father and sisters *have* murdered Branán, they could only have done it after five past seven this morning, after he got back from Las Palmas.'

Maureen took a deep breath. 'You said if I co-operated, like, you'd let me off.'

'I said that the courts would probably go easy on you, that's all.'

'I will co-operate, but only if you don't press any charges against me at all. You couldn't charge me with theft, any road, because you can't be guilty of stroking something when you was given it.'

'So you're admitting that Assistant Commissioner O'Reilly gave you the briefcase with twenty thousand euros in it?'

'Only if you don't charge me with nothing.'

'All right,' said Katie. 'You have a deal, conditional on what you tell me.'

'O'Reilly calls me and says that he wants me to meet you and spin you that story about Branán being done for, and how I wanted my revenge for it, and the arms shipment and all.'

'You and Branán – are you really doing a line?'

'We've been going out together for yonks there.'

'And your father and sisters don't mind?'

'Not at all, like, because it's a way of keeping our two families in touch with each other, even if most of them hate each other's guts, and wouldn't piss on each other if they was on fire. Like if the Callahans have some deal in mind and the O'Flynns happen to have the same deal in mind, we both get to know about it and so we don't tread on each other's toes, like, do you know what I mean?'

'You mean if you're both thinking of robbing the same charity shop, you don't both turn up there at the same time?'

'I'm admitting to nothing like that. My family never robbed a charity shop and never would. Holy Mary, what do you take us for?'

'I'm just giving you a hypothetical example, Maureen. But go on.'

Maureen looked dubious for a moment, but then she said, 'Okay... O'Reilly offers me ten thousand euros to tell you that story. I say twenty, and he says fifteen, but I stick to twenty and in the end he says yes, he can just about scrape that up, because it's worth it. So the rest you know.'

'So you never spoke to any undercover detective from the SDU?'

Maureen shook her blonde bob, but Katie said, 'Would you just say "no" out loud, please, Maureen, because we're recording this.'

'No. I never met nobody like that, and do you think I'd tell them goms anything if I did? All I did was tell you what O'Reilly told me to tell you.'

'So there is no arms shipment?'

'We was out of that business a long time ago, after the Good Friday Agreement. Not that I'm admitting that we was ever in it.'

'But this arms shipment that you told me was delivered this morning to Sarsfield Court Industrial Estate – that doesn't exist?'

'No, it does not.'

'So nobody's coming from Armagh this afternoon to make you an offer for Skorpion machine pistols?'

'No, nobody at all.'

'So what's the significance of half-past three? Surely if Assistant Commissioner O'Reilly was trying to get me to set up an abortive raid on an empty warehouse, any time would have done.'

'I have to admit that was my idea,' said Maureen. She stopped looking so petulant and actually managed a self-satisfied little smirk. 'It was my idea but O'Reilly went for it big time. We've only just taken over the lease of the warehouse, like, and at the moment it's empty. But my sister Saoirse has the twin boys Tom and Patrick and it was their birthdays this week, so we decided that the warehouse would be a grand location for a party, seeing as how there's thirty or forty kids to entertain. Inside there's tables set up and the place is all decorated with balloons and paper chains, and there's going to be clowns and magicians and O'Brady's performing dogs.'

Katie sat back. 'I have to hand it to you, Maureen. That was a stroke of genius. I can see the headlines now. "Armed Gardaí Raid Kiddie's Birthday Party". I would have been lucky not to have been sacked on the spot and lose my pension.'

'O'Reilly did give me the impression that he wasn't too fond of you, like, I have to tell you.'

'That's the understatement of the century.'

Detective Ó Doibhilin raised one eyebrow as if to say 'That just about wraps that up, then, doesn't it? Don't ask me what in the name of God how you're going to handle this now.'

'That's all I can tell you,' said Maureen. 'Are you going to let me go now?'

'Yes, Maureen,' Katie told her, 'you can go. I have one stipulation, though: you're not to mention any of this to anybody. Especially the media. Like, ever, for the rest of your life.'

'My father and my sisters know all about it. I had to warn them that the guards were going to come bursting in when they were all singing "Happy Birthday to You".

'Well, tell them to keep it to themselves, too, or I'll pull you straight back in again for wasting police time and any other charge I can think of.'

Maureen nodded towards the briefcase. 'What about my twenty thousand?'

'I hope you're not serious. That money is evidence. And you didn't exactly earn it, did you, because you got found out.'

'That wasn't my fault. O'Reilly knew that Branán was on his holliers but he said I should tell you that he was dead.'

'Me and the moth went to Gran Canaria for a week once,' put in Sergeant Daley. mournfully, taking off his glasses. 'There isn't too much difference between that and being dead.'

* * *

After Maureen Callahan had left, Detective Ó Doibhilin took the briefcase back to the Technical Bureau to have the money and the interior lining tested for any signs of fingerprints or DNA that might prove that Assistant Commissioner O'Reilly had handled it.

Katie meanwhile went back up to her office to check if Lorcan Fitzgerald had rung Conor back. As she was walking past Assistant Commissioner O'Reilly's office, she saw that his door was open, and she could hear somebody moving around inside. She wondered if Jimmy O'Reilly had seen Maureen Callahan being arrested by Detective Ó Doibhilin, and had come back to the station to find out if she had told Katie about him paying her off. She knocked, and opened the door wider.

Nobody answered, so she went inside. Standing behind Jimmy O'Reilly's desk she found his former civilian assistant, James Elvin. He had the looks of a young Leonardo DiCaprio, with brushed-up blond hair, and before she had discovered that he was Jimmy O'Reilly's lover, Katie had quite fancied him. He had a black waterproof jacket draped over his arm and he was holding a pair of yellow leather boots. With his free hand he was leafing through Jimmy O'Reilly's desk diary.

As soon as Katie came into the office, he quickly closed the diary and stepped away from the desk – grinning guiltily, because he knew that he had been caught in the act.

'DS Maguire!' he said. 'How's it going on?'

'I thought you didn't work here any more,' said Katie.

'No, I don't. But Assistant Commissioner O'Reilly said I could come by the station and pick up this jacket and these boots I left behind.'

'What, and look through his diary, too?'

'I was curious to know how long he was going to be away, that's all.'

'Monday he'll be back. Why?'

'I need to talk to him face-to-face.'

'I see. I won't ask you what about.'

'I'm leaving Cork, that's all. As a matter of fact I'm leaving the country altogether. I've found myself a job with a law firm in Amsterdam that's desperate for an English-speaking secretary.'

'I wish you luck, then.'

James Elvin hesitated for a moment, and then he said, 'I don't want to hurt him, like. But I thought it best to make a clean break, you know. Rather than pretend that things could go on like they were before.'

'I'm not sure I know what you mean.'

'You know full well that he was borrowing money from Bobby Quilty so that I could settle the debts that I'd run up gambling.

The things he said about you, I wouldn't repeat them to a priest in confession.'

'Don't worry. He's said plenty to my face. I think "witch" was about the least worst name that he called me.'

'I can't change my ways,' said James Elvin. 'I've tried, believe me. I've even been to the Gamblers Anonymous. But I suppose you could say that I'm hopelessly addicted. The problem is – now that Bobby Quilty's gone to meet his Maker – Jimmy has nobody else that he can borrow the money off. Sorry, I didn't mean any disrespect – Assistant Commissioner O'Reilly.'

Katie could see that he had tears in his eyes. He wiped them with his sleeve, and then he said, 'I asked him for ten thousand only a few days ago. I *begged* him, like. I was almost on my knees. There's fellers from the Diamond Club who say they're going to break my legs if I don't pay at least half of what I owe them. But he said no, he couldn't manage it, he needed the money for something more important. We had a real fierce argument about it. I said to him, what's more important to you than me? But he wouldn't say. So afterwards I thought, I'm glad to be going. The feller that runs the law firm in Amsterdam, he says he can help me financially, if you follow me. And all the debts I've run up in Cork, I can leave them behind and forget about them, because they'll never find out where I've disappeared to.'

'Holy Mother of God,' said Katie. 'You're some chiselling little bastard, aren't you?'

James Elvin sniffed, and shrugged. 'I know that, DS Maguire. You don't have to tell me. But that's me, that's the way I am, and there's nothing I can do about it. The only thing is, I'm shitting myself about telling Jimmy because I know he'll do ninety, and then he'll probably cry, and I don't want to leave him like that.'

Katie said, very quietly, 'Why don't you write him a note, James, telling him that you have started a new life? Tell him how much you appreciate everything that he's done for you, and that you're going to miss him, but you're sure that he'll soon be able to find somebody else to take your place. Write him a note like that, and

I'll give it to him, and then you won't have to face him raging at you or bursting into tears.'

'You'd do that for me? Even though I've been such a bastard?'

'James, there's such a thing in this world as forgiveness. Write the note and bring it along to my office. Then off you go to Amsterdam and forget about Cork and your gambling debts and Assistant Commissioner O'Reilly.'

'Thank you,' said James Elvin, although he was so choked up that he could hardly get the words out.

Katie walked along to her office feeling treacherous, in a way, but also triumphant. She couldn't wait to see Jimmy O'Reilly's face when she presented him with his own briefcase, with his twenty thousand euros still in it, and a note from James Elvin saying that he was leaving him.

* * *

Conor was still waiting for a return call from Lorcan Fitzgerald, and Detective Scanlan was looking bored.

Katie said, 'Okay, Let's leave it for now. Conor – so long as you keep that phone with you. Maybe Fitzgerald's busy napping dogs right now, or maybe he's just not interested in your Neapolitan mastiff. If that's the case, we'll have to track him down some other way. Michael – you go home now and get your head down. Pádraigin, go and get yourself something to eat.'

'What about you?' asked Conor, when Detectives Ó Doibhilin and Scanlan had gone.

'I thought you and me could go to Ramen for some Asian street food. It's only a couple of minutes down the road.'

'That sounds like a plan. Breakfast seems like a long time ago now.'

They walked together down Anglesea Street to Ramen, with its red-painted frontage and a notice-board outside saying *Buy One For The Price Of Two And Get One Free.* It was crowded inside, and noisy, and filled with the smells of wok-fried vegetables and garlic. They managed to find a place to sit on one of the long wooden benches, and order themselves some beef khao pad and prawn firecracker and teriyaki. Conor ordered a Tiger beer but Katie stuck to sparkling water.

Conor laid the mobile phone on the table beside him in case Lorcan Fitzgerald rang.

'I missed you last night, Katie,' he told her.

'I missed you too.'

'So when are you and I going to be able to get together again?'

She reached across and gently touched his cheek. She loved his face. It was so strong, and clearly formed, and in his eyes she could see such sparkle and sincerity. Her husband Paul had been handsome when she first met him, but too many years of Satzenbrau and take-away curries had made him rounder, with a double chin, and his eyes had always been shifty, like his character. John had looked almost godlike when she first met him, with his black curly hair and his muscular body, but now of course he was physically ruined.

Fate had brought her Conor at the wrong time in her life – while she still had John to look after – but she had such a strong feeling that he could be the right man for her. His lovemaking had been so strong but so considerate, and more than anything else he made her laugh, and feel happy.

'I can come back to the guest house with you this evening,' she said. 'I can't stay all night, though, as much as I'd like to.'

'I thought you said you had someone to take care of your dog. What's his name – Barney?'

'I do. But I have other things to attend to.'

'Like?'

'Like checking my mail and watering my plants and making sure the house is tidy. Also, my father lives in Monkstown on the opposite side of the river and I have to go and see if he needs anything.'

'Okay, fair play. I suppose that sometimes post and plants and parents have to take priority over passion.'

She gave him a light, playful slap. He caught hold of her wrist, and held it firmly, and looked steadily into her eyes. He didn't have to say anything. She could sense that he was feeling a stirring sensation between his legs just by holding her, because she was feeling the same. *My God,* she thought, *this is something special. This is something very, very special.*

'Come with me this afternoon,' she said. 'I'm going up to Sarsfield Court, for a birthday party.'

'A birthday party? Aren't you on duty?'

'You'll see,' she said, as their food arrived in cardboard take-away boxes. She picked up her chopsticks and gave him a particular look that John always used to call her Irish Sea look. Because her eyes were so green, he said that it made him feel that he was looking out to sea – a calm sea, but a sea with unexplored depths, where sunken treasure lay, but riptides, too.

They ate, and talked, and laughed, but still the phone didn't ring.

Thirty-three

Only about ten minutes after they had returned from lunch, Dr Kelley arrived at the station. She came up to Katie's office in a bundled-up camelhair coat and a floppy tweed hat, carrying a white cardboard box.

'I had three tries at this before I managed to get it right,' she said. 'But I'm pure pleased with what I've managed to produce.'

She set the box down on the low glass-topped table by the couches, and opened the lid. Inside, carefully wrapped up in tissue paper, were five knife-blades, all made of dark grey plastic. Two of the blades were flat, like conventional knife-blades, but the other three were thick and multi-faceted, more like lemon-squeezers than knives.

'These were all 3-D printed using high-definition acrylate,' Dr Kelley explained. 'I could have used metal, but I wanted to achieve the finest detail possible. If you can find the original weapon, you'll be able to compare the tiniest scratches and nicks in the blade, and identify it beyond any possible dispute.'

'You have two here that look like ordinary knives,' said Katie. 'What are these triangular ones?'

'These two flat blades were replicated from the wound that the knife inflicted when it was first pushed into the victim's perineum. After that first penetration, though, the blade was rotated in an anti-clockwise direction inside his body, and these other three blades are representations of the damage that was done.'

'Jesus,' said Conor. 'That wouldn't have done his love life much good.'

Katie examined all of the blades and then put them back in the box. 'That's fantastic, Dr Kelley. You're a genius. As you say, all we have to do now is find the original knife.'

Dr Kelley looked at her watch. 'I'm off back to Dublin now, but I expect that I'll be back – either me myself or one of my fellow pathologists. You Corkonians seem to be making a habit of killing each other these days, in one unusual way or another.'

She left, and Katie said to Conor, 'Twenty past two. I have to go down and give our escorts a quick briefing, and then we can head off to Sarsfield Court.'

'We're going to a birthday party and we have to have escorts?'

'Only to be on the safe side. They're not exactly what you'd call close friends, the characters holding the party. As a matter of fact, they're downright dangerous.'

Katie went down to see Superintendent Pearse, who was sitting in his office having a shouting match with somebody on the phone.

'I fecking *told* him I had to have that warrant issued today! I made it totally transparently crystal clear! So where's he disappeared off to? Joseph and Mary and the Wain, I can't believe it!'

When he had slammed the phone down, Katie gave him a smile and said, 'I'll be heading off to Sarsfield Court in a minute. Do you have your men free?'

'I'll call them in now, Katie. Sorry for the shouting. Those eejits across at the District Court couldn't organise a you-know-what in a you-know-where.'

He made the call and after two or three minutes two burly uniformed gardaí came in, both of them wearing holsters with Sig-Sauer automatic pistols. One of them had a face so red he looked as if he were about to explode at any moment, but Katie guessed that he had probably been sunning himself on Gran Canaria, too.

'I'm calling in to a children's birthday party at Sarsfield Court Industrial Estate,' Katie told them. 'I'm afraid I'm not at liberty yet to tell you exactly why, but I can tell you who the organisers are. The Callahan family. Yes, *that* Callahan family – I'm not surprised you're pulling faces. I have to give them a bit of a caution, so they won't be very happy out, so I'd appreciate it if you'd stand behind me looking formidable. Just give them the impression that you'll whip out your handcuffs if any of those Callahans gives me the slightest bother.'

Conor was waiting for her by the front desk.

'All set?' he asked her.

'All set. There's only one stop I want to make on the way.'

They went outside to the car park and climbed into Katie's blue Focus. As she drove across Parnell Bridge the two armed gardaí followed close behind her in a black unmarked Volvo. She drove across to Oliver Plunkett Street, where she parked, and then she and Conor walked to Maylor Street. They reached Smyths Toy Store and Katie went straight in.

'A toy shop?' said Conor.

'It's a children's birthday party we're going to. We can't turn up without presents.'

* * *

The yard outside the green-painted warehouse was crowded with vehicles, most of them SUVs, so Katie had to park in the roadway. The two armed gardaí parked across the entrance, in case anybody wanted to leave in a hurry.

Katie walked up to the front door, carrying a large yellow Smyths bag, with Conor beside her and the two gardaí a few steps behind. There were two big men standing beside the door, one of whom Katie recognised as a former bouncer from the Voodoo Rooms. He recognised her, too, because he stepped forward with his hand held out. He was wearing a black T-shirt with a white picture of Jimi Hendrix on it.

From inside the warehouse Katie could hear loud music, and children shouting, and a man's amplified voice. It sounded as if they were playing musical chairs.

'Sorry, folks, this is a private party going on here,' the bouncer told her. 'No uninvited guests allowed in.'

'Is Maureen here yet?' Katie asked him. 'If Maureen's here, tell her that Detective Superintendent Maguire is paying the Callahans a friendly social call. And I have birthday presents for Tom and Patrick.'

The bouncer looked dubious, but his companion said, 'Go on, Vinny, for Christ's sake. Go tell her.'

The bouncer went inside, and they waited for a few minutes before he came out again and said, 'Maureen says it's okay. You can come on in.'

Katie and Conor stepped in through the warehouse door while the two armed gardaí waited outside. The noise inside the warehouse was deafening. Three long tables had been set out with plates of sausage rolls and Tayto crisps and cupcakes, and the children were running around them shrieking and laughing. Scores of multi-coloured balloons were hanging from the ceiling, as well as paper-chains and streamers. 'Wake Me Up' by Avicii was playing from two loudspeakers at top volume, and a man in a red-and-yellow clown outfit was dancing to it, and juggling Indian clubs.

On the right-hand side of the warehouse a fourth table had been set for adults, and there were at least twenty of them, with bottles of beer and wine and whiskey. Most of them were women, but there were six or seven men, and Katie knew most of them, because at one time or another she had arrested and questioned them and charged them. One of the women she recognised as the wife of a man who had been sent to prison only three weeks ago for beating a teenager with a hammer on Carey Street and causing him irreparable brain damage.

Sitting at the front of this table was Danny Callahan, the father of the Callahan clan, white-haired, with a bristly white moustache. He was wearing a baggy grey tracksuit and he had the appearance of a long-retired boxer. Next to him was Bree, Maureen's oldest sister, with frizzy blonde curls and lips painted a garish scarlet. Bree was bulging out of a green velvet dress, with huge bare arms and enormous breasts, and she was drinking

Magners cider out of a bottle. Next to Bree sat Maureen, glaring at Katie as if she were daring her to say anything that would upset her family.

All of the adults stared at Katie with intense hostility as she approached them. Katie kept on smiling, but saying nothing because the music was so loud and they wouldn't have been able to hear her. When 'Wake Me Up' had finished, Danny Callahan called over to the young DJ on the opposite side of the warehouse, 'Give us a moment's hush, would you, Lloyd?' and then the only noise came from the children.

'What are you after, Mrs Maguire?' asked Danny. 'We're having a private birthday party here. I don't recall myself inviting any shades.'

Katie said, 'I've brought birthday presents for the boys. And I wanted to have a word with all of you, just to avoid any misunderstandings.'

'What manner of misunderstandings would those be, then?'

'Any misunderstandings that might arise from the little trick that Maureen tried to play on me. I gather you all know about her falsely trying to arrange for me to mount a full-scale Garda raid on this birthday party, and I expect that she's explained to you the arrangement that she and I have come to. In case she hasn't made it abundantly clear to you, I've withdrawn all charges against her on the condition that her attempt to deceive me is never mentioned by her or by any of you, and I mean like *ever*. If I hear one whisper of it – and believe me I get to hear every single whisper that goes around Cork – then I'll be having no hesitation in charging her with extortion and wasting police time.'

She opened the Smyths bag and took out two bright green Splash Attack water pistols. She held them out to Danny but he wouldn't lift his hands to take them, so she set them down on the table next to the whiskey bottles.

'Maureen tried to make me believe that you were expecting a shipment of guns here today. For a while, I nearly believed her. And do you know why I believed her? Because the Callahans have been dealing in illegal guns for years, and I know for a fact that you're still doing it.

'But these two children's scuttering guns are the only shipment of arms you're going to be getting today, or any other day. After the way you've tried to set me up, I'm going to make sure that my detectives keep the closest watch on you, twenty-four seven, and if they get so much as a hint that you're bringing in more guns, or more explosives, I'm going to crack down on you so hard that the next birthday party you'll be attending for Tom and Patrick will be their twenty-first, and that's if you're lucky.'

All the time she was talking, Danny was fiddling with his signet rings, twisting them around and around. To Katie, that was an indication that he was doing everything he could to keep his temper bottled up. He wouldn't usually let anybody speak to him like that, let alone a woman, and let alone a guard, and let alone a woman guard.

When she had finished, though, he jerked his head towards Conor. 'This your feller?' he asked her.

Katie didn't answer, but Danny turned to Conor and said, 'If she's your sly lack, boy, this Mrs Maguire, I suggest to you that you watch out for her day and night, every day of the week, equally close as she's going to be watching us Callahans. That's all I'm going to say.'

'Are you threatening me, Mr Callahan?' said Katie.

'You think whatever takes your fancy,' Danny told her, and shouted out, 'Lloyd! You can start up the music again now! Loud as you like!'

Staying any longer would simply have been provocative, so Katie said to Conor, 'Come on. I think I've made my point,' and the two of them walked out of the warehouse and back into the open air. They found the two bouncers smoking and chatting to the two armed gardaí as if they were old acquaintances they had met in a pub.

Katie and Conor returned to their car, turned around, and drove back through Sallybrook towards the city. Katie glanced into her rear-view mirror from time to time to make sure that the gardaí were keeping up with them.

'That was impressive,' said Conor. 'Look at you... your hands aren't even shaking.'

'They don't frighten me all that much, the Callahans,' said Katie. 'They're old-school, like the O'Flynns. They can do some fierce terrible things to people who cross them – setting fire to them and nailing them to trees – well, and shooting them in the head if they're lucky. But they're wide when it comes to the law, unlike some of the young headers we have to deal with these days. They're so high on drugs, some of these kids, they never think about the consequences of killing someone, no matter who they are. Civilian, guard, they just don't care.'

Conor said, 'Are you done for the day, or do you have to go back to the station?'

'That's it for now,' said Katie. 'My hands may not be shaking, but my nerves could do with a scoop.'

* * *

They stopped for a drink at Dan Lowery's pub on MacCurtain Street. It was a small, intimate pub, its shelves crowded with bottles and souvenirs and vases of dried flowers, and its walls hung with mirrors and framed advertisements for Murphy's stout. Katie liked to go there because it was so discreet and because its stained-glass windows meant that nobody could see her from the street.

That was the same reason it was favoured by Eamonn 'Foxy' Collins, once one of Cork's most prosperous drug dealers. He was there today at his usual table in the back room, along with a young brunette in a fur-collared anorak who looked about half his age, and a shaven-headed minder in a maroon leather jacket. Eamonn was dressed as smartly as usual, in a tailor-made three-piece suit, and he nodded a greeting to Katie as she walked in with Conor.

'What's the craic, Detective Superintendent?' he called out, knowing full well that she would be annoyed to be identified out loud in front of the other customers – although at this time of the afternoon there were only six or seven other drinkers in the front bar.

'You know what's going on more than I do, Eamonn,' she replied.

'Foxy' stood up and came over to her table. His ginger hair was brushed up and she thought that it was whiter than the last time she had seen him.

He leaned over towards her and said, in a low voice, 'I'll tell you something for nothing, DS Maguire. I'm out of the business now. I swear on the tomb of Saint Patrick. There's too much competition these days, and it's fierce unregulated. Somebody's fetching tons of the stuff into the city and selling it on the streets at knock-off prices, and I got tired of competing. I was like Brown Thomas trying to compete with Poundsworth.'

'Yes, I heard you'd retired from dealing,' said Katie. 'You're still running your insurance business, though?'

'Foxy' gave her a grin. 'Everybody needs protection, don't they? And the guards can't be everywhere at once.'

Conor interrupted and said, 'What would you like to drink, Katie?'

'Oh, my apologies for interrupting you,' said 'Foxy'. 'This your new feller, is it? Aren't you going to introduce me?'

'No,' said Katie.

'Foxy' held out his hand to Conor and said, 'Well, boy, whoever you are, it's a pleasure to meet you. I'm Eamonn Collins, a very long-time acquaintance of your delightful lady-friend here.'

Conor shook his hand and smiled. 'I expect I'll find out when you've sat down again if it was a pleasure to meet you, too.'

'Foxy' leaned over to Katie again. 'You need to find out who's supplying this stuff, DS Maguire, and I'm serious now. Almost all of it is cut or contaminated with Christ alone knows what and the kids are going to start dropping like flies. At least when I was in the business my product was all good quality. The only clients who passed away on me were the ones who took too much of it, because it was so pure and they were enjoying it so much and you can't blame me for that.'

'Don't worry, Eamonn,' said Katie. 'I'm sure Saint Peter will take that into account when you reach the pearly gates.'

Eamonn returned to his table and Conor went to the bar and ordered their drinks. When he came back, he said, 'I have to say, Katie, you have some very interesting friends.'

'"Foxy" Collins is no friend of mine,' said Katie. 'He's one of the few gangsters in Cork who makes my blood run cold. I don't know for sure how many people he's had killed, but it wouldn't surprise me if it runs into double figures.'

'And you've never been able to nail him for it?'

'Conor – if he makes *my* blood run cold, what effect do you think he has on any witnesses? He's right, though. I have to find out where all these drugs are coming from. At least one of those six students at Greenmount could have died, and for all I know there are scores of heroin addicts lying dead in their squats and they don't have anybody to wonder why they've gone missing.'

Conor raised his glass of Murphy's. 'Oh well,' he said. 'Here's to survivors everywhere. And us.'

* * *

They went back to Conor's room at the Gabriel Guest House. As soon as Conor had closed the door and locked it, he took Katie in his arms and kissed her, so deeply and for so long that they were both breathless.

'I dreamed about this last night,' he said. He pulled off his windcheater and wrestled himself out of his navy-blue sweater and tossed them on to the armchair. Then he took off Katie's coat, and her jacket, and kissed her again, running his fingers up into her hair at the back of her neck.

'God almighty, you don't know how much I want you,' he said. 'You're beautiful. You're like a merrow, do you know that? You put a spell on me.'

'Not too much like a merrow, I hope,' smiled Katie, kissing the tip of his nose and his lips and stroking his beard. 'I don't have a tail and I don't smell like mackerel.'

He took off her sweater and then her bra, and then they both raced to strip themselves naked. They tumbled together on to the bed, and Katie kissed him again and again, and gripped his hardened penis in her hand as if she had a right to it, as if she were the queen of lovemaking and this was her sceptre.

She lay on her back and opened up her legs, but instead of climbing on top of her, Conor lay beside her and massaged her breasts, tugging her nipples until they stiffened. Then he ran his hand down her stomach and started to stroke her clitoris with his middle fingertip. At the same time he kissed her shoulder and then the side of her neck and then her cheek.

Katie turned her head to smile at him, and he smiled back at her. She could tell by the tension in his muscles and the stiffness of his penis how much he was aching to slide himself inside her, but in his eyes she saw calm, and a look of deep fulfilment, as if he had found at last the woman that he had always dreamed about, and he never wanted their lovemaking to end.

His fingertip went on playing with her clitoris until it was as stiff as a bird's beak, and her vagina was wet and slippery. Conor eased his right hand under the cheek of her bottom and dipped his index finger into her, to lubricate it, and then he started to massage her anus. The sensation made Katie roll her hips, urging him to push his finger inside her.

'Conor,' she breathed. She was gasping now, and her face felt flushed. 'Oh, Conor, oh, God, you're amazing.'

His finger went up inside her anus as far as it would go, and stirred her around and around, and then he lifted her thigh and she could feel the swollen head of his penis between the lips of her vulva. All she wanted now was for him to fill her completely. He was just about to thrust when his mobile phone started ringing – the mobile phone that he had been given to talk to Lorcan Fitzgerald.

Katie opened her eyes, and suddenly she was back in reality.

'Answer it,' she told him. 'Answer it, Conor – *quick*!'

Conor was totally confused. 'Jesus, Katie.'

'*Answer it!*' she gasped, lifting herself away from him so that he had to take out his finger, and sitting up.

He stumbled off the bed and picked his windcheater up off the chair, scrambling through the pockets to find his phone. It was still ringing when he found it, and prodded the screen to answer it. Katie thought: *Please remember that you're Redmond O'Dea*.

'Hallo there,' he said, and she was relieved to hear him put on his Tipperary accent. 'Yes, sir. Yes. This is Redmond, yes.'

He was still kneeling on the floor but he turned around to Katie and gave her a thumbs-up.

'They're all fine dogs, sir, yes, sir, I can promise you that,' he said, after a while. 'The Neapolitan mastiff in particular. Oh yes, sir. You can imagine the fights you could have with him, like. You could set three pit bulls up against him, and he'd tear the fecking lungs out of all of them, so he would.'

He listened for a while longer, and then he said, 'Okay. That's grand. I'll meet you there, Wednesday at twelve, and I'll bring the dogs with me. No, that's no bother at all. Thanks for ringing back, Lorcan. I'll see you then.'

He dropped the mobile phone on to the chair and stood up. Katie had always thought that John looked like a Greek god, because he used to be so muscular, but Conor was lean and slim and hairy and all he needed was a crown of thorns and a spear-wound in his side to look like Jesus. His penis had half-subsided now but it was still swollen.

'Well?' she said.

'Lorcan Fitzgerald is very interested in the dogs I have to offer him. He's checked with Bartley Doran to make sure I'm sound. He wants to meet at twelve on Tuesday and guess where… Bartley Doran's place.'

'That's fantastic,' said Katie. 'We can have a reception committee waiting for him.'

Conor climbed back on to the bed and put his arms around her but Katie looked at her watch and said, 'I'm sorry, Conor. I really need to be heading off.'

'What? You're not serious, are you?'

'I'm sorry, but I'm really pushed for time and the traffic's going to be a nightmare. I shouldn't really have come here in the first place.'

'Oh, Katie, come on. We were almost there. You can't leave a fellow half-satisfied. It's bad for his tubes.'

Katie kissed him and said, 'You're wonderful, Conor, and I adore you. But I have to come into the station for a couple of hours tomorrow morning and I can meet you after. Then we can spend the whole afternoon together.'

'You mean it? The whole afternoon?'

Katie kissed him again. 'The whole afternoon. I promise.'

Conor kissed her back, and then, very gently, with both hands, he took hold of her thighs and opened her legs wide. He bent his head down and licked her lasciviously, and sucked her, and when he looked up again he said, 'There. At least I'll be able to taste you tonight. I won't brush my teeth till the morning.'

As she drove home to Cobh, Katie thought: *Why did I leave him like that? I was enjoying his lovemaking, too – in fact I was loving it – and I didn't really have to go.*

She wondered if she was frightened of how strongly she was attracted to him, and of losing control.

Sometimes you need to let yourself go, Katie Maguire. You don't have to be a detective superintendent when you're naked, and in bed with a man who excites you so much. Or maybe you do.

Thirty-four

Gerry Mulvaney was woken up by somebody shaking his shoulder and saying, 'Gerry! Come on, Gerry! Wake up, boy! You can't sleep all day!'

He opened his eyes. He saw a middle-aged woman with chaotic hair, grinning at him. He looked all around him and saw that he was lying in a room with pale green walls. No pictures, only pale green walls. A yellowish blind was drawn halfway down the window and he could hear that it was raining outside, and see raindrops dancing on the windowsill.

His brain felt as if it had turned into cotton wool. He couldn't think where he was, or why he was here. He couldn't even remember what his name was. He was aware of a dull throbbing pain in his lower right leg, below the knee, but it was a distant pain, almost as if his right leg belonged to somebody else, and he was feeling the pain sympathetically.

'Where – where the feck am I?' he said, slurrily. Even his lips felt as if they belonged to somebody else.

'You're in St Giles' Clinic, don't you remember?'

'No. I don't. And who the feck are you?'

'Oh get away with you, Gerry. I'm Grainne. You've known me for years. Listen look – here's himself. He'll tell you what the score is.'

A tall thin man leaned over Gerry like the jib of a crane. Gerry squeezed his eyes tight shut, and then opened them again, and now he began to piece together where he was, and what had happened to him, and who these people were.

'*Gearoid*,' he croaked. 'What are you doing to me, Gearoid? What you said before, about making me disabled and all, you wasn't being serious, was you, boy?'

'I told you, Gerry. I'm making you useful. Much more useful than you ever were before.'

'My fecking leg hurts.'

'It will, for a while yet, but don't worry. We'll be giving you the morphine to keep your suffering down to a minimum.'

'I want to get out of here, Gearoid. I want to go back to my kennels. How can I be selling Lorcan's dogs for him while you have me in here? Jesus, haven't you done enough to me? I never let you down before.'

'Well, I know that, Gerry,' said Gearoid. 'But you let us down this one time, and very badly, and how can I be sure that you won't let us down like that again? There's too much at stake here, Gerry.'

'What have you done to my leg? You haven't cut it off, have you?'

'Mother of God, Gerry, nothing so drastic as that. All I've done is taken out the bones below the knee.'

'You've *what*? How in the name of feck am I going to be able to walk, if you've taken my fecking bones out? Can't you put them back in again?'

'Sorry, no. Once I've taken them out, that's irreversible, and in any event Dermot will have disposed of them by now. Crushed them in the wood-chipper. Besides which, Gerry, you won't be required to walk in your new role in life. In fact it's preferable if you can't. Your new role in life requires you to be chronically disabled.'

Gerry tried to lift himself up, but he didn't have the strength. 'Please, Gearoid. Don't do this to me. I'll do anything you want – anything.'

'I know you would, Gerry, but what I want is for you to be crippled for life. That's the only way you're going to be of any use to me from now on.'

Gerry's eyes filled with tears, and he gave a deep, throat-wrenching sob. He tried to say something else to Gearoid, but he was so frightened and distressed that he couldn't speak.

Gearoid said, 'Grainne, will you tell Dermot to bring in the wheelchair now.' Then he leaned over Gerry again. 'What we're going to do now, Gerry, is show you some of your fellow travellers. You'll be taking some regular trips to England, once or twice a week at least, and I'd like you to see some of the people who'll be going with you, before you can't see them any more.'

'What – what do you mean by that?' Gerry choked out.

'You're going to be blinded, Gerry. You have to be. The people in England we're doing business with, they insist on it. Otherwise there's always a risk that you could identify them in a court of law, and that would be a disaster. For them, of course, but for me, too. My entire operation would collapse, and we're talking millions, Gerry – millions. Far more than your eyesight is worth, let me tell you.'

'You said before that I could choose! Blind or deaf, that's what you said! If it comes to that, I'd rather be deaf than fecking blind!'

'Yes, I said you could choose, Gerry, but like the scientist you are, you chose not to choose. Instead you tried to throw yourself out of the window and cost me two hundred euros in replacement glass. So I'm choosing for you, and I choose not only to take the bones out of your arms and your legs, but to make you blind and deaf. You'll still be able to feel, and to think, and to eat and drink and go through all of the other bodily functions, but you'll be trapped in your own little world, Gerry, and it'll be darkness and silence for the rest of your life.'

Gerry, again, was speechless, although his eyes were brimming with tears and his Adam's apple was working up and down with terror and self-pity.

Dermot came into the room pushing a wheelchair. Between them, he and Gearoid lifted Gerry off the bed and lowered him into it. He was wearing only a black T-shirt and a large white pair of adult incontinence pants. His left leg was bandaged and supported by a blue wraparound McDavid shin splint. He stopped sobbing once he was sitting in the wheelchair and wiped his eyes with the back of his hand, but he still wasn't able to speak.

'Come on, then, Gerry, let's take the grand tour,' said Gearoid. 'I just want you to appreciate that you're not the only one who's helping us out with this great enterprise of ours. By the time we've finished, we'll be the biggest importer of narcotics in the country. We'll make those gangs up in Dublin look like amateurs.'

Dermot pushed the wheelchair along the upstairs corridor until they reached a large room at the back of the house which overlooked the garden. The walls were plain, with no pictures on them, and there was no television, although there was a Bose music player on a side-table with a small stack of CDs beside it. Outside, it was raining hard, and all the laurel bushes were dripping.

There were seven armchairs in the room, arranged in a semi-circle, with their backs to the window. In four of these armchairs sat Siobhán and Fiontán, as well as another woman, dark-haired, a little older than Siobhán, and another young man, with a large nose and a blue shaven head with a deep red crescent-shaped cleft in it.

'Here they are, Gerry, your fellow heroes and heroines,' said Gearoid. 'There's two more, but Fearghal's having a bit of a sleep before we send him off to the UK this afternoon, and Kieran's still recovering from having his pelvis split apart. You were lucky by comparison. I didn't have to send my trusty helpers out to run you down. And when I mean run you down, that's what they do, they chase you in their car and they run you down.'

Dermot pushed Gerry up to Siobhán's chair. Siobhán was wearing a thick black polo-neck sweater and a baggy pair of jeans, and socks, but no shoes. Her head was lowered as if she were asleep, but as Gerry was pushed nearer she raised it, with a jerk, as if she could see him.

'This is Siobhán,' said Gearoid. 'She can hear you, but she's blind, and she can't say hello – or anything else, come to that. But she's done one run for us already, and we're very happy with her. She's pretty, don't you think? And when the customs officers see a pretty girl like Siobhán, stricken by blindness and such total disability, they're all the more inclined to wave the ambulance through without turfing her out of it so that they can search it.'

Siobhán made a gargling sound in her throat, but it was impossible to tell if she were trying to speak, or if she were doing nothing more than swallowing an excess of saliva.

Next, Gerry was pushed up to face Fiontán.

'For feck's sake take me out of here,' said Gerry. 'I don't need to see any more, Gearoid. This is doing nothing at all but putting the fear of God into me. Jesus, Gearoid, I can't face you turning me into one of these people. I'd rather you killed me. I mean it. Why don't you just fecking kill me?'

'Because dead people can't pay back what they owe, Gerry, and dead people are no use to me at all. I could fit out a hearse, I suppose, to carry drugs in, but how many times do you think I could ship your dead body to England and back before Revenue started sniffing at it and growing more than a mite suspicious?'

Fiontán's head was tilted back, and he was dribbling and twitching with nervous spasms. The brunette woman kept turning her head from side to side, and she was clearly aware that there was somebody else in the room, although she could neither see them nor hear them. The young man with the cleft in his head sat utterly still, his blind blue eyes staring at nothing, but endlessly grinding his teeth.

'This is Breda, and this is Val,' said Gearoid. 'You'll be making the journey with one or other of them from time to time, so it's good for you to have an idea of what they look like.'

Gerry closed his eyes. He obviously knew that it was useless for him to repeat 'kill me', so he said nothing. Gearoid had already lamed him. If he blinded him and deafened him and made it impossible for him to speak, that would be just like being dead, except that he would still be alive.

'Right,' said Gearoid. 'I think it's time to make a start on you, Gerry. Will you take him through to the operating room, Dermot, and strap him on the table? I'll be with you in a minute. I have to ring my mother. She hasn't been feeling too bright lately.'

'*Gearoid*,' said Gerry, but that was all.

Dermot pushed him back along the corridor and into the room that Gearoid used as an operating theatre. Gerry had stopped crying now, and he was starting to feel numb, as if none of this was really happening. The numbness was partly caused by the morphine that he had been given to suppress the pain in his leg, and partly by his brain defending him against the horror of what was going to be done to him.

Grainne helped Dermot to heave Gerry out of the wheelchair and on to the operating table. Dermot fastened a wide black canvas strap around his thighs, and tightly buckled it up, and then he forced his arms down by his sides and buckled a second canvas strap across his midriff.

'Not hurting you at all, the straps?' Dermot asked him.

'Get away to feck with you, Dermot,' Gerry retorted. 'As if you give a shite.'

They waited for Gearoid to join them. Gerry lay helplessly bound to the table, staring up at the ceiling, while Dermot jabbed at his mobile phone and Grainne hummed 'Red Is The Rose'. For a moment, Gerry thought that she was humming it only to mock him, because he had sung it to his girlfriend Aoife when he had proposed to her, more years ago than he could count. Aoife had died of ovarian cancer when she was only thirty-seven, and Gerry had never remarried. After Aoife had gone, his only companions had been his dogs, and most of those he had never much cared for.

Oh, Aoife, if you could see me now, that boy who sang to you.

Gearoid came into the room. He didn't speak as he took down his green surgical gown from the hook by the door and pushed his arms into it. Grainne tied it up for him at the back. Then he put on his surgeon's cap, and his mask, although he didn't pull his mask up over his face. He leaned over Gerry and smiled and said, 'You won't be needing the anaesthetic for this, Gerry. This is a very simple procedure and in spite of what you might think, it doesn't hurt too much. So I'm told, anyway, not having experienced it for myself.'

He beckoned Dermot to come around to the top end of the operating table. 'Grab a hold of Gerry's ears for me, Dermot, and hold his head still. This won't take long but we don't want him shaking his head around like a wet retriever.'

He opened Gerry's right eye wide with his index finger and his thumb, and then he turned to Grainne and said, 'Pass me the speculum, will you?'

She handed him a wire speculum, and he inserted it under Gerry's eyelid to prevent him blinking. Gerry grunted and tried to twist his head to one side but Dermot was gripping his ears far too tight.

'Spoon,' said Gearoid, and Grainne gave him a long-handled surgical spoon, with a very small bowl at the end of it.

Gearoid said to Gerry, 'This is what we call enucleation, Gerry. As I said, it's probably one of the most painless ways of blinding you. I've tried all kinds of different methods, like caustic liquids and penetrating the eyeball with a pointed instrument, but I think you'll agree with me that this is the least traumatic.'

He inserted the spoon into Gerry's eye socket, wiggling it slightly so that it cupped the back of the eyeball. Gerry gasped, and panted. He would have screamed, but he didn't have enough air in his lungs.

Very slowly, and with a soft sucking sound, Gearoid scooped Gerry's glistening eyeball out of its socket. It stared at him without expression on the end of his spoon, still fastened to the thin pink optic nerve.

'Scissors,' he said, and Grainne passed him a pair of scissors with small curved blades. He snipped the optic nerve, which shrivelled back into Gerry's empty eye socket like a worm with its head cut off.

Gearoid carefully removed the speculum and Gerry's eyelid drooped shut, although blood slid out from under it, diluted by his tears.

'There... that wasn't so bad, was it, Gerry?' said Gearoid. He held up Gerry's right eye in front of his left one, so that he could see it. Still panting with shock, Gerry stared at it in disbelief.

'What did Humphrey Bogart say at the end of *Casablanca*?' said Gearoid. "Here's looking at you, kid."'

Gerry exhaled loudly through his nose, and then his left eye closed, too. Grainne prodded him, and when she got no response, she said, 'Look, he's passed out. Did you *have* to do that, like – show him his eye? Hasn't he suffered enough trauma already, for the love of God, what with his leg.'

Gearoid pulled down his face mask. 'Come on, Grainne. What's the point of punishing someone if they don't see how they're being punished? He could have ruined everything. He could have cost us millions. We could have ended up doing ten years in jail because of him.'

Dermot was growing impatient for a smoke. 'He's wiped,' he said. 'How much longer do I have to keep holding on to his ears for?'

Gearoid looked down at Gerry. His cheeks were still rough and scarlet but the rest of his face was chalky white, so that he looked like a comatose clown. Gearoid thought for a few seconds and then said, 'Kidney bowl,' to Grainne. She held the bowl out for him and he dropped Gerry's eye into it. The eye stared at the bottom of the bowl as if it didn't understand what it was doing there.

'All right,' said Gearoid. 'Let's extract the other eye while we're at it. There'll be too much for us to do this afternoon getting the ambulance ready.'

He pulled up his mask again, held out his hand, palm upwards, and said, 'Spoon.'

Thirty-five

Katie had intended to arrive at the station early that morning, but she overslept and didn't arrive until 10:15, yawning and carrying a cup of strong black coffee. Her only breakfast had been two oat-and-honey bars which she had eaten in the car.

John had called out for her three or four times during the night. First he had complained that he was suffering excruciating phantom pain in his legs. Then his throat had been burning with a raging thirst and he had drunk all of his water. Next his bedcover had slipped off on to the floor and he was shivering with cold, but his legs had been hurting too much for him to get out of bed and pick it up. After that he had been woken up by a nightmare that Katie had been badly injured at work and he had wanted to make sure that it wasn't true.

As she drove into the city, in a downpour that was almost blinding, she had received a message from the chief technical officer Bill Phinner to call him as soon as she could. Once she had reached her office, she took off her hooded raincoat and shook it, fluffed up her hair, and then rang him.

He came up carrying the brown leather briefcase. She couldn't tell from his expression what his test results might have been, because he always looked miserable, as if he couldn't understand why God had put him on this earth to perform such a grisly job.

'How's it going on, Bill?' Katie asked him.

Bill set the briefcase down on her desk and clicked it open. The bundles of money were still inside, covered in bubble-wrap.

'Like er, we found traces of saliva and phlegm on the interior lining of the briefcase and also on some of the banknotes, which would indicate that whoever was handling them sneezed while they were doing it. We also found two grey human hairs.'

'So who are we looking for? Somebody old, with a cold?'

'As per your instructions, we compared the saliva with a swab taken from Assistant Commissioner O'Reilly's telephone handset, and we also took a sample from a toothbrush in his toilet. The hairs we compared with hairs that we found on the back of his chair and also on the carpet under his desk.'

'And?'

'There's no doubt about it at all. If Jimmy O'Reilly didn't fill that briefcase with money himself, then he was unquestionably present while somebody else was doing it. And sneezed.'

Katie sat down. She felt as if all her suspicions had been vindicated, but she also felt deflated and more than a little apprehensive. She wished in a way that Bill had said that there was no evidence that Jimmy O'Reilly had packed that money for Maureen Callahan, because now she was faced with having to confront him, and the dilemma of whether or not she should report him to the GSOC.

She thought it was sad, too, that Jimmy O'Reilly hated her so much, and found her so threatening. She hadn't told anyone about his relationship with James Elvin, but he obviously found it intolerable that she knew about it. His plan to discredit her had been absurd and ill thought-out, but if she hadn't taken the precaution of tracking Maureen Callahan's car, and if Kyna hadn't almost miraculously produced that photograph of Branán O'Flynn in Las Palmas, he still could have damaged her career so drastically that she would have had to resign.

'What's the story behind this, ma'am?' asked Bill. 'I asked Ó Doibhilin but he said to ask you.'

'Let's just say that it's very complex,' said Katie. 'Apart from that, I don't know what the consequences are going to be. We took the hair and saliva samples from Jimmy O'Reilly's office without his knowledge or consent. However they're both non-intrusive samples and I'm sufficiently senior to have authorised it and I have every reason to believe that an offence has been committed.'

'Really? What nature of offence, exactly?'

'I'm going to be discussing this with Jimmy O'Reilly face-to-face, Bill, and we'll see where we go from there. Meanwhile if you can keep this whole thing to yourself.'

'Well, that won't be difficult since I have no idea what "this whole thing" actually is. But I assume that if I looked into a crystal ball I might see a violent collision between "shite" and "fan" in the very near future.'

'You have it, Bill. Thank you. I'll keep you up to date.'

* * *

Half an hour later, Conor rang her and asked her if she still had the afternoon free.

'So far as I know. I have some paperwork to catch up with, but after that, yes.'

'Maybe we could have lunch together. Where's good on a Sunday?'

'Perrott's Garden Bistro at the Hayfield Manor if you can get us in. They're usually very busy, but their Sunday lunch is fantastic.'

'I'll see what I can do. Is it okay if I mention your name? And your rank?'

'Don't you dare. If they're all booked up we'll go for a Thai.'

It took her only another hour to go through all of her files and all her reports. She checked with Detective Dooley on Keeno's condition at the Mercy, but he told her that there was still no change.

'No better, but no worse. Who knows? He might stay like that for ever. Stuck between heaven and hell, like, and welcomed by neither.'

She also checked to see if any members of the public had responded to their new appeal for witnesses to the stabbing of Martin Ó Brádaigh, but none had.

She had almost finished going through her budget figures when Detective Scanlan knocked at her door.

'Pádraigin,' said Katie, putting down her pen. 'I didn't think you were working today.'

'It was the best day to catch that priest you wanted me to talk to, Father Brennan. He was fierce evasive, and he wouldn't talk at all about what happened when he visited the Knocknaheeny Youth Project. I went very easy on him, though, and I've arranged to talk to him again. I think I'll get more out of him next time, when he's not so defensive. I didn't want to scare him into wiping his laptop, either.'

'So have you finished for today?'

'I have, yes. But I was surprised to see Assistant Commissioner O'Reilly just now. I thought I heard you say that he was in Dublin this weekend.'

'He's here? Now?'

'I saw him go into his office. I said good morning but he didn't even look at me. I'd say he's real thwarted about something.'

Katie opened her desk drawer and took out the note that James Elvin had written for Jimmy O'Reilly. Then she pulled a pair of forensic gloves out of her jacket pocket, snapped them on, and picked up the briefcase. Detective Scanlan looked at her, puzzled.

'What?' she said. 'Have I said something?'

'You'll find out soon enough,' Katie told her, with the grimmest of smiles. 'Or maybe not. It depends.'

Detective Scanlan went back to the squad room to fetch her coat, while Katie walked down the corridor to Assistant Commissioner O'Reilly's office. The door was closed so she rapped on it, hard. At first there was no answer, so she rapped again.

'Who is it?' Jimmy O'Reilly called out, impatiently. 'I'm up the walls right now.'

Katie opened the door and went in. Jimmy O'Reilly was standing behind his desk, holding his phone to his ear. He was wearing a dishevelled light grey suit, and he had loosened his black Freemasons tie.

'Hold on a moment, David,' he said. 'I have a visitor.' Then to Katie, he said, 'What is it you want, Katie? I have my solicitor on the phone here.'

Katie held up the briefcase. Jimmy O'Reilly stared at it, and then he said, 'David? Listen, David, something's come up. I'll ring you back in just a while.'

He put down the phone. 'What do you expect me to say?' he asked Katie.

'I'm sure you'll say nothing,' said Katie. 'Nothing to incriminate yourself, anyway.'

'So what are you holding up that briefcase for?'

'You know why, sir.'

'I never saw that briefcase before in my life.'

'So you filled it with twenty thousand euros with your eyes closed, did you?'

'I don't know what you're talking about. My God, you'd do anything to stir up trouble for me, wouldn't you?'

'If anybody's an expert on stirring up trouble, I'd say that it's you. Well, maybe you're not. Paying off Maureen Callahan to fool me into thinking that there was an arms shipment, that wasn't too expert, was it? And trying to fix it so that I organised a raid on a children's birthday party? Forget about my reputation. What if a child had been hurt, or even killed?'

'I still have no idea what you're talking about.'

'I've had this briefcase and the banknotes inside it checked by Bill Phinner's technical experts for DNA. It matches your DNA, sir, I'm sorry to say. Do you remember sneezing while you were wrapping up that money?'

Katie and Jimmy O'Reilly stared at each other for almost a quarter of a minute without saying anything. They both knew what Jimmy O'Reilly had tried to set up, and that he had failed, and they both knew that there was no point in him trying to deny it.

'I'll, ah – I'll, ah – be having that briefcase back now, if you don't mind, Katie,' said Jimmy O'Reilly, holding out his hand.

'No, sir. This is evidence.'

'It's my briefcase, for Christ's sake, and the money inside it is also mine. It cost me dear, raising that money, I can tell you, in more ways than one. I can't afford to lose it.'

'I'm fully aware of that, sir,' said Katie. She took James Elvin's note out of her inside pocket and put it down on his desk. He frowned at it, and said, 'What's that?' but then he saw his name *Jimmy* scrawled on it, in blue ballpen. He looked up at Katie and his face was stricken.

Katie said, 'Look, listen, I'll leave you in peace to read what it says. Then maybe you and I can have a talk later about what steps we're going to take next. I'll be here for the next half-hour, then I'm leaving for the rest of the day.'

Jimmy O'Reilly didn't answer her, and made no move to pick up James Elvin's note. Katie left his office and walked back to her own, half-expecting him to come running after her down the corridor to snatch the briefcase out of her hand. She even looked over her shoulder, but although his office door remained half-open, he didn't appear.

She sat at her desk and waited for twenty minutes, although she was more than ready to leave. She thought that she should at least give Jimmy O'Reilly the time for what she had said to him to sink in – that, and James Elvin's note that he was leaving him.

She stood up, opened her black patent shoulder-bag and took out her hairbrush and her make-up. She was pouting at herself in her mirror to apply some fresh lipstick when Jimmy O'Reilly suddenly materialised in her office doorway like a beamed-up character out of *Star Trek*.

He walked up to her until he was almost close enough to take the lipstick out of her hand. His default expression was miserable, but she had never seen him look like this before. He had a strange unfocused look in his eyes as if he were drunk, but he didn't smell of drink, only faintly of stale cigarettes and body odour.

He lifted his left hand and thoughtfully stroked his chin, his eyes half-closed, while he kept his right hand behind his back.

'Do you know what they say?' he whispered. He was so quiet that she could hardly hear him. 'They say that every man has a Nemesis, and that Nemesis punishes every man who happens to be blessed with good fortune.'

'Listen, sir – ' Katie began. She wanted to tell him that he had given her no choice, but he lifted his finger to his lips and said, '*Shhh! You* listen.'

He came even closer, and Katie couldn't back away because her leg was already pressed against her desk.

'You, Katie Maguire, you're my Nemesis,' he continued. 'I had one of the most respected positions in the Garda. I had a young man who adored me. Then *you* came into my life, and now I have nothing at all.'

'Sir – I'm sure we can come to some kind of a compromise about what you tried to set up with Maureen Callahan,' said Katie. 'If you never try to do anything like that again, there's no reason why we can't put it behind us. Everybody makes rash decisions at times, and you were very angry with me. I understand that.'

'But you'll always have that threat hanging over me, won't you? You're not only my Nemesis, you're my sword of Damocles! I'm supposed to be your superior officer, but how can I act like your superior officer when I know that you could ruin me at a moment's notice – because I said something that upset you, or because you disagreed with one of my orders, or for no other reason except you were having your monthly?'

'Sir—'

'Ever since I first met you, Katie, I disliked you. I disliked your cleverness, and your self-satisfaction, and the fact that they promoted you only because you're a woman. And that's what I dislike about you most of all – you're a woman.'

Katie was about to say something else to calm him down when he produced a nickel-plated Sig-Sauer automatic from behind his back. Katie recognised it immediately: it had been presented to him for twenty-five years' service. He lifted it up so that it was pointing toward the ceiling, and ostentatiously cocked it.

Three alternatives flashed into Katie's mind. She could try to twist the gun out of his hand, although he might be able to angle it towards her while they were struggling and pull the trigger. Either that, or she could drop sideways to the floor, pulling out her own gun while she did so, and shoot him, if he didn't shoot her first. Then again, she could kick him, as hard as she had kicked Keeno, but because he was standing so close it would be difficult for her to swing her leg for enough momentum.

'I hope... I hope from the bottom of my heart that you never forget this,' said Jimmy O'Reilly.

Before Katie could grab his wrist he opened his mouth wide, stuck the muzzle of the gun between his white false teeth and fired. There was an ear-splitting bang and the back of his head burst open, spraying blood and brains across the plain beige carpet in a wide fan shape. There was even a fine haze of blood on the opposite wall, beside the couches, over Katie's framed certificates.

For a split-second, Jimmy O'Reilly was staring at Katie with the saddest, most desperate look in his eyes that she had ever seen, and then he toppled over backwards with his arms flapping like a man falling off a cliff. He hit the carpet with a thud and lay still.

Inspector O'Rourke was the first one to come running into Katie's office. He must have just come in from outside, because his windcheater was sparkling with raindrops.

Katie was still standing beside her desk, with her hand pressed over her mouth in shock.

'Jesus Christ,' said Inspector O'Rourke. Katie could tell that he was making an instant assessment of what might have happened. He saw that Katie wasn't armed and that the nickel-plated Sig-Sauer was lying on the floor where Jimmy O'Reilly had dropped it.

'Don't tell me he's topped himself, right in front of you.'

Katie nodded, and then she turned and walked stiff-legged to her toilet. She went inside and brought up three heaving splashes of coffee and chewed-up oats into her washbasin.

She lifted her head and stared at herself in the mirror. She was surprised by how calm and unruffled she looked, although her lipstick was smudged.

She went back into her office. Inspector O'Rourke had been joined by Detective Sergeant Begley and Detective Markey and four uniformed gardaí. They were all standing around the doorway looking stunned.

Inspector O'Rourke was prodding at his mobile phone. He looked up and said, 'Are you right, ma'am?'

'I'm okay,' said Katie. 'You'd best call Bill Phinner up here to take some pictures, and an ambulance, and Dr Cullinane.' Dr Cullinane was the Cork City Coroner, and she would require formal proof of Jimmy O'Reilly's identity, and evidence of his cause of death.

'I've called Bill already,' said Inspector O'Rourke. 'He's coming up here himself, along with a couple of his technical experts. I'm just ringing for a white van now. Dr Cullinane won't be in her office today but I'll leave her a message so.'

It was then that Katie's own phone played "Tá Mo Chleamhnas a Dhéanamh". She answered it immediately and it was Conor.

'I've managed to book us a table at the Hayfield, although it took some persuasion. When will you be finished?'

'I won't be, Conor, not today. I'm sorry. We've had a bit of a tragedy here, to be honest with you.'

'A tragedy? What do you mean? What kind of a tragedy?'

'There's only one kind of tragedy, isn't there? The kind that never should have happened, but did.'

Thirty-six

Ger backed the ambulance up to the porch of St Giles' Clinic and Milo opened the doors. It was raining so hard now that it was almost laughable, and water was clattering down the side of the porch from a broken gutter.

Gearoid looked at his watch and said, 'Where in God's name has Lorcan got to? He said that he'd be here by two-thirty at the latest.'

'He probably went down to Bandon to see that woman of his,' said Grainne. She was dressed already in her paramedic's uniform, and she was smoking a last cigarette before she climbed into the ambulance.

'No, no. He's finished with that one,' said Gearoid. 'He only used her so that he could work out how to break into her kennels. Well, to be fair, that wasn't the only reason. It seems like she wasn't getting much from her husband, and she was a bit of a tornado in bed.'

'I know he's your brother but he worries me sometimes,' said Grainne. 'He lets his heart rule his head, do you know what I mean, and he lets his mickey rule both of them.'

Just as she said that, the black Opel turned into the driveway with its headlights on and parked beside the ambulance. Lorcan climbed out and hurried towards them through the rain.

'I'm not going to ask you where you've been,' said Gearoid.

'That's a mercy. I've been down to Riverstick, as a matter of fact, to feed Gerry's dogs. They were starving, most of them. I think I can sell one or two of them, but the rest I'll have to take up to Bartley, to use as bait.'

'I hope he'll pay you for them.'

'Sure I won't be asking him for money. All he has to do is give me a few tips on which are the gamer dogs, and then I'll be going to Egypt for my holliers, first class.'

'Egypt? You don't want to be going there. It's full of terrorists.'

'You think I'm scared of terrorists?'

Siobhán was wheeled out of the front door and then Dermot and Milo lifted her into the back of the ambulance. Dermot went back inside and came out a few moments later pushing Fearghal on a trolley. Milo helped him to lift him into the ambulance, too. Fearghal was staring upwards all of the time, as if he expected to see angels descending from the clouds, and he was making an extraordinary whirring sound in the back of his throat.

'You know what that feller reminds me of?' said Lorcan. 'A fecking grasshopper I once ran over with my lawnmower, and chopped its legs off. It made that noise exactly.'

Grainne climbed into the back of the ambulance and Milo closed the doors.

Gearoid said to Lorcan, 'Chill your gills this trip, and I mean it. Wardy's had a new delivery in from Rotterdam and he says it's huge. You may have to go over to Essex again the middle of the week, but we should have the second ambulance up and running by then. It only needs a new alternator, and Sonny says he can fit that in tomorrow.'

'Tuesday I'll be going up to Tipp, to Bartley's place,' Lorcan told him. 'There's some kennel owner from Carrigahorig who says he has a Neapolitan mastiff for sale, for fighting.'

'Jesus,' said Gearoid. 'They're enormous, those Neapolitan mastiffs, when they're fully grown.'

'That's why I'm interested. You could fecking rake it in with a monster of a dog like that, in betting stakes.'

Gearoid patted Lorcan on the shoulders and then he said, 'Any road, it's time for you to go. I don't think this weather's going to be improving, and I heard there's new roadworks past Kilmacthomas.'

Milo came up to them and said, 'Are we out the gap, then? This rain's going to get worse before it gets better.'

Lorcan went back to his car. Before Grainne climbed into the back of the ambulance, she flicked her cigarette butt away, blew out smoke, and said to Gearoid, 'I don't know. I read my Tarot cards last night and I have a fierce quare feeling about this trip.'

Gearoid shook his head in amusement. 'Grainne, if I had believed in everything that fortune-tellers told me, I never would have done anything with my life, ever. I would have stayed in bed and lived on take-aways, too scared to go out.'

'A fortune-teller warned you to beware of a baby, didn't she? You told me that yourself.'

'I only told you that to prove how easy it is to read anything into what fortune-tellers warn you about. We believe what we want to believe, and we turn a blind eye to everything else.'

'Just like poor old Gerry,' said Grainne. She stepped up into the ambulance and Milo closed the doors behind her. Gearoid stood in the porch and watched as the black Opel and the ambulance drove out of the clinic on to the Middle Glanmire Road and then turned sharp left into Lover's Walk.

Dermot sniffed and said, 'You'll be wanting to go up and see to Gerry. He woke up ten minutes ago and he's been throwing a ghand ever since so I had to use the ball gag to shut him up.'

'In that case, I think it's time I took out his tongue,' said Gearoid. 'I think we've all heard enough from Gerry Mulvaney to last us a lifetime.'

* * *

They had only driven a short distance past Tivoli Docks when the ambulance's engine started to make loud knocking noises. The knocking grew louder and louder until it reverberated through the whole body of the ambulance and Grainne shouted out from the back, 'What's wrong, Ger? Pull over, for the love of God, we're getting mangalated here!'

Ger turned the ambulance into the narrow driveway that led to the Lota Brothers of Charity. Lorcan drew his car in close behind them. He came hurrying up to the ambulance in the rain, just as Ger and Milo climbed out.

'What have you stopped for?' he shouted, above the swishing of passing cars.

'Sounds like the big end's gone,' said Ger. 'There's no way this feller's going to England – not today, any road.'

'I don't fecking believe this,' said Lorcan. 'We have a shipment to pick up that's worth hundreds of thousands, and now we can't do it because a crappy second-hand ambulance has broken down.'

Ger pushed his wet fringe out of his eyes. 'Spot on,' he said, with complete equanimity. 'You have it exactly.'

'Christ on a bicycle,' said Lorcan. 'We'll just have to turn round and go back to the clinic. I'll ring Gearoid and see if we can't get one of the other ambulances going.'

'The only one that's halfway near ready needs a new alternator,' Ger told him. 'The other one, they haven't finished fitting out the inside yet. There wouldn't be nowhere to stash the stash, like.'

'I don't fecking believe this!'

'There's nothing we can do about it, boy,' said Milo, as placidly as Ger.

'You're right, we'll have to go back,' said Lorcan. 'But Jesus – Gearoid's going to go mental.'

He returned to his car while Ger and Milo climbed back into the ambulance. Ger turned the key in the ignition and the starter-motor whinnied, but all that happened was a loud and very final-sounding *clonk*.

'Sure lookit, it's banjaxed,' said Milo. 'Totally and utterly banjaxed. I'll have to ring Sonny to come out and give us a tow.'

Lorcan came back again and knocked on the driver's door window. 'What in the name of Jesus is going on?' he demanded. Ger opened the door and climbed out again.

'Won't start,' he said. 'Milo's calling Sonny to give us a tow back to Montenotte.' As he spoke, though, he looked over Lorcan's shoulder and said, 'Sketch, boy. Shades.'

'What?' said Lorcan, turning around to see a Garda Nissan Terrano pulling in behind his Opel. 'Oh shite. That's all we fecking need.'

Two gardaí came walking towards them, putting on their caps. One was a tall, burly man; the other was a small blonde woman.

Lorcan said to Ger, out of the corner of his mouth, 'You don't know me, okay? You broke down and I'm a just passing motorist who stopped to see if I could give you some assistance. Do you have that? Because I'm out of here now.'

Milo came around the ambulance and he quickly repeated the same words to him. 'If they think we're travelling together they'll want to know why, and who I am, and right now I can't think of any plausible explanation.'

'What's the problem here?' asked the male garda, as he approached. 'This is the road to the Brothers of Charity campus, are you aware of that, and I'm afraid you're obstructing it.'

'Oh, right, the Brothers of Charity,' said Milo. 'They're the ones who look after the loonies, aren't they? Well, I'm sorry about that, but our ambulance has broken down and we're waiting on a tow.'

Lorcan said, 'I only stopped to see if there was anything I could do to help, but these fellers seem to have it under control. So I'll be heading off, okay?'

'Yes, okay,' the garda told him, and Lorcan walked back to his car, climbed into it, and drove off. He could have turned around at the next roundabout, which was only a hundred metres further up the road, but he didn't want the guards to see him going back the way he had come, so he turned left to return to Montenotte through Glanmire Village.

Milo said to the gardaí, 'I've rung Sonny Powers from Powers Motors in Togher, and he's promised us a tow truck asap. So we won't be blocking up this entrance for too much longer.'

'Where were you heading?' the female garda asked him.

'Oh, well, Rosslare, like, for the ferry. We were on our way to a rehab clinic in England. It's a regular run we have to make. We take our patients there for specialist therapy which unfortunately is not available to them here in Cork.' That was the line that Gearoid had made him learn word for word, in case they were ever questioned by the Garda or by Revenue.

'Do you have any patients on board now?'

'Only the two. But they'll be grand altogether for the moment. There's a nurse in there with them in case they need anything, you know like a drink or any medicamation.'

'Would you open the doors, please, so that we can see them?'

'Well, now, I wouldn't want to be disturbing them. They're probably out for the count, do you know what I mean? We always give them a sedative before they travel, so they don't get distressed. Like I said, they'll be grand altogether.'

'Would you open the doors, please, so that we can see them?' the female garda repeated.

Milo wiped the rain from his forehead with the back of his hand. 'They have serious disabilities, the both of them. I can't be responsible if they have some kind of a seizure.'

'Open the doors, sir,' said the male garda.

'If you insist,' said Milo, and puffed out his cheeks in resignation. He opened the doors, and then stepped away. Inside, Grainne was sitting between Siobhán and Fearghal, and she stood up apprehensively as the two gardaí came up close to the back of the ambulance. Fearghal was sitting strapped in a harness in a metal chair, while Siobhán was lying on the trolley, covered in a pale blue blanket. Both of them were awake, and when Siobhán heard the doors open and the sound of traffic and rain outside, she flapped her arms, and managed to make a honking noise in the back of her throat.

'Poor creature, she's fierce easily upset by strangers,' said Grainne.

Fearghal remained motionless, staring at the darkness inside his head.

'Would you put down the steps, please,' said the female garda.

Grainne was about to protest, but Milo caught her eye and shook his head. Gearoid had warned him to keep any encounters with guards or customs inspectors as low-key as possible. '*Get up their nose, Milo, and they'll start sniffing around.*'

Milo lowered the steps and the female garda climbed inside the back of the ambulance. She looked closely at Fearghal first, and waved her hand in front of his face. 'He's very unresponsive, isn't he?'

'Blind, deaf, and double amputee,' said Grainne. 'He was in a road accident when he was twelve. Both of his parents were killed so he was lucky.'

The garda said nothing, although it was plain from her expression what she was thinking. If Fearghal was lucky, God have mercy on anybody less fortunate than he was.

Next the garda turned to Siobhán.

'What about her?'

'Brain tumour,' said Grainne. 'She's blind, and unable to speak, or walk, or grasp anything in her hands. It's a very sad case because she's a fine half, isn't she?'

Siobhán was aware that the garda was standing close to her, and again she honked and flapped her arms. Grainne laid her hand on her forehead and said, 'Ssh, now, darling. It's only the guards making sure that you're being well taken care of.'

The female garda took out her iPhone and quickly prodded it. When she found what she was looking for, she swiped her finger quickly to the left. She peered intently at the screen for a moment, and then she glanced down at Siobhán, and then she put her phone back in her pocket.

'I'm very concerned about this young woman's condition,' she said. 'I'm calling for an ambulance to take her to the University Hospital.'

'What?' said Grainne. 'You can't do that. She's legally in the care of St Giles' Clinic. We have all of her records and all of her medication, and we know exactly how to deal with her anxiety fits, which they won't know how to do at the hospital. You'll be putting her life at risk if you take her.'

The female garda ignored her and called emergency services. Out in the rain, her male colleague had been taking pictures of the ambulance, as well as Milo and Ger. When he saw her talking on her iPhone, he said, 'What's the story, Róisin?'

'This young woman looks like she's suffering some kind of an episode,' said the female garda. 'I've called for a white van to take her into CUH.'

She turned to Grainne and said, 'What's her name, please?'

'I don't have to tell you that. And I'm protesting most strongly about you taking her.'

'Please tell me her name. Does she have next of kin that I can get in touch with? I'd like their contact details too.'

'I can't tell you anything without the permission of the doctor in charge of St Giles'. This is outrageous, do you know? This is totally outrageous.'

'So what's the name of the doctor in charge of St Giles'? We can ring him and get his permission right now.'

'Dr Fitzgerald. Dr Gearoid Fitzgerald. But he'll tell you the same as me. Siobhán is our patient and you have no right at all to take her out of our care. He'll make sure that your boss gives you down the banks for doing this, I swear to God.'

'Oh. So her first name's Siobhán? What's her surname?'

'That was a slip of the tongue, like. It might be Siobhán but then again it might not. And I'm not giving you any more information whatsoever. So there you have it.'

The female garda stepped down from the ambulance. She looked up at the male garda with the rain dripping from the peak of his cap and she gave him a look which she had given him more than once before when they had been on patrol together. She was wordlessly letting him know that there was more to her calling an ambulance than she had told him in front of Grainne.

Milo said, 'What's going on here? Grainne?'

'You'd best ring Gearoid,' said Grainne. 'These guards want to take Siobhán to CUH. They've already sent for an ambulance.'

Milo looked at the two gardaí and then he turned around to Ger. All Ger could do was pull a face and shrug. They both knew that if they tried to obstruct the guards in the course of carrying out their duty, they could be arrested.

Grainne said, 'Holy Saint Mary, I'll ring him myself. Give me your phone, Milo. I left mine at the clinic.'

She rang the clinic's number, but it was engaged. She waited, and rang again, and it was still engaged. Before she could try a third time, they saw blue lights flashing through the rain, and an ambulance appeared, and parked beside the St Giles' Clinic ambulance.

As two paramedics climbed out, Milo said to Ger, 'Come on, boy. There's feck all we can do about this. Let's get out of the rain.'

Thirty-seven

Katie spent the whole afternoon at the station while her office was photographed and Assistant Commissioner O'Reilly's body removed on a trolley, covered with a sheet. He would be taken to the mortuary for a post-mortem examination tomorrow by Dr Kelley or one of her associates, while his gun would be tested by Bill Phinner's team for fingerprints and DNA, just to make sure that Katie hadn't fired it.

Although it was considered highly unlikely that Katie had shot him, the animosity between them was common knowledge at Anglesea Street, and she was experienced enough at analysing crime scenes to have made it appear that he had committed suicide, even if she had killed him herself.

Chief Superintendent MacCostagáin was off today, so she commandeered his office while her own was being cleaned, and she rang him at home to tell him what had happened.

'God, you're not serious,' he said. It was teatime now and he sounded as if he had a mouth full of shortbread.

As simply as she could, Katie told him about Jimmy O'Reilly's plan to compromise her career, and about his doomed relationship with James Elvin, and how he had borrowed money from Bobby Quilty.

'Katie, you should have told me all this before. You know that.'

'You may not believe me, sir, but I didn't want to ruin him. All right, he was behaving like a complete browl, but he was in love with James, and you know the stupid things that people sometimes do when they're in love. And for all that he detested me and would have liked to have seen me sacked, he had a fantastic track record in the force, and he was a very good assistant commissioner.'

'How about his family? Have they been notified?'

'Yes, sir. His parents are deceased but he has two brothers and three sisters, and Inspector O'Rourke has been getting in touch with them.'

'I've called the Commissioner's office and told one of her assistants all about it. The media will have to be informed, of course, but it's up to her how she wants to announce it. She'll need to be fierce diplomatic with this one. If it comes out that he was gay, then there's not much we can do about it, except to say that we don't judge our senior officers on their sexual orientation, but only on their performance.'

Katie thought of Kyna when he said that, but of course she said nothing.

Half an hour later, she was called by Eithne, who had been working all weekend to finish her likeness of the dognapper whose brain had been blown out by Eoin Cassidy.

'I'm pure pleased with it,' she said. 'He really *looks* like a dognapper. I'm going to scan it now and email it to you.'

'How are you feeling?' Katie asked her.

'Sad. Bereft. But this work keeps my mind off it, like. It's so grisly that I have to concentrate completely, which I couldn't do if I was flower-arranging, say, or baking cakes.'

'Good girl yourself,' said Katie, gently. 'I can't wait to see what your dome-headed dognapper looks like.'

When Eithne's scan came through, Katie sat back in Chief Superintendent MacCostagáin's large leather chair and stared at it for a long time. Although he was a man, the dead dognapper's face reminded her of her geography teacher at school – furtive and ferrety and occasionally cruel, reducing some girls to tears. She would contact Mathew McElvey in the press office tomorrow and have this sent out to the media.

At 5:10 pm, Conor rang her.

'How's the tragedy coming along?' he asked her.

'Still tragic. But I've just about finished for the day.'

'I don't suppose I can interest you in a drink and dinner with your favourite pet detective.'

'No, Conor, I'm sorry. I'm flah'd out, to be crude about it. I'm going to go home and have a hot bath and watch some stupid television.'

'At least have a quick drink with me before you go. I missed you today. I really, really missed you.'

Katie kept on staring at the dead dognapper. Eithne had caught a deeply unsettling expression in his eyes, as if he could actually see her staring at him, and intended to do something extremely unpleasant to her for being so inquisitive.

'One drink, then,' she said. 'I'll meet you in the Market Tavern across the road.'

* * *

Conor was already sitting at the back of the pub when she arrived. He stood up and held out his arms for her, and even though she had promised herself that she wouldn't show him how devastated she had been by Jimmy O'Reilly shooting himself in front of her, she burst into tears when he held her and her mouth was dragged down by a painful, ugly sob.

The barman stood and watched them with polite curiosity as Conor hugged her and shushed her. At last, when they separated, and Katie took out a crumpled handkerchief to wipe her eyes, he called out, 'Detective Superintendent? You'll be wanting your usual?'

Katie nodded and smiled and sat down with Conor under a framed photograph of Muhammad Ali. He laid his hands on top of hers and said, 'So what's this tragedy? It must have been a fierce tragic tragedy to upset *you* so much, Madam Hardboiled Detective.'

She told him, although she spoke very quietly and made sure that the barman couldn't overhear her. When she had finished, Conor could only sit back and say, 'Jesus H. Christ. No wonder you're shaken.'

'This is totally confidential, though, Conor. Noirin O'Sullivan will probably be making a statement to the media tomorrow, but until then you mustn't mention it to a soul.'

'You can trust me, Katie, you know that.'

Katie finished her first vodka and tonic in three distressed gulps, and then asked the barman for another. She tried to change the subject and talk to Conor about anything else except Jimmy O'Reilly, but all she could see in her mind's eye was the way he had looked at her after he had blown the back of his head off. Dead, of course, but sad to be dead, and it was only because of Katie that he had killed himself.

After her third drink, she squeezed Conor's hand and said, 'I'll have to be heading off home now. It's going to be a long day tomorrow.'

The pub had gradually become crowded while they were sitting there, and the last thing she wanted was to hear laughter and people telling jokes.

Conor said, 'You're not going to drive yourself, are you? You must be over the limit by now.'

'I'll be grand altogether, Conor. Don't you worry about me. I'll see you in the morning.'

'Katie – you can't drive yourself home. It's not only the drink. You're very tired and upset and it's easy to make a misjudgement when you're feeling like that. And look outside, it's pelting down. Six point seven on the Fliuch Scale, at least.'

Katie couldn't help smiling. *Fliuch* meant simply 'wet'. 'Fair play,' she said. 'I'll call for a taxi.'

'I'll drive you home myself. I've had only the one pint of Murphy's. Maybe I can even persuade you to let me stay the night.'

What Conor was suggesting sounded desperately attractive. If ever she had needed somebody to hold her tight in the middle of the night and comfort her, it was now. And she had to admit that she *was* slightly steamed.

'There's only one thing,' she said. 'I have a friend staying with me at the moment. He's recuperating after both his legs were amputated. A carer looks after him during the day, but I have to keep my ears open for him during the night.'

'He had both of his legs amputated?'

'It's a long story. But in a roundabout way, like, I feel responsible for what happened, and that's why I've been taking care of him.'

Conor shook his head. 'Jesus, Katie. It seems to me like you've got the whole damn world on your shoulders. Let me drive you home.'

Katie took a last sip of her drink, although there was nothing in the glass now but ice and a slice of lime. 'Yes,' she said. 'I'd like that. And I'd appreciate that, too. And I'd be pure grateful.'

They hurried across the junction to the Garda station car park, keeping close together under Katie's umbrella. As well as the pelting rain, the wind was beginning to gust. It was what her late husband Paul used to call 'dead umbrella weather' because the streets were littered with €4 umbrellas from Centra, all inside-out.

They climbed into Katie's Focus. Conor could barely squeeze himself behind the wheel and so he had to shift the driving-seat back as far as it would go. He leaned across and kissed her and said, 'I didn't realise how little you are.'

'Big enough to arrest you for seducing a Garda officer under the influence of Smirnoff.'

Conor drove them across the river and back to Cobh. Katie felt exhausted but she didn't want to close her eyes. Visibility was down to less than a hundred metres, even with the windscreen wipers flapping madly, and she was almost blinded by glaring headlights.

'I think it's God,' said Conor, as they passed the Passage West ferry terminal. 'He adjusts the weather to match our feelings. Have you ever once been to a funeral when it wasn't raining stair rods?'

They turned into Katie's front drive. As soon as Bridie opened the front door, Barney came out with his tail wagging wildly.

'This is Barney,' said Katie. 'Barney, this is Conor. Give him your best snuffle.'

Conor bent down and patted Barney and tugged at his ears, which Barney always loved. 'Oh, you're a grand feller you are!'

said Conor. 'Look at the lovely glossy coat on you. Almost the same colour as your mistress's hair.'

'I'm Bridie,' said Bridie, and raised her eyebrows at Katie as if to say 'Well, *he's* a sexy biscuit.' Katie could also sense that – with Conor here – she was hesitant to talk to her about John.

They took off their coats and went into the living-room.

'This is pure minimalist,' said Conor. 'Exactly how I would have imagined your house. Everything well under control – even the pictures on their walls.'

'To tell you the truth I think it's far too bare,' Katie told him. 'I'd love it a bit more cluttered but I never have the time to go out buying knick-knacks.'

Bridie said, 'He's asleep now, himself, and I can't see him waking up until morning. He had the phantom pain again this afternoon. It was something terrible so I dosed him with the maximum codeine that I could give him.'

'Otherwise?' Katie asked her. Bridie knew that she was inquiring about his mood.

'One minute up, like, the next minute down. Then back up again. He's still very optimistic about the future if you know what I mean.' Saying that, she glanced at Conor again, who was sitting on the couch and giving Barney a neck-rub. Barney was staring at him with adoring eyes. Katie had always believed that dogs can sense when somebody genuinely loves them, and when they're pretending. Barney had always been highly suspicious of strangers, especially if he thought that they might be threatening Katie in any way, but she had never seen him take to anybody so quickly.

'I'll be off, then,' said Bridie. 'Enjoy your evening, won't you?'

Katie prised off her shoes. 'Oh, that's a relief,' she said. 'How about some music and a nightcap?'

'Haven't you had enough?' said Conor.

'Probably, yes,' she said, climbing on to the couch and kissing him. 'But I feel like one more now I'm home, and I've some Murphy's in the fridge if you'd like one.'

'Go on, then. After the day you've had, I think you're forgiven.'

Katie put on the CD of soothing Celtic harp and flute music which she played to herself whenever her day had been stressful. She went into the kitchen and poured out a stout for Conor and then came back in and poured out a large glass of vodka for herself.

'You're going to have a fierce hangover tomorrow morning,' said Conor.

'It won't make a doonchie bit of difference, my darling,' said Katie. 'My whole job is a hangover at the moment. Some days I think that there's nothing else in the world that I'd rather be doing, but today I wish I was doing anything else but. At least if I was working behind the perfume counter in Brown Thomas or serving meals in Isaac's I wouldn't have people blowing their heads off right in front of me.'

Conor put his drink down, took her face in his hands as gently and reverently as if it were a communion chalice, and kissed her. She closed her eyes and opened her lips so that his tongue could tangle with hers, and then explore the inside of her mouth. She didn't want him to stop, because as long as he was kissing her she didn't have to think about anything else.

They sat and talked and kissed while the harp and flute music played soft and plaintive in the background, and Barney lay on the floor close to the couch, not sleeping, but obviously feeling contented, as if he were part of a family again.

'You must be hungry,' said Katie, sitting up straight. 'Here I am, being so selfish. Just because my stomach's all tied up in knots.'

'I wouldn't say no to a sandwich of something,' said Conor.

'There's some bacon-and-egg pie that Bridie made for lunch today if you don't mind that.'

'That sounds perfect.'

Katie went back to the kitchen and cut Conor a large slice of bacon-and-egg pie, which she garnished with cherry tomatoes and coleslaw. She brought it into the living-room on a place-mat and gave Conor a knife and fork. Then she sat close to him again and watched him eat. She loved the look of him so much that she couldn't resist touching his ear and kissing him.

'I know a joke about this,' said Conor, pointing to the pie with his knife.

'You know a joke about bacon-and-egg pie? Then tell me. Anything to get my mind off Jimmy O'Reilly.'

'There was two young Cork lads visiting Dublin and they went into this café. It was much posher than they were used to but they were starving. After they'd perused the menu, this very pretty young waitress comes up to them and says, "What'll you have?" and Seamus says, "I'd love a quickie." Well, the waitress can't believe her ears, so she says, "*What* did you say?" and Seamus tells her, "I'd really love a quickie." The waitress says, "You're disgusting," and storms off to fetch the manager. It's then that Brendan leans over to Seamus and says, "I think it's pronounced *quiche*."'

Katie looked at Conor a few seconds without saying anything and then she laughed.

'Mother of God,' she said. 'I never thought I'd end up today by laughing. You're a tonic, Conor, you truly are.'

'Oh, but they weren't stupid, those Cork lads. They paid for the quiche but they sneaked out without eating it.'

Katie slapped Conor's shoulder and said, 'You're mad. I think I love you.'

* * *

It was almost eleven o'clock by the time the music finished. Katie sat up and said, 'Come on, let's go to bed. I have to be up before fonya-haun tomorrow. There's going to be so much to do.'

She showed Conor into her bedroom so that he could undress. She made sure that Barney had water for the night and then she switched on the alarm. Before she returned to the bedroom she quietly opened the nursery door to make sure that John was still sleeping and that he hadn't dropped his bedcover on to the floor. He was lying on his back, his face very pale, and breathing almost silently.

My God, she thought, *haven't I ruined your life. You should never have come near me.*

Perhaps Jimmy O'Reilly had been right, and she *was* Nemesis. Not only his, but of every man who came close.

Conor was down to his white Calvin Klein briefs by the time she came back. She couldn't help noticing how much he was bulging.

'How's your friend?' he asked her.

'Oh, he's okay. Dead to the world.'

She quickly undressed herself. When she was naked, Conor put his arms around her, and stroked her bare back, and lightly kissed her forehead and her eyelids and her nose and then her lips. She tugged down his briefs and held him for a moment, but then she said, 'Let's take a shower and get some sleep.'

'That's the second-best suggestion I thought you'd come up with,' said Conor.

They showered together, and Katie lent Conor her toothbrush to clean his teeth, and then they climbed into bed. Katie was feeling dizzy from all of the vodka she had drunk and she was relieved when Conor came up close behind her and held her tight, because it stopped the bed from tilting up and down.

'Goodnight,' she said. 'And thank you. And God bless.'

His hand was cupping her breast and she could feel his erection against the small of her back as smooth and as hard as a polished bone. She knew how much he wanted to make love to her, but he was also considerate enough to let her close her eyes and try to get some sleep.

'*Oíche mhaith, codladh maith, agus aisling an-milis*,' he breathed into the hair behind her ear.

* * *

She was woken by the sound of a door opening. She opened her eyes and lay there, listening intently. It had stopped raining and the night was silent, except for Conor's steady breathing against her bare shoulder. The moon had risen, and was shining through the thin linen curtains, so that the bedroom was lit almost as brightly as daylight.

She lifted her head a little so that she could see her bedside clock. 2:47. Her mouth was dry and she was beginning to feel a headache behind her eyes, and she knew she should have drunk at least a pint of water before she went to bed.

She was about to ease herself out of bed and go to the kitchen when she heard a bump, followed by another bump, and then another, unsteady but insistent.

Dear Jesus, it was John. He had left the nursery and was walking down the hallway on his stumps. She needed to get up quickly and stop him from coming into the bedroom.

It was too late. As she tried to lift Conor's heavy arm off her without waking him, the bedroom doorknob turned, and the door slowly opened.

Katie dropped her head back on to the pillow and closed her eyes. Whatever John's reaction was going to be when he saw Conor lying next to her, she didn't want to confront him, or tell him to get out of her bedroom, not now, in the middle of the night.

The door opened wider and she heard two more bumps as he came into the room. He stopped, but she could hear him panting from the effort of having walked down the hallway.

Please don't say anything. Please just turn around and go back to bed and sob and rage and hate me as much as I deserve you to hate me. But please don't wake up Conor and please don't make some appalling scene.

She heard one more stumbling bump as John came closer. He was obviously trying to see who was lying next to her with his dark-haired arm around her. The panting continued, a little harsher now, and quicker.

Almost half a minute went by. Then she heard John turn around and slowly balance his way out of the bedroom. He closed the door behind him, very quietly.

Tears slid out of Katie's eyes and she had to bite her knuckle to stop herself from sobbing out loud. Her lungs hurt from suppressing her grief. All she could think of now was John painfully returning to his bed, having seen for himself now that she no longer loved him.

'He's still very optimistic about the future, if you know what I mean.'

Yes, Bridie, I know what you mean. I also know what it means to hurt him so badly that he will probably want to do nothing but die.

Thirty-eight

Conor was still sleeping at 6:15 when Katie climbed out of bed. She made as little noise as she could as she opened her wardrobe and took out her clothes and dressed. Today she wore a charcoal-grey merino sweater and a black trouser-suit. She was in mourning, and she was mourning more than the suicide of Jimmy O'Reilly.

She looked into the nursery but John was still asleep, too. She was reluctant to go in, but she crept halfway across the room so that she was close enough to hear him breathing.

At 6:35 she went back into her bedroom with a glass of grapefruit juice and a mug of coffee for Conor. She switched on the lights and even though it was still dark outside and the sun wouldn't rise for another hour and twenty minutes, she opened the curtains.

Conor opened his eyes and blinked at her as if he didn't recognise her. 'What?' he said, and looked around him.

'It's morning,' she told him. 'I have to be at the station before eight. We can have some breakfast when we get there.'

'I was having a dream,' said Conor. 'I was dreaming that I was running down a hillside with a pack of hounds, and we were chasing after this fellow. The hounds were baying and we were running as fast as we could but we never seemed to be able to catch up with him.'

Katie sat on the bed and kissed him. 'That was a dream of sexual frustration.'

He kissed her back. 'If that was only a dream, how come I'm still sexually frustrated now that I've woken up?'

'Maybe tonight,' said Katie. 'Let me see what the day brings first.'

Bridie arrived at seven and at seven-thirty Mrs Tierney from next door came to take Barney for his morning walk. Conor gave Barney a last affectionate ear-tugging and Barney seemed reluctant to leave him.

'You've made a friend for life there, Conor,' said Bridie.

Before she left for Anglesea Street, Katie went in to the nursery again to see John. This time he was awake, and he had switched on his bedside lamp. His face was expressionless, as if he hadn't yet decided if he should look wounded, or angry, or contemptuous, or forgiving, or something else altogether.

'How are you feeling?' she asked him. 'Do you still have pain in your legs?'

'What legs?' he said, flatly.

'They'll be fitting your first prosthetics this week. You said yourself that it would make all the difference.'

'Maybe it's too late for anything to make a difference.'

'John—' Katie began, but she couldn't think what to say to him. *Sorry*? because she wasn't sorry – not for having slept with Conor, anyway. *I still love you, but not in the way I used to*? because that would be a lie, too.

'Have a good day,' he told her. 'Will I be seeing you this evening, or what will you be doing?' He nodded his head towards the open door as if to indicate that he was asking her about Conor.

'I don't know yet. We're up the walls right now. I'll try to get back early, though. There's some things I need to talk to you about.'

'Oh, really? Don't put yourself out. I may not have legs but I have all the time in the world.'

Katie bent over him as if to kiss his forehead but he sharply turned his face away.

'I'll see you after so,' she told him.

Conor was waiting for her beside her car. He held up her keys and said, 'Do you want to drive?'

'No. You can, if you like. It makes for a pleasant change, having somebody else in the driving-seat.'

* * *

She had been sitting at her desk for only five minutes before Detective Sergeant Begley knocked at her door. He still had a yellowish bruise on his forehead from Keeno's head-butting, but otherwise he looked fit and rested. He also looked excited.

'Good to have you back, Sean,' said Katie. 'What's the story?'

'They told me all about Jimmy O'Reilly so soon as I came in this morning. Holy Mary, ma'am, I can't even find the words.'

'No, I know. It hasn't leaked out yet, but I expect the Commissioner will be making a formal announcement later today.'

'You're all right yourself, though? Apart from the shock of it, like.'

'Apart from having drunk a scatter of vodkas last night and feeling as sick as a plane to Lourdes – yes, Sean, I'm grand altogether.'

'Pleased to hear it, ma'am. But come here till I tell you this. Inspector Mulhare has just called me. I mean, literally two minutes ago. Two of his traffic cops attended a private ambulance which was broken-down on the N8 yesterday afternoon, round about fifteen-thirty – mostly because it was blocking up the entrance to the Lota Brothers of Charity. The cops found two disabled patients on board, a young girl and a young fellow, and when they took a lamp at them to make sure they were okay, guess who the young girl was?'

'Sean, it's a little early for guessing games, and like I say, I'm feeling a little delicate.'

'Siobhán O'Donohue, that's who it was – that girl reported missing after Hallowe'en night at the Eclipse Club. One of the traffic cops recognised her immediately.'

'But – what, she was *disabled*? Siobhán O'Donohue wasn't disabled, was she?'

'She wasn't when she went missing but she is now. And I mean gravely disabled. She's blind, she's unable to speak, and she's lost the use of both hands. Both legs have been badly fractured and not set properly, so she can't walk, either.'

'Mother of God. What action did he take? The traffic cop?'

'It was a she, actually. Garda Róisin O'Malley. She didn't want to alert the nurse who was taking care of Siobhán that she recognised her – not until she'd been able to confirm her identity one hundred per cent. So she made out that she was worried that Siobhán looked as if she was having a seizure and called for a regular ambulance to take her to the Wilton Hilton.'

'That was smart thinking. But now we know that it's definitely her?'

'Her mother was called in late last night, and she identified her. Not only that, but one of Bill Phinner's technical experts took a DNA test, too, to make absolutely sure, and that proved ninety-nine-point-nine per cent positive. Inspector Mulhare had the results of that only about ten minutes ago, which is why he called me.'

'So Siobhán can't speak? She can't tell us how she became disabled?'

'No. But the technical expert took a rake of photographs. He'll have them all sorted and downloaded in a half-hour or so, and you'll be able to see what she looks like for yourself. The technical expert told Mulhare that in his opinion none of her disabilities appeared to be genetic, or caused by illness or accident. That's all except for her legs, which look as if they've been crushed somehow, but which weren't properly reset – not as they should have been, and which any hospital would have done for her.'

'So her disabilities could have been inflicted on her deliberately?'

'That was the technical expert's opinion, yes, ma'am. He said he was sure of it. But not by any amateur, either. She's been given a throat operation and he said the stitching was expert – like, only a trained medical professional could have done it.'

'This private ambulance – who did it belong to? And the nurse – where was she from? And what about the young man who was in it, along with Siobhán? I presume Garda O'Malley has filed her report about it.'

'She has, yes. It's up now, if you want to read it.'

Katie switched on her desktop PC. She logged on to the latest reports that had been entered in the past twelve hours by all of the gardaí stationed at Anglesea Street and scrolled through until she reached the entry from Garda O'Malley. It was accompanied by the photographs of the ambulance that Garda O'Malley's fellow traffic garda had taken while she was inside it, talking to Grainne.

'Well, now, is this a coincidence or what?' she said. 'St Giles' Clinic. The very same St Giles' Clinic who claimed they knew nothing about the mysterious taxi-ride taken by Gerry Mulvaney.'

She scrolled down further, to Garda O'Malley's written report. Out loud, she read, 'The female medic protested at our removal of the young woman and said that the director of St Giles' Clinic Dr Gearoid Fitzgerald would be lodging a formal complaint. She said: "I will make sure that your boss gives you down the banks."'

It was then that Moirin put her head around the door. 'Excuse me for eavesdropping,' she said. 'Did I hear you say "Dr Gearoid Fitzgerald"?'

'Yes, you did,' said Katie. 'Why?'

'I don't mean to butt in or anything, ma'am, but when I heard the name Dr Gearoid Fitzgerald—'

'What is it, Moirin? Do you know him? Come on in and tell me.'

Moirin came into Katie's office and Katie was concerned to see that she was looking quite upset.

'It's only the very name of him gives me the shivers,' she said.

'Here, sit down,' said Katie, and led her over to the couches under the window. Detective Sergeant Begley came to join them, but sat a little way away so that Moirin wouldn't feel crowded.

'I never saw anything about it in the papers or on the TV, so it must have been kept very quiet,' said Moirin.

'Go on,' Katie coaxed her, and took hold of her hand.

'It was my cousin Rose,' said Moirin. 'She was pregnant with her third, and she'd been told already that the baby was a girl, but she had the Down's syndrome. Rose was sad about that, of course, but every life is a life, and she was pure prepared to raise and nurture the little child and do whatever she could to make her happy. She and her husband Denny even had a name for her, Aibhlinn, because that means a child that is longed for.'

She paused, and wiped a tear from her eye with her fingertips. Katie squeezed her hand but waited for her to compose herself.

'Little Aibhlinn was three weeks premature and struggling when she was born. They took her into intensive care but Rose was told that it was touch and go. What she didn't know was that Dr Fitzgerald's wife was giving birth at the same time, and that *her* little boy was born with a hole in his heart, and wasn't expected to live more than a day or two.

'As it was, little Aibhlinn passed away, although the cause of death was never made clear to Rose at all. And to this day I don't think anybody exactly knows how he did it, but it seems like Dr Fitzgerald falsified some papers which gave him permission to take the poor little girl's heart, and to transplant it into his own child, which he did.

'Rose and Denny still believe that he murdered little Aibhlinn, suffocated her maybe, so that he could save his own son.'

'I've never heard about this, ever,' said Katie. 'When did this happen? And where? If Dr Fitzgerald forged any legal documents, that should have been reported to us straight away.'

'It was three-and-a-half years ago, at the University Maternity Hospital. Rose and Denny only found out by accident that little Aibhlinn's heart had been stolen from her. One of the junior nurses happened to say that she must be in Heaven because she had given her heart so that another child could live a full life. They made a complaint, and the Medical Council made a full enquiry, like. After about nine months they were told that Dr Fitzgerald had been struck off the register.'

Katie turned to Detective Sergeant Begley. 'Struck off, but now he has his own clinic. I suppose he could have applied to be re-registered.'

'I can check with the Medical Council. If he's still practising as a doctor without being registered we can lift him for fraud.'

'He wouldn't have needed to re-register if he's simply running a care home for people with severe disabilities. But after what you've told me about Siobhán O'Donohue, it seems like he might be disabling his patients himself. Now, why in God's name would he want to do that? It might make sense if he was extracting fees from their relatives for looking after them, but Siobhán's parents didn't even know where she was.'

'We're only going to get the answer to that if we ask him,' said Detective Sergeant Begley.

'Exactly. Has he called CUH to ask how his patient is, and when he might expect her to be returned to his clinic?'

'There was a call, yes, from some woman called Grainne Buckley.'

'Oh, right. That was the same woman who came back to us about Gerry Mulvaney's taxi fare. What did she have to say?'

'She only asked how their patient was faring. Didn't mention her by name. The hospital passed the call to Garda O'Malley, and Garda O'Malley told her that she was recovering and that the hospital would ring her back as soon as she was fit enough to be collected.'

'That Garda O'Malley sounds fierce crabbit altogether. It wouldn't surprise me if she's doing my job in a few years' time.'

'So what's the plan?' asked Detective Sergeant Begley.

'Let me talk to Bill Phinner first about Siobhán's disabilities and how his expert thinks they might have been inflicted. I might even go to see Siobhán for myself. Then we can work out what we're going to do next. But I don't want this going off at half-cock. If Dr Fitzgerald is clever enough to have got away with murdering somebody else's baby, then he could have a very plausible excuse for mutilating Siobhán.'

Moirin said, 'If he did what Rose and Denny believe he did, then he's long overdue for punishment, that's all I can say.'

* * *

Katie went down to the Technical Bureau and found Bill Phinner in his office. He was mournfully reading through an MRI scan report on a homeless man who had been found dead on Saturday morning in the only doorway in Crane Lane, in the city centre.

'Ah – it's yourself, ma'am,' said Bill. 'I've been expecting you. You've come about the missing young woman with all the injuries.'

'Injuries?' said Katie.

'You can scarce call them disabilities. Here, take a look. I was just about to send these up to you anyway.'

He inserted a CD into his computer and brought up a series of photographs of Siobhán O'Donohue lying on a bed in the hospital's recovery room. Katie pulled over a chair and sat beside him, so that she could see the images more clearly. Siobhán's eyes were the first image – brown eyes staring blindly at nothing at all.

'There's no obvious external damage to her eyes,' said Bill. 'Apart from that she has no cataracts, neither of her retinas are detached, and both macula are perfect, with no degeneration and no holes. We'll need an MRI scan for tell for sure, but our guess is that her optic nerve has been severed.'

Next he showed her Siobhán's throat, and the neat sutures in it. 'Again, we need a scan to confirm it, but this suturing is consistent with a throat operation such as a laryngectomy,and she's been stitched up by somebody who really knows what they're doing.'

'Like Dr Gearoid Fitzgerald, for example.'

'Stop! Gearoid Fitzgerald? He's not your suspect, is he?'

'He could be. Do you know him?'

'Gearoid Fitzgerald? One of the best surgeons in the country, he was, before he suddenly decided to retire. I met him a few times. Strange character, though, very driven. I don't know why he gave it all up so early. One day he was right on top of his game, the next day, *pff*, he was gone.'

'I know why he went, but I'll tell you that in a minute,' said Katie. 'Let me have a look at the rest of these pictures first.'

Bill brought up the photographs of Siobhán's legs, and close-ups of her knees, which were swollen and lumpy and almost twice as wide as they should have been. 'By the look of it, she was crushed by something fierce heavy. My opinion is that she was run over by a vehicle of some sort. The injuries are consistent with that.'

'When will you be doing your scans?'

'Sometime later today, hopefully. If not, tomorrow morning. She had a minor myocardial infarction shortly after Tyrone had examined her, and so we're liaising with CUH. They have her on a heart monitor just at the moment.'

'After what's been done to her, I'm surprised she's still living and breathing. But let me tell you about Dr Fitzgerald.'

When she had described why Dr Fitzgerald had been struck off, Bill sat back and let out a long, soft whistle.

'Do you know, in a funny sort of a way, that doesn't surprise me about him at all. Every time I talked to him I had the feeling that he considered himself superior to the rest of us poor mortals. He held up his hands to me once and said, "You see these? These have the power of life or death." I'll bet he thought that poor little baby with the Down's syndrome could never expect the same quality of life as his son, so for him it was no contest. It wouldn't surprise me in the slightest if he murdered her – maybe even took out her heart while she was still alive.'

'We don't know that, Bill, and we'll never be able to prove it.'

'I'm only saying that it wouldn't surprise me. Any road – what are you going to do now? Arrest him?'

'I'll be sending a couple of officers up to his clinic to keep an eye on it, but I'm going to hold off lifting him until I've received the results of your MRIs. I want to have watertight evidence that Siobhán was wilfully maimed, and as far as possible that it was Dr Fitzgerald who did it. If her optic nerves have been severed without any obvious damage to her eyes, that would have taken a high degree of surgical skill, wouldn't it? So unless there's another surgeon working at St Giles' Clinic that we're not aware of, it must have been him.'

'Okay, then. I've asked Dr Moran to call me as soon as Siobhán has recovered enough to be scanned. I've sent you all of these photos now, and as soon as Tyrone's written up his report I'll send you that too.'

Katie stood up and nodded at the MRI report that Bill had been looking through when she came in. 'Is that the fellow in Crane Lane you're reading about? Any idea what the cause of death was?'

'Take your pick. Cirrhosis of the liver, ulcerated stomach lining, bowel tumour, kidney stones and deep vein thrombosis.'

'No evidence of foul play, though?'

'No,' said Bill. 'Just a foul life, that's all.'

Thirty-nine

Although it was only 10:30 in the morning, Eoin was already drunk. He was sitting in the living-room in the same red check shirt that he had been wearing for the past three days, and the fly of his jeans was undone. His hair was matted and he was unshaved, and he smelled strongly of body odour.

He was staring at the television with the volume turned right down so that it was almost inaudible. In his right hand he was holding a cigarette with a long crooked ash on it. In his left hand he was holding an empty half-bottle of Paddy's whiskey.

Cleona came in through the front door, wearing her long khaki raincoat and rushers. She took off her rushers in the hallway and then she came into the living-room, unbuttoning her coat.

'Is that all you're going to do all day?' she asked Eoin. 'Sit there like a zombie watching *1000 Heartbeats* with the sound off?'

'What the feck else is there do?' Eoin retorted. 'The kennels have gone down the tubes. If you can suggest some other line of work that I'm qualified for, then send me your suggestions on a postcard, please.'

'We can rebuild the business, Eoin. We still have seven dogs to take care of, and we can advertise for more. It'll take a little time, but maybe if we changed the name.'

'To what? Dognappers' Delight? Nobody's going to trust us again. We might as well give those seven dogs back to their owners and close down for good and all.'

'Eoin, look at the state of you. You haven't shaved and there's a smell of benjy off you. You're totally wrecked. You have to pull yourself together for the love of God, otherwise we're going to go bankrupt and find ourselves sleeping on the streets.'

Eoin let the ash from his cigarette drop on to the carpet. 'Pull myself together? I've lost twenty-six valuable dogs and the insurance are quibbling because the alarms weren't switched on. I'm still on police bail for blowing that scumbag's head off. I was forced to watch my wife being shagged right in front of me by some lowlife, and I can't get the picture of it out of my head. And you want me to pull myself together? Get real, Cleona, for feck's sake. We're finished here. And we're finished too. You and me.'

Cleona sat down beside him and put her hand on his shoulder, but he pushed it off.

'What do you mean, we're finished? We *can* get over this, Eoin. All we have to do is be strong.'

'You're codding me, aren't you? Every time you take off your clothes, all I can see is that bastard sticking his disgusting micky into you. All right, you've told me, you've washed and you've washed and you've washed any trace of him away, but you can't wash my brain, girl. All the soap in the whole fecking world is never going to wash that picture out of my head.'

'Eoin, give it time. You're still suffering from shock. But maybe a shock is what you and me both needed. Things haven't been going well between us for a long time now, have they? I mean, admit it. Even before this happened, we hardly ever made love any more, did we? And we were always having ructions about the smallest things.'

Eoin thought for a while, and then he tried to stand up. He promptly sat down again, but then he held on to the arm of the couch and managed to pull himself upright. He stood swaying for a while, and belched, and then he started to make his way towards the door.

'Where are you going?' Cleona asked him.

'I'm going to drain the main vein, if you must know. Then I'm going into Ballinspittle to buy myself a couple more bottles of forgetting juice.'

'You're not driving, the state you're in.'

'What's it to you? Why don't you go find that scumbag who shagged you and beg him for some more?'

With that, he staggered across the hallway to the toilet, crashing into the door before he managed to turn the handle. Once he was inside, he started to urinate loudly and at great length, and Cleona could hear that most of it was clattering on to the floor. She got up and quickly tiptoed into the kitchen. She took the car keys down from the hook beside the door and dropped them into the drawer where she kept all her cooking utensils.

By the time Eoin came out of the toilet she was back in the living-room. She hadn't turned up the television or switched channels, because she knew that Eoin would only throw a rabie if she did, as if he wasn't going to throw enough of a rabie when he found that the car keys were gone.

He struggled into his black waterproof jacket and then he went into the kitchen. She heard him scuffling around and muttering to himself, and then he came back into the living-room.

'Where's the car keys, Clee?'

'How should I know? You were the last one to drive it.'

'I hung them up on the hook. I always hang them up on the hook. Where the feck are they?'

'I don't know, Eoin. Up in Nelly's room behind the wallpaper, I expect.'

'Don't get fecking funny with me, girl. You've hid them, haven't you? You've fecking hid them. Well, I'm giving you three, and then I want them right here in my hand.'

'I don't have them, Eoin, and in any case you're not fit to ride a kiddie's scooter, let alone drive a car. If you don't kill yourself you'll kill somebody else, and then you'll really be in trouble with the law.'

Eoin came up to her chair, seized hold of her wrists, and pulled her up on to her feet.

'Eoin! You're hurting me! Let go!'

He stared at her with red-rimmed eyes. His breath smelled like rotten chicken.

'Where are the fecking car keys, Clee? This is the last time I'm asking you nicely, because if I have to ask you again, I'll have to slap you. You understand me?'

'Eion, I have no notion at all where they are. Now let go of my wrists, will you? You're going to be giving me bruises.'

'Bruises?' spat Eoin. 'What do you think you've given me? Nothing but fecking grief, ever since we started this business. Always fecking nag, nag, nag.'

'I've never nagged you. It's all been too much for you, that's all. I always told you that we needed help but you never listened. You've been running yourself into the ground.'

Eoin closed his eyes for a few seconds. Then he opened them again and screeched out, '*Where – are – the – fecking – keys?*'

'For the last time, Eoin, I have no idea,' said Cleona, trying to stay calm. 'Now why don't you sit down and I'll make you a good strong mug of coffee and you can sober yourself up?'

Without hesitation, Eoin let go of her wrists and punched her on the left cheekbone. She dropped abruptly back into her chair, lifting her hand to her eye, but Eoin dragged her up on to her feet again, and punched her on the right breast, and then her stomach, and then her stomach again.

'*No*!' she screamed at him, shielding her stomach with both hands and backing away from him. '*No, Eoin! Don't! Don't hit me again!*'

But Eoin was mad with drink and adrenalin and he went for her again, punching her stomach so that she doubled up and fell awkwardly sideways on to the floor, hitting her head against the leg of the couch.

'*Eoin! No!*' she begged him, as he tried to heave her up on to her feet again. '*I'm pregnant!*'

Eoin lurched back, knocking the television off its table with a loud crash. There was a crackle and then its screen went blank.

'What – *what* did you just say?' Eoin demanded.

'I'm pregnant, Eoin. I'm expecting a baby.'

'How can you be pregnant? It isn't possible! We haven't—'

He stopped, and when he spoke again, his voice was very quiet and blurred, like somebody speaking through a thick woollen scarf. 'We haven't—'

Cleona grasped the arm of the couch and pulled herself up to sit on it. Her left eye was already swollen and closing, and she was holding her stomach in pain.

Eoin looked down at the television, and then he looked back at her. 'It's not mine, is it?'

Cleona wouldn't answer.

'It's not mine, is it, you slut? Go on, admit it! It can't be mine! So whose is it?'

'You've hurt me, Eoin,' said Cleona. 'You've really, really hurt me.'

'And you don't think you deserve it? You slut! You fecking *slut*! You're sitting there with another man's wain inside of you, and you're moaning that I've hurt you? Jesus Christ in Heaven, what do you think you've done to me?'

Cleona winced and closed her eyes, keeping her arms wrapped around her midriff. Eoin leaned over her and shouted in her ear, 'Whose is it, Clee? Whose little bastard is it? How many other scumbags have you been poking? Jesus, what a deceitful whore you are! Whose is it?'

'What difference does it make?' whispered Cleona. 'It's a baby, it's a new life, that's all.'

'What *difference* does it make? You're fecking joking, aren't you? What *difference* does it make? Don't you remember the vow you made when we got married? "I promise to be true to you in good times and in bad?" Remember saying that, Clee? But you let some other scumbag poke you, and not only that, you're expecting his baby! So whose baby is it? Come on, tell me who he is!'

Cleona gave him the smallest shake of her head. She was concentrating too much on the pain that she was feeling in her stomach, and suddenly she convulsed and brought up a handful of pale grey sick, half phlegm and half porridge.

'Holy Mary Mother of God you fecking disgust me,' said Eoin. 'Are you going to tell me who the father is, or what? Or will I have to beat it out of you?'

Cleona wiped her hand on the cushion and started to sob. Eoin stood watching her for a moment with his mouth turned down in revulsion, and then he stalked stiff-legged out of the room, hitting his shoulder against the doorframe. He went out into the hallway and then Cleona heard him open the front door. A damp, chilly draught blew in from the yard outside, a draught that smelled of recent rain and dogs.

After a while she managed to stand up and shuffle to the kitchen. She bent over the sink, staring one-eyed at the plughole while her stomach tightened and she brought up more sick.

Please dear God let my baby be safe. Please calm Eoin down and make him understand how desperately I needed a man who made me feel young and attractive again. I know how much I've betrayed my marriage vow to him, dear God, but please make sure my baby hasn't been hurt.

She was still leaning over the sink when she heard the front door slam so hard that the flower-vase on the windowsill beside it dropped on to the floor.

'Clee?' said Eoin, in a bloated voice. He was obviously looking into the living-room to see if she was there.

She didn't answer, but eventually he came along the hallway and appeared in the kitchen door. She slowly stood up straight, with a cold sensation sliding down her spine, because he was carrying the long three-pronged pitchfork they used to spread out the straw.

'Eoin?' she said. 'What's that for?'

He took a drunken step forwards, as if the floor were sloping like the deck of a ship. He held up the pitchfork and said, 'Persuasion, that's what it's for.'

'Eoin, you're really scaring me. Please take that thing away. Please.'

Eoin stared at her intently but his eyes seemed to be unfocused. 'It's only to persuade you to tell me who the father is. Tell me who the father is and I'll take it away.'

'I told you. What difference does it make who the father is? And anyway, I don't see him any more.'

'How long was it going on for? And when? All those times I had to go away for the night, I suppose? Those times I had to go to Kerry and Galway, and that dog show in Killarney. Was that when you were shagging him? I bet it was. And I bet you and him, you were laughing your heads off that I didn't know. Did you suck his micky? Have I been kissing your lips and all the time they were the same lips that sucked another man's micky? Jesus, I'll never be able to wash away the taste of him, will I? You whore.'

'Eoin, please take that away. I'm hurting bad enough as it is. I think I might have to call for the doctor.'

Eoin levelled the pitchfork at her and took two steps nearer. Cleona backed away until she had reached the kitchen wall and could back away no further.

'Tell me his name,' said Eoin. He made a jabbing gesture with the pitchfork and shouted, '*Tell me his fecking name, Cleona! Tell me his name!*'

'*Lorcan!*' Cleona screamed at him. '*It was Lorcan Fitzgerald!*'

Eoin seemed to be stunned. He opened and closed his mouth, and then he said, 'Lorcan Fitzgerald? That grey-haired feen who kept coming around and asking if we had any dogs for sale?'

Cleona nodded, too tearful to speak.

Eoin started to inhale deeply, his chest swelling up more and more every time he drew in breath. His face was bright red with rage and alcohol and he looked as if he could actually explode and spatter the kitchen walls with his flesh and blood, like a suicide bomber.

Without a word, though, he rammed the three prongs of the pitchfork into Cleona's stomach, with one of them piercing the back of her right hand. He stabbed her with such force that the points of the prongs were only stopped by the kitchen wall behind her.

Cleona gasped, but that was the only sound she made. Eoin pulled out the pitchfork, although he had jammed it into her stomach so hard that he had to tug it from side to side to get it completely free.

Cleona held out a hand for him to support her, but he backed away, and she dropped to her knees on the kitchen floor with blood flooding the front of her pale beige sweater.

'My baby,' she sobbed. 'Oh, dear Christ. My baby.'

She fell forward and lay on the floor shivering. Again she stretched out one hand as if she wanted Eoin to take hold of it and help her, but again he backed away. After a few moments more, he walked out of the kitchen and threw the pitchfork down in the hallway. Then he went into the living-room and picked up the phone.

He dialled 112 and when the emergency operator answered, he said, 'My name is Eoin Cassidy. My address is Sceolan Kennels, Ballinroe East.'

'Yes, Eoin, thank you. But what's your emergency?'

Eoin lifted his left hand and looked at his wedding-ring, turning it this way and that. Then he said, 'I don't know if you'd call it an emergency, exactly. But I've just killed another man's child.'

Forty

Katie had a quick lunch with Conor upstairs at the Electric restaurant on South Mall Street. They sat by the window overlooking the river, with the spires of St Finbarr's cathedral in the middle distance, and the sky filled with huge white cumulus clouds. She had wanted to come here because it was lively and busy and normal, although she still wasn't very hungry.

Conor didn't ask her how she was feeling, but then he didn't have to. He had been to the Dog Unit's kennels that morning to see the dogs that Sergeant Browne had rounded up for him, and he talked about them instead. He described them with such affection that he could have been talking about children that he was thinking of adopting.

'Those bull terriers were so tough and aggressive and snarly, but as soon as you patted them and stroked them and gave him a Molly and Murphy dog biscuit they were the softest dogs you ever met.'

'Well, you have a way with them, Conor. I've seen it for myself. It's the same way you have with me, except I don't think I fancy a dog biscuit.'

They both had only starters – Katie ordered the salmon gravadlax and Conor chose the Clonakilty black pudding with parsnip and apple purée. Although they said very little to each other, anybody watching them would have sensed the bond that was growing between them. The waitress treated them almost as if they were newly-weds.

After lunch they walked back to Anglesea Street, but Katie

stopped and kissed Conor halfway along Copley Street, before they came within sight of the Garda station.

'I shouldn't be too late tonight,' she told him. 'I'll see you later so.'

'I'm counting on it, Katie, believe me.'

As soon as she returned to her office, Detective Scanlan came in to see her.

'Glad you're back, ma'am, we have a woman downstairs who says she recognises the picture that they published in the *Examiner* this morning, the fellow who had his head shot off at Sceolan Kennels. Sergeant Begley's talking to her now.'

'Begley can deal with her, can't he?'

'He could of course, but she's very emotional about it and she has absolute proof that it's him. She's his mother.'

'His mother? Serious?'

'She reads the paper online every morning and there was her own son on the front page. She took a screenshot and compared it with her photo album.'

'Getting very technological, the older generation,' said Katie. 'All right, let's go down and see her.'

She and Detective Scanlan went down together to one of the interview rooms. Detective Sergeant Begley was sitting with a white-haired woman in a dark brown overcoat with a rabbit-fur collar, clutching a large brown handbag on her knees. Katie guessed she must be in her mid-seventies, and that she must have been very pretty once, but she had one of those round babyish faces that rarely ages very well.

Detective Sergeant Begley stood up and said, 'This is Mrs Teagan O'Connor, ma'am. Mrs O'Connor – this is Detective Superintendent Maguire.'

Mrs O'Connor looked up tearfully. On the table in front of her was her printed-out screenshot of Eithne's likeness of the dead dognapper, as well as an old leather-bound photograph album.

Katie sat down beside her and picked up the screenshot.

'This is your son?' she asked, gently.

Mrs O'Connor nodded, and wiped her eyes, and sniffed. 'Brendan. He's the eldest of five. Look – see.'

She slid the photograph album across the table and pointed to a large black-and-white photograph of five young men standing and sitting in a garden. In the middle of the group, and the tallest of all of them, was the man whose face Eithne had re-created from the fragments of his shattered head. The resemblance was so marked that there was no doubt in Katie's mind that it was him.

'So, Teagan, tell me about him,' said Katie.

'I was already saying to your sergeant here that Brendan was always trouble, mixing with a bad crowd ever since he was a teenager. If there was a knock at the door and it was a guard, it was always Brendan who'd been caught getting a langie off of a bus along Pana, or denting people's cars playing long slogs down the end of Glandore Park.'

'How old was he?'

'Thirty-six next Good Friday.'

'The night he was shot – did you know where he was, and what he was up to?'

'I had no clue whatsoever at all. I hadn't seen him at all for three weeks at least. He lives with his girlfriend Oona up in Onslow Gardens, with their three kids and all. She's a right brasser that Oona and she and me never got on at all, which is why I don't see so much of him.'

'Did you have any notion at all that he was involved with a gang of dog thieves?'

Mrs O'Connor took a tissue out of her handbag and loudly blew her nose. 'I knew that he had some fierce rough pals who were all mixed up with dog-racing and all like that. He had a pit bull dog of his own which I couldn't stick at all. Horrible beast, always pulling away at its leash like it couldn't wait to jump up and take a bite out of your neck.'

'Do you know who any of these rough pals were?'

'Some of them, yes. Two or three of them he'd known ever since he was knee high to a high knee – old bunscoil pals like Kevin

Brodie and Paddy Adams. But lately in the past few months there was one feen he was always talking about, do you know what I mean, and seemed pure impressed by. The last two times I went round to his house to see the grandchildren he was there, this fellow, acting like he owned the place. He had the grey hair and the grey suit and a sneery way of talking, like he was the only one who knew anything at all and the rest of the world was nothing but eejits. Brendan said he was a well-known dog-breeder.'

'What was his name? Do you know?'

'Lorcan, that was his Christian name. I never heard his surname.'

'I see. Have you seen or heard anything from this Lorcan since Brendan was killed?'

'Nothing. Not a word. Of course I didn't know until this morning that anything had happened to Brendan, did I? It wasn't unusual for me not to hear from him a month at a time, and Oona never rang me to ask where he was. Maybe she knew that he'd been killed, like, but if she *did* know, she never bothered to tell me about it.'

'Did Brendan tell you anything else about Lorcan, apart from him being a dog-breeder? Did he tell you where he lived, for instance?'

'No. Although there was one thing he did say about him. My older sister Vera was sick with the flu last July and it was taking her for ever to get over it. When I told Brendan about it he said that Lorcan's brother was a famous doctor and runs his own clinic, and if she didn't get better soon he could maybe arrange for her to visit him.'

Katie looked at Detective Sergeant Begley and although he didn't look back at her, she could tell by the way his eyes widened that he was thinking the same as she was. Brendan's friend Lorcan was Lorcan Fitzgerald the dognapper, and not only that, the odds were high that Lorcan Fitzgerald's brother was Dr Gearoid Fitzgerald, of St Giles' Clinic.

'Thank you, Teagan,' she said. 'I think that's all I need to ask you for the time being, except for Oona's address. We'll be going to have a chat with her, of course. Is it okay if we make a copy of your photo album?'

Mrs O'Connor nodded. 'What about Brendan's remains?' she asked. 'What's going to happen about his funeral?'

'His remains are still in the mortuary at the University Hospital, and I'm afraid they'll have to stay there until the coroner has held a full inquest. After that – well, I suppose that's something that you and Oona will have to arrange between you.'

'Holy Saint Patrick. The very sight of her makes me craw sick. If it wasn't for the grandchildren I'd be delighted never to clap eyes on her again, or to smell that Estée Lauder she sprays all over herself, a whole bottle at a time I shouldn't wonder.'

When Detective Scanlan had led Mrs O'Connor away, Katie and Sergeant Begley sat looking at the screenshot and the photo album and said nothing to each other for over a minute.

'That forensic artist really has some talent, doesn't he?' said Detective Sergeant Begley at last, picking up the screenshot. 'He's caught this Brendan spot on – and when you consider that there was only half of his head left.'

'That artist is a she, and her name's Eithne O'Neill,' said Katie. 'She's young, and, yes, she's brilliant. But this is a turn-up for the books, isn't it? Lorcan Fitzgerald and Dr Gearoid Fitzgerald being brothers. I mean, it *must* be him, mustn't it? How many other Dr Fitzgeralds run their own clinics in Cork?'

'I sometimes think that God sends us these complimications just for a laugh,' said Detective Sergeant Begley. 'Have you had any thoughts yet about how you're going to deal with Dr Fitzgerald?'

'I'm going over to CUH this afternoon to see the girl that we took from his ambulance, and then I'll work out the best way of taking it from there. We have the clinic under surveillance of course and there's no sign yet that he's thinking of making a run for it – so maybe it wasn't him who mutilated this girl, and all he's been doing is taking care of her. But I don't want to spook him, and I can't afford another fiasco like Operation Trident.'

'Operation Trident wasn't your fault, ma'am. We all know that Bobby Quilty was tipped off.'

'All the same, Sean, I'm taking this one cautious step at a time. If it *wa*s Dr Fitzgerald who operated on her, I want to make sure that he doesn't see anywhere but the inside of a cell on Rathmore Road for the rest of his days.'

* * *

Katie and Detective Scanlan were met at CUH by Dr Donal Moran, a short, affable man with oversized spectacles and freckles. Katie thought that he looked more like a stand-up comedian than a cardiac specialist. He took them up to the room where Siobhán had been recovering, chatting all the way. A uniformed garda was sitting outside the door, reading a copy of *Motoring Life*. He jumped to his feet immediately when he saw Katie coming along the corridor.

'All quiet?' Katie asked him.

'Yes, ma'am. A couple of chatty nurses, that's all.'

Dr Moran took Katie and Detective Scanlan in to Siobhán's room. The calico blind was drawn halfway down so it was dim in there, and Siobhán was still on a cardiac monitor with a built-in defibrillator in case she showed any signs of a relapse. She lay propped up by two large pillows, ivory-faced, her hair clean and brushed, her eyes wide open. She was so still and her breathing was so silent that she could have been a waxwork.

A young nurse was sitting in the corner by the window and she got up and brought over two chairs for Katie and Detective Scanlan so that they could sit on either side of Siobhán's bed.

'Siobhán,' said Dr Moran, softly. 'It's Dr Moran again. I've brought somebody in to talk to you. It's two Garda officers, Detective Superintendent Maguire and Detective Scanlan. Would you nod your head please if you understand me?'

Siobhán nodded.

Katie reached out and held Siobhán's right hand, although it felt very cold and Siobhán didn't respond to her touch at all.

'Siobhán,' she said. 'I'm a detective superintendent, as Dr Moran told you, but I'd like you to think about me as Katie. My colleague here is Pádraigin. We're here to find out what's happened to you, and who hurt you like this. When we know for sure who it is, we're going to arrest them and charge them and make sure that they're sent to jail.'

Siobhán blinked, but remained utterly still.

'Was it Dr Gearoid Fitzgerald who blinded you and took away your voice?'

Tears welled up in the corner of Siobhán's eyes and she nodded.

'Do you know why you were being taken to the UK?'

Siobhán nodded again.

'Was it for medical treatment? That's what we were told by the nurse who was with you.'

Siobhán shook her head.

'So it wasn't for medical treatment?'

Siobhán shook her head even more strenuously this time.

'Siobhán, sweetheart, do you think you can spell out for me why you were being taken to the UK? If I go through all of the letters of the alphabet, will you nod when I reach the right letter? I don't mind how long it takes. All I care about is punishing Dr Fitzgerald.'

Katie turned around to ask for a tissue to wipe Siobhán's eyes but the nurse was already standing behind her to hand her one.

'Are you ready?' Katie asked her, when she had patted the tears from her cheeks. Siobhán nodded and so Katie began. 'A – B – C – D—'

At 'D', Siobhán nodded and stopped her, so she started again. When she reached 'R' she nodded again, and yet again when she got to 'U'.

'Is it drugs?' said Katie.

Siobhán nodded.

'So it was nothing to do with treating you at all? They were smuggling drugs?'

Siobhán nodded again.

It took over two more hours, with Katie reciting the alphabet over and over, and Siobhán nodding whenever she came to the right letter, and Detective Scanlan writing down her evidence in her notebook. Eventually, Siobhán was growing too tired to continue, but she had told Katie everything that she had overheard about the drugs that Dr Fitzgerald had been running, and the name of the man called 'Wardy'. She also told her that there were other patients at St Giles' Clinic who had been deliberately maimed.

Dr Moran had been called away to deal with an emergency, but the young nurse sat in the corner of the room listening to Siobhán's nodded testimony with mounting horror.

At last Katie said, 'Listen, Siobhán, we won't press you any more today. But tomorrow we'll have to come back with a camera crew so that we can make a video of what you've just told us. I'm sorry that we have to make you go through it all over again, but if we have a video we can show it to a judge and get a search warrant for the clinic and a warrant to arrest Dr Fitzgerald. Is it okay with you if we do that?'

Siobhán nodded.

* * *

As they drove back to Anglesea Street, Detective Scanlan said, 'Jesus – how could anybody have mutilated a beautiful young girl like that, just for the sake of drugs?'

'You know the answer to that as well as I do, Pádraigin. They don't have the slightest feeling for anybody else's lives. If they did, they wouldn't be peddling narcotics. But if Dr Fitzgerald has been bringing in drugs in his ambulances, I'm beginning to think that we might have solved the question of how Cork is being flooded with the stuff.'

'But why does he have to blind people, and cripple them?'

'Do you remember those Dutch smugglers a couple of years ago who got caught sneaking cocaine and heroin into the UK in a fleet of fake ambulances? The prosecution reckoned they'd brought in more than four hundred million pounds' worth of drugs before they were caught. When the British crime agency stopped one of their ambulances, they found it was rammed to the roof with drugs, all hidden behind secret panels. There was about thirty-eight million pounds' worth, in only one ambulance.'

'Yes, I remember reading about that,' said Detective Scanlan. 'But those Dutch fellows – they didn't mutilate anyone, did they, as far as I know?'

'No, they didn't. Sure, they had fake patients in their ambulances, the same as Dr Fitzgerald. But that was one of the ways the British crime agency caught them. Once the ambulances had reached their destination, their officers lamped the so-called patients strutting away, perfectly healthy, and counting out the money that they'd been paid for pretending that they were disabled.'

'Oh, God,' said Detective Scanlan. 'So what you're thinking is – Dr Fitzgerald didn't want to be caught out the same way? That's why he's made his patients genuinely disabled?'

'Why else?' said Katie. 'Why else do you think he broke poor Siobhán's legs? So she couldn't run away. And why else do you think he blinded her? So she couldn't see where she was or what was going on around her, or identify any faces. And why else did he cut her vocal cords? So she couldn't speak and tell anybody who had hurt her. He made sure her hands were useless, too, so she couldn't even write down anything to incriminate him. The one big mistake he made was to spare her hearing. If he had deafened her, punctured her eardrums or whatever, she wouldn't have been able to communicate with us at all.'

'What's that saying? "A nod is as good as a wink to a blind horse." To tell you the truth, I never really understood what that meant.'

'It means exactly what Siobhán was able to do for us today. When you already suspect that something's going on, it takes only the slightest signal for you to be assured that it's true. A nod, or a wink. In Siobhán's case, a few nods did it.'

'I feel for her,' said Detective Scanlan. 'I really and truly feel for her. Myself, I think I'd rather be dead than be like her. It's a living death, isn't it?'

* * *

Chief Superintendent MacCostagáin called for Katie when she arrived back at the station. She was intending to talk to him anyway, because she wanted to set up a full-scale raid on St Giles' Clinic as soon as she had a warrant from a District Court judge. Her rank as detective superintendent gave her the authority to search premises without a warrant if she considered that there was sufficient evidence of a crime being committed, but there was so much at stake here that she wanted to make sure that she couldn't be challenged in court for not following procedure. Apart from that, she was still haunted by the humiliating failure of Operation Trident.

'Ah, Katie,' said Chief Superintendent MacCostagáin, as soon as she came into his office. 'I have to warn you that there's going to be a full investigation into Jimmy O'Reilly's suicide.'

'Really?' she said, sitting down. 'I didn't expect anything else.'

'There was some suggestion from Dublin that you should be suspended until the whole matter is completely cleared up, but I told them that we have too much on our plates just now and I couldn't spare you. The forensics clearly show that you never handled Jimmy's firearm and that the angle of the shot was entirely consistent with a self-inflicted wound, so they agreed that you could stay on the job. But there *will* be a hearing, if only to satisfy the Phoenix Park bureaucracy.'

'In a way, do you know, I wish that a hearing wasn't necessary,' said Katie. 'Jimmy and I didn't get along at all, and he could be a real *aingiseoir* at times, but I don't want to see him humiliated, especially now that he's passed.'

'Well, you know what they say. Life is a vale of misery, or a word to that effect, and then you die.'

'It is for poor Siobhán O'Donohue,' said Katie. She told Chief Superintendent MacCostagáin how she had interviewed Siobhán, and how she planned to make a video recording of her responses. She also told him that the dead dognapper had been identified as Brendan O'Connor, and that his mother's evidence had further strengthened the evidence that Lorcan Fitzgerald was responsible for the raid on Sceolan Kennels.

When she told him that there was a strong possibility that Lorcan Fitzgerald and Dr Gearoid Fitzgerald were brothers, all he could say was, 'Christ in Heaven. What a cat's malack. I agree with you that we need to stick close to the book on this one. Drug dealers and doctors can always afford the most expensive lawyers, and in this case your suspect happens to be both.'

Katie said, 'I have Scanlan checking the birth and electoral records to make absolutely certain, but I'm pretty sure that they are related. What I'm really interested to find out now is whether the dognapping and the drug dealing are in any way connected, or whether they're running them as two separate rackets.'

'All I can say, Katie, is good luck to you so. You can tell Michael Pearse that I've authorised a search of St Giles' Clinic, as and when the warrant's issued. I imagine you'll be calling in the RSU, too, as a precaution. You have your arrest of Lorcan Fitzgerald pretty much sewn up, don't you, with your fighting dogs and all? And you've liaised with Superintendent O'Neill in Tipperary Town?'

'We're all set to go on that,' Katie assured him. 'Wednesday at noon, at the horrible Bartley Doran's place. I don't think I've looked forward to lifting anybody so much for a long time.'

'Now, then, Katie. Aren't you always saying yourself that the name of the game is "objectivity".'

'Not when you've seen a poodle ripped to pieces for the fun of it.'

They were still talking when Detective Sergeant Begley knocked at the door.

'Apologies for interrupting you, but I've had a call from Inspector O'Brien in Bandon. About twenty minutes ago they arrested Eoin Cassidy from Sceolan Kennels. They have him on charges of murder and attempted murder.'

'What?' said Katie. 'For shooting the dognapper? Don't tell me his wife's changed her mind about giving evidence against him.'

'No, not at all. It's his wife he tried to murder,' said Detective Sergeant Begley. 'Apparently he found out she was pregnant by another man and so he stabbed her with a pitchfork and killed the baby. The wife herself is in a serious but stable condition at the Mercy.'

'Mother of God,' said Katie. 'If only she'd agreed to give evidence about him when she had the chance.'

'Oh, there's more to it than that,' said Detective Sergeant Begley. 'Guess who the father was? She admitted it to him before he stabbed her. Lorcan Fitzgerald.'

'The Grey Man,' said Katie. 'I'll bet you a million euros that was why he was having an affair with her. He was probably checking up on what dogs they were keeping at the kennels, and what they were worth, and how to turn the alarms off, too. God, some men are such bastards, aren't they?'

'Don't look at me,' said Detective Sergeant Begley.

* * *

She rang Conor at 6:15 pm and told him that she was finished for the day. Maybe he could meet her at Henchy's and they could have a drink before going back to his guest house.

'That is far and away the best idea I've heard all day,' he told her.

'In that case I'll ring Bridie and ask her if she can stop over the night to take care of John. I'll get back to you in a minute.'

She was about to ring Bridie when her phone warbled, and when she picked it up and said, 'DS Maguire,' it was Bridie.

'Bridie! I was just about to call you! Is everything okay?'

Bridie sounded out of breath. 'Sorry to bother you, ma'am, but it's John. He's been very down all day, barely saying a word. In the end he told me that he'd surprised you with this new fellow of yours Conor and that all his hopes for the future had been dashed, like.'

'Go on,' said Katie.

'I popped down to Centra just now to buy some fresh milk and the paper and when I got back I checked John's medication to have it ready for the evening and all the boxes of codeine were gone. I went into his room and he was sitting there with all the codeine tablets on the bedside table next to him, over fifty of them, and a glass of orange juice.

'He said his life wasn't worth the living without you and that he was going to take all of the tablets and I shouldn't try to stop him. Of course I scooped them up and took them away. I can't say if he was really intending to kill himself, but he's fierce depressed, I can tell you that.'

Katie pressed the heel of her hand against her forehead. 'Okay, Bridie,' she said, tiredly. 'I'm finished here at the station so I'll come home and have a talk with him. I'll be with you in forty minutes so.'

She sat back for a moment and then she called Conor.

'Don't tell me,' he said. 'Somebody's robbed the AIB and you can't come and meet me.'

'Well, it's worse than that. But, no, I can't meet you. Not tonight. Maybe tomorrow, with any luck.'

'That's all right, darling. I know how demanding your job is. I'm prepared to wait for you.'

Katie took a deep breath. 'I have to warn you, Conor. It's always going to be like this.'

'I understand that, Katie, completely. But that's what I love about you. I never came across a woman in my life before with such dedication to other people.'

'I'll ring when I'm free, sweetheart,' said Katie, and put down the phone.

Forty-one

When she arrived home, John was sitting in the living-room watching television. She found Bridie and Barney in the kitchen.

'How is he?' she asked Bridie.

'Let's say that he's less than happy,' said Bridie. 'I don't think that he's seriously suicidal, otherwise he would have swallowed all of those codeines before I came back from the shop. But I've seen this so many times before. It's a cry for help, do you know what I mean? "Look at me, I'm disabled, I'm ruined, and even the people who used to love me don't love me any more."'

Katie said, 'It's not only his legs, Bridie. John and I broke up several times before. We loved each other, I'm not saying we didn't, but we had different paths in life, that's all. We never could have been happy together.'

'Are you going to tell him that? Because even now he still seems to think that there's a chance.'

'Thank you, Bridie,' said Katie. 'You can go home now. I'll have a chat with John and see if we can work something out.'

When Bridie had left, Katie went into the living-room and sat down on the couch beside John.

'I suppose Bridie told you about the pills,' he said, without looking at her.

'Of course she did. I'm paying for her to take care of you.'

'I thought about taking them, I have to admit. But then I thought about you, and all of the stress that you must be under. You never talk about it, that's the trouble. You never tell me what you're dealing with, at work. I mean, murderers, and rapists, and drug smugglers, and frauds. And you never say a word. How can we possibly have any future together if you won't even tell me what you've been doing, during the day?'

'I can't tell you, John. It's confidential.'

'So – even when we're married – it's still going to be confidential?'

Merciful Heaven, thought Katie. *He still believes that we're going to be married. He's seen me in bed with Conor, and he still believes that he and I are going to be spending the rest of our lives together.*

'All right,' she said. 'See how much you can stomach of this. I'm investigating St Giles' Clinic, in Montenotte, because we have evidence that the doctor in charge is using ambulances to smuggle drugs from the UK into Cork.'

'Ambulances? Serious?'

'That's right. It looks like he's building up a fleet of ambulances which are specially fitted out to hold millions of euros' worth of heroin and cocaine and God knows what else. He's making sure that they're getting through customs without being searched because they have severely disabled patients on board.'

'Oh, like me, you mean?'

'You're not as severely disabled as these people. They're blind, and incapable of speech, and none of them can walk. We believe that the doctor in charge has been maiming them himself. We've already rescued one girl and she's given me a lot of evidence about what he's been doing.'

'So – have you arrested him?'

'We will do, but we need to make sure that our evidence is rock solid. We're going to interview the girl that we rescued tomorrow morning, but we have to make sure that it was Dr Fitzgerald who blinded her and mutilated her.'

'That's his name, is it, Dr Fitzgerald?'

'John, I shouldn't have told you any of this. It's all strictly confidential. But I want you to understand that it's not the stress of my job that's driven us apart, and it's not you losing your legs, either. We're two different people, with different ideas and different destinies ahead of us.'

'Just because we're different, Katie, that doesn't mean we can't have a happy life together. Millions of people are happy together, even if they don't see eye to eye at all.'

Katie took hold of his hand. It didn't feel familiar any more, not like her lover's hand. It was like holding the hand of a complete stranger.

'Let's just see how things work out, John, all right? You'll have your new legs this week, won't you? Please promise me you won't try to take those pills again.'

John turned to her and there was a look in his eyes which she had never seen before. Cunning, as if he had decided on some plan of action, but wasn't prepared to tell her what it was.

'I promise – if you promise to marry me.'

'What's the point of my promising to marry you if you can't promise that you'll still be alive?'

John was silent for a while, but then he lifted Katie's hand away from his and said, 'You were going to spend the night with him tonight, weren't you? That Conor.'

'John – I came home to make sure that you weren't still bent on taking your own life.'

That seemed to satisfy John, because he said, 'Okay,' very quietly, and turned up the volume on the television so that he could listen to *Nationwide*.

* * *

Lorcan said, 'Jesus, Gearoid, they must suspect something, the state of her.'

Gearoid turned away from his office window. He had been watching Sonny Powers from Powers Motors working on the broken-down ambulance. It was already dark outside, but Sonny had three halogen lamps around him, which reminded Gearoid of an operating theatre.

'They can suspect all they like, but they won't be able to prove anything,' he said, quite calmly. 'If they come here to question me about her condition, all I have to say is that she was left here in that condition by God alone knows who, abandoned on the front porch, and that out of the goodness of our hearts we took her in.'

'And you think they'll swallow that? For real?'

'What choice will they have? I don't have to say anything at all, if I don't want to. That's my legal right. And how are they going to prove who operated on her?'

'Oh, come on. Who in the world but you could have cut her vocal cords and severed her optic nerves? Who else would have had a reason to?'

'That's not the point, Lorcan. All I have to do is deny it. Siobhán can't give evidence because she can't speak and she can't write and since she's totally blind how is she going to identify me in a court of law?'

Lorcan took out a pack of cigarettes and lit one, and blew out of a long stream of smoke. 'All I can say is, boy, you have some fecking nerve.'

'In surgery, you have to. Everybody trusts surgeons, but if they only knew for instance what a fine line it is between successfully stitching up an aortic aneurysm and a catastrophic haemorrhage, they wouldn't feel even a tenth so confident. But there you are. All a surgeon can do is hold his nerve and do his best. Emotion never comes into it. If your patients survive, that's very good for your track record. If they die, well, that's life. You sterilise your scalpels and go on to the next one.

'Besides,' he said, turning back to the window, 'we're already making a fortune out of this business and I'm certainly not going to give it up now. Not because of some stupid mechanical failure.'

'Fair play to you, Gearoid,' said Lorcan, looking around for an ashtray. 'When does Sonny think he's going to have the ambulance up and running again?'

'Tomorrow morning at the latest. I've already told Wardy we're going to be a day late. Are you going to be okay to go over there with them?'

'I've arranged to meet some kennel owner from North Tipp

to check out some dogs he has for sale, but I can put it off until later in the week.'

'That's grand. From what Wardy was telling me, the latest shipment is all first-class quality and he estimates that one run alone will net us forty to fifty thousand. I promise you this, Lorcan, by the middle of the summer we're going to be the dominant supplier in the whole of Munster.'

Lorcan sucked at his cigarette, and then he said, 'I can feel a trip to Charles Hurst the Ferrari dealers coming on.'

'No, you don't. The way you survive in this business is to keep your profile low and your bake tight shut.'

* * *

After John had gone to bed, Katie sat up in her pink pyjamas to finish her drink. She switched off the television so that the only sound was the clinking of ice in her glass. Barney lay sleeping on the carpet close beside her, although he kept twitching and snuffling as if he were dreaming. It was clear to her now that she would have to make arrangements for John to be taken into a convalescent home. She had agreed to look after him because she felt so guilty about him losing his legs, but she was only causing him emotional agony on top of the physical pain that he was already suffering. She would call his therapist in the morning and see what they could recommend.

Once she had finished her drink she switched off the lights and shut Barney in the kitchen. Although she went to bed she couldn't fall asleep, and she lay there staring into total darkness like Siobhán.

About an hour later she heard John cry out. She stayed where she was, but after another twenty minutes he cried out again, like a small boy who has lost his mother in Dunne's Stores. She threw back her duvet and went to see what he wanted.

Forty-two

It was raining the next morning, fine and soft, not a dead-umbrella day, but drenching enough, and it was forecast to last until late afternoon. Katie left the house early, before John was awake. As she drove, she thought again about sending him into care, and she knew that she had made the right decision. His continued presence was causing her almost as much stress and pain as he was going through.

As she turned into the car park at Anglesea Street, her iPhone pinged. She had the first of her twice-daily updates from Detective Ó Doibhilin on Keeno. *Stable but still in coma.* She wondered if Keeno might stay asleep for the next twenty years, and wake up to find that Katie had retired from the force to marry Conor, and that she had three or four children, and that all of his dognapping cronies were either dead or serving time on Rathmore Road.

When she sat down at her desk and started on her paperwork and messages, Moirin came in with a cup of coffee for her. Moirin didn't mention Dr Fitzgerald, but as she was going back to her office, Katie said, 'Moirin – just to let you know – we're getting ourselves all geared up to arrest Dr Fitzgerald. Don't you worry – he's going to get what he deserves.'

'Well, I know my cousin Rose will be happy out, if he's punished at last for what he's done,' said Moirin. 'Myself, I don't think I'll believe it until I hear with my own ears the judge saying that he's guilty and sends him to prison for ten years or more. That could have been my niece, that little Aibhlinn. Down's baby or not, she could have had a pure happy life.'

A few minutes later, Detective Dooley came in, accompanied by a bald middle-aged man, who was grinning with nervousness. He was wearing a belted raincoat and carrying a broad-brimmed hat pressed to his chest, and Katie thought that he looked as if he had stepped right out of a 1920s photograph of the Cork IRA.

'Morning, ma'am,' said Detective Dooley. 'This here is Mr Patrick Byrne. Mr Byrne – this is Detective Superintendent Maguire. Mr Byrne saw that bulletin on the news last night about Martin Ó Brádaigh and he reckons he witnessed that incident himself.'

'A very good morning to you, detective superintendent,' said Mr Byrne. 'Not weatherwise, I have to admit, but otherwise.'

'Come on in,' said Katie, and led Mr Byrne over to the couches under the window. Mr Byrne perched himself right on the edge of one of them and laid his hat in his lap.

'Sorry, my coat's a little wet.'

'Don't worry about that,' said Katie. 'Tell me exactly what you saw.'

'Like er, I didn't realise until I saw it on the telly last night that it was of any importance at all,' said Mr Byrne. 'Me and the missus was on our way to Rosslare, like, to spend a few days with our youngest daughter in London. We was driving along when we came across this black car slapbang in the middle of the road, like, and in front of this black car there was an ambulance, and in front of *that* there was another car. We had to stall for a moment before we could overtake because there was a few cars coming the other way, so when we did pass we was going fairly slow.

'At first we thought there might have been an accident, like, do you know what I mean, what with there being an ambulance there. But we couldn't see nobody injured or nothing, and there was no paramedics there, only these two fellers.'

'So you saw two men there? What were they doing? Were they arguing?'

'Not at all, by the looks of it. They was standing close together, face to face, as if they was having what you might call an intimate conversation. Very close together.'

'Can you remember what they looked like? Would you recognise them, if you saw them again?'

'One was wearing a grey coat, and he had this curly grey hair. I couldn't see his face because he had his back turned to me. The other feller was big, much bigger than the grey-haired feller, but I couldn't see his face, either, because the grey feller's head was in the way.'

'What about the cars? You say there was a black one. What about the other one?'

'I can't recall, to be honest with you,' said Mr Byrne. 'Maybe silvery, or silvery-blue.'

'And the ambulance? Was that a regular ambulance, yellow with green squares on it?'

'Not at all, no. It was white, white all over. It had some lettering on the side of it but I didn't have the time to read it. I did see a picture on it, though – like a monk holding on to some kind of animal, and the animal had an arrow sticking out of it. I remember that, because I thought that was kind of a quare picture to be painted on the side of an ambulance.'

Katie stood up, went over to her desk and switched on her PC. She Googled an image of St Giles, nursing an injured hart. Mr Byrne stood up, too, taking out a pair of half-glasses. He put them on and peered at the computer screen with his head tilted back.

'Spot on,' he said. 'That's exactly the same picture almost.'

'Thank you, Mr Byrne,' said Katie. 'You've been extremely helpful.'

'Did something happen to one of them fellers?' asked Mr Byrne. 'Is that why you was asking for witnesses?'

'Yes. A short time after you saw them, one of them was run over by a truck and killed. The big one.'

'Holy Mary. That's terrible. May his soul rest in peace.'

Detective Dooley escorted Mr Byrne out of the station, and then immediately came back. 'Would you believe it?' he said. 'St Giles' Clinic rears its ugly head again. And the Grey Man, too. Or another grey man. Or do you think that's just a coincidence?'

'You know that I don't believe in coincidences, Robert. All I want to find out now is what that ambulance was doing there, and what the grey-haired man and Martin Ó Brádaigh were discussing so intimately, and whether the grey-haired man stabbed him or not, and how Martin Ó Brádaigh came to be run down by a Paddy's Whiskey truck.'

She lifted her raincoat off its hook and said, 'I'll be going over to CUH now with Pádraigin Scanlan to make that video of poor Siobhán O'Donohue. Once we have that, I think we'll be more than ready to go to a judge for a search warrant for St Giles' Clinic, and arrest warrants for Dr Gearoid and Lorcan Fitzgerald.'

* * *

'Bridie!' called John. He was sitting at the kitchen table with a bowl of porridge in front of him which he had barely touched, and a mug of tea.

Bridie came in from the living-room and said, 'What is it, John? What's the matter? Don't you care for the porridge? I put cream in it so.'

'I'm not very hungry, Bridie, to be honest with you. I'm feeling too tense. Katie wants you to take me to this private clinic this morning to have an assessment.'

'What? What are you talking about? She never said nothing to me.'

'I expect she forgot. She has her hands full at the moment and I'm the last of her worries.'

'So you don't want that?' Bridie asked him. She took his bowl of porridge away, ate a spoonful of it herself, and then turned on the tap and washed the rest of it down the sink.

'It's because of yesterday, the pills and all,' said John. 'She thinks that my medication may be wrong. Maybe it's making me depressed when I shouldn't be. I mean, you know me, I'm always looking on the bright side, aren't I? As soon as I have my prosthetic legs I'll be nearly the man I used to be, and Katie and I will get back together. So she's suggested that I have some blood tests, and my reflexes checked, and maybe even a brain scan.'

'Well, that's news to me,' said Bridie. 'Where does she want you to have these done?'

'St Giles' Clinic, it's on Middle Glanmire Road, in Montenotte. They specialise in taking care of people with severe disabilities. People like me.'

'And she wants me to take you there this morning? Has she made an appointment?'

'I don't think you need one. You just walk in and they assess you on the spot.'

Bridie said, 'I'd best ring her, you know, just to make sure.'

'You won't get through to her, Bridie. She's in court all morning and most of the afternoon. I'm really surprised that she didn't tell you about it, but I know that she wants me to have it done.'

'Well, all right, then,' said Bridie. 'I suppose that it's a good idea. I don't want to come back from getting the messages one day and find that you need your stomach pumping, or that you've gone to meet your Creator.'

John said, 'Grand. I'll just go to the jacks and then I'll put on my coat and we can go.'

* * *

They drove through the mizzle in Bridie's ten-year-old Ford Galaxy, and all the way to the outskirts of Cork Bridie never stopped talking. John remained silent. He was too busy thinking about what he was going to say to the owners of St Giles' Clinic to persuade them to take him in.

'How long is this assessment going to take?' Bridie asked him, as they turned off the main road and drove up between the high stone walls of Lover's Walk. 'If it's hours, like, I could go into town and look round the shops, couldn't I? I haven't had the chance to do that for ages. I could really do with some new bras, if you don't mind my saying so.'

'We'll have to see,' said John. He had come up with the idea of having himself admitted to St Giles' after Katie had told him last night about her investigation into Dr Fitzgerald, although his plan was still only half thought-out. He hadn't been at all sure that he would be able to convince Bridie to drive him here, but she had obviously relished the opportunity to get out of the house for a few hours.

'Here it is,' she said, turning into Middle Glanmire Road and up the steep-sloping driveway into St Giles' Clinic. She stopped outside the front porch and pulled on the handbrake. There was nobody around except for a mechanic in a grubby blue boiler suit, who was tinkering with an ambulance around the side of the house. There were two ambulances parked right behind it – one with plastic sheeting over the windscreen to protect it while it was being resprayed, and one yellow ambulance with green Battenberg squares on it, and the lettering *Emergency: Lifeline Ambulance Service.*

'You can wheel me inside, Bridie,' said John. 'Whatever you do, though, don't mention Katie's name or who she is. Tell them a friend of yours saw the St Giles' Clinic website, and suggested you bring me here to be taken care of. If it gets out that Katie's been second-guessing the doctors at the University Hospital, or that she's been having trouble with a suicidal boyfriend... well, you can imagine what the *Irish Times* would make of it.'

'So what do you want me to say?'

'Tell them that, up until now, you've been looking after me yourself, but now it's becoming a bit too much of a burden for you, so you'd like them to assess me to see if I'm eligible for care at St Giles'. Tell them that I have no living relatives, which is true, but also say that they can send their invoice for their assessment and any other treatment to Caremark. Katie's told me that she'll pay for any new medication and any therapy, if I need it.'

'But doesn't that sound like I'm asking them to take care of you permanent-like?'

'It does, yes. But if they think that I might be coming here to live, they'll give me a very thorough assessment. They look after people who don't have any hope of recovery, so when they see that all I need is a change in my medication, that's what they'll tell me. Give them your mobile number when you go in, and when they've finished assessing me they can call you and you can come and collect me.'

Bridie looked dubious about this, but then she shrugged and said, 'All right. If this is what Katie wants. She's footing the bill, after all.'

She lifted John's wheelchair out of the back of her Galaxy and brought it around to the passenger side so that he could swing himself into it. Then she pushed him up to the clinic's front door and rang the bell.

Nobody answered, so she rang again. Immediately, Grainne opened the door. She looked flushed, as if she had been interrupted in the middle of an argument. She stared at John, and then she raised her eyes to Bridie and said, 'Yes? What is it? What do you want?'

'We've, ah – we've come for an assessment,' said Bridie. 'Well, John here – not me. He's come for an assessment.'

'I'm sorry,' said Grainne. 'I have no idea what you're talking about. What kind of assessment?'

'To see if you could take him in, like. A friend of mine said she'd seen your website and that's what you do. Take in people like John – people with the serious disabilities.'

John deliberately didn't say anything, and didn't look up at Grainne.

'Well, yes, we do,' said Grainne. 'But it depends on their background. We only take in severely disabled people who can't find care from anywhere else. People with no family to take care of them. People with no funding. We're a charity, really.'

'John has no relatives. I work for Caremark and I've been looking after him, but he's been very depressed because of his disability. It's reached the point where he's been thinking of ending it all, if you know what I mean. If you could give him an assessment to see what's the best way that we can take care of him – well, that could even save his life.'

Grainne didn't answer immediately, but even though he was pretending that he was staring blankly at nothing at all, John could see from the way that her eyes were darting from side to side that she was thinking very hard.

'Dr Fitzgerald isn't here at the moment,' she told Bridie, after a while. 'It would be up to him to assess whether your John was suitable for us. But – what time is it? – he'll be back in less than half an hour, I expect. He's only seeing his bank manager. Is it possible that you can wait?'

'Could I leave John here, and then you can ring me when he's been assessed?'

'Well... all right. I don't see why not. He doesn't have any special needs, does he? I mean, he's continent? And he's not carrying any communicable diseases?'

Grainne bent down and spoke to John very slowly and clearly. 'Are you happy with that, John? If you wait here for a little while for Dr Fitzgerald?'

John glanced up at her and whispered, '*Yes.*'

Forty-three

Bridie gave Grainne her mobile number, and then she said, 'G'luck, John, I'll see you after.' She walked quickly back to her Galaxy, climbed into it and reversed down the driveway. It was then that John realised how pleased she was to have some free time away from him. All that nursing, all that sympathetic listening to his feelings about Katie – she had done that only because she was paid to do it, and not because she really cared about him. In a strange way, it made him feel worse than walking into Katie's bedroom in the middle of the night and finding her asleep with another man.

'What's your name, then?' Grainne asked him. 'We'll be filling in the proper registration forms for you if Dr Fitzgerald decides that we should assess you.'

'John,' said John, in a slow, thick voice, as if his tongue were swollen.

'Yes, I heard John. But John what?'

'Meagher. John Meagher.'

'And how old are you John?'

'Thirty-six. I think so, any road.'

'Where have you been living, John?'

'With Bridie. In Cobh. She saw me at the hos – she saw me at the hospital – and she took pity on me. Because of my legs. Because of my *no* legs.'

'What happened to your legs, John? How did you lose them?'

'Accident. Fell – fell off my motorbike. Hit my head too.' John pointed to his left temple and said, 'I had a bleed. Now I can't remember things so good.'

Grainne patted him on the shoulder and said, 'That's grand altogether, John. I think that Dr Fitzgerald may well want to give you some tests, so that we can admit you.'

John gave her a sloping smile as if he didn't really understand her. She released the brake on his wheelchair, turned him around, and pushed him down the hallway and into the large reception room. The window into which Gerry Mulvaney had thrown himself was still boarded up.

'I doubt if Dr Fitzgerald will be longer than a half-hour,' said Grainne. 'Can I fetch you anything in the meantime? A glass of water maybe? How about today's paper?'

Grainne's initial reaction to John's appearance at the front door had been bordering on the outright hostile, but now it seemed that she couldn't do enough to make him feel welcome. This was just what he had been hoping for. With any luck, it might give him the opportunity to look around the clinic and see if there were any more patients who had been deliberately mutilated like Siobhán. How grateful Katie would be, if he could. Not only would it save her from having to mount an expensive Garda search of the premises, it would prove to her that even without his legs he was still a man, with strength and initiative. When they had first become lovers, she frequently used to tell him that he looked like a Greek god. Maybe the god had been cut down to size, but everything else about him was intact. *I could still make love to you, Katie, like I used to, if only you would let me.*

After about ten minutes, Grainne came back into the reception room and said, 'Dr Fitzgerald just rang me. He'll be back in about twenty-five minutes. Are you still okay for the moment? I have to pop around to the shop but I won't be long. If there's anything you need urgent shout out for Dermot. He's in the kitchen at the back, clearing out the wastepipe. The things that people tip down the sink, you wouldn't credit it.'

She went away again, leaving the door a few centimetres ajar. John waited for a while, and then wheeled himself up to it, and listened. At first he could hear nothing except a water-tank rumbling somewhere. That was probably caused by Dermot, whoever Dermot was, flushing out the wastepipe. Then, very faintly, he heard somebody howling.

He eased himself out of the wheelchair and stood on his stumps. He opened the door a little wider, and he could distinctly hear howling. Or maybe it was singing. It was the most extraordinary noise that he had ever heard a human being make, so maybe it wasn't a human being at all, but some kind of animal. But what animal could howl, and then utter a shrill and repetitive whirring sound, and then a series of deep, tragic sobs?

He stepped out awkwardly into the hallway, almost losing his balance. There was nobody around, and even the water-tank had stopped rumbling. Directly opposite the reception room was a wide staircase, with mahogany newel posts in the shape of cruel-eyed eagles. The howling was coming from the first floor – thinner and sadder now, but definitely human.

John steadied himself by holding on to the doorframe, and then he stumbled across the hallway until he reached the staircase. He rested for a moment, panting, but from upstairs now he could hear another voice. It sounded like a woman keening at a funeral, and it went on and on, joining the howling and the whirring and the sobbing. John felt as if he had tricked his way into a madhouse, or a house that was crowded with grieving ghosts.

Holding on to the banister rail, he climbed up the stairs until he reached the first-floor landing. He stopped to rest again, and catch his breath. It was gloomy up here, with a shiny parquet floor, and it smelled of oak and furniture polish and antiseptic. He stumped slowly along the corridor, keeping one hand against the wall to stop himself from falling over.

The howling was coming from inside the first door that he reached. Howling, and then sobbing, and then that extraordinary whirring. The woman's keening was coming from further along the corridor, and John had never heard such grieving in his life.

He glanced behind him to make sure that he wasn't being watched or followed, and then he opened the first door. The inside of the room was dim, because the blind was drawn down. Up against the opposite wall stood a large hospital-type bed, with a bedside table, and a plain plywood wardrobe. Lying on the bed was a fiftyish-looking man with two thick white surgical pads covering his eyes. His face was sallow and his chin was covered with prickly white stubble. The pale beige blanket that covered him from the waist down was humped up, and John could see the outline of a metal frame that was obviously intended to keep the pressure of the bedclothes off his legs.

He must have heard John come bumping into the room, because he suddenly stopped howling, and listened. Then he made a gargling sound, as if he were being sick, although nothing came out of his mouth.

John went up to the side of the bed and cautiously touched the man's hand. The man jumped, as if he had been given an electric shock, and gargled again.

'Ssh, it's okay,' John told him. 'My name's John and I've come here to find out what's happened to you.'

The man let out a cackle, more like a chicken than a man.

'Can you speak at all?' John asked him.

The man shook his head.

'What I have to find out is, how did you get this way? Did you have an illness, like cancer or something?'

The man shook his head again, and pink dribble ran from the side of his mouth.

'Did you have an accident?'

Another shake.

'So this was done to you deliberately?'

Nod.

'What? You can't speak, and you've been blinded? Did Dr Fitzgerald do this to you?'

Another nod, frantic this time.

John said, 'Listen... I'm going to check up on that woman I can hear down the corridor. Then I'm going to call the guards. My partner's a senior detective. She knows what's been happening here, and she's going to make sure that Dr Fitzgerald pays for what he's done to you.'

The man gargled again, and then let out a chirrup. John couldn't work out what Dr Fitzgerald might have done to him to make him sound like this. He could tell that the man was desperately trying to talk to him, but he was completely incapable of speech, and almost drowning in blood-streaked saliva.

'I'll be back, I promise you,' he said, and balanced his way out of the room and into the corridor. The woman had stopped keening, but she was still making sad honking noises. John was sure that he could hear another man sobbing, too. *Jesus*, he thought. *Talk about the house of horrors. This place is hell on earth.*

He opened the door of the woman's room. It was completely dark in there, so he groped for the light-switch and turned on the overhead light. A young red-haired women was lying in bed at the side of the room. Her eyes were closed but she was honking and moaning and it was obvious that she wasn't asleep. John approached her and touched her bare shoulder, and she flinched, but she kept on honking, and gave him no indication at all that she knew he was there.

She was quite pretty, with a heart-shaped face and freckles across the bridge of her nose, and John guessed that she couldn't have been older than fifteen or sixteen.

'Can you hear me?' he asked her.

She didn't answer, so he leaned over her and spoke clearly and loudly in her left ear. 'Can you hear me at all?'

He waited, but she still didn't respond, so he assumed that she was either deaf or mentally impaired. He laid his hand on her shoulder again, trying to make her aware that he was here, and that he had come to help her. It was then that she lifted her left arm out from underneath the blanket, and he saw that her hand had been amputated, and she had nothing on the end of her arm but a smooth round wrist. He raised the blanket and saw that her right hand, too, had been amputated.

He took a staggering step back. At the end of the bed the blanket was lying flat, so he lifted it up there. Both of the girl's feet had been amputated, ending at the ankles.

John didn't have to see any more. He couldn't guess how many disabled people Dr Fitzgerald was keeping in his clinic altogether, but it was enough for him to have seen two – especially since one of them had nodded his assent that it had been Dr Fitzgerald who had mutilated him.

He left the girl's room, closing the door as quietly as he could, and started to walk back towards the staircase. He had almost reached it when he heard the front door open, and voices in the hallway, a man and a woman's. He couldn't distinctly hear what they were saying at first, but he recognised Grainne's voice.

They came nearer to the bottom of the staircase. He slowly retreated, still holding on to the wall to keep his balance.

'So who brought him here?' asked the man.

'He has a young female carer,' said Grainne. 'She works for Caremark, but I think she took it on herself to take care of him because he's a good-looking feen and she felt fierce sorry for him. But now she's finding him too much to cope with.'

'It's the same old story, isn't it? People never realise how taxing it's going to be, looking after a chronically disabled person day and night, week in and week out. And if they take good care of them, and don't conveniently allow them to die of thirst, or malnutrition, or the bedsores – well, it can seem like they have to take care of them for ever.'

'He's here, in the reception room,' said Grainne, opening the door. 'John – Dr Fitzgerald is back! Give him a moment to take off his coat and he'll be with you directly.'

John backed further away, along the corridor. He was grinding his teeth, which he always did when he was stressed. Maybe there was another way out of here, a servants' staircase, a fire escape, something like that, but even if there was, it would be almost impossible for him to get away on his stumps. It would be agonisingly painful, too.

He heard Grainne say, 'He's not there. Gearoid! I left him waiting in the reception room.'

'Maybe he went to water the horses.'

'But his wheelchair's still here. He's lost his legs from the knees downwards. I didn't think for a moment that he could walk.'

Grainne walked to the end of the hallway, opened a door, closed it, and then came back again. 'No, he's not in there. Dermot!'

'What is it now?'

'Have you seen a feen with no legs walking around?'

'No, but I once saw a feller with no fingers scratching his arse.'

'Oh, for the love of Jesus, Dermot, this isn't funny. He was supposed to be waiting in the reception room for Dr Fitzgerald to come back from town, but now he's not there any more.'

'Maybe he got tired of waiting and just decided he'd had enough.'

'What, and walked out, without any legs? Head off, will you.'

It was then that Dr Fitzgerald said, 'Maybe he heard some of the patients calling out. You know what a Godawful racket they can make. Maybe he went upstairs to see what all the noise was about. If he's thinking of being admitted here, after all, he'd want to find out what he was letting himself in for, wouldn't he? I use earplugs myself, at night, especially when it's a full moon and Dermot turns himself into a werewolf.'

His words may have sounded like banter, but even from up here on the landing John could tell by his tone of voice that Dr Fitzgerald was irritated, and very serious. He had no doubt at all that he would be coming upstairs in a moment, just to make sure that John hadn't been poking around. If he was running a major drugs-smuggling racket, as Katie suspected, he wouldn't be the kind of man who left anything to chance.

John retreated further down the corridor, opening one door after another. In each gloomy room, there was a hospital bed, and somebody lying in it, either asleep and snoring or awake and moaning. At the end of the corridor there was a green stained-glass window with a wistful-looking merrow on it, sitting on a rock. Next to that, a door led into Dr Fitzgerald's operating room, with its stainless-steel sink and its stainless-steel side-table and its cases of surgical instruments. John could hear footsteps coming up the stairs, so he hobbled into this room and closed the door. If he stood close to the wall behind the door, and somebody opened it to take a quick sconce inside, maybe they wouldn't see him, especially since there were so many surgical gowns hanging on the back of it.

His stumps were hurting badly now, and he had to take a few seconds to squeeze his eyes tight shut and try to suppress the pain. When it had eased a little, he took his mobile phone out of his pocket and dialled Katie's number.

He could see that her phone was ringing, but she didn't answer. *Please let her not be driving, or in a meeting, or interrogating somebody. I need her now.*

He dialled her number a second time. Now he could hear footsteps coming along the corridor, and doors opening and closing. Dr Fitzgerald must be looking into each patient's room to see if he was there.

'John?' said Katie. 'What is it? I'm at CUH. We're just about to start filming our video.'

'I'm at St Giles' Clinic,' John whispered.

'What? Could you speak up, please? There's an awful lot of people talking at once and I can't hear you.'

'I'm at St Giles' Clinic,' he repeated, but only a little louder.

'What in the name of God are you doing there? Where's Bridie?'

'Bridie's gone shopping.'

'*What?* She's left you at St Giles' Clinic and gone shopping? Are you codding me, John?'

'No, darling. I'm stone-cold serious. I persuaded Bridie to fetch me here. I thought it would save you having to raid the place.'

'John, I can't believe what you're telling me. Please say that this is a joke.'

'I've seen them for myself, Katie. There's a fellow here who can't speak and it looks like he might have been blinded, and there's a young girl with no hands and no feet. I haven't had time to check them all, but you can hear them screaming and crying and wailing. I tell you, it sounds like Purgatory.'

'You have to get out of there now, John. I mean it. Get out of there now and ring Bridie and tell her to come back and pick you up, urgent. I'll call her myself, too.'

'I can't get out. Dr Fitzgerald's come back and he's looking for me.'

'So where are you?'

'I'm hiding myself in some kind of an operating room, upstairs.'

'Then stay there. I have two surveillance officers directly outside and they'll come in to get you right now. Stay there and don't move but if Dr Fitzgerald finds you and wants to know what you're doing there, don't say a word. Act like you can't speak. For God's sake don't tell him that you were looking around for evidence.'

John said, 'I've fucked this up, haven't I?'

'Don't worry about that,' said Katie. 'Just stay where you are and keep this phone open. I'm having Pádraigin call the surveillance officers right this second.'

John was about to describe to Katie exactly where he was, in the room next to the stained-glass window, when the door opened and Dr Fitzgerald came in. He was still wearing his long black raincoat and from John's point of view he appeared so tall and attenuated with his hawklike nose and his swept-back hair that he could have been a vampire.

John pressed himself back against the wall but Dr Fitzgerald turned around and saw him immediately.

'Who are you and who are you talking to?' he snapped, in his dry, schoolmasterly voice.

John said nothing, so Dr Fitzgerald came up to him and twisted his mobile phone out of his hand. His fingers were long and very strong and John was too weakened by his medication to resist him.

Dr Fitzgerald peered at the screen with his lips tightly pursed and then he held the phone up to his ear.

'John?' said Katie. 'John, what's happening? The surveillance officers won't be more than a couple of minutes.'

Dr Fitzgerald prodded the phone to end the call and then slung it sideways across the room.

'So who are you?' he said. 'Don't tell me you're a guard. I know the Garda recruit men with no brains but I didn't realise they're taking on men with no legs.'

John still didn't answer, so Dr Fitzgerald took hold of his sleeve and dragged him, stumbling, out of the corner.

'Get back downstairs,' he ordered him. 'Get back downstairs and if any guards come knocking at the door, tell them that you're fine and that there's nothing wrong.'

It took all of his self-control for John not to shout back at Dr Fitzgerald, but he had to recognise that without his legs he was physically powerless, and that anything he said would only cause Katie more horrendous complications. Slowly and painfully, and trailing his hand along the wall, he hobbled his way back towards the staircase. Grainne was waiting for him there, with her arms folded, and a disgusted expression on her face, as if he were a child and she couldn't believe how badly he had let her down.

Meanwhile, Dr Fitzgerald opened up one of his cases of surgical instruments and selected a number 12 blade, which was curved like a hook. He fitted it on to a scalpel handle and then he left the operating room without closing the door behind him, and walked swiftly along the corridor with his raincoat rustling.

John heard him coming up behind him but didn't turn around. He was concentrating too hard on reaching the staircase, and his stumps were now giving him so much pain that he was biting his tongue.

Dr Fitzgerald came close up behind him and without saying a word he reached around in front of him and cut his throat. He sliced so deeply into his neck muscles that John's head dropped backwards and almost fell off, and a huge spout of blood gushed out of his carotid artery and soaked his jacket, as well as splattering on to the parquet floor.

'Holy Jesus!' Grainne cried out.

Dr Fitzgerald gave John a kick in the small of his back so that he fell against the skirting-board. John shuddered violently and his right hand reached out as if he were trying to save himself from sliding into death, but then he lay still. Dr Fitzgerald tossed his scalpel on top of him.

'God in Heaven, what did you do that for?' said Grainne.

'We're found out, Grainne. He was phoning the guards when I caught him. They're on their way now.'

Dermot had heard Grainne crying out, and he came stamping up the stairs to see what was going on. When he caught sight of John's half-decapitated body he said, 'Holy Saint Joseph.'

Dr Fitzgerald was behaving with ice-cold hysteria. He turned away from John's body and then he turned back again, holding up his bloodstained right hand.

'I'll wash my hands,' he said. 'I'll have to wash my hands and then we'll get out of here as quick as we can.'

'What about him?' said Dermot, pointing at John's body. 'You can't just leave him lying there, can you?'

'We can dispose of him,' said Dr Fitzgerald. 'Where are Ger and Milo?'

'You know where they are,' Dermot told him. 'You sent them out to see if they could pick up another patient, to replace Siobhán. They're probably sitting in a layby on the Western Road, smoking their heads off and looking out for some student they can run over.'

'Well, call them,' said Dr Fitzgerald. 'No – on the other hand, don't call them. They'll only complicate things. Is that ambulance repaired yet?'

'I think so. I heard Sonny revving the engine outside, so I reckon he must have fixed it.'

'Right. Okay. Dermot – you go and check that it's up and running. Then we can take this fool away and get rid of him. Grainne, there's a blue plastic sheet in the operating theatre, under the table at the side. Bring it out, will you, so that we can wrap him up? We don't want any more blood on the floor than we have already. Once we've taken him outside, Dermot, if you can get out the bucket and the mop.'

Grainne said, 'Gearoid, what about all the patients? If the guards are coming, they're going to find all the patients, aren't they?'

'I'm not worried about the patients. They're all alive, aren't they, even if they're not kicking. There's no way that the guards can prove that we disabled them. We're taking care of them, aren't we? We're giving them better care than they could ever expect anywhere else.'

'*We* didn't disable them, Gearoid,' said Grainne. '*You* did.'

'Don't give me that, Grainne. You aided and abetted. Who handed me the spoon when I was taking out Gerry Mulvaney's eyeballs?'

At that moment, the doorbell rang, and rang again, and again, and there was a loud hammering on the front door.

'That'll be the guards,' said Dr Fitzgerald. He held up his bloody hand again. 'I must wash my hands. Grainne – you go and answer the door. Stall them. Tell them that everything's grand and deny that this fellow ever came here. No, don't do that. The woman on the phone said surveillance officers. That probably means that they've been watching us, and so they will have seen him arrive here.'

The doorbell was now rung continuously, and the hammering was even louder.

'Jesus wept,' said Dermot. 'Any second now they'll be knocking it down with one of them battery rams.'

'Go on, Grainne, go and open the door for them,' said Dr Fitzgerald. 'Tell them that he's upstairs, right in the middle of a medical assessment, and that we'll be bringing him down in just a few minutes. Then take them into the reception room and lock them in. That should give us enough time to get away.'

'Gearoid, this is madness,' said Grainne. 'We're never going to get away with this. Not in a million years.'

'*Will you answer the door and do what I tell you!*' Dr Fitzgerald screamed at her. '*If they can't find his body they can't prove anything!*'

Grainne shrugged, and looked at John lying up against the wall, with his head tilted away from his neck and his hair matted with blood. 'If that's what you want, Gearoid. But it wasn't me who cut that feen's throat, no matter what you say about aiding and abetting.'

She went downstairs. As she walked along the hallway she called out, 'All right! All right! I'm coming for the love of God! Hold your whisht awhile will you!'

Dr Fitzgerald turned to Dermot and said, 'Go out the kitchen way and see if the ambulance is ready. If it is, come back up and we'll carry this fool outside.'

'And where are you thinking of taking him?' asked Dermot. 'We can't just turn up at St Finbarr's Cemetery and politely ask them to bury him for us, can we?'

'If you bury bodies they can be found, can't they?' said Dr Fitzgerald, still holding up his hand. 'But if they've been eaten, they can never be found, can they?'

'You're joking, aren't you? What are you going to do, cut him up and put him on the barbecue?'

'Of course not. We'll take him up to Ballyknock. Lorcan's up there already. We can give him to Bartley Doran's dogs as bait.'

'Now I know you're joking.'

'Dermot, I was never more serious in my life. Now get down there, will you, and make sure the ambulance is ready.'

Forty-four

Katie was speeding back into the city on the South Link road when Detective Sergeant Begley called her.

'One of the surveillance officers who was watching St Giles' has just been in touch. He says that they were let into the clinic, but asked to wait for a few minutes, because your John was right in the middle of a medical assessment. Next thing they knew they looked out of the window and saw an ambulance shooting off. They were going to go after it but found that they'd been locked in.'

'Oh, this gets better by the minute,' said Katie. 'I'm guessing that it was one of the clinic's own ambulances – the white St Giles' ones, with the picture of St Giles on it?'

'That's right. We haven't clocked it yet but they can't get far. They might as well have tried to get away in an ice-cream van.'

'What about John? Is he still there?'

'No sign of him, ma'am, but there's a whole mess of blood in the first-floor corridor.'

'Mother of God,' said Katie, and felt a deep sickening sensation in her stomach. As soon as John had rung her and told her that he was inside St Giles' Clinic, she had known that this would end badly.

'There's five patients there altogether, four male and one female,' said Detective Sergeant Begley. 'They're all blind and all severely disabled. I've contacted the Mercy and they'll be sending a couple of ambulances to pick them up. O'Donovan and Markey are on their way up to Montenotte now, along with eight uniforms. I've informed Bill Phinner, too, and he's sending up a technical team.'

'But there was nobody else there at the clinic? No nurses – no office staff?'

'Nobody, ma'am. The two surveillance officers said they were let in by a very charming woman, which is why they didn't suspect that they were being duped.'

'And they allowed her to lock them in? I think we'll have to send them back to Templemore for retraining.'

She reached Anglesea Street and turned into the station car park. She could have gone up to St Giles' Clinic herself, but she trusted Detectives O'Donovan and Markey. Now that a large quantity of blood had been found, it was technically a crime scene, and they were quite capable of following procedure. Apart from that, if it was John's blood, which it very well might be, she didn't want to see it. She wasn't squeamish, but she didn't want her last abiding memory of the man she had once loved to be a lake of blood in some unfamiliar house.

As she walked across the station's reception area, she saw to her surprise that Conor was sitting there. He dropped the newspaper that he had been reading and came across to her.

'What are you doing here?' she asked him.

'Waiting for you, believe it or not. I had to come into town anyway and I was wondering if you might be able to spare half an hour for coffee. Your assistant told me that you were at the hospital, but she said you shouldn't be too long, so here I am.'

'I'm sorry, Conor, I have a crisis on my hands just now,' Katie told him. 'John has done something very stupid and now I'm worried that he might have been hurt, or even killed, God forbid.'

Conor followed her to the lift, but when the door opened he said, 'Listen, I don't want to be in your way. Call me later if you can. I'll go and see how Sergeant Browne's getting along with my fighting dogs.'

'No, come up for a moment, and I'll tell you what's happening. If something really bad has happened to John, I could use some moral support.'

They went up in the lift. Conor saw Katie biting at the side of her thumbnail and said, 'He's more than a friend, isn't he? Or used to be. Am I right? And that's why you've been looking after him.'

Katie gave him nothing but a brief smile to acknowledge that he was right. Then she walked along to her office and he followed her.

Before she did anything else, she rang Bridie, for the fifth time. All she heard was Bridie's answering service, asking her to leave a message after the tone.

Conor sat down and said, 'So what's happened? How do you know that John's been hurt?'

Katie was in the middle of telling him about the call that she had received from John while he was hiding at St Giles' Clinic, when her phone rang.

'Ma'am? DS Begley. We've located the ambulance. We thought it might have been heading for Ringaskiddy or Rosslare, to get on a ferry, or possibly due north to the border. But it's been spotted by a Tipp patrol and it was driving through Cashel town centre. They must have gone all the way up by the back roads, Goatenbridge and Ballybacon, that way.'

'Cashel? Are they following it now?'

'At a fierce discreet distance, yes – waiting for our instructions on how to proceed.'

'They've been seen in Cashel,' Katie told Conor, covering the phone with her hand. Then, to Detective Sergeant Begley, 'Which way are they heading now?'

There was a long pause, and then Detective Sergeant Begley said, 'Palmer's Hill. No – they've turned off now, to the right-hand side, down some unmarked track.'

Katie said to Conor, 'They're heading for Bartley Doran's place. They must be. Why in the name of Jesus are they going there? Come on, I'm going up there now myself. Will you come with me? If there's dogs involved I'd like to have you there.'

She called Superintendent Pearse and told him where she was going, and why, and asked for half-a-dozen uniformed gardaí and an armed response unit. She asked him also to contact Superintendent O'Neill at Tipperary Town to keep him up to date on what she was doing, and request some back-up, if he could spare it.

'Don't I get a gun?' asked Conor, as they went back downstairs and hurried out in the car park.

'If there's any danger of shooting, I'll lend you a ballistic vest.'

'Oh, okay. But that's not quite so exciting as having a gun.'

'Believe me, Conor, there is nothing exciting about shooting somebody. It's just about the most dreadful thing that I've ever had to do.'

* * *

They didn't follow the winding route through the South Tipperary countryside that the St Giles' Clinic ambulance must have taken. Instead, Katie drove at high speed up the M8, the same road that she and Conor had used when they went up to Ballyknock to visit Guzz Eye McManus.

In spite of the fine rain that was still falling, she drove at nearly 170 kph on the motorway, and it took them less than thirty minutes before she turned off for Palmer's Hill. The Tipperary patrol car was parked beside the entrance to the narrow lane that led up to Bartley Doran's property, with two gardaí sitting in it. Katie got out and went to talk to them, explaining that back-up was already on the way.

It was less than ten minutes before three more patrol cars arrived, two from Cork and one from Tipperary Town, as well as an Emergency Response Unit, in a Volvo SUV, carrying four armed officers dressed from head to foot in black.

Katie called all the gardaí to gather around her. The soft rain kept falling and sparkled on her dark red hair.

'As far as we know, the ambulance that we've been pursuing has been used to smuggle drugs from the UK to Cork. We believe the man behind the operation is Dr Gearoid Fitzgerald, a surgeon who was struck off the medical register but who started up his own clinic, presumably as a cover for his drug operation.

'We suspect that he's been deliberately mutilating people so that they can appear to be seriously disabled patients, and thereby avoiding a thorough search of his ambulances by customs officers. He knows now that we've discovered what he's doing, which is why he's made a run for it today. I can't say that I'm sure why he's come here. This is the home of a man who trains dogs for dog fighting. But Dr Fitzgerald's brother Lorcan is involved in dognapping and dog fighting, and so it's possible that he's here today, too.

'We're here to arrest Dr Fitzgerald and any members of his clinical staff who may have come along with him. I'm not expecting any fierce resistance but these are serious criminals we're dealing with here so be wide.'

She paused, and then she said, 'There's one thing. There may be a disabled man on board in a serious condition who has lost a lot of blood. I've organised an ambulance which will be here very soon, but if you find him please let me know as soon as you can. That's all. Let's go.'

The convoy of Garda vehicles jostled their way slowly down the lane to the rusty metal gate outside Bartley Doran's farmyard. The St Giles' Clinic ambulance was parked on the left-hand side, close to the barn. Katie and Conor climbed out of Katie's car, and as they did so, Bartley himself came limping out of his house with his blackthorn stick.

'What the feck is all this?' he demanded, waving with his stick at the three patrol cars and the ERU Volvo.

'We've come for Dr Fitzgerald,' said Katie, taking out her ID and showing it to him.

Bartley stared at her, and then at Conor. 'So, you two were shades all the time. I thought you both had a smell of bacon about you, but I thought that if the Guzz trusted you, then you must be straight.'

'Will you open the gate, please, Mr Doran,' said Katie. 'We don't want any trouble. We're only looking for Dr Fitzgerald, and any of his staff who might have come with him.'

'I'll tell you what you can do, girl,' said Bartley, spitting on the ground. 'You and all of your piggy pals here can go away to feck. Go on, the lot of you. Away to feck with you. This is my land and you're not setting foot on it.'

'Please open the gate, Mr Doran.'

Bartley turned around and started to limp back towards his house. 'Gearoid!' he shouted out. 'Lorcan! There's a whole herd of pigs have showed up!'

'So – Lorcan's here too,' Katie said to Conor. 'That's probably why he came here.' She turned around to the garda standing behind her and said, 'Would you do the honours, please?'

The garda beckoned to his partner and his partner opened the boot of their patrol car and came across with a large pair of bolt-cutters. He cut through the chain on Bartley Doran's gate and pushed it wide open. Then the whole posse of them spread out and walked towards the house, with Katie in the middle and the four ERU officers on either side, holding their Heckler and Koch MP7 submachine-guns across their chests.

Katie said to Conor, 'Stay behind me, Conor. Just in case.'

'That's the first time in my life that a woman has ever said that to me,' said Conor. 'The first time she's meant it, anyway.'

They were still thirty metres from the front of the house when the front door was thrown open and Grainne appeared. She came walking towards them with her hands held up. She was followed by Dermot, in a thick grey roll-neck sweater and jeans that were still heavily stained with blood.

'We give up!' called Grainne, in a high, shrill voice. 'Look, we're coming quietly!'

As soon as Dermot had stepped down from the porch, however, Lorcan came out of the front door, with Gearoid close behind him. Like two escaping thieves in a melodramatic play, they ran along the front of the house and across the scrubby grass patch that led to the barn.

The uniformed gardaí started to run after them, with the armed officers jogging close behind. But Grainne crossed diagonally in front of them, waving her arms and shrieking, '*No! No! It's not them you want! It's us!*'

Dermot made a half-hearted attempt to obstruct one of the gardaí, too, but the officer pushed him hard in the chest and he fell backwards on to the muddy tarmac, and lay there with his arms spread, as if he had really had enough, and couldn't be bothered to get up.

Gearoid and Lorcan had reached the front of the barn, and they were obviously intending to continue along the sheds where Bartley kept his dogs, but one of the ERU officers fired an ear-splitting shot into the air and shouted, '*Stop!*'

Gearoid and Lorcan both stopped, looking confused. Katie was running up to them, with Conor next to her, and she thought that she had them now. As he turned around, though, Gearoid saw that the barn door was right behind them. He pushed it open and tugged Lorcan by the sleeve to follow him inside. They slammed the door behind them, and they were gone.

By now, Bartley had come out of the house again and was standing on the edge of the porch. When he saw Gearoid and Lorcan disappear into the barn, he screamed out, '*No, Gearoid, no! Not in the barn! Not in the fecking barn for feck's sake!*'

He started to limp towards the barn himself, until Katie shouted at him, 'Stop! Stay where you are, Bartley! You keep out of this!'

'But it's the dogs!' Bartley shouted back at her. 'They have the fecking dogs in there and they're having a mass bump!'

'That's a mock-fight, Katie, to make them more aggressive,' said Conor. 'I wouldn't go in there, if I were you.'

'I have to,' Katie told him, tersely.

As they neared the barn, they could hear dogs barking in a frenzy, and men shouting. Katie beckoned the ERU officers and said, 'We're going inside, but cover us. If any of those dogs looks like it's out of control, don't hesitate to shoot it. You'll probably be doing it a favour.'

One of the black-uniformed officers pushed at the door, but it seemed that it was bolted from the inside. He kicked it, and it gave way a little, so he kicked it again even harder, and it shuddered open. Holding up his submachine-gun, he stepped inside. Katie went in after him, followed by another armed officer, and Conor, and three gardaí.

Bartley's three young helpers were there, inside the makeshift ring of crates, and they were each desperately holding on to two pit-bull terriers – six slavering dogs between them. Each pit-bull had a chain leash, which was wrapped around the young men's wrists, but they were straining against their leashes so violently that the young men could barely keep on their feet. The dogs' eyes were bulging, their teeth were bared, and their mouths were dripping with foam and blood. Two of them had their ears in bloody tatters, and all of them had teeth-marks and rips along their flanks. The penis of one of them was dangling by a fleshy thread of skin.

They must have been fighting each other before Gearoid and Lorcan had come stumbling into the barn, but now they were all pulling strenuously at their leashes to get at them, because they must have thought that they were bait, and much easier to attack. They may also have smelled that they were frightened, and that could have aroused their blood-lust even more.

'Gearoid and Lorcan Fitzgerald!' Katie shouted out. She could barely make herself heard over the pit-bulls barking.

'You can't prove anything!' Dr Fitzgerald shouted back. It was almost a scream. 'You can't prove anything!'

'What have you done with John Meagher?' Katie shouted. 'Where is he? What have you done with him?'

'You can't prove anything!' Dr Fitzgerald repeated. Then he held up both of his hands and said, 'I'm entitled! Don't you know that? I'm entitled! God gave me these hands! These hands hold life and death! I'm entitled!'

Lorcan called out, 'He's right! We've never done nothing! You can't arrest us when we've done nothing!'

Dr Fitzgerald started to back away, and Katie could see that there was another door at the other end of the barn. She said to the two gardaí close beside her, 'Can you restrain both of them and fetch them outside? I can't read them their rights in here. They'll complain to their lawyers they couldn't hear them!'

The gardaí unclipped their handcuffs from their belts, and started to walk around the circle of wooden crates towards Gearoid and Lorcan. Before they could reach them, though, two of the pit-bulls pulled so hard on their chains that the young man holding them fell forward on to his knees. The dogs dragged him right across the ring, and both of them bounded over the crates, one after the other, so that the young man collided with them and lost his grip on their chains.

Gearoid staggered backwards and tried to beat the dogs off, but both of them launched themselves at him, snarling and snapping and tearing at his sleeves and his hands. He fell on to the sawdust-covered floor and they went for his head, their teeth ripping at his ears and his nose and his cheeks. He screamed, and tried to roll himself free, but the pit-bulls were determined to wrench the flesh from his face.

Lorcan kicked the dogs as hard as he could, again and again. He kicked them in their ribs, and in their testicles, and in the side of their heads, but they had endured worse kicks than that in their lives and they ignored him.

'Shoot them!' Katie shouted. Two of the armed gardaí came up close to the pit-bulls as they struggled and wrestled with Gearoid on the floor, pointing their automatic pistols at them, but hesitant to fire in case they hit Gearoid. Katie pulled her own revolver out of its holster but that was only because the other four pit-bulls were mad with excitement now, leaping up into the air and barking and pulling at their chains so hard that they were nearly strangling themselves.

It was then that Conor walked quickly around the ring and stood behind the two armed gardaí. He did nothing for a few seconds, simply standing there, but then he put two fingers between his lips and let out a weird, piercing whistle. Nothing happened at first, but then he whistled again and both dogs stopped biting at Gearoid's face and lifted their heads and looked at him.

Even the dogs in the ring quietened down when they heard him whistle, although two of them kept on barking alternately, as if they were some kind of threatening double-act.

Conor said, 'Come on, you two. *Am chun tú a chodladh.* Time for you to sleep.'

The two dogs stood in front of him with those bulging eyes, their jaws dripping with Gearoid's blood, their docked tails twitching. They stared at him as if they couldn't understand what he was or where he had come from.

'Now you can do it,' said Conor. The two armed gardaí stood either side of him, holding their automatics in both hands. They pointed them directly between the pit-bulls' eyes, and fired, one after the other. The pit-bulls' heads burst open like watermelons and they dropped sideways on to the floor, one on top of the other, their legs quivering.

The shots had been deafening, and the other four pit-bulls became hysterical, throwing themselves around so wildly that one of the young men was knocked off his feet and barely managed to keep hold of them. Gearoid tried to sit up, making a bubbling noise between lips that were hanging free from his face like thin strips of raw liver. His nose had been bitten off, leaving a dark triangular hole, and the skin and flesh had been torn from his cheeks, so that the white bones were visible. He lifted one hand, but then he fell back on to the floor and lay there, shaking.

Lorcan looked down at his brother, and then turned around and stared at Katie with almost theatrical malevolence. He walked stiffly towards her, but as he came nearer, a garda stepped forward and said, 'That's close enough, sham.'

'It's *you*, isn't it?' he said, ignoring the garda and still staring at Katie. 'I've heard about you. You think you were sent from Heaven to judge the rest of humanity. You think you're fecking immortal. Well, here's my answer to that misconception, detective not-so-superintendent.'

He reached inside his jacket and out flashed his triangular knife. The garda lunged forward to grab his wrist but Katie was quicker. She lifted her revolver and shot him point-blank in the chest.

Lorcan looked at her in amazement. Then he looked at his knife, and dropped it on to the floor. He sagged to his knees, with blood running out of the side of his mouth. Then, abruptly, he coughed more blood, and slowly lay down on his side, as if he were settling himself in bed for the night.

Katie could hear nothing at all. The garda was saying something to her but she could see only his lips moving. She raised her hand to acknowledge him, and then she turned around and stepped out of the barn, into the rain.

Conor followed her. He stood close to her but he obviously didn't want to hold her in his arms, not in front of all of these gardaí.

'How did you do that?' she said, at last, although she was still half-deaf.

'What, the whistling, with the dogs? I suppose I can understand dogs better than I can understand people, that's all.'

Katie looked up at him. She had raindrops in her eyelashes. 'I don't understand people at all, Conor. Not in the slightest.'

She was still standing there when a garda came across from the farmyard where the St Giles' Clinic ambulance was parked. He had white hair and grey eyes and he looked very grim-faced.

'We've searched the ambulance, ma'am, and in the back we found a deceased individual. From your description of his condition – his amputated legs, like – we believe it to be John Meagher.'

'I see,' said Katie. 'Do you have any idea how he might have died?'

'Throat cut, ma'am, I'm sorry to say.'

She looked up at Conor. She felt numb now, as well as deaf.

'Why would they bring his body here, of all places?' she asked him. Then she faintly heard the pit-bulls barking inside the barn, and she said, 'Don't answer that.'

Her iPhone rang. It was Bridie, and she sounded bewildered.

'I went back to pick up John after I'd done my shopping, and there was nobody there but loads of guards who wouldn't tell me nothing. What's happened to him? He's all right, isn't he?'

'Yes, Bridie. He's grand altogether. He's not suffering any more, anyway.'

'I'm sorry, Katie. I don't quite know what you mean.'

'That doesn't surprise me at all, Bridie. I'm not sure that I do, either.'

Forty-five

The next morning was cold, but at least it was dry and sunny. Katie's first meeting of the day was with Chief Superintendent MacCostagáin, to discuss the details of John's murder and the shootings at Bartley Doran's farm, and how they were going to present these to the media.

Dr Gearoid Fitzgerald had survived his mauling by the pit-bull terriers, but he was being treated in the Mercy for catastrophic facial injuries. 'If only he could operate on himself,' said Chief Superintendent MacCostagáin, wryly. 'He's about the only surgeon in the country with the skill to make himself look halfway normal again.'

Lorcan Fitzgerald had survived, too, with a punctured lung, and he was recovering in CUH. When he was ready to be discharged he would be arrested for dognapping and with grievously wounding Martin Ó Brádaigh. The knife that he had taken out to stab Katie had matched the plastic knife that Dr Kelley had 3D-printed, in every microscopic detail.

Katie still faced an enquiry into the suicide of Assistant Commissioner O'Reilly, and she had handed in her revolver until an investigation had been completed into the shooting of Lorcan Fitzgerald.

'You've been through a fierce difficult time, Katie,' said Chief Superintendent MacCostagáin, as she went to his office door. She could feel how much he wanted to put his arm around her, and give her a reassuring hug. 'You have a couple of weeks of time off owing to you, don't you? Why don't you take it?'

'I'll think about it,' she said. 'Let me bury John first. There's nobody else to do it.'

She went up to her office, and to her surprise, Kyna was there, drinking coffee and talking to Moirin.

'I'm sorry,' said Kyna. 'Moirin fetched this coffee for you, but we didn't know how long you'd be.'

Moirin stood up and said, 'I'll get you another one. It's no bother.'

When she had gone, Katie held Kyna tightly and they kissed.

'From what Moirin told me, it sounds like you've been through hell and back,' said Kyna.

'I'm not sure I'm back yet. Do you know when you're starting?'

'Monday. Believe it or not, I can't wait.'

'There's one thing you have to know,' said Katie, sitting down at her desk. 'This pet detective I've been working with, Conor. Well – we've become very close.'

'Oh, yes?' said Kyna. 'How close is very close?'

'Let's just say that if he asked me—'

'You'd marry him?'

'I'm not sure I want to get married again. Not yet, anyway. But I wouldn't say no if he suggested that we move in together.'

Kyna raised her eyebrows and turned her head to look out of the window. The sun was shining on the Elysian tower, it reflected on to her face.

'Kyna—' said Katie. 'If working here again is going to be painful for you—'

'No, no. Not at all,' said Kyna, turning around again and smiling. 'I've told you before. I've thought about this over and over. I've thought about us. I've thought about my feelings for you, and I can cope.'

'You'll find somebody else. I'm sure of it.'

'Yes, I probably will,' said Kyna. 'It's a little sad, though. It doesn't matter how pretty she is, this somebody else, or how lovable, she'll never be Katie Maguire.'

* * *

Just after 4:00 pm she decided to call it a day. She told Moirin that she could leave early, too, and then she rang Conor and asked him if he would like to go for a drink with her. She needed to sit down with him and talk about everything that had happened yesterday at Bartley Doran's farm. He had seen John's body in the back of the ambulance, but she hadn't wanted to look, and now she wished that she had.

Conor agreed to come down to the city and meet her at the Long Valley.

'I think I need to talk it all over, too,' he told her. 'I had a nightmare last night about those pit-bulls looking up at me and then their heads blowing up.'

Katie put on her coat but then her phone rang. It was Detective Ó Doibhilin, and he sounded serious.

'It's Keeno,' he said. 'He passed away about twenty minutes ago. Aortic embolism, that's what the doctor told me.'

'All right, Michael,' said Katie. 'Thanks for telling me.'

'They won't blame you for killing him, will they? I mean, it was self-defence, like, wasn't it?'

'It depends what the coroner has to say.'

'I would have been perfectly happy to kick his head in, myself.'

'I know. But it's not up to us to be the judges. Nor the executioners, either.'

Wearily, she put down the phone, checked in her handbag to see that she had everything she needed, switched off her office lights and went downstairs. It occurred to her as she went down in the lift that if ever she wanted to spend a night with Conor, she wouldn't have to worry about going home and looking after John. It made her feel guilty, thinking that, but she also couldn't help feeling relieved.

As she crossed the reception area towards the main doors she saw a tall, handsome woman in a camelhair coat waiting by the front desk. The officer behind the desk was engaged in what looked like a long phone conversation, nodding and writing down notes.

Katie went up to the woman and said, 'Can I help you?'

The woman smiled. Katie guessed that she was about forty, but her make-up was immaculate and she had striking blue eyes, slightly starey, as if she was wearing contact lenses, and blue enamel earrings.

'I don't know,' she said. 'I'm looking for Conor Ó Máille.'

Katie said, 'He's not here at the moment, I'm afraid, and he won't be here for the rest of today. Do you want me to tell him who called?'

'That's kind of you, yes,' said the woman. 'I'm his wife.'